One of Nevil Shute's most famous novels is the story of a harrowing wartime experience, and of a search that led half-way around the world.

She was one of eighty women captured by the Japanese and herded along the jungle trails in a "death march" that would cover 1200 miles. He was an Australian soldier, a prisoner of war who had tried to steal food for her and was caught and crucified by his Japanese guards.

Together they had shared a few days of happiness and danger—hours she would never forget. And so, when she came to inherit the legacy, she set out on the long journey, following the memory of a lost love to Malaya and beyond . . . seeking the fate of a man.

Also by Nevil Shute
Published by Ballantine Books:

ON THE BEACH

A TOWN
LIKE ALICE

Originally published as "The Legacy"
NEVIL SHUTE

BALLANTINE BOOKS • NEW YORK

ISBN 0-345-30565-5

This edition published by arrangement with William Morrow and Company, Inc.

Manuufactured in the United States of America

Published in Great Britain by William Heinemann, Ltd., London, under the title *A Town Like Alice*.

The quotation from "When You Are Old," by W. B. Yeats, on the title page is from his *Poems*, copyright 1906 by The Macmillan Company and used with their permission.

First American Printing: January, 1963
Fifth Printing: November 1981

First Canadian Printing: March, 1963
Fourth Canadian Printing: February, 1967

A TOWN
LIKE ALICE

Chapter I

JAMES MACFADDEN died in March 1905 when he was forty-seven years old; he was riding in the Driffield Point to Point.

He left the bulk of his money to his son Douglas. The Macfaddens and the Dalhousies at that time lived in Perth, and Douglas was a school friend of Jock Dalhousie who was a young man then, and had gone to London to become junior partner in a firm of solicitors in Chancery Lane, Owen, Dalhousie, and Peters. I am now the senior partner, and Owen and Dalhousie and Peters have been dead for many years, but I never changed the name of the firm.

It was natural that Douglas Macfadden should put his affairs into the hands of Jock Dalhousie, and Mr. Dalhousie handled them personally till he died in 1928. In splitting up the work I took Mr. Macfadden on to my list of clients, and forgot about him in the pressure of other matters.

It was not until 1935 that any business for him came up. I had a letter from him then, from an address in Ayr. He said that his brother-in-law, Arthur Paget, had been killed in a motor car accident in Malaya and so he wanted to re-draft his will to make a trust in favour of his sister Jean and her two children. I am sorry to say that I was so ignorant of this client that I did not even know he was unmarried and had no issue of his own. He finished up by saying that he was too unwell to travel down to London, and he suggested that perhaps a junior member of the firm might be sent up to see him and arrange the matter.

This fitted in with my arrangements fairly well, because when I got this letter I was just leaving for a fortnight's fishing holiday on Loch Shiel. I wrote and told him that I would visit him on my way south, and I put the file concerning his affairs in the bottom of my suitcase to study one evening during my vacation.

When I got to Ayr I took a room at the Station Hotel, because in our correspondence there had been no suggestion that he could put me up. I changed out of my plus-fours into a dark business suit, and went to call upon my client.

He did not live at all in the manner I had expected. I did not know much about his estate except that it was probably well over twenty thousand pounds, and I had expected to find my client living in a house with a servant or two. Instead, I discovered that he had a bedroom and a sitting-room on the same floor of a small private hotel just off the sea front. He was evidently leading the life of an invalid though he was hardly more than fifty years old at that time, ten years younger than I was myself. He was as frail as an old lady of eighty, and he had a peculiar grey look about him which didn't look at all good to me. All the windows of his sitting-room were shut and after the clean air of the lochs and moors I found his room stuffy and close; he had a number of budgerigars in cages in the window, and the smell of these birds made the room very unpleasant. It was clear from the furnishings that he had lived in that hotel and in that room for a good many years.

He told me something about his life as we discussed the will; he was quite affable, and pleased that I had been able to come to visit him myself. He seemed to be an educated man, though he spoke with a marked Scots accent. "I live very quietly, Mr. Strachan," he said. "My health will not permit me to go far abroad. Whiles I get out upon the front on a fine day and sit for a time, and then again Maggie—that's the daughter of Mrs. Doyle who keeps the house—Maggie wheels me out in the chair. They are very good to me here."

Turning to the matter of the will, he told me that he had no close relatives at all except his sister, Jean Paget. "Forbye my father might have left what you might call an indiscretion or two in Australia," he said. "I would not say that there might not be some of those about, though I have never met one, or corresponded. Jean told me once that my mother had been sore distressed. Women talk about these things, of course, and my father was a lusty type of man."

His sister Jean had been an officer in the W.A.A.C.s in the 1914-1918 war, and she had married a Captain Paget in the spring of 1917. "It was not a very usual sort of marriage," he said thoughtfully. "You must remember that my sister Jean had never been out of Scotland till she joined the army, and the greater part of her life had been spent in Perth. Arthur Paget was an Englishman from Southampton, in Hampshire. I have nothing against Arthur, but we had all naturally thought that Jean would have married a Scot. Still, I would not say but it has been a happy marriage, or as happy as most."

After the war was over Arthur Paget had got a job upon a rubber estate in Malaya somewhere near Taiping, and Jean, of course, went out there with him. From that time Douglas Macfadden had seen little of his sister; she had been home on leave in 1926 and again in 1932. She had two children, Donald born in 1918 and Jean born in 1921; these children had been left in England in 1932 to live with the Paget parents and to go to school in Southampton, while their mother returned to Malaya. My client had only seen them once, in 1932 when their mother brought them up to Scotland.

The present position was that Arthur Paget had been killed in a motor accident somewhere near Ipoh; he had been driving home at night from Kuala Lumpur and had driven off the road at a high speed and hit a tree. Probably he fell asleep. His widow, Jean Paget, was in England; she had come home a year or so before his death and she had taken a small house in Bassett just outside Southampton to make a home for the children and to be near their schools. It was a sensible arrangement, of course, but it seemed to me to be a pity that the brother and the sister could not have arranged to live nearer to each other. I fancy that my client regretted the distance that separated them, because he referred to it more than once.

He wanted to revise his will. His existing will was a very simple one, in which he left his entire estate to his sister Jean. "I would not alter that," he said. "But you must understand that Arthur Paget was alive when I made that will, and that in the nature of things I expected him to be alive when Jean inherited from me, and I expected that he would be there to guide her in matters of business. I shall not make old bones."

He seemed to have a fixed idea that all women were unworldly creatures and incapable of looking after money; they were irresponsible, and at the mercy of any adventurer. Accordingly, although he wanted his sister to have the full use of his money after his death, he wanted to create a trust to ensure that her son Donald, at that time a schoolboy, should inherit the whole estate intact after his mother's death. There was, of course, no special difficulty in that. I presented to him the various pros and cons of a trust such as he envisaged, and I reminded him that a small legacy to Mrs. Doyle, in whose house he had lived for so many years, might not be out of place provided that he was still living with them at the time of his death. He agreed to that. He told me then that he had no close relations living, and he asked me if I would undertake to be the sole trustee of his estate and the executor of his will. That is the sort of business a family solicitor frequently takes on his shoulders, of course. I told him that in view of my age he should appoint a co-trustee, and he agreed to the insertion of our junior partner, Mr. Lester Robinson, to be co-trustee with me. He also agreed to a charging clause for our professional services in connection with the trust.

There only remained to tidy up the loose ends of what was, after all, a fairly simple will. I asked him what should happen if both he and his sister were to die before the boy Donald was twenty-one, and I suggested that the trust should terminate and the boy should inherit the estate absolutely when he reached his majority. He agreed to this, and I made another note upon my pad.

"Supposing then," I said, "that Donald should die before his mother, or if Donald and his mother should die in some way before you. The estate would then pass to the girl, Jean. Again, I take it that the trust would terminate when she reached her majority?"

"Ye mean," he asked, "when she became twenty-one?"

I nodded. "Yes. That is what we decided in the case of her brother."

He shook his head. "I think that would be most imprudent, Mr. Strachan, if I may say so. No lassie would be fit to administer her own estate when she was twenty-one. A lassie of that age is at the mercy of her sex, Mr. Strachan, at the mercy of her sex. I would want the trust to continue for much longer than that. Till she was forty, at the very least."

From various past experiences I could not help agreeing with him that twenty-one was a bit young for a girl to have absolute control over a large sum of money, but forty seemed to me to be excessively old. I stated my own view that twenty-five would be a reasonable age, and very reluctantly he receded to thirty-five. I could not move him from that position, and as he was obviously tiring and growing irritable I accepted that as the maximum duration of our trust. It meant that in those very unlikely circumstances the trust would continue for twenty-one years from that date, since the girl Jean had been born in 1921 and it was then 1935. That finished our business and I left him and went back to London to draft out the will, which I sent to him for signature. I never saw my client again.

It was my fault that I lost touch with him. It had been my

habit for a great many years to take my holiday in the spring, when I would go with my wife to Scotland for a fortnight's fishing, usually to Loch Shiel. I thought that this was going on for ever, as one does, and that next year I would call again upon this client on my way down from the north to see if there was any other business I could do for him. But things turn out differently, sometimes. In the winter of 1935 Lucy died. I don't want to dwell on that, but we had been married for twenty-seven years and—well, it was very painful. Both our sons were abroad, Harry in his submarine on the China Station and Martin in his oil company at Basra. I hadn't the heart to go back to Loch Shiel, and I have never been to Scotland since. I had a sale and got rid of most of our furniture, and I sold our house on Wimbledon Common; one has to make an effort at a time like that, and a clean break. It's no good going on living in the ashes of a dead happiness.

I took a flat in Buckingham Gate opposite the Palace stables and just across the park from my club in Pall Mall. I furnished it with a few things out of the Wimbledon house and got a woman to come in and cook my breakfast and clean for me in the mornings, and here I set out to re-create my life. I knew the pattern well enough from the experience of others in the club. Breakfast in my flat. Walk through the Park and up the Strand to my office in Chancery Lane. Work all day, with a light lunch at my desk. To the club at six o'clock to read the periodicals, and gossip, and dine, and after dinner a rubber of bridge. That is the routine that I fell into in the spring of 1936, and I am in it still.

All this, as I say, took my mind from Douglas Macfadden; with more than half my mind upon my own affairs I could only manage to attend to those clients who had urgent business with my office. And presently another interest grew upon me. It was quite obvious that war was coming, and some of us in the club who were too old for active military service began to get very interested in Air Raid Precautions. Cutting the long story short, Civil Defence as it came to be called absorbed the whole of my leisure for the next eight years. I became a Warden, and I was on duty in my district of Westminster all through the London blitz and the long, slow years of war that followed it. Practically all my staff went on service, and I had to run the office almost single-handed. In those years I never took a holiday, and I doubt if I slept more than five hours in any night. When finally peace came in 1945 my hair was white and my head shaky, and though I improved a little in the years that followed I had definitely joined the ranks of the old men.

One afternoon in January 1948 I got a telegram from Ayr. It read,

> REGRET MR DOUGLAS MACFADDEN PASSED AWAY LAST
> NIGHT PLEASE INSTRUCT RE FUNERAL.
> DOYLE, BALMORAL HOTEL, AYR.

I had to search my memory, I am afraid, to recollect through the war years who Mr. Douglas Macfadden was, and then I had to turn to the file and the will to refresh my memory with the details of what had happened thirteen years before. It seemed rather odd to me that there was nobody at Ayr who could manage the funeral business. I put in a trunk call to Ayr right away and very soon I was speaking to Mrs. Doyle. It was a bad line, but I understood that she knew of no relations; apparently Mr. Macfadden had had no visitors for a very long time. Clearly, I should have to go to Ayr myself, or else send somebody. I had no urgent engagements for the next two days and the matter seemed to be a little difficult. I had a talk with Lester Robinson, my partner who had come back from the war as a Brigadier, and cleared my desk, and took the sleeper up to Glasgow after dinner that night. In the morning I went down in a slow train to Ayr.

When I got to the Balmoral Hotel I found the landlord and his wife in mourning and obviously distressed; they had been fond of their queer lodger and it was probably due in a great part to their ministrations that he had lived so long. There was no mystery about the cause of death. I had a talk with the doctor and heard all about his trouble; the doctor had been with him at the end, for he lived only two doors away, and the death certificate was already signed. I took a brief look at the body for identification and went through the various formalities of death. It was all perfectly straightforward, except that there were no relations.

"I doubt he had any," said Mr. Doyle. "His sister used to write to him at one time, and she came to see him in 1938, I think it was. She lived in Southampton. But he's had no letters except just a bill or two for the last two years."

His wife said, "Surely, the sister died, didn't she? Don't you remember him telling us, sometime towards the end of the war?"

"Well, I don't know," he said. "So much was happening about that time. Maybe she did die."

Relations or not, arrangements had to be made for the funeral, and I made them that afternoon. When that was done I settled down to look through the papers in his desk. One or two of the figures in an account book and on the back of the counterfoils of his cheque-book made me open my eyes; clearly I should have to have a talk with the bank manager first thing next morning. I found a letter from his sister dated in 1941 about the lease of her house. It threw no light, of course, upon her death, if she was dead, but it did reveal significant news about the children. Both of them were in Malaya at that time. The boy Donald, who must have been twenty-three years old then, was working on a rubber plantation near Kuala Selangor. His sister Jean had gone out to him in the winter of 1939, and was working in an office in Kuala Lumpur.

At about five o'clock I put in a trunk call to my office in London, standing in the cramped box of the hotel, and spoke to my partner. "Look, Lester," I said. "I told you that there was some difficulty about the relations. I am completely at a loss up here, I'm sorry to say. Provisionally, I have arranged the funeral for the day after tomorrow, at two o'clock, at St. Enoch's cemetery. The only relations that I know of live, or used to live, in Southampton. The sister, Mrs. Arthur Paget, was living in 1941 at No. 17 St. Ronans Road, Bassett—that's just by Southampton somewhere. There were some other Paget relations in the district, the parents of Arthur Paget. Mrs. Arthur Paget—her Christian name was Jean —yes, she was the deceased's sister. She had two children, Donald and Jean Paget, but they were both in Malaya in 1941. God knows what became of them. I wouldn't waste much time just now looking for them, but would you get Harris to do what he can to find some of these Southampton Pagets and tell them about the funeral? He'd better take the telephone book and talk to all the Pagets in Southampton one by one. I don't suppose there are so very many."

Lester came on the telephone to me next morning just after I got back from the bank. "I've nothing very definite, I'm afraid, Noel," he said. "I did discover one thing. Mrs. Paget died in 1942, so she's out of it. She died of pneumonia through going out to the air-raid shelter—Harris got that from the hospital. About the other Pagets, there are seven in the telephone directory and we've rung them all up, and they're none of them anything to do with your family. But one of them, Mrs. Eustace Paget, thinks the family you're looking for are the Edward Pagets, and that they moved to North Wales after the first Southampton blitz."

"Any idea whereabouts in North Wales?" I asked.

"Not a clue," he said. "I think the only thing that you can do now is to proceed with the funeral."

"I think it is," I replied. "But tell Harris to go on all the same, because apart from the funeral we've got to find the heirs. I've just been to the bank, and there is quite a sizable estate. We're the trustees, you know."

I spent the rest of that day in packing up all personal belongings and letters and papers to take down to my office. Furniture at that time was in short supply, and I arranged to store the furniture of the two rooms, since that might be wanted by the heirs. I gave the clothes to Mr. Doyle to give away to needy people in Ayr. Only two of the budgerigars were left; I gave those to the Doyles, who seemed to be attached to them. Next morning I had another interview with the bank manager and telephoned to book my sleeper on the night mail down to London. And in the afternoon we buried Douglas Macfadden.

It was very cold and bleak and grey in the cemetery, that January afternoon. The only mourners were the Doyles, father, mother, and daughter, and myself, and I remember thinking that it was queer how little any of us knew about the man that we were burying. I had a great respect for the Doyle family by that time. They had been overwhelmed when I told them of the small legacy that Mr. Macfadden had left them and at first they were genuinely unwilling to take it; they said that they had been well paid for his two rooms and board for many years, and anything else that they had done for him had been because they liked him. It was something, on that bitter January afternoon beside the grave, to feel that he had friends at the last ceremonies.

So that was the end of it, and I drove back with the Doyles and had tea with them in their sitting-room beside the kitchen. And after tea I left for Glasgow and the night train down to London, taking with me two suitcases of papers and small personal effects to be examined at my leisure if the tracing of the heir proved to be troublesome, and later to be handed over as a part of the inheritance.

In fact, we found the heir without much difficulty. Young Harris got a line on it within a week, and presently we got a letter from a Miss Agatha Paget, who was the headmistress of a girls' school in Colwyn Bay. She was a sister of Arthur

Paget, who had been killed in the motor accident in Malaya. She confirmed that his wife, Jean, had died in Southampton in the year 1942, and she added the fresh information that the son, Donald, was also dead. He had been a prisoner of war in Malaya, and had died in captivity. Her niece, Jean, however, was alive and in the London district. The headmistress did not know her home address because she lived in rooms and had changed them once or twice, so she usually wrote to her addressing her letters to her firm. She was employed in the office of a concern called Pack and Levy Ltd, whose address was The Hyde, Perivale, London, N.W.

I got this letter in the morning mail; I ran through the others and cleared them out of the way, and then picked up this one and read it again. Then I got my secretary to bring me the Macfadden box and I read the will through again, and went through some other papers and my notes on the estate. Finally I reached out for the telephone directory and looked up Pack and Levy Ltd to find out what they did.

Presently I got up from my desk and stood for a time looking out of the window at the bleak, grey, January London street. I like to think a bit before taking any precipitate action. Then I turned and went through into Robinson's office; he was dictating, and I stood warming myself at his fire till he had finished and the girl had left the room.

"I've got that Macfadden heir," I said. "I'll tell Harris."

"All right," he replied. "You've found the son?"

"No," I said. "I've found the daughter. The son's dead."

He laughed. "Bad luck. That means we're trustees for the estate until she's thirty-five, doesn't it?"

I nodded.

"How old is she now?"

I calculated for a minute. "Twenty-six or twenty-seven."

"Old enough to make a packet of trouble for us."

"I know."

"Where is she? What's she doing?"

"She's employed as a clerk or typist with a firm of handbag manufacturers in Perivale," I said. "I'm just about to concoct a letter to her."

He smiled. "Fairy Godfather."

"Exactly," I replied.

I went back into my room and sat for some time thinking out that letter; it seemed to me to be important to set a formal tone when writing to this young woman for the first time. Finally I wrote,

Dear Madam,

It is with regret that we have to inform you of the death of Mr. Douglas Macfadden at Ayr on January 21st. As Executors to his will we have experienced some difficulty in tracing the beneficiaries, but if you are the daughter of Jean (nee Macfadden) and Arthur Paget formerly resident in Southampton and in Malaya, it would appear that you may be entitled to a share in the estate.

May we ask you to telephone for an appointment to call upon us at your convenience to discuss the matter further? It will be necessary for you to produce evidence of identity at an early stage, such as your birth certificate, National Registration Identity Card, and any other documents that may occur to you.

I am,

    Yours truly,

        for Owen, Dalhousie and Peters,

            N. H. STRACHAN

She rang me up the next day. She had quite a pleasant voice, the voice of a well-trained secretary. She said, "Mr. Strachan, this is Miss Jean Paget speaking. I've got your letter of the 29th. I wonder—do you work on Saturday mornings? I'm in a job, so Saturday would be the best day for me."

I replied, "Oh yes, we work on Saturday mornings. What time would be convenient for you?"

"Should we say ten-thirty?"

I made a note upon my pad. "That's all right. Have you got your birth certificate?"

"Yes, I've got that. Another thing I've got is my mother's marriage certificate, if that helps."

I said, "Oh yes, bring that along. All right, Miss Paget, I shall look forward to meeting you on Saturday. Ask for me by name, Mr. Noel Strachan. I am the senior partner."

She was shown into my office punctually at ten-thirty on Saturday. She was a girl or woman of a medium height, dark-haired. She was good looking in a quiet way; she had a tranquillity about her that I find difficult to describe except by saying that it was the grace that you see frequently in women of a Scottish descent. She was dressed in a dark blue coat and skirt. I got up and shook hands with her, and gave her the chair in front of my desk, and went round and sat down myself. I had the papers ready.

"Well, Miss Paget," I said. "I heard about you from your aunt—I think she is your aunt? Miss Agatha Paget, at Colwyn Bay."

She inclined her head. "Aunt Aggie wrote and told me that she had had a letter from you. Yes, she's my aunt."

"And I take it that you are the daughter of Arthur and Jean Paget, who lived in Southampton and Malaya?"

She nodded. "That's right. I've got the birth certificate and mother's birth certificate, as well as her marriage certificate." She took them from her bag and put them on my desk, with her identity card.

I opened these documents and read them through carefully. There was no doubt about it; she was the person I was looking for. I leaned back in my chair presently and took off my spectacles. "Tell me, Miss Paget," I said. "Did you ever meet your uncle, who died recently? Mr. Douglas Macfadden?"

She hesitated. "I've been thinking about that a lot," she said candidly. "I couldn't honestly swear that I have ever met him, but I think it must have been him that Mother took me to see once in Scotland, when I was about ten years old. We all went together, Mother and I and Donald. I remember an old man in a very stuffy room with a lot of birds in cages. I think that was Uncle Douglas, but I'm not quite sure."

That fitted in with what he had told me, the visit of his sister with her children in 1932. This girl would have been eleven years old then. "Tell me about your brother Donald, Miss Paget," I asked. "Is he still alive?"

She shook her head. "He died in 1943, while he was a prisoner. He was taken by the Japs in Singapore when we surrendered, and then he was sent to the railway."

I was puzzled. "The railway?"

She looked at me coolly, and I thought I saw tolerance for the ignorance of those who stayed in England in her glance. "The railway that the Japs built with Asiatic and prisoner-of-war labour between Siam and Burma. One man died for every sleeper that was laid, and it was about two hundred miles long. Donald was one of them."

There was a little pause. "I am so sorry," I said at last. "One thing I have to ask you, I am afraid. Was there a death certificate?"

She stared at me. "I shouldn't think so."

"Oh . . ." I leaned back in my chair and took up the will. "This is the will of Mr. Douglas Macfadden," I said. "I have a copy for you, Miss Paget, but I think I'd better tell you what it contains in ordinary, non-legal language. Your uncle made two small bequests. The whole of the residue of the estate was left in trust for your brother Donald. The terms of the trust were to the effect that your mother was to enjoy the income from the trust until her death. If she died before your brother attained his majority, the trust was to continue until he was twenty-one, when he would inherit absolutely and the trust would be discharged. If your brother died before inheriting, then you were to inherit the residuary estate after your mother's time, but in that event the trust was to continue till the year 1956, when you would be thirty-five years old. You will appreciate that it is necessary for us to obtain legal evidence of your brother's death."

She hesitated, and then she said, "Mr. Strachan, I'm afraid I'm terribly stupid. I understand you want some proof that Donald is dead. But after that is done, do you mean that I inherit everything that Uncle Douglas left?"

"Broadly speaking—yes," I replied. "You would only receive the income from the estate until the year 1956. After that, the capital would be yours to do what you like with."

"How much did he leave?"

I picked up a slip of paper from the documents before me and ran my eye down the figures for a final check. "After paying death duties and legacies," I said carefully, "the residuary estate would be worth about fifty-three thousand pounds at present-day prices. I must make it clear that that is at present-day prices, Miss Paget. You must not assume that you would inherit that sum in 1956. A falling stock market affects even trustee securities."

She stared at me. "Fifty-three thousand pounds?"

I nodded. "That seems to be about the figure."

"How much a year would that amount of capital yield, Mr. Strachan?"

I glanced at the figures on the slip before me. "Invested in trustee stocks, as at present—about £1550 a year, gross income. Then income tax has to be deducted. You would have about nine hundred a year to spend, Miss Paget."

"Oh . . ." There was a long silence; she sat staring at the desk in front of her. Then she looked up at me, and smiled. "It takes a bit of getting used to," she remarked. "I mean, I've always worked for my living, Mr. Strachan. I've never thought that I'd do anything else unless I married, and that's only a different sort of work. But this means that I need never work again—unless I want to."

She had hit the nail on the head with her last sentence. "That's exactly it," I replied. "Unless you want to."

"I don't know what I'd do if I didn't have to go to the office," she said. "I haven't got any other life . . ."

"Then I should go on going to the office," I observed.

She laughed. "I suppose that's the only thing to do."

I leaned back in my chair. "I'm an old man now, Miss Paget. I've made plenty of mistakes in my time and I've learned one thing from them, that it's never very wise to do anything in a great hurry. I take it that this legacy will mean a considerable change in your circumstances. If I may offer my advice, I should continue in your present employment for the time, at any rate, and I should refrain from talking about your legacy in the office just yet. For one thing, it will be some weeks before you get possession even of the income from the estate. First we have to obtain legal proof of the death of your brother, and then we have to obtain probate and realize a portion of the securities to meet estate and succession duties. Tell me, what are you doing with this firm Pack and Levy?"

"I'm a shorthand-typist," she said. "I'm working now as secretary to Mr. Pack."

"Where do you live, Miss Paget?"

She said, "I've got a bed-sitting room at No. 43 Campion Road, just off Ealing Common. It's quite convenient, but of course I have a lot of my meals out. There's a Lyons just round the corner."

I thought for a minute. "Have you got many friends in Ealing? How long have you been there?"

"I don't know very many people," she replied. "One or two families, people who work in the firm, you know. I've been there over two years now, ever since I was repatriated. I was out in Malaya, you know, Mr. Strachan, and I was a sort of prisoner of war for three and a half years. Then when I got home I got this job with Pack and Levy, and I've been there ever since."

I made a note of her address upon my pad. "Well, Miss Paget," I said, "I should go on just as usual for the time being. I will consult the War Office on Monday morning and obtain this evidence about your brother as quickly as I can. Tell me his name, and number, and unit." She did so, and I wrote them down. "As soon as I get that, I shall submit the will for probate. When that is proved, then the trust commences and continues till the year 1956, when you will inherit absolutely."

She looked up at me. "Tell me about this trust," she asked. "I'm afraid I'm not very good at legal matters."

I nodded. "Of course not. Well, you'll find it all in legal language in the copy of the will which I shall give you, but what it means is this, Miss Paget. Your uncle, when he made this will, had a very poor opinion of the ability of women to manage their own money. I'm sorry to have to say such a thing, but it is better for you to know the whole of the facts."

She laughed. "Please don't apologize for him, Mr. Strachan. Go on."

"At first, he was quite unwilling that you should inherit the capital of the estate till you were forty years old," I said. "I contested that view, but I was unable to get him to agree to any less period than the present arrangement in the will. Now, the object of a trust is this. The testator appoints trustees—in this case, myself and my partner—who undertake to do their best to preserve the capital intact and hand it over to the legatee—to you—when the trust expires."

"I see. Uncle Douglas was afraid that I might spend the fifty-three thousand all at once."

I nodded. "That was in his mind. He did not know you, of course, Miss Paget, so there was nothing personal about it. He felt that in general women were less fit than men to handle large sums of money at an early age."

She said quietly, "He may have been right." She thought for a minute, and then she said, "So you're going to look after the money for me till I'm thirty-five and give me the interest to spend in the meantime? Nine hundred a year?"

"If you wish us to conduct your income tax affairs for you, that would be about the figure," I said. "We can arrange the payments in any way that you prefer, as a quarterly or a monthly cheque, for example. You would get a formal statement of account half-yearly."

She asked curiously, "How do you get paid for doing all this for me, Mr. Strachan?"

I smiled. "That is a very prudent question, Miss Paget. You will find a clause in the will, No. 8, I think, which entitles us to charge for our professional services against the income from the trust. Of course, if you get into any legal trouble we should be glad to act for you and help you in any way we could. In that case we should charge you on the normal scale of fees."

She said unexpectedly, "I couldn't ask for anybody better." And then she glanced at me, and said michievously, "I made some enquiries about this firm yesterday."

"Oh . . . I hope they were satisfactory?"

"Very." She did not tell me then what she told me later, that her informant had described us as, "As solid as the Bank of England, and as sticky as treacle." "I know I'm going to be in very good hands, Mr. Strachan."

I inclined my head. "I hope so. I am afraid that at times you may find this trust irksome, Miss Paget; I can assure you that I shall do my utmost to prevent it from becoming so. You will see in the will that the testator gave certain powers to the trustees to realize capital for the benefit of the legatee in cases where they were satisfied that it would be genuinely for her advantage."

"You mean, if I really needed a lot of money—for an operation or something—you could let me have it, if you approved?"

She was quick, that girl. "I think that is a very good example. In case of illness, if the income were insufficient, I should certainly realize some of your capital for your benefit."

She smiled at me, and said, "It's rather like being a ward in Chancery, or something."

I was a little touched by the comparison. I said, "I should feel very much honoured if you care to look at it that way, Miss Paget. Inevitably this legacy is going to make an upset in your condition of life, and if I can do anything to help you in the transition I should be only too pleased." I handed her her copy of the will. "Well, there is the will, and I suggest you take it away and read it quietly by yourself. I'll keep the certificates for the time being. After you've thought things over for a day or two I am sure that there will be a great many questions to which you will want answers. Would you like to come and see me again?"

She said, "I would. I know there'll be all sorts of things I want to ask about, but I can't think of them now. It's all so sudden."

I turned to my engagement diary. "Well, suppose we meet again about the middle of next week." I stared at the pages. "Of course, you're working. What time do you get off from your office, Miss Paget?"

She said, "Five o'clock."

"Would six o'clock on Wednesday evening suit you, then? I shall hope to have got somewhere with the matter of your brother by that time."

She said, "Well, that's all right for me, Mr. Strachan, but isn't it a bit late for you? Don't you want to get home?"

I said absently, "I only go to the club. No, Wednesday at six would suit me very well." I made a note upon my pad, and then I hesitated. "Perhaps if you are doing nothing after that you might like to come on to the club and have dinner in the Ladies' Annexe," I said. "I'm afraid it's not a very gay place, but the food is good."

She smiled, and said warmly, "I'd love to do that, Mr. Strachan. It's very kind of you to ask me."

I got to my feet. "Very well, then, Miss Paget—six o'clock on Wednesday. And in the meantime, don't do anything in a great hurry. It never pays to be impetuous. . . ."

She went away, and I cleared my desk and took a taxi to the club for lunch. After lunch I had a cup of coffee and slept for ten minutes in a chair before the fire, and when I woke up I thought I ought to get some exercise. So I put on my hat and coat and went out and walked rather aimlessly up St. James' Street and along Piccadilly to the Park. As I walked, I wondered how that fresh young woman was spending her week-end. Was she telling her friends all about her good luck, or was she sitting somewhere warm and quiet, nursing and cherishing her own anticipations, or was she on a spending spree already? Or was she out with a young man? She would have plenty of men now to choose from, I thought cynically, and then it struck me that she probably had those already because she was a very marriageable girl. Indeed, considering her appearance and her evident good nature, I was rather surprised that she was not married already.

I had a little talk that evening in the club with a man who is in the Home Office about the procedure for establishing the death of a prisoner of war, and on Monday I had a number of telephone conversations with the War Office and the Home Office about the case. I found, as I had suspected, that there was an extraordinary procedure for proving death which could be invoked, but where a doctor was available who had attended the deceased in the prison camp the normal certification of death was the procedure to adopt. In this instance there was a general practitioner called Ferris in practice at Beckenham who had been a doctor in Camp 206 in the Takunan district on the Burma-Siam railway, and the official at the War Office advised me that this doctor would be in a position to give the normal death certificate.

I rang him up next morning, and he was out upon his rounds. I tried to make his wife understand what I wanted but I think it was too complicated for her; she suggested that I should call and see him after the evening surgery, at half past six. I hesitated over that because Beckenham is a good long way out, but I was anxious to get these formalities over quickly for the sake of the girl. So I went out to see this doctor that evening.

He was a cheerful, fresh-faced man not more than thirty-five years old; he had a keen sense of humour, if rather a macabre one at times. He looked as healthy and fit as if he had spent the whole of his life in England in a country practice. I got to him just as he was finishing off the last of his patients, and he had leisure to talk for a little.

"Lieutenant Paget," he said thoughtfully. "Oh yes, I know. Donald Paget—was his name Donald?" I said it was. "Oh, of course, I remember him quite well. Yes, I can write a death certificate. I'd like to do that for him, though I don't suppose it'll do him much good."

"It will help his sister," I remarked. "There is a question of an inheritance, and the shorter we can make the necessary formalities the better for her."

He reached for his pad of forms. "I wonder if she's got as much guts as her brother?"

"Was he a good chap?"

He nodded. "Yes," he said. "He was a delicate-looking man, dark and rather pale, you know, but he was a very good type. I think he was a planter in civil life—anyway, he was in the Malay volunteers. He spoke Malay very well, and he got along in Siamese all right. With those languages, of course, he was a very useful man to have in the camp. We used to do a lot of black market with the villagers, the Siamese outside, you know. But quite apart from that, he was the sort of officer the men like. It was a great loss when he went."

"What did he die of?" I asked.

He paused with his pen poised over the paper. "Well, you could take your pick of half a dozen things. I hadn't time to do a post-mortem, of course. Between you and me, I don't really know. I think he just died. But he'd recovered from enough to kill a dozen ordinary men, so I don't know that it really matters what one puts down on the certificate. No legal point depends upon the cause of death, does it?"

"Oh, no," I said. "All I want is the death certified."

He still paused, in recollection. "He had a huge tropical ulcer on his left leg that we were treating, and that was certainly poisoning the whole system. I think if he'd gone on we'd have had to have taken that leg off. He got that because he was one of those chaps who won't report sick while they can walk. Well, while he was in hospital with the ulcer, he got cerebral malaria. We had nothing to treat that damn thing with till we got around to making our own quinine solutions for intravenous injection; we took a frightful risk with that, but there was nothing else to do. We got a lot through it with that, and Paget was one of them. He got over it quite well. That was just before we got the cholera. Cholera went right through the camp—hospital and everything. We couldn't isolate the cases, or anything like that. I never want to see a show like that again. We'd got nothing, *nothing*, not even saline. No drugs to speak of, and no equipment. We were making bedpans out of old kerosene tins. Paget got that, and would you believe it, he got over cholera. We got some prophylactic injections from the Nips and we gave him those; that may have helped. At least, I think we gave him that—I'm not sure. He was very weak when that left him, of course, and the ulcer wasn't any too good. And about a week after that, he just died in the night. Heart, I fancy. I'll tell you what I'll do. I'll put down for Cause of Death—Cholera. There you are, sir. I'm sorry you had to come all this way for it."

As I took the certificate I asked curiously, "Did you get any of those things yourself?"

He laughed. "I was one of the lucky ones. All I got was the usual dysentery and malaria, the ordinary type malaria, not cerebral. Overwork was *my* trouble, but other people had that, too. We were in such a jam, for so long. We had hundreds of cases just lying on the floor or bamboo charpoys in palm huts—it was raining almost all the time. No beds, no linen, no equipment, and precious few drugs. You just couldn't rest. You worked till you dropped asleep, and then you got up and went on working. You never came to an end. There was never half an hour when you could slack off and sit and have a smoke, or go for a walk, except by neglecting some poor sod who needed you very badly."

He paused. I sat silent, thinking how easy by comparison my own war had been. "It went on like that for nearly two years," he said. "You got a bit depressed at times, because you couldn't even take time off to go and hear a lecture."

"Did you have lectures?" I asked.

"Oh yes, we used to have a lot of lectures by the chaps in camp. How to grow Cox's Orange Pippins, or the T.T. motor cycle races, or Life in Hollywood. They made a difference to the men, the lectures did. But we doctors usually couldn't get to them. I mean, it's not much of an alibi when someone's in convulsions if you're listening to a lecture on Cox's Orange Pippins at the other end of the camp."

I said, "It must have been a terrible experience."

He paused, reflecting. "It was so beautiful," he said. "The Three Pagodas Pass must be one of the loveliest places in the world. You've got this broad valley with the river running down it, and the jungle forest, and the mountains . . . We used to sit by the river and watch the sun setting behind the mountains, sometimes, and say what a marvellous place it would be to come to for a holiday. However terrible a prison camp may be, it makes a difference if it's beautiful."

When Jean Paget came to see me on Wednesday evening I was ready to report the progress I had made. First I went through one or two formal matters connected with the winding up of the estate, and then I showed her the schedule of the furniture that I had put in store at Ayr. She was not much interested in that. "I should think it had all better be sold, hadn't it?" she remarked. "Could we put it in an auction?"

"Perhaps it would be as well to wait a little before doing that," I suggested. "You may want to set up a house or a flat of your own."

She wrinkled up her nose. "I can't see myself wanting to furnish it with any of Uncle Douglas' stuff, if I did," she said.

However, she agreed not to do anything about that till her own plans were more definite, and we turned to other matters. "I've got your brother's death certificate," I said, and I was going on to tell her what I had done with it when she stopped me.

"What did Donald die of, Mr. Strachan?" she asked.

I hesitated for a moment. I did not want to tell so young a woman the unpleasant story I had heard from Dr. Ferris. "The cause of death was cholera," I said at last.

She nodded, as if she had been expecting that. "Poor old boy," she said softly. "Not a very nice way to die."

I felt that I must say something to alleviate her distress. "I had a long talk with the doctor who attended him," I told her. "He died quite peacefully, in his sleep."

She stared at me. "Well then, it wasn't cholera," she said. "That's not the way you die of cholera."

I was a little at a loss in my endeavour to spare her unnecessary pain. "He had cholera first, but he recovered. The actual cause of death was probably heart failure, induced by the cholera."

She considered this for a minute. "Did he have anything else?" she asked.

Well, then of course there was nothing for it but to tell her everything I knew. I was amazed at the matter-of-fact way in which she took the unpleasant details and at her knowledge of the treatment of such things as tropical ulcers, until I recollected that this girl had been a prisoner of the Japanese in Malaya, too. "Damn bad luck the ulcer didn't go a bit quicker," she said coolly. "If there'd been an amputation they'd have had to evacuate him from the railway, and then he wouldn't have got the cerebral malaria or the cholera."

"He must have had a wonderfully strong constitution to have survived so much," I said.

"He hadn't," she said positively. "Donald was always getting coughs and colds and things. What he *had* got was a wonderfully strong sense of humour. I always thought he'd come through, just because of that. Everything that happened to him was a joke."

When I was a young man, girls didn't know about cholera or great ulcers, and I didn't quite know how to deal with her. I turned the conversation back to legal matters where I was on firmer ground, and showed her how her case for probate was progressing. And presently I took her downstairs and we got a taxi and went over to the club to dine.

I had a reason for entertaining her, that first evening. It was obvious that I was going to have a good deal to do with this young woman in the next few years, and I wanted to find out about her. I knew practically nothing of her education or her background at that time; her knowledge of tropical diseases, for example, had already confused me. I wanted to give her a good dinner with a little wine and get her talking; it was going to make my job as trustee a great deal easier if I knew what her interests were, and how her mind worked. And so I took her to the Ladies' Annexe at my club, a decent place where we could dine in our own time without music and talk quietly for a little time after dinner. I find that I get tired if there is a lot of noise and bustling about, as in a restaurant.

I showed her where she could go to wash and tidy up, and while she was doing that I ordered her a sherry. I got up from the table in the drawing room when she came to me, and gave her a cigarette, and lit it for her. "What did you do over the weekend?" I asked as we sat down. "Did you go out and celebrate?"

She shook her head. "I didn't do anything very much. I'd arranged to meet one of the girls in the office for lunch on

Saturday and to go and see the new Bette Davis film at the Curzon, so we did that."

"Did you tell her about your good fortune?"

She shook her head. "I haven't told anybody." She paused, and sipped her sherry; she was managing that and her cigarette quite nicely. "It seems such an improbable story," she said, laughing. "I don't know that I really believe in it myself."

I smiled with her. "Nothing is real till it happens," I observed. "You'll believe that this is true when we send you the first cheque. It would be a great mistake to believe in it too hard before that happens."

"I don't," she laughed. "Except for one thing. I don't believe you'd be wasting so much time on my affairs unless there was something in it."

"It's true enough for that." I paused, and then I said, "Have you thought yet what you are going to do in a month or two when the income from the trust begins? Your monthly cheque, after the tax has been deducted, will be about seventy-five pounds. I take it that you will hardly wish to go on with your present employment when those cheques begin to come in?"

"No . . ." She sat staring for a minute at the smoke rising from her cigarette. "I don't want to stop working. I wouldn't mind a bit going on with Pack and Levy just as if nothing had happened, if it was a job worth doing," she said. "But—well, it's not. We make ladies' shoes and handbags, Mr. Strachan, and small ornamental attaché cases for the high-class trade—the sort that sells for thirty guineas in a Bond Street shop to stupid women with more money than sense. Fitted vanity cases in rare leathers, and all that sort of thing. It's all right if you've got to earn your living, working in that sort of place. And it's been interesting, too, learning all about that trade."

"Most jobs are interesting when you're learning them," I said.

She turned to me. "That's true. I've quite enjoyed my time there. But I couldn't go on now, with all this money. One ought to do something more worth while, but I don't know what." She drank a little sherry. "I've got no profession, you see—only shorthand and typing, and a bit of book-keeping. I never had any real education—technical education, I mean. Taking a degree, or anything like that."

I thought for a moment. "May I ask a very personal question, Miss Paget?"

"Of course."

"Do you think it likely that you will marry in the near future?"

She smiled. "No, Mr. Strachan, I don't think it's very likely that I shall marry at all. One can't say for certain, of course, but I don't think so."

I nodded without comment. "Well then, had you thought about taking a university course?"

Her eyes opened wide. "No—I hadn't thought of that. I couldn't do it, Mr. Strachan—I'm not clever enough. I couldn't get into a university." She paused. "I was never higher than the middle of my class at school, and I never got into the Sixth."

"It was just a thought," I said. "I wondered if that might attract you."

She shook her head. "I couldn't go back to school again now. I'm much too old."

I smiled at her. "Not quite such an old woman as all that," I observed.

For some reason the little compliment fell flat. "When I compare myself with some of the girls in the office," she said quietly, and there was no laughter in her now, "I know I'm about seventy."

I was finding out something about her now, but to ease the situation I suggested that we should go in to dinner. When the ordering was done, I said, "Tell me what happened to you in the war. You were out in Malaya, weren't you?"

She nodded. "I had a job in an office, with the Kuala Perak Plantation Company. That was the company my father worked for, you know. Donald was with them, too."

"What happened to you in the war?" I asked. "Were you a prisoner?"

"A sort of prisoner," she said.

"In a camp?"

"No," she replied. "They left us pretty free." And then she changed the conversation very positively, and said, "What happened to you, Mr. Strachan? Were you in London all the time?"

I could not press her to talk about her war experiences if she didn't want to, and so I told her about mine—such as they were. And from that, presently, I found myself telling her about my two sons, Harry on the China Station and Martin in Basra, and their war records, and their families, and children. "I'm a grandfather three times over," I said ruefully. "There's going to be a fourth soon, I believe."

She laughed. "What does it feel like?"

"Just like it did before," I told her. "You don't feel any different as you get older. Only, you can't do so much."

Presently I got the conversation back on to her own affairs. I pointed out to her what sort of life she would be able to lead upon nine hundred a year. As an instance, I told her that she could have a country cottage in Devonshire and a little car, and a daily maid, and still have money to spare for a moderate amount of foreign travel. "I wouldn't know what to do with myself unless I worked at something," she said. "I've always worked at something, all my life."

I knew of several charitable appeals who would have found a first-class shorthand-typist, unpaid, a perfect godsend, and I told her so. She was inclined to be critical about those. "Surely, if a thing is really worth while, it'll pay," she said. She evidently had quite a strong business instinct latent in her. "It wouldn't need to have an unpaid secretary."

"Charitable organizations like to keep the overheads down," I remarked.

"I shouldn't have thought organizations that haven't got enough margin to pay a secretary can possibly do very much good," she said. "If I'm going to work at anything, I want it to be something really worth while."

I told her about the almoner's job at a hospital, and she was very much interested in that. "That's much more like it, Mr. Strachan," she said. "I think that's the sort of job one might get stuck into and take really seriously. But I wish it hadn't got to do with sick people. Either you've got a mission for sick people or you haven't, and I think I'm one of the ones who hasn't. But it's worth thinking about."

"Well, you can take your time," I said. "You don't have to do anything in a hurry."

She laughed at me. "I believe that's your guiding rule in life—never do anything in a hurry."

I smiled. "You might have a worse rule than that."

With the coffee after dinner I tried her out on the Arts. She knew nothing about music, except that she liked listening to the radio while she sewed. She knew nothing about literature, except that she liked novels with a happy ending. She liked paintings that were a reproduction of something that she knew, but she had never been to the Academy. She knew nothing whatsoever about sculpture. For a young woman with nine hundred a year, in London, she knew little of the arts and graces of social life, which seemed to me to be a pity.

"Would you like to come to the opera one night?" I asked. She smiled. "Would I understand it?"

"Oh yes. I'll look and see what's on. I'll pick something light, and in English."

She said, "It's terribly nice of you to ask me, but I'm sure you'd be much happier playing bridge."

"Not a bit," I said. "I haven't been to the opera or anything like that for years."

She smiled. "Well, of course I'd love to come," she said. "I've never seen an opera in my life. I don't even know what happens."

We sat talking about these things for an hour or more, till it was half past nine and she got up to go; she had three quarters of an hour to travel out to her suburban lodgings. I went with her, because she was going from St. James' Park Station, and I didn't care about the thought of so young a woman walking across the park alone late at night. At the station, standing on the dark, wet pavement by the brightly lit canopy, she put out her hand.

"Thank you so much, Mr. Strachan, for the dinner, and for everything you're doing for me," she said.

"It has been a very great pleasure to me, Miss Paget," I replied, and I meant it.

She hesitated, and then she said, smiling, "Mr. Strachan, we're going to have a good deal to do with each other. My name is Jean. I'll go crackers if you keep on calling me Miss Paget."

"You can't teach an old dog new tricks," I said awkwardly.

She laughed. "You said just now you don't feel any different as you get older. You can try and learn."

"I'll bear it in mind," I said. "Sure you can manage all right now?"

"Of course. Good night, Mr. Strachan."

"Good night," I said, lifting my hat and dodging the issue. "I'll let you know about the opera."

In the following weeks while probate was being granted I took her to a good many things. We went together to the opera several times, to the Albert Hall on Sunday afternoons, and to art galleries and exhibitions of paintings. In return, she took me to the cinema once or twice. I cannot really say that she developed any very great artistic appreciation. She liked paintings more than concerts. If it had to be music she preferred it in the form of opera and the lighter the better; she liked to have something to look at while her ears were assailed. We went twice to Kew Gardens as the spring came on. In the course of these excursions she came several times to my flat in Buckingham Gate; she got to know the kitchen, and made tea once or twice when we came in from some outing together. I had never entertained a lady in that flat before except my daughters-in-law, who sometimes come and use my spare room for a night or two in London.

Her business was concluded in March, and I was able to send her her first cheque. She did not give up her job at once, but continued to go to the office as usual. She wanted, very wisely, to build up a small reserve of capital from her monthly cheques before starting to live on them; moreover, at that time she had not made up her mind what she wanted to do.

That was the position one Sunday in April. I had arranged a little jaunt for her that day; she was to come to lunch at the flat and after that we were going down to Hampton Court, which she had never seen. I thought that the old palace and the spring flowers would please her, and I had been looking forward to this trip for several days. And then, of course, it rained.

She came to the flat just before lunch, dripping in her dark blue raincoat, carrying a very wet umbrella. I took the coat from her and hung it up in the kitchen. She went into my spare room and tidied herself; then she came to me in the lounge and we stood watching the rain beat against the Palace stables opposite, wondering what we should do instead that afternoon.

We had not got that settled when we sat down to coffee before the fire after lunch. I had mentioned one or two things but she seemed to be thinking about other matters. Over the coffee it came out, and she said,

"I've made up my mind what I want to do first of all, Mr. Strachan."

"Oh?" I asked. "What's that?"

She hesitated. "I know you're going to think this very odd. You may think it very foolish of me, to go spending money in this way. But—well, it's what I want to do. I think perhaps I'd better tell you about it now, before we go out."

It was warm and comfortable before the fire. Outside the sky was dark, and the rain streamed down on the wet pavements.

"Of course, Jean," I replied. "I don't suppose it's foolish at all. What is it that you want to do?"

She said, "I want to go back to Malaya, Mr. Strachan. To dig a well."

Chapter 2

I SUPPOSE there was a long pause after she said that. I remember being completely taken aback, and seeking refuge in my habit of saying nothing when you don't know what to say. She must have felt reproof in my silence, I suppose, because she leaned towards me, and she said, "I know it's a funny thing to want to do. May I tell you about it?"

I said, "Of course. Is this something to do with your experiences in the war?"

She nodded. "I've never told you about that. It's not that I mind talking about it, but I hardly ever think about it now. It all seems so remote, as if it was something that happened to another person, years ago—something that you'd read in a book. As if it wasn't me at all."

"Isn't it better to leave it so?"

She shook her head. "Not now, now that I've got this money." She paused. "You've been so very kind to me," she said. "I do want to try and make you understand."

Her life, she said, had fallen into three parts, the first two so separate from the rest that she could hardly reconcile them with her present self. First, she had been a schoolgirl living with her mother in Southampton. They lived in a small, three-bedroomed house in a suburban street. There had been a period before that when they had all lived in Malaya, but they had left Malaya for good when she was eleven and her brother Donald was fourteen, and she had only confused memories of that earlier time. Apparently Arthur Paget had been living alone in Malaya when he met his death, his wife having brought the children home.

They lived the life of normal suburban English children, school and holidays passing in a gentle rhythm with the one great annual excitement of three weeks' holiday in August in the Isle of Wight, at Seaview or at Freshwater. One thing differentiated them slightly from other families, in that they all spoke Malay. The children had learned it from the amah, of course, and their mother encouraged them to continue talking it in England, first as a joke and as a secret family language, but later for a very definite reason. When Arthur Paget drove his car into the tree near Ipoh he was travelling on the business of his company, and his widow became entitled to a pension under the company scheme. He had been a competent and a valuable man. The directors of the Kuala Perak Plantation Company, linking compassion with their quest for first-class staff, wrote to the widow offering to keep a position for the boy Donald as soon as he became nineteen. This was a good opening and one that they all welcomed; it meant that Donald was headed for Malaya and for rubber planting as a career. The Malay language became a matter of importance in giving him a good start, for very few boys of nineteen going to the East for their first job can speak an Oriental language. That shrewd Scotswoman, their mother, saw to it that the children did not forget Malay.

Jean had liked Southampton well enough, and she had had a happy childhood there in a gentle orbit of home, school, the Regal cinema, and the ice skating rink. Of all these influences the one that she remembered best was the ice rink, connected in her mind inevitably with Waldteufel's Skaters' Waltz. "It was a lovely place," she said, staring reminiscently into the fire. "I suppose it wasn't much, really—it was a wooden building, I think, converted out of something that had been put up in the first war. We skated there about twice a week ever since I can remember, and it was always lovely. The music, and the clean, swift movement, and all the boys and girls. The coloured lights, the crowd, and the ring of skates. I got quite good at it. Mummy got me a costume—black tights and bodice, and a little short skirt, you know. Dancing was wonderful upon the ice. . . ."

She turned to me. "You know, out in Malaya, when we were dying of malaria and dysentery, shivering with fever in the rain, with no clothes and no food and nowhere to go, because no one wanted us, I used to think about the rink at Southampton more than anything. It was a sort of symbol of the life that used to be—something to hold on to in one's mind." She paused. "Directly I got back to England I went back to Southampton, as soon as I could—I had something or other to do down there, but really it was because all through those years I had promised myself that one day I would go back and skate there again. And it had been blitzed. It was just a blackened and a burnt-out shell—there's no rink in Southampton now. I stood there on the pavement with the taxi waiting behind me with my boots and skates in my hand, and I couldn't keep crying with the disappointment. I don't know what the taxi driver thought of me."

Her brother had gone out to Malaya in 1937 when Jean

was sixteen. She left school at the age of seventeen and went to a commercial college in Southampton, and emerged from it six months later with a diploma as a shorthand-typist. She worked then for about a year in a solicitor's office in the town, but during this year a future for her in Malaya was taking shape. Her mother had kept in contact with the Chairman of the Kuala Perak Plantation Company, and the chairman was very satisfied with the reports he had of Donald from the plantation manager. Unmarried girls were never very plentiful in Malaya, and when Mrs. Paget approached the Chairman with a proposal that he should find a job for Jean in the head office at Kuala Lumpur it was considered seriously. It was deemed undesirable by the Company that their managers should marry or contract liaisons with native women, and the obvious way to prevent it was to encourage unmarried girls to come out from England. Here was a girl who was not only of a family that they knew but who could also speak Malay, a rare accomplishment in a shorthand-typist from England. So Jean got her job.

The war broke out while all this was in train, and to begin with, in England, this war was a phoney war. There seemed no reason to upset Jean's career for such a trivial matter; moreover, in Mrs. Paget's view Jean was much better in Malaya if war was to flare up in England. So Jean left for Malaya in the winter of 1939.

For over eighteen months she had a marvellous time. Her office was just round the corner from the Secretariat. The Secretariat is a huge building built in the more spacious days to demonstrate the power of the British Raj; it forms one side of a square facing the Club across the cricket ground, with a perfect example of an English village church to one side. Here everybody lived a very English life with tropical amenities; plenty of leisure, plenty of games, plenty of parties, plenty of dances, all made smooth and easy by plenty of servants. Jean boarded with one of the managers of the Company for the first few weeks; later she got a room in the Tudor Rose, a small private hotel run by an English-woman which was, in fact, more or less a chummery for unmarried girls employed in the offices and the Secretariat.

"It was just too good to be true," she said. "There was a dance or a party every single night of the week. One had to cry off doing something in order to find time to write a letter home."

When war came with Japan it hardly registered with her as any real danger, nor with any of her set. December the 7th

1941 brought America into the war and so was a good thing; it meant nothing to the parties in Kuala Lumpur except that young men began to take leave from their work and to appear in uniform, itself a pleasurable excitement. Even when the Japanese landed in the north of Malaya there was little thought of danger in Kuala Lumpur; three hundred miles of mountain and jungle was itself a barrier against invasion from the north. The sinking of the *Prince of Wales* and the *Repulse* was a catastrophe that didn't mean a thing to a girl of nineteen who had just rejected her first proposal.

Soon the married women and the children were evacuated to Singapore, in theory at any rate. As the Japanese made headway down the peninsula with swift encirclements through jungle that no troops had ever penetrated before, the situation began to appear serious. There came a morning when Jean's chief, a Mr. Merriman, called her into the office and told her bluntly that the office was closing down. She was to pack a suitcase and go to the station and take the first train down to Singapore. He gave her the name of their representative at an address off Raffles Place, and told her to report there for a passage home. Five other girls employed in the office got the same orders.

The Japanese at that time were reported to be near Ipoh, about a hundred miles to the north.

The serious nature of the position was obvious to everyone by then. Jean went to the bank and drew out all her money, about six hundred Straits dollars. She did not go to the station, however; if she had, it is doubtful whether she would have been able to get down to Singapore because the line by that time was completely blocked with military traffic coming up to the Front. She might have got away by road. Instead of that, she went to Batu Tasik to see Mrs. Holland.

Batu Tasik is a place about twenty miles north-west of Kuala Lumpur, and Mr. Holland was a man of forty, the manager of an opencast tin mine. He lived in quite a pleasant bungalow beside the mine with his wife Eileen and their children, Freddie aged seven, Jane aged four, and Robin who was ten months old. Eileen Holland was a comfortable, motherly woman between thirty and thirty-five years old. The Hollands never went to parties or to dances; they were not that sort. They stayed quietly at home and let the world go by them. They had invited Jean to come and stay with them soon after she arrived, and she had found their company restful. She had been to see them several times after that, and once, when she had had a slight attack of dengue, she had spent a week with them recuperating. In Kuala Lumpur on the previous day she had heard that Mr. Holland had brought his family into the station but had been unable to get them on the train, so they had all gone home again. Jean felt she could not leave without seeing the Hollands and offering her help with the children; Eileen Holland was a good mother and a first-rate housewife, but singularly unfitted to travel by herself with three children in the turmoil of evacuation.

Jean got to Batu Tasik fairly easily in a native bus; she arrived about lunch time and she found Mrs. Holland alone with the children. All trucks and cars belonging to the mine had been taken by the army, and the Hollands were left with their old Austin Twelve with one tyre worn down to the canvas and one very doubtful one with a large blister on the wall. This was the only vehicle that they now had for their evacuation, and it didn't look too good for taking the family to Singapore. Mr. Holland had gone into Kuala Lumpur to get two new outer covers; he had gone in at dawn and Mrs. Holland was already in a state of flutter that he had not come back.

In the bungalow everything was in confusion. The amah had gone home or had been given notice, and the house was full of suitcases half packed, or packed and opened again. Freddie had been in the pond and was all muddy, Jane was sitting on her pot amongst the suitcases, crying, and Mrs. Holland was nursing the baby and directing the cooking of lunch and attending to Jane and worrying about her husband all at the same time. Jean turned to and cleaned up Freddie and attended to Jane, and presently they all had lunch together.

Bill Holland did not come till nearly sunset, and he came empty-handed. All tyre stocks in Kuala Lumpur had been commandeered. He had found out, however, that a native bus was leaving for Singapore at eight in the morning, and he had reserved seats for his family on that. He had had to walk the last five miles for lack of any other transport, and walking five miles down a tarmac road in the middle of the afternoon in the heat of the tropics is no joke; he was soaked to the skin and with a raging thirst, and utterly exhausted.

It would have been better if they had started for Kuala Lumpur that night, but they didn't. All movement on the roads at night was prohibited by the military, and to start out in the Austin in the dark would have been to risk a burst of fire from trigger-happy sentries. They decided to leave at dawn which would give plenty of time to get to Kuala Lumpur before eight. Jean stayed the night with them in the bungalow, wakeful and uneasy. Once in the middle of the night she heard Bill Holland get up and got out into the verandah; peering out through her mosquito net she could see him standing motionless against the stars. She climbed out from under the net and slipped on her kimono; in Malaya one sleeps with very little on. She walked along the verandah to him. What is it?" she whispered.

"Nothing," he said. "Just thought I heard something, that's all."

"Someone in the compound?"

"No—not that."

"What?"

"I thought I heard guns firing, very far away," he said. "Must have been fancy." They stood tense and listening against the great noise of the crickets and the frogs. "God," he said presently, "I wish it was dawn."

They went back to bed. That night the Japanese advance patrols infiltrated behind our forces lining the Bidor and penetrated as far as Slim River, less than fifty miles away.

They were all up before dawn and loading up the Austin in the first grey light; with three adults and three children and the luggage for all of them the Austin was well loaded down. Mr. Holland paid the boys off and they started down the road for Kuala Lumpur, but before they had gone two miles the tyre that was showing canvas burst. There was a strained pause then while they worked to put the spare on, the one with the blister on the wall; this took them for another half mile only before going flat. In desperation Mr. Holland went on on the rim; the wire wheel collapsed after another two miles, and the Austin had run to its end. They were then about fifteen miles from Kuala Lumpur, and it was half past seven.

Mr. Holland left them with the car and hurried down the road to a plantation bungalow about a mile away; there was no transport there, and the manager had left the day before. He came back disappointed and anxious, to find the children fretful and his wife only concerned to get back to their bungalow. In the circumstances it seemed the best thing to do. Each of the adults took one child, and carrying or leading it they set out to walk the five miles home again, leaving the luggage in the car, which they locked.

They reached home in the first heat of the day, utterly exhausted. After cold drinks from the refrigerator they all lay down for a little to recover. An hour later they were roused by a truck stopping at the bungalow; a young officer came hurrying into the house.

"You've got to leave this place," he said. "I'll take you in the truck. How many of you are there?"

Jean said, "Six, counting the children. Can you take us into Kuala Lumpur? Our car broke down."

The officer laughed shortly. "No, I can't. The Japs are at Kerling, or they were when I last heard. They may be further south by now." Kerling was only twenty miles away. "I'm taking you to Panong. You'll get a boat from there to get you down to Singapore." He refused to take the truck back for their luggage, probably rightly; it was already loaded with a number of families who had messed up their evacuation, and the Austin was five miles in the direction of the enemy.

Kuala means the mouth of a river, and Kuala Panong is a small town at the entrance to the Panong River. There is a District Commissioner stationed there. By the time the truck reached his office it was loaded with about forty men, women, and children picked up for forcible evacuation from the surrounding estates. Most of these were Englishwomen of relatively humble birth, the wives of foreman engineers at the tin mines or gangers on the railway. Few of them had been able to appreciate the swiftness and the danger of the Japanese advance. Plantation managers and those in the Secretariat and other Government positions had had better sources of information and more money to spend, and these had got their families away to Singapore in good time. Those who were left to be picked up by truck at the last moment were the least competent.

The truck halted at the D.C.'s office and the subaltern went inside; the D.C. came out presently, a very worried man, and looked at the crowded women and children, and the few men amongst them. "Christ," he said quietly as he realized the extent of the new responsibility. "Well, drive them to the accounts office over there; they must sit in the verandah for an hour or two and I'll try and get something fixed up for them. Tell them not to wander about too much." He turned back into the office. "I can send them down in fishing boats, I think," he said. "There are some of those left. That's the best I can do. I haven't got a launch."

The party were unloaded on to the verandah of the accounts office, and here they were able to stretch and sort themselves out a little. There were chatties of cold water in the office and the verandah was shady and cool. Jean and Bill Holland left Eileen sitting on the verandah with her back against the wall with the children about her, and walked into the village to buy what they could to replace the luggage they had lost. They were able to get a feeding bottle for the baby, a little quinine, some salts for dysentery, and two tins of biscuits and three of tinned meat; they tried for mosquito nets, but they were all sold out. Jean got herself a few needles and thread, and seeing a large canvas haversack she bought that, too. She carried that haversack for the next three years.

They went back to the verandah about tea time and displayed their purchases, and had a little meal of biscuits and lemon squash.

Towards sunset the lighthouse keepers at the river mouth telephoned to the D.C. that the *Osprey* was coming into the river. The *Osprey* was the Customs launch that ran up and down the coast looking for smugglers from Sumatra across the Malacca Strait; she was a large diesel-engined vessel about a hundred and thirty feet long, normally stationed at Penang; a powerful, seagoing ship. The D.C.'s face lit up; here was the solution to his problems. Whatever was the mission of the *Osprey* she must take his evacuees on board, and run them down the coast out of harm's way. Presently he left his office, and walked down to the quay to meet the vessel as she berthed, to interview the captain.

She came round the bend in the river, and he saw that she was loaded with troops, small stocky men in grey-green uniforms with rifles and fixed bayonets taller than themselves. With a sick heart he watched her as she came alongside, realizing that this was the end of all this endeavor.

The Japanese came rushing ashore and arrested him immediately, and walked him back up the jetty to his office with guns at his back, ready to shoot him at the slightest show of resistance. But there were no troops there to resist; even the officer with the truck had driven off in an attempt to join his unit. The soldiers spread out and occupied the place without a shot; they came to the evacuees sitting numbly in the verandah of the accounts office. Immediately, with rifles and bayonets levelled, they were ordered to give up all fountain pens and wrist watches and rings. Advised by their men folk, the women did so silently, and suffered no other molestation. Jean lost her watch and had her bag searched for a fountain pen, but she had packed it in her luggage.

An officer came presently, when night had fallen, and inspected the crowd on the verandah in the light of a hurricane lamp; he walked down the verandah thrusting his lamp forward at each group, a couple of soldiers hard on his heels with rifles at the ready and bayonets fixed. Most of the children started crying. The inspection finished, he made a little speech in broken English. "Now you are prisoners," he said. "You stay here tonight. Tomorrow you go to prisoner camp perhaps. You do good things, obedience to orders, you will receive good from Japanese soldiers. You do bad things, you will be shot directly. So, do good things always. When officer come, you stand up and bow, always. That is good thing. Now you sleep."

One of the men asked, "May we have beds and mosquito nets?"

"Japanese soldiers have no beds, no mosquito nets. Perhaps tomorrow you have beds and nets."

Another said, "Can we have some supper?" This had to be explained. "Food."

"Tomorrow you have food." The officer walked away, leaving two sentries on guard at each end of the verandah.

Kuala Panong lies in a marshy district of mangrove swamps at the entrance to a muddy river; the mosquitoes are intense. All night the children moaned and wailed fretfully, preventing what sleep might have been possible for the adults. The night passed slowly, wearily on the hard floor of the verandah; between the crushing misery of captivity and defeat and the torment of the mosquitoes few of the prisoners slept at all. Jean dozed a little in the early hours and woke stiff and aching and with swollen face and arms as a fresh outburst from the children heralded the more intense attack from the mosquitoes that comes in the hour before the dawn. When the first light came the prisoners were in a very unhappy state.

There was a latrine behind the accounts office, inadequate for the numbers that had to use it. They made the best of that, and there was nothing then to do but to sit and wait for what would happen. Holland and Eileen made sandwiches for the children of tinned meat and sweet biscuits, and after this small breakfast they felt better. Many of the others had some small supplies of food, and those that had none were fed by those who had. Nothing was provided for the prisoners that morning by the Japanese.

In the middle of the morning an interrogation began. The prisoners were taken by families to the D.C.'s office, where a

Japanese captain, whom Jean was to know later as Captain Yoniata, sat with a lieutenant at his side, who made notes in a child's penny exercise book. Jean went in with the Hollands; when the captain enquired who she was she explained that she was a friend of the family travelling with them, and told him what her job was in Kuala Lumpur. It did not take very long. At the end the captain said, "Men go to prisoner camp today, womans and childs stays here. Men leave in afternoon, so you will now say farewell till this afternoon. Thank you."

They had feared this, and had discussed it in the verandah, but they had not expected it would come so soon. Holland asked, "May we know where the women and children will be sent to? Where will their camp be?"

The officer said, "The Imperial Japanese Army do not make war on womans and on childs. Perhaps not go to camp at all, if they do good things, perhaps live in homes. Japanese soldiers always kind to womans and to childs."

They went back to the verandah and discussed the position with the other families. There was nothing to be done about it, for it is usual in war for men to be interned in separate camps from women and children, but none the less, it was hard to bear. Jean felt her presence was unwanted with the Holland family, and went and sat alone on the edge of the verandah, feeling hungry and wondering with gloom tempered by the buoyancy of youth, what lay ahead of her. One thing was certain; if they were to spend another night upon the verandah she must get hold of some mosquito repellent. There was a chemist's shop just up the village that they had visited the afternoon before; it was probable that in such a district he had some repellent.

As an experiment she attracted the attention of the sentry and pointed to her mosquito bites; then she pointed to the village and got down from the verandah on to the ground. Immediately he brought his bayonet to the ready and advanced towards her; she got back on to the verandah in a hurry. That evidently wouldn't do. He scowled at her suspiciously, and went back to his position.

There was another way. The latrine was behind the building up against a wall; there was no sentry there because the wall prevented any exit from the accounts office except by going round the building to the front. She moved after a time and went out of the back door. Sheltered from the view of the sentries by the building, she looked around. There were some children playing in the middle distance.

She called softly in Malay, "Girl. You, you girl. Come here."

The child came towards her; she was about twelve years old. Jean asked, "What is your name?"

She giggled shyly, "Halijah."

Jean said, "Do you know the shop that sells medicine? Where a Chinese sells medicine?"

She nodded. "Chan Kok Fuan."

Jean said, "Go to Chan Kok Fuan, and if you give my message to him so that he comes to me, I will give you ten cents. Say that the Mem has Nyamok bites"—she showed her bites—"and he should bring ointments to the verandah, and he will sell many to the Mems. Do this, and if he comes with ointments I will give you ten cents."

The child nodded and went off. Jean went back to the verandah and waited; presently the Chinaman appeared carrying a tray loaded with little tubes and pots. He approached the sentry and spoke to him, indicating his wish to sell his wares; after some hesitation the sentry agreed. Jean got six tubes of repellent and the rest was swiftly taken by the other women. Halijah got ten cents.

Presently a Japanese orderly brought two buckets of a thin fish soup and another half full of boiled rice, dirty and unappetizing. There were no bowls or utensils to eat with. There was nothing to be done but to eat as best they could; at that time they had not fallen into the prisoner's mode of life in which all food is strictly shared out and divided scrupulously, so that some got much more than others, who got little or none. There were still food supplies, however, so they fell back on the biscuits and the private stocks to supplement the ration.

That afternoon the men were separated from their families, and marched off under guard. Bill Holland turned from his fat, motherly wife, his eyes moist. "Good-bye, Jean," he said heavily. "Good luck." And then he said, "Stick with them, if you can, won't you?"

She nodded. "I'll do that. We'll all be in the same camp together."

The men were formed up together, seven of them, and marched off under guard.

The party then consisted of eleven married women and two girls, Jean and an anaemic girl called Ellen Forbes who had been living with one of the families; she had come out to be married, but it hadn't worked out. Besides these there were nineteen children varying in age from a girl of fourteen to babies in arms; thirty-two persons in all. Most of the women could speak no language but their own; a few of them, including Eileen Holland, could speak enough Malay to control their servants, but no more.

They stayed in the accounts office for forty-one days.

The second night was similar to the first, except that the doors of the offices were opened for them and they were allowed to use the rooms. A second meal of fish soup was given to them in the evening, but nothing else whatever was provided for their use—no beds, no blankets, and no nets. Some of the women had their luggage with them and had blankets, but there were far too few to go round. A stern-faced woman, Mrs. Horscfall, asked to see the officer; when Captain Yoniata came she protested at the conditions and asked for beds and nets.

"No nets, no beds," he said. "Very sorry for you. Japanese womans sleep on mat on floor. All Japanese sleep on mat. You put away proud thoughts, very bad thing. You sleep on mat like Japanese womans."

"But we're English," she said indignantly. "We don't sleep on the floor like animals!"

His eyes hardened; he motioned to the sentries, who gripped her by each arm. Then he hit her four stinging blows upon the face with the flat of his hand. "Very bad thoughts," he said, and turned upon his heel, and left them. No more was said about beds.

He came to inspect them the next morning and Mrs. Horsefall, undaunted, asked for a water supply; she pointed out that washing was necessary for the babies and desirable for everyone. A barrel was brought into the smallest office that afternoon and was kept filled by coolies; they turned this room into a bathroom and wash house. In those early days most of the women had money, and following the example of Chan Kok Fuan the shopkeepers of the village came to sell to the prisoners, so they accumulated the bare essentials for existence.

Gradually they grew accustomed to their hardships. The children quickly learned to sleep upon the floor without complaint; the young women took a good deal longer, and the women over thirty seldom slept for more than half an hour without waking in pain—but they did sleep. It was explained to them by Captain Yoniata that until the campaign was over the victorious Japanese had no time to construct prison camps for women. When all Malaya had been conquered they would be moved into a commodious and beautiful camp which would be built for them in the Cameron Highlands, a noted health resort up in the hills. There they would find beds and mosquito nets and all the amenities to which they were accustomed, but to earn these delights they must stay where they were and do good things. Doing good things meant getting up and bowing whenever he approached. After a few faces had been slapped and shins had been kicked by Captain Yoniata's army boots, they learned to do this good thing.

The food issued to them was the bare minimum that would support life, and was an unvarying issue of fish soup and rice, given to them twice a day. Complaint was useless and even dangerous; in view of Captain Yoniata these were proud thoughts that had to be checked for the moral good of the complainant. Meals, however, could be supplied by a small Chinese restaurant in the village, and while money was available most of the families ordered one cooked meal a day from this restaurant.

They received no medical attention and no drugs whatsoever. At the end of a week dysentery attacked them, and the nights were made hideous by screaming children stumbling with their mothers to the latrine. Malaria was always in the background, held in check by the quinine that they could still buy from Chan Kok Fuan at an ever-increasing price. To check the dysentery Captain Yoniata reduced the soup and increased the rice ration, adding to the rice some of the dried, putrescent fish that had formerly made the soup. Later, he added to the diet a bucket of tea in the afternoon, as a concession to English manners.

Through all this time, Jean shared with Mrs. Holland the care of the three Holland children. She suffered a great deal from weakness and a feeling of lassitude induced, no doubt, by the change in diet, but she slept soundly most nights until wakened, which was frequently. Eileen Holland suffered much more. She was older, and could not sleep so readily upon the floor, and she had lost much of the resilience of her youth. She lost weight rapidly.

On the thirty-fifth day, Esmé Harrison died.

Esmé was a child of eight. She had had dysentery for some time and was growing very thin and weak; she slept little and cried a great deal. Presently she got fever, and for two days ran a temperature of a hundred and four as the malaria rose in her. Mrs. Horsefall told Captain Yoniata that the child must see a doctor and go to a hospital. He said he was very sorry, but there was no hospital. He would try and get a doctor, but the doctors were all fighting with the victorious army of the Emperor. That evening Esmé entered on a series of convulsions, and shortly before dawn she died.

She was buried that morning in the Moslem cemetery behind the village; her mother and one other woman were allowed to attend the burial. They read a little of the service out of a Prayer Book before the uncomprehending soldiers and Malays, and then it was over. Life went on as before in the accounts office, but the children now had nightmares of death to follow them to sleep.

At the end of six weeks Captain Yoniata faced them after the morning inspection. The women stood worn and draggled in the shade of the verandah facing him, holding the children by the hand. Many of the adults, and most of the children, by that time were thin and ill.

He said, "Ladies, the Imperial Japanese Army has entered Singapore, and all Malaya is free. Now prisoner camps are being built for men and also for womans and childs. Prisoner camps are at Singapore and you go there. I am very sad your life here has been uncomfortable, but now will be better. Tomorrow you start to Kuala Lumpur, not more than you can go each day. From Kuala Lumpur you go by train to Singapore, I think. In Singapore you will be very happy. Thank you."

From Panong to Kuala Lumpur is forty-seven miles; it took a minute for his meaning to sink in. Then Mrs. Horsefall said, "How are we to travel to Kuala Lumpur? Will there be a truck?"

He said, "Very sorry, no truck. You walk, easy journeys, not more than you can go each day. Japanese soldier help you."

She said, "We can't walk, with these children. We *must* have a truck."

These were bad thoughts, and his eyes hardened. "You walk," he repeated.

"But what are we to do with all the luggage?"

He said, "You carry what you can. Presently the luggage is sent after you." He turned, and went away.

For the remainder of the day they sat in stunned desperation; those who had luggage sorted helplessly through their things, trying to make packs that would hold the essentials and yet which would not be too heavy. Mrs. Horsefall, who had been a schoolmistress in her time and had assumed the position of leader, moved among them, helping and advising. She had one child herself, a boy of ten called John; her own position was better than most, for it was possible for a woman to carry the necessities for one boy of that age. The position of the mothers with several younger children was bad indeed.

Jean and Mrs. Holland had less of a problem, for having lost their luggage they had less to start with and the problem of selection did not arise. They had few clothes to change into, and what they had could easily go into Jean's haversack. They had acquired two blankets and three food bowls between them, and three spoons, and a knife and a fork; they decided to make a bundle of these small possessions in the blankets, and they had a piece of cord to tie the bundle with and to make a sling, so that one could carry the haversack and one the bundle. Their biggest problem was their shoes, which had once been fashionable and were quite unsuitable for marching in.

Towards evening, when the children had left them and they were alone with the baby in a corner, Mrs. Holland said quietly, "My dear, I shan't give up, but I don't think I can walk very far. I've been so poorly lately."

Jean said, "It'll be all right," although deep in her mind she knew that it was not going to be all right at all. "You're much fitter than some of the others," and this possibly was true. "We'll have to take it very slowly, because of the children. We'll take several days over it."

"I know, my dear. But where are we going to stay at night? What *are* they going to do about that?"

Nobody had an answer to that one.

Rice came to them soon after dawn, and at about eight o'clock Captain Yoniata appeared with four soldiers, who were to be their guard upon the journey. "Today you walk to Ayer Penchis," he said. "Fine day, easy journey. Good dinner when you get to Ayer Penchis. You will be very happy."

Jean asked Mrs. Horsefall, "How far is Ayer Penchis?"

"Twelve or fifteen miles, I should think. Some of us will never get that far."

Jean said, "We'd better do what the soldiers do, have a rest every hour. Hadn't we?"

"If they'll let us."

It took an hour to get the last child out of the latrine and get the women ready for the march. The guards squatted on their heels; it was a small matter to them when the march started. Finally Captain Yoniata appeared again, his eyes hard and angry. "You walk now," he said. "Womans remaining here are beaten, beaten very bad. You do good thing and be happy. Walk now."

There was nothing for it but to start. They formed into a little group and walked down the tarmac road in the hot sun, seeking the shade of trees wherever they occurred. Jean walked with Mrs. Holland, carrying the bundle of blankets slung across her shoulders as the hottest and the heaviest load, and leading the four-year-old Jane by the hand. Seven-year-old Freddie walked beside his mother, who carried the baby, Robin, and the haversack. Ahead of them strolled the Japanese sergeant; behind came the three privates.

The women went very slowly, with frequent halts as a mother and child retired into the bushes by the roadside. There was no question of walking continuously for an hour and then resting; the dysentery saw to that. For those who were not afflicted at the moment the journey became one of endless, wearisome waits by the roadside in the hot sun, for the sergeant refused to allow the party to move on while any remained behind. Within the limits of their duty the Japanese soldiers were humane and helpful; before many hours had passed each was carrying a child.

Slowly the day wore on. The sergeant made it very clear at an early stage that there would be no food and no shelter for the party till they got to Ayer Penchis, and it seemed to be a matter of indifference to him how long they took to get there. They seldom covered more than a mile and a half in the hour, on that first day. As the day went on they all began to suffer from their feet, the older women especially. Their shoes were quite unsuitable for walking long distances, and the heat of the tarmac swelled their feet, so that before long many of them were limping with foot pains. Some of the children went barefoot and got along very well. Jean watched them for a time, then stooped and took her own shoes off, savouring the unaccustomed road surface gingerly with her bare feet. She walked on carrying her shoes, picking her way with her eyes upon the ground, and her feet ceased to pain her though from time to time the tarmac grits hurt her soft soles. She got along better barefoot, but Eileen Holland refused to try it.

They stumbled into Ayer Penchis at about six o'clock that evening, shortly before dark. This place was a Malay village which housed the labour for a number of rubber plantations in the vicinity. The latex-processing plant of one stood near at hand and by it was a sort of palm-thatch barn, used normally for smoking sheets of the raw rubber hung on horizontal laths. It was empty now and the women were herded into this. They sank down wearily in a stupor of fatigue; presently the soldiers brought a bucket of tea and a bucket of rice and dried fish. Most of them drank cup after cup of the tea, but few had any appetite for the food.

With the last of the light Jean strolled outside and looked around. The guards were busy cooking over a small fire; she approached the sergeant and asked if she might go into the village. He understood that, and nodded; away from Captain Yoniata discipline was lax.

In the village she found one or two small shops, selling clothes, sweets, cigarettes, and fruit. She saw mangoes for sale, and bought a dozen, chaffering over the price with the Malay woman to conserve her slender cash. She ate one at once and felt better for it; at Kuala Panong they had eaten little fruit. She went back to the barn and found that the soldiers had provided one small lamp with an open wick fed by coconut oil.

She distributed her mangoes to Eileen and the Holland children and to others, and found they were a great success. Armed with money from the women she went down to the village again and got four dozen more, and presently all the women and children were in mango up to the ears. The soldiers came in with another bucket of tea and got a mango each for their pains, and so refreshed, the women were able to eat most of the rice. Presently they slept, exhausted, weak, and ill.

The barn was full of rats, which ran over them and round them all night through. In the morning it was found that several of the children had been bitten.

They woke aching in new places with the stiffness and fatigue of the day before; it did not seem possible that they could march again. The sergeant drove them on; this time the stage was to a place called Asahan. It was a shorter stage than the day before, about ten miles, but it had need to be, because they took as long getting to it. This time the delay was chiefly due to Mrs. Collard. She was a heavy woman of about forty-five with two children, Harry and Ben, aged about ten and seven. She had suffered from both malaria and dysentery at Panong, and she was now very weak; she had to stop and rest every ten minutes, and when she stopped they all stopped since the sergeant would not allow them to separate. She was relieved of all load and the younger women took turns to walk by her and help her along.

By the afternoon she had visibly changed colour; her

somewhat ruddy face had now gone a mottled blue, and she was complaining constantly of pains in her chest. When they finally reached Asahan she was practically incapable of walking alone. Their accommodation was another rubber-curing barn. They half carried Mrs. Collard into it and sat her up against the wall, for she said that lying down hurt her, and she could not breathe. Somebody went to fetch some water, and bathed her face, and she said, "Thank you, dearie. Give some of that to Harry and Ben, there's a dear." The woman took the children outside to wash them, and when she came back Mrs. Collard had fallen over on her side, and was unconscious. Half an hour later she died.

That evening Jean got more fruit for them, mangoes and bananas, and some sweets for the children. The Malay woman who supplied the sweets refused to take money for them. "No, mem," she said. "It is bad that Nippon soldiers treat you so. This is our gift." Jean went back to the barn and told the others what had happened, and it helped.

In the flickering light of the cooking fire outside the barn Mrs. Horsefall and Jean held a conference with the sergeant, who spoke only a very few words of English. They illustrated their meaning with pantomime. "Not walk tomorrow," they said. "No. Not walk. Rest—sleep—tomorrow. Walk tomorrow, more women die. Rest tomorrow. Walk one day, rest one day."

They could not make out if he understood or not. "Tomorrow," he said, "woman, in earth."

It would be necessary to bury Mrs. Collard in the morning. This would prevent an early start, and would make a ten-mile stage almost impossible. They seized upon this as an excuse. "Tomorrow bury woman in earth," they said. "Stay here tomorrow."

They had to leave it so, uncertain whether he understood or not; he squatted down on his heels before the fire with the three privates. Later he came to Jean, his face alight with intelligence. "Walk one day, sleep one day," he said. "Womans not die." He nodded vigorously, and she called Mrs. Horsefall, and they all nodded vigorously together, beaming with good nature. They were all so pleased with each other and with the diplomatic victory that they gave him a banana as a token of esteem.

All that day Jean had walked barefoot; she had stubbed her toes two or three times and had broken her toenails, but she felt fresher that evening than she had felt for a long time. The effect of the march upon the women began to show itself that night in very different forms, according to their age. The women under thirty, and the children, were in most cases actually in better condition than when they left Panong; they were cheered by the easier discipline, and stimulated by the exercise and by the improvement in the diet brought by fruit and sweets. The older women were in much worse case. For them exhaustion outweighed these benefits, they lay or sat listlessly in the darkness, plagued by their children and too tired to eat. In many cases they were too tired even to sleep.

In the morning they buried Mrs. Collard. There was no burial ground at hand but the Malay headman showed them where they could dig the grave, in a corner of the compound near a rubbish heap. The sergeant got two coolies and they dug a shallow grave; they lowered Mrs. Collard into it covered by a blanket, and Mrs. Horsefall read a little out of the Prayer Book. Then they took away the blanket because they could not spare that, and the earth was filled in. Jean found a carpenter who nailed a little wooden cross together for them, and refused payment; he was a Moslem or perhaps merely an animist, but he knew what the Tuans did for a Christian burial. They wrote JULIA COLLARD on it and the date of death with an indelible pencil hoping it would survive the rain, and then they had a long discussion over the text to put underneath it. This interested every woman in the party, and kept them happy and mentally stimulated for half an hour. Mrs. Holland, rather surprisingly, suggested Romans, 14, 4; "Who art thou that judgest another man's servant? to his own master he standeth or falleth," meaning the sergeant who had made them march that day. But the other women did not care for that, and finally they compromised on "Peace, perfect peace, with loved ones far away." That pleased everybody.

They sat around and washed their clothes after the burial was over. Soap was getting very scarce amongst them, but so was money. Mrs. Horsefall held a sort of meeting after rice and examined the money situation; half the women had no money left at all, and the rest had only about fifteen dollars between them. She suggested pooling this, but the mothers who had money left preferred to keep it for their own children; as there was so little in any case it did not seem worth while to worry them by making an issue of it. They all agreed, however, to share rations equally, and after that their feeding times were much better organized.

Captain Yoniata turned up about midday, driving in

Kuala Lumpur in the District Commissioner's car. He stopped and got out, angry to find that they were not upon the road. He abused the sergeant for some minutes in Japanese; the man stood stiffly to attention, not saying a word in explanation or defence. Then he turned to the women. "Why you not walk?" he demanded angrily. "Very bad thing. You not walk, no food."

Mrs. Horsefall faced him. "Mrs. Collard died last night. We buried her this morning, over there. If you make us walk every day like this, we shall all die. These women aren't fit to march at all. You know that."

"What woman die of?" he enquired. "What illness?"

"She had dysentery and malaria, as most of us have had. She died of exhaustion after yesterday's march. You'd better come inside and look at Mrs. Frith and Judy Thomson. They couldn't possibly have marched today."

He walked into the barn, and stood looking at the two or three women sitting listless in the semi-darkness. Then he said something to the sergeant and went back to his car. At the door he turned to Mrs. Horsefall. "Very sad woman die," he said. "Perhaps I get a truck in Kuala Lumpur. I will ask." He got into the car and drove away.

His words went round the women quickly; he had gone to get a truck for them, and they would finish the journey to Kuala Lumpur by truck; there would be no more marching. Things weren't so bad, after all. They would be sent by rail from Kuala Lumpur to Singapore, and there they would be put into a proper camp with other Englishwomen, where they could settle down and organize their lives properly, and get into a routine that would enable them to look after the children. A prison camp would have a doctor, too, and there was always some kind of a hospital for those who were really ill. They became much more cheerful, and the most listless ones revived, and came out and washed and made themselves a little more presentable. Their appearance was a great concern to them that afternoon. Kuala Lumpur was their shopping town where people knew them; they must get tidy before the truck came for them.

Captain Yoniata appeared again about an hour before sunset; again he spoke to the sergeant, who saluted. Then he turned to the women. "You not go to Kuala Lumpur," he said. "You go to Port Swettenham. English destroy bridges, no railway to Singapore no good. You go to Port Swettenham now, and then ship to Singapore."

There was a stunned silence. Then Mrs. Horsefall asked,

"Is there going to be a truck to take us to Port Swettenham?"

He said, "Very sorry no truck. You walk slow, easy stages. Two days, three days, you walk to Port Swettenham. Then ship take you to Singapore."

From Asahan to Port Swettenham is about thirty miles. She said, "Captain Yoniata, please be reasonable. Many of us are quite unfit to walk any further. Can't you get some transport for the children, anyway?"

He said, "Englishwomans have proud thoughts, always. Too good to walk like Japanese womans. Tomorrow you walk to Bakri." He got into his car and went away; that was the last they ever saw of him.

Bakri is eleven miles in the general direction of Port Swettenham. The change in programme was the deepest disappointment to them, the more so as it showed irresolution in their destiny. Mrs. Holland said despairingly, "I don't see why he shouldn't have known at Panong that the bridges were down, and not sent us to Kuala Lumpur at all. It makes one wonder if there's going to be a ship when we get to Port Swettenham . . ."

There was nothing for it, and next morning they started on the road again. They found that two of the privates had been taken away, and one remained to guard them, with the sergeant. This was of no consequence to their security because they had no desire to attempt to escape, but it reduced by half the help the guards had given them in carrying the younger children, so that it threw an extra burden on the mothers.

That day for the first time Jean carried the baby, Robin. Mrs. Holland was walking so badly that she had to be relieved. She still carried the haversack and looked after Freddie, but Jean carried the bundle of blankets and small articles, and the baby, and led Jane by the hand. She went barefoot as before; after some experiments she found that the easiest way to carry the baby was to perch him on her hip, as the Malay women did.

The baby, curiously, gave them the least anxiety of any of the children. They fed it on rice and gravy from the fish soup or stew, and it did well. Once in the six weeks it had seemed to be developing dysentery and they had given it a tiny dose or two of Glauber's salts, and it recovered. Mosquitoes never seemed to worry it, and it had not had fever. The other children were less fortunate. Both had had dysentery from time to time, and though they seemed now to be free of it they had gone very thin.

They slept that night in the bungalow that had belonged to the manager of the Bakri tin mine, an Englishman. In the seven or eight weeks since he had abandoned it it had been occupied by troops of both sides and looted by the Malays; now little remained of it but the bare walls. Marvellously, however, the bath was still in order though filthily dirty, and there was a store of cut wood for the furnace that heated water. The sergeant, true to his promise, allowed them a day of rest here, and they made the most of the hot water for washing their clothes and themselves. With the small improvement in conditions their spirits revived.

"I should think there'd be hot water on the ship," said Mrs. Holland. "There usually is, isn't there?"

They marched again next day to a place called Dilit; this was mostly a day spent marching down cart tracks in the rubber plantations. The tracks were mostly in the shade of the trees and this made it pleasant for them, and even the older women found the day bearable. They had some difficulty in finding the way. The sergeant spoke little Malay and had difficulty in understanding the Malay women latex tappers that he asked for directions from time to time. Jean found that she could understand the answers that the women gave, and could converse with them, but having got the directions they required she had some difficulty in making the sergeant understand. They reached an agreement by the end of the day that she should talk to the women, who talked to her less shyly in any case, and she developed a sign language which the sergeant understood. From that time onwards Jean was largely responsible for finding the shortest way for the party to go.

In the middle of the afternoon Ben Collard, the younger son of Mrs. Collard who had died, trod on something while walking barefoot in the grass that bit him with poison fangs, and got away. He said afterwards that it looked like a big beetle; possibly it was a scorpion. Mrs. Horsefall took charge and laid him on the ground and sucked the wound to draw the poison from it, but the foot swelled quickly and the inflammation travelled up the leg to the knee. It was obviously painful and he cried a great deal. There was nothing to be done but carry him, and this was no easy matter for the women in their feeble condition because he was a boy of seven and weighed five stone. Mrs. Horsefall carried him for an hour and after that the sergeant took him and carried him the rest of the way. By the time they got to Dilit the ankle was enormous and the knee was stiff.

At Dilit there was no accommodation for them and no food. The place was a typical Malay village, the houses built of wood and palm thatch raised about four feet from the ground on posts, leaving a space beneath where dogs slept and fowls nested. They stood or sat wearily while the sergeant negotiated with the Malay headman: very soon he called for Jean, and she joined the trilingual discussion. The village had rice and could prepare a meal for them, but the headman wanted payment, and was only with difficulty induced to agree to provide rice for so many on the word of the sergeant that they would be paid some day. As regards accommodation he said flatly that there was none, and the party must sleep under the houses with the dogs and poultry; later he agreed to move the people from one house, so that the thirty prisoners had a roof to sleep under on a floor about fifteen feet square.

Jean secured a corner for their party, and Eileen Holland settled in to it with the children and the baby. A few feet from them Mrs. Horsefall was working on Ben Collard. Somebody had some permanganate crystals and someone else an old razor blade; with this they cut the wound open a little, in spite of the child's screams, and put in crystals and bound it up; then they applied hot fomentations. There was nothing Jean could do, and she wandered outside.

There was a sort of village kitchen, and here the Japanese private was superintending the activities of women of the village who were preparing rice. At a house near by the headman was sitting at the head of the steps leading up to his house, squatting on his heels and smoking a long pipe: he was a grey-haired old man wearing a sarong and what once had been a khaki drill jacket. Jean crossed to him and said rather shyly in Malay, "I am sorry we have been forced to come here, and have made trouble for you."

He stood up and bowed to the Mem. "It is no trouble," he said. "We are sorry to see Mems in such a state. Have you come far?"

She said, "From Bakri today."

He made her come up into the house: there was no chair and she sat with him on the floor at the doorless entrance. He asked their history, and she told him what had happened, and he grunted. Presently the wife came from within the house bearing two cups of coffee without sugar or milk; Jean thanked her in Malay, and she smiled shyly, and withdrew into the house again.

Presently the headman said, "The Short One"—he meant

the Japanese sergeant—"says you must stay here tomorrow."

Jean said, "We are too weak to march each day. The Japanese allow us to rest a day between each day of marching. If we may stay here tomorrow it will help us a great deal. The sergeant says he can get money for the food."

"The Short Ones never pay for food," the headman said. "Nevertheless, you shall stay."

She said, "I can do nothing but thank you."

He raised his grey old head. "It is written in the Fourth Surah, 'Men's souls are naturally inclined to covetousness; but if ye be kind towards women and fear to wrong them, God is well acquainted with what ye do.' "

She sat with the old man till rice was ready; then she left him and went to her meal. The other women looked at her curiously. "I saw you sitting with the headman, chatting away," said one. "Just as if you were old chums."

Jean smiled. "He gave me a cup of coffee."

"Just fancy that! There's something in knowing how to talk to them in their own language, isn't there? What did he talk about?"

Jean thought for a minute. "This and that—about our journey. He talked about God a little."

The woman stared at her. "You mean, his own God? Not the real God"?

"He didn't differentiate," Jean said. "Just God."

They rested all next day and then marched to Klang, three or four miles outside Port Swettenham. Little Ben Collard was neither better nor worse; the leg was very much swollen. The chief trouble with him now was physical weakness: he had eaten nothing since the injury for nothing would stay down, and none of the children by that time had any reserves of strength. The headman directed the villagers to make a litter for him in the form of a stretcher of two long bamboo poles with spreaders and a woven palm mat between, and they put him upon this and took turns at carrying it.

They got to Klang that afternoon, and here there was an empty schoolhouse: the sergeant put them into this and went off to a Japanese encampment near at hand, to report and to arrange rations for them.

Presently an officer arrived to inspect them, marching at the head of a guard of six soldiers. This officer, whom they came to know as Major Nemu, spoke good English. He said, "Who are you people? What do you want here?"

They stared at him. Mrs. Horsefall said, "We are prisoners,

from Panong. We are on our way to the prisoner-of-war camp in Singapore. Captain Yoniata in Panong sent us here under guard, to be put on a ship to Singapore."

"There are no ships here," he said. "You should have stayed in Panong."

It was no good arguing, nor had they the energy. "We were sent here," she repeated dully.

"They had no right to send you here," he said angrily. "There is no prison camp here."

There was a long, awkward silence: the women stared at him in blank despair. Mrs. Horsefall summoned up her flagging energy again. "May we see a doctor?" she asked. "Some of us are very ill—one child especially. One woman died upon the way."

"What did she die of?" he asked quickly. "Plague?"

"Nothing infectious. She died of exhaustion."

"I will send a doctor to examine you all. You will stay here for tonight, but you cannot stay for long. I have not got sufficient rations for my own command, let alone feeding prisoners." He turned and walked back to the camp.

A new guard was placed upon the schoolhouse: they never saw the friendly sergeant or the private again. Presumably they were sent back to Panong. A Japanese doctor, very young, came to them within an hour; he had them all up one by one and examined them for infectious disease. Then he was about to take his departure, but they made him stay and look at little Ben Collard's leg. He ordered them to continue with the hot fomentations. When they asked if he could not be taken in to hospital he shrugged his shoulders and said, "I enquire."

They stayed in that schoolhouse under guard, day after day. On the third day they sent for the doctor again for Ben Collard was obviously worse. Reluctantly the doctor ordered his removal to the hospital in a truck. On the sixth day they heard that he had died.

Jean Paget crouched down on the floor beside the fire in my sitting-room; outside a change of wind had brought the London rain beating against the window.

"People who spent the war in prison camps have written a lot of books about what a bad time they had," she said quietly, staring into the embers. "They don't know what it was like, *not* being in a camp."

Chapter 3

THEY stayed in Klang eleven days, not knowing what was to become of them. The food was bad and insufficient, and there were no shops in the vicinity: if there had been shops they could not have done much with them, because their money was now practically gone. On the twelfth day Major Nemu paraded them at half an hour's notice, allocated one corporal to look after them, and told them to walk to Port Dickson. He said that there might be a ship there to take them down to Singapore; if there was not they would be walking in the general direction of the prison camps.

That was about the middle of March 1942. From Klang to Port Dickson is about fifty miles, but by this time they were travelling more slowly than ever. It took them till the end of the month; they had to wait several days in one village because Mrs. Horsefall went down with malaria and ran a temperature of a hundred and five for some time. She recovered and was walking, or rather tottering, within a week, but she never recovered her vigour and from that time onwards the leadership fell more and more upon Jean's shoulders.

By the time they reached Port Dickson their clothes were in a deplorable condition. Very few of the women had a change of any sort, because burdens had been reduced to an absolute minimum. Jean and Mrs. Holland had nothing but the thin cotton frocks that they had worn since they were taken; these were now torn and ragged from washing. Jean had gone barefoot since the early stages of the march and intended to go on without shoes: she now took another step towards the costume of the Malay woman. She sold a little brooch for thirteen dollars to an Indian jeweller in Salak, and with two of the precious dollars she bought a cheap sarong.

A sarong is a skirt made of a tube of cloth about three feet in diameter; you get into it and wrap it round your waist like a towel, the surplus material falling into pleats that permit free movement. When you sleep you undo the roll around your waist and it then lies over you as a loose covering that you cannot roll out of. It is the lightest and coolest of all garments for the tropics, and the most practical, being simple to make and to wash. For a top, she cut down her cotton frock into a sort of tunic which got rid of the most tattered part, the skirt, and from that time she was cooler and more at ease than any of them. At first the other women strongly disapproved of this descent to native dress: later most of them followed her example as their clothes became worn out.

There was no haven for them at Port Dickson, and no ship. They were allowed to stay there, living under desultory guard in a copra barn, for about ten days; the Japanese commander then decided that they were a nuisance, and put them on the road to Seremban. He reasoned, apparently, that they were not his prisoners and so not his responsibility; it was the duty of those who had captured them to put them into camp. His obvious course was to get rid of them and get them out of his area before, by their continued presence, they forced him to divert food and troops and medical supplies from the Imperial Japanese Army to sustain them.

At Siliau, between Port Dickson and Seremban, tragedy touched the Holland family, because Jane died. They had stayed for their day of rest in a rubber-smoking shed: she had developed fever during the day's march and one of the two Japanese guards they had at that time had carried her for much of the day. Their thermometer had been broken in an accident a few days before and they had now no means of telling the temperature of malaria patients, but she was very hot. They had a little quinine left and tried to give it to her, but they could not get her to take much of it till she grew too weak to resist, and then it was too late. They persuaded the Japanese sergeant to allow them to stay at Siliau rather than to risk moving the child, and Jean and Eileen Holland stayed up with her, sleepless, fighting for her life in that dim, smelly place where the rats scurried round at night and hens walked in and out by day. On the evening of the second day she died.

Mrs. Holland stood it far better than Jean had expected that she would. "It's God's will, my dear," she said quietly, "and He'll give her Daddy strength to bear it when he hears, just as He's giving us all strength to bear our trials now." She stood dry-eyed beside the little grave, and helped to make the little wooden cross. Dry-eyed she picked the text for the cross: "Suffer little children to come unto Me." She said quietly, "I think her Daddy would like that one."

Jean woke that night in the darkness, and heard her weeping.

Through all this the baby, Robin, throve. It was entirely
fortuitous that he ate and drank nothing but food that had
been recently boiled; living on rice and soup, that happened
automatically, but may have explained his relative freedom
from stomach disorders. Jean carried him every day, and her
own health was definitely better than when they had left
Panong. She had had five days of fever at Klang, but
dysentery had not troubled her for some time, and she was
eating well. With the continual exposure to the sun she was
getting very brown, and the baby that she carried on her hip
got browner.

Seremban lies on the railway, and they had hoped that
when they got there there would be a train down to Singapore. They got to Seremban about the middle of April, but
there was no train for them; the railway was running in a
limited fashion but probably not through to Singapore. Before very long they were put upon the road to Tampin, but
not till they had lost another member of the party.

Ellen Forbes was the unmarried girl who had come out to
get married and hadn't, a circumstance that Jean could well
understand by the time she had lived in close contact with
her for a couple of months. Ellen was a vacuous, undisci-
plined girl, good-humoured, and much too free with Japanese
troops for the liking of the other women. At Seremban they
were accommodated in a schoolhouse on the outskirts of the
town, which was full of soldiers. In the morning Ellen simply
wasn't there, and they never saw her again.

Jean and Mrs. Horsefall asked to see the officer and stated
their case, that a member of their party had disappeared,
probably abducted by the soldiers. The officer promised to
make enquiries, and nothing happened. Two days later they
received orders to march down the road to Tampin, and
were moved off under guard.

They stayed at Tampin for some days, and got so little
food there that they practically starved; at their urgent en-
treaty the local commandant sent them down under guard
to Malacca, where they hoped to get a ship. But there was no
ship at Malacca and the officer in charge there sent them
back to Tampin. They plodded back there in despair; at
Alor Gajah Judy Thomson died. To stay at Tampin meant
more deaths, inevitably, so they suggested it was better for
them to continue down to Singapore on foot, and a corporal
was detailed to take them on the road to Gemas.

In the middle of May, at Ayer Kuning, on the way to
Gemas, Mrs. Horsefall died. She had never really recovered

from her attack of malaria or whatever fever it was that had attacked her two months previously; she had had recurrent attacks of a low fever which had made Jean wonder sometimes if it was malaria that she had had at all. Whatever it was it had made her very weak; at Ayer Kuning she developed dysentery again, and died in two days, probably of heart failure or exhaustion. The faded little woman, Mrs. Frith, who was over fifty and always seemed to be upon the point of death and never quite made it, took over the care of Johnnie Horsefall and it did her a world of good; from that day Mrs. Frith improved and gave up moaning in the night.

They got to Gemas three days later; here as usual in towns they were put into the schoolhouse. The Japanese town major, a Captain Nisui, came to inspect them that evening; he had known nothing about them till they appeared in his town. This was quite usual and Jean was ready for it; she explained that they were prisoners being marched to camp in Singapore.

He said, "Prisoner not go Singapore. Strict order. Where you come from?"

She told him. "We've been travelling for over two months," she said, with the calmness born of many disappointments. "We must get into a camp, or we shall die. Seven of us have died upon the road already—there were thirty-two when we were taken prisoner. Now there are twenty-five. We can't go on like this. We *must* get into camp at Singapore. You must see that."

He said, "No more prisoner to Singapore. Very sorry for you, but strict order. Too many prisoner in Singapore."

She said, "But, Captain Nisui, that can't mean women. That means men prisoners, surely."

"No more prisoner to Singapore," he said. "Strict order."

"Well, can we stay here and make ourselves a camp, and have a doctor here?"

His eyes narrowed. "No prisoner stay here."

"But what are we to do? Where can we go?"

"Very sad for you," he said. "I tell you where you go tomorrow."

She went back to the women after he had gone. "You heard all that," she said calmly. "He says we aren't to go to Singapore after all."

The news meant very little to the women; they had fallen into the habit of living from day to day, and Singapore was very far away. "Looks as if they don't want us any where," Mrs. Price said heavily. "Bobbie, if I see you teasing Amy again I'll wallop you just like your father. Straight, I will."

Mrs. Frith said, "If they'd just let us alone we could find a little place like one of them villages and live till it's all over."

Jean stared at her. "They couldn't feed us," she said slowly. "We depend upon the Nips for food." But it was the germ of an idea, and she put it in the back of her mind.

"Precious little food we get," said Mrs. Frith. "I'll never forget that terrible place Tampin in all my born days."

Captain Nisui came the next day. "You go now to Kuantan," he said. "Woman camp in Kuantan, very good. You will be very glad."

Jean did not know where Kuantan was. She asked, "Where is Kuantan? Is it far away?"

"Kuantan on coast," he said. "You go there now."

Behind her someone said, "It's hundreds of miles away. It's on the east coast."

"Okay," said Captain Nisui. "On east coast."

"Can we go there by railway?" Jean enquired.

"Sorry, no railway. You walk, ten, fifteen miles each day. You get there soon. You will be very happy."

She said quietly, "Seven of us are dead already with this marching, Captain. If you make us march to this place Kuantan more of us will die. Can we have a truck to take us there?"

"Sorry, no truck," he said. "You get there very soon."

He wanted them to start immediately, but it was then eleven in the morning and they rebelled. With patient negotiation Jean got him to agree that they should start at dawn next day; this was the most that she could do. She did, however, get him to provide a good supper for them that night, a sort of meat stew with the rice, and a banana each.

From Gemas to Kuantan is about a hundred and seventy miles; there is no direct road. They left Gemas in the last week of May; on the basis of their previous rate of progress Jean reckoned that it would take them six weeks to do the journey. It was by far the longest they had had to tackle; always before there had been hope for transport of some sort at the end of fifty miles or so. Now six weeks of travelling lay ahead of them, with only a vague hope of rest at the end. None of them really believed that there were prison camps for them at Kuantan.

"You made a mistake, dearie," said Mrs. Frith, "saying

what you did about us staying and making a camp here. I could see he didn't like that."

"He just wants to get rid of us," Jean said wearily. "They don't want to bother with us—just get us out of the way."

They left next morning with a sergeant and a private as a guard. Gemas is a railway junction and the East Coast railway runs north from there; the railway was not being used at all at that time, and there was a rumour that the track was being taken up and sent to some unknown strategic destination in the north. The women were not concerned with that; what concerned them was that they had to walk along the railway line, which meant walking in the sun most of each day, and there was no possibility of getting a ride in a train.

They went on for a week, marching about ten miles every other day; then fever broke out among the children. They never really knew what it was; it started with little Amy Price who came out in a rash and ran a high temperature, with a running nose. It may have been measles. It was impossible in the conditions of their life to keep the children segregated, and in the weeks that followed it spread from child to child. Amy Price slowly recovered, but by the time she was fit to walk again seven of the other children were down with it. There was nothing they could do except to keep the tired, sweating little faces bathed and cool, and change the soaked clothes for what fresh ones they could muster. They were at a place called Bahau when the sickness was at its height, living at the station in the ticket office and the waiting room, and on the platform. They had bad luck because there had been a doctor in Bahau three days before they arrived, a Japanese army doctor. But he had gone on in his truck in the direction of Kuala Klawang, and though they got the headman to send runners after him they never made contact with him. So they had no help.

At Bahau four children died, Harry Collard, Susan Fletcher, Doris Simmonds who was only three, and Freddie Holland. Jean was most concerned with Freddie, as was natural, but there was so little she could do. She guessed from the first day of fever that he was going to die; by that time she had amassed a store of sad experience. There was something in the attitude of people, even tiny children, to their illness that told when death was coming to them, a listlessness, as if they were too tired to make the effort to live. By that time they had all grown hardened to the fact of death. Grief and mourning had ceased to trouble them;

death was a reality to be avoided and fought, but when it came—well, it was just one of those things. After a person had died there were certain things that had to be done, the straightening of the limbs, the grave, the cross, the entry in a diary saying who had died and just exactly where the grave was. That was the end of it; they had no energy for afterthoughts.

Jean's care now was for Mrs. Holland. After Freddie was buried she tried to get Eileen to care for the baby; for the last few weeks the baby had been left to Jean to feed and tend and carry, and she had grown very much attached to it. With both the older children dead Jean gave the baby, Robin, back to its mother, not so much because she wanted to get rid of it as because she felt that an interest must be found for Eileen Holland, and the baby would supply it. But the experiment was not a great success; Eileen by that time was so weak that she could not carry the baby on the march, and she could not summon the energy to play with it. Moreover, the baby obviously preferred the younger woman to its mother, having been carried by her for so long.

"Seems as if he doesn't really belong to me," Mrs. Holland said once. "You take him, dear. He likes being with you." From that time on they shared the baby; it got its rice and soup from Eileen, but it got its fun from Jean.

They left four tiny graves behind the signal box at Bahau and went on down the line carrying two litters of bamboo poles; the weakest children took turns in these. As was common on this journey, they found the Japanese guards to be humane and reasonable men, uncouth in their habits and mentally far removed from western ideas, but tolerant to the weaknesses of women and deeply devoted to children. For hours the sergeant would plod along carrying one child piggyback and at the same time carrying one end of the stretcher, his rifle laid beside the resting child. There was the usual language difficulty. The women by that time were acquiring a few words of Japanese, but the only one who could talk Malay fluently was Jean, and it was she who made enquiries at the villages and sometimes acted as interpreter for the Japanese.

Mrs. Frith surprised Jean very much. She was a faded, anaemic little woman of over fifty. In the early stages of the journey she had been very weak and something of a nuisance to them with her continued prognostications of evil; they had trouble enough in the daily round without looking forward and anticipating more. Since she had adopted Johnnie Horsefall Mrs. Frith had taken on a new lease of life; her health had improved and she now marched as strongly as any of them. She had lived in Malaya for about fifteen years; she could only speak a few words of the language but she had a considerable knowledge of the country and its diseases. She was quite happy that they were going to Kuantan. "Nice over there, it is," she said. "Much healthier than in the west, and nicer people. We'll be all right once we get over there. You see."

As time went on, Jean turned to Mrs. Frith more and more for comfort and advice in their predicaments.

At Ayer Kring Mrs. Holland came to the end of her strength. She had fallen twice on the march and they had taken turns in helping her along. It was impossible to put her on the litter; even in her emaciated state she weighed eight stone, and they were none of them strong enough by that time to carry such a load very far. Moreover, to put her on a litter meant turning a child off it, and she refused even to consider such a thing. She stumbled into the village on her own feet, but by the time she got there she was changing colour as Mrs. Collard had before her, and that was a bad sign.

Ayer Kring is a small village at a railway station; there were no station buildings here, and by negotiation the headman turned the people out of one house for them, as had been done several times before. They laid Mrs. Holland in a shady corner and made a pillow for her head and bathed her face; they had no brandy or any other stimulant to give her. She could not rest lying down and insisted on sitting up, so they put her in a corner where she could be supported by the walls. She took a little soup that evening but refused all food. She knew herself it was the end.

"I'm so sorry, my dear," she whispered late in the night. "Sorry to make so much trouble for you. Sorry for Bill. If you see Bill again, tell him not to fret. And tell him not to mind about marrying again, if he can find somebody nice. It's not as if he was an old man."

An hour or two later she said, "I do think it's lovely the way baby's taken to you. It *is* lucky, isn't it?"

In the morning she was still alive, but unconscious. They did what they could, which wasn't very much, but her breathing got weaker and weaker, and at about midday she died. They buried her in the Moslem village cemetery that evening.

At Ayer Kring they entered the most unhealthy district

they had passed through yet. The central mountains of Malaya were now on their left hand, to the west of them as they marched north, and they were coming to the head waters of the Pahang River which runs down to the east coast. Here the river spreads out into numerous tributaries, the Menkuang, the Pertang, the Belengu, and many others, and these tributaries running through flat country make a marshy place of swamps and mangroves that stretched for forty miles along their route, a country full of snakes and crocodiles, and infested with mosquitoes. By day it was steamy and hot and breathless; at night a cold wet mist came up and chilled them unmercifully.

By the time they had been two days in this country several of them were suffering from fever, a fever that did not seem quite like the malaria that they were used to, in that the temperature did not rise so high; it may have been dengue. They had little by that time to treat it with, not so much because they were short of money as because there were no drugs at all in the jungly villages that they were passing through. Jean consulted with the sergeant, who advised them to press on, and get out of this bad country as soon as possible. Jean was running a fever herself at the time and everything was moving about her in a blur; she had a cracking headache and it was difficult to focus her eyes. She consulted with Mrs. Frith, who was remarkably well.

"What he says is right, dearie," Mrs. Frith declared. "We won't get any better staying in this swampy place. I think we ought to walk each day, if you ask me."

Jean forced herself to concentrate. "What about Mrs. Simmonds?"

"Maybe the soldiers would carry her, if she gets any worse. I don't know, I'm sure. It's cruel hard, but if we've got to go we'd better go and get it over. That's what I say. We shan't do any good hanging around here in this nasty place."

They marched each day after that, stumbling along in fever, weak, and ill. The baby, Robin Holland, that Jean carried got the fever; this was the first ailment it had had. She showed it to the headman in the village of Mentri, and his wife produced a hot infusion of some bark in a dirty coconut shell; Jean tasted it and it was very bitter, so she judged it to be a form of quinine. She gave a little to the baby and took some herself; it seemed to do them both good during the night. Before the day's march began several of the women took it, and it helped.

It took them eleven days to get through the swamps to the higher ground past Temerloh. They left Mrs. Simmonds and Mrs. Fletcher behind them, and little Gillian Thomson. When they emerged into the higher, healthier country and dared to stay a day to rest, Jean was very weak but the fever had left her. The baby was still alive, though obviously ill; it cried almost incessantly during its waking hours.

It was Mrs. Frith who now buoyed them up, as she had depressed them in the earlier days. "It should be getting better all the time, from now on," she told them. "As we get nearer to the coast it should get better. It's lovely on the east coast, nice beaches to bathe on, and always a sea breeze. It's healthy, too."

They came presently to a very jungly village on a hilltop; they never learned its name. It stood above the river Jengka. By this time they had left the railway and were heading more or less eastwards on a jungle track that would at some time join a main road that led down to Kuantan. This village was cool and airy, and the people kind and hospitable; they gave the women a house to sleep in and provided food and fresh fruit, and the same bark infusion that was good for fever. They stayed there for six days revelling in the fresh, cool breeze and the clear, healthy nights, and when they finally marched on they were in better shape. They left a little gold brooch that had belonged to Mrs. Fletcher with the headman as payment for the food and kindness that they had received, thinking that the dead woman would not have objected to that.

Four days later, in the evening, they came to Maran. A tarmac road runs through Maran crossing the Malay Peninsula from Kuantan to Kerling. The road runs through the village, which has perhaps fifty houses, a school, and a few native shops. They came out upon the road half a mile or so to the north of the village; after five weeks upon the railway track and jungle paths it overjoyed them to see evidence of civilization in this road. They walked down to the village with a fresher step. And there, in front of them, they saw two trucks and two white men working on them while Japanese guards stood by.

They marched quickly towards the trucks, which were both heavily loaded with railway lines and sleepers; they stood pointing in the direction of Kuantan. One of them was jacked up on sleepers taken from the load, and both of the white men were underneath it working on the back axle. They wore shorts and army boots without socks; their bodies were brown with sunburn and very dirty with the muck from the back axle. But they were healthy and muscular men, lean, but in good physical condition. And they were white, the first white men that the women had seen for five months.

They crowded round the trucks; their guard began to talk in staccato Japanese with the truck guards. One of the men lying on his back under the axle, shifting spanner in hand, glanced at the bare feet and the sarongs within his range of vision and said slowly, "Tell the mucking Nip to get those mucking women shifted back so wc can get some light."

Some of the women laughed, and Mrs. Frith said, "Don't you go using that language to me, young man."

The men rolled out from under the truck and sat staring at the women and the children, at the brown skins, the sarongs, the bare feet. "Who said that?" asked the man with the spanner. "Which of you speaks English?" He spoke deliberately in a slow drawl, with something of a pause between each word.

Jean said, laughing, "We're all English."

He stared at her, noting the black hair plaited in a pigtail, the brown arms and feet, the sarong, the brown baby on her hip. There was a line of white skin showing on her chest at the V of her tattered blouse. "Straits born?" he hazarded.

"No fear," he said in his deliberate way. "We're Aussies."

Ile got to his feet; he was a fair-haired powerfully built man about twenty-seven or twenty-eight years old. "Dinky-die?" he said.

She did not understand that. "Are you prisoners?" she asked.

He smiled slowly. "Are we prisoners?" he repeated. "Oh my word."

There was something about this man that she had never met before. "Are you English?" she asked.

"No fear," he said in his deliberate way. "We're Aussies."

She said, "Are you in a camp here?"

He shook his head. "We come from Kuantan," he said. "But we're driving trucks all day, fetching this stuff down to the coast."

She said, "We're going to Kuantan, to the women's camp there."

He stared at her. "That's crook for a start," he said slowly. "There isn't any women's camp at Kuantan. There isn't any regular prisoner camp at all, just a little temporary camp for us because we're truck drivers. Who told you that there was a women's camp at Kuantan?"

"The Japanese told us. They're supposed to be sending us there." She sighed. "It's just another lie."

"The bloody Nips say anything." He smiled slowly. "I thought you were a lot of boongs," he said. "You say you're English, dinky-die? All the way from England?"

She nodded. "That's right. Some of us have been out here for ten or fifteen years, but we're all English."

"And the kiddies—they all English too?"

"All of them," she said.

He smiled slowly. "I never thought the first time that I spoke to an English lady she'd be looking like you."

"You aren't exactly an oil painting yourself," Jean said.

The other man was talking to a group of the women; Mrs. Frith and Mrs. Price were with Jean. The Australian turned to them. "Where do you come from?" he enquired.

Mrs. Frith said, "We got took in Panong, over on the west coast, waiting for a boat to get away."

"But where did you come from now?"

Jean said, "We're being marched to Kuantan."

"Not all the way from Panong?"

She laughed shortly. "We've been everywhere—Port Swettenham, Port Dickson—everywhere. Nobody wants us. I reckon that we've walked nearly five hundred miles."

"Oh my word," he said. "That sounds a crook deal to me. How do you go on for tucker, if you aren't in a camp?"

She did not understand him. "Tucker?"

"What do you get to eat?"

"We stay each night in a village," she said. "We'll have to find somewhere to stay here. Probably in a place like this it'll be the school. We eat what we can get in the village."

"For Christ's sake," he said. "Wait while I tell my cobber." He swung round to the other. "You heard about the crook deal that they got?" he said. "Been walking all the time since they got taken. Never been inside a prison camp at all."

"They've been telling me," the other said. "The way these bloody Nips go on. Makes you chunda."

The first man turned back to Jean. "What happens if any of you get sick?"

She said cynically, "When you get sick, you get well or you die. We haven't seen a doctor for the last three months and we've got practically no medicines left, so we mostly die. There were thirty-two of us when we were taken. Now we're seventeen."

The Australian said softly, "Oh my word."

Jean said, "Will you be staying here tonight?"

He said, "Will you?"

"We shall stay here," she said. "We shall be here tomorrow too, unless they'll let us ride down on your trucks. We can't march the children every day. We walk one day and rest the next."

He said, "If you're staying, Mrs. Boong, we're staying too. We can fix this bloody axle so as it will never roll again, if needs be." He paused in slow thought. "You got no medicines?" he said. "What do you want?"

She said quickly, "Have you got any Glauber's salts?"

He shook his head. "Is that what you want?"

"We haven't got any salts at all," she said. "We want quinine, and something for all these skin diseases that the children have got. Can we get those here?"

He said slowly, "I'll have a try. Have you got any money?"

Mrs. Frith snorted, "After being six months with the Japs? They took everything we had. Even our wedding rings."

Jean said, "We've got a few little bits of jewellery left, if we could sell some of those."

He said, "I'll have a go first, and see what I can do. You get fixed up with somewhere to sleep, and I'll see you later."

"All right."

She went back to their sergeant and bowed to him because that pleased him and made things easier for them. She said, "Gunso, where yasme tonight? Children must yasme. We see headman about yasme and mishi?"

He came with her and they found the headman, and negotiated for the loan of the school building for the prisoners, and for the supply of rice for mishi. They did not now experience the blank refusals that they formerly had met when the party was thirty strong; the lesser numbers had made accommodation and food much easier for them. They settled into the school building and began the routine of chores and washing that occupied the bulk of their spare time. The news that there was no women prisoners' camp in Kuantan was what they had all secretly expected, but it was a disappointment, none the less. The novelty of the two Australians made up for this, because by that time they were living strictly from day to day.

At the trucks the Aussies got back to their work. With heads close together under the axle, the fair-haired man that Jean had talked to said to his cobber, "I never heard such a crook deal. What can we do to fix this bastard so as we stay here tonight? I said I'd try and get some medicines for them."

They had already rectified the binding brake that had heated up the near-side hub and caused the stoppage. The other said, "Take the whole bloody hub off for a dekko, 'n pull out the shaft from the diff. That makes a good show of dirty bits. Means sleeping in the trucks."

"I said I'd try and get some medicines." They worked on for a little.

"How you going to do that?"

"Petrol, I suppose. That's easiest."

It was already growing dark when they extracted four feet of heavy metal shafting, splined at both ends, from the back axle; dripping with black oil they showed it to the Japanese corporal in charge of them as evidence of their industry. "Yasme here tonight," they said. The guard was suspicious, but agreed; indeed, he could do nothing else. He went off to arrange for rice for them, leaving them in charge of the private who was with him.

On the excuse of a benjo, the fair-haired man left the trucks and in the half light retired behind a house. He slipped quickly down behind a row of houses, and came out into the street a couple of hundred yards down, towards the end of the village. Here there was a Chinaman who ran a decrepit bus; the Australian had noted this place on various journeys through Maran; they plied regularly up and down this road.

In his deliberate manner he said quietly, "Johnnie, you buy petrol? How much you give?" It is extraordinary how little barrier an unknown language makes between a willing buyer and a willing seller. At one point in the negotiation they resorted to the written word, and the Australian wrote GLAUBER'S SALTS and QUININE and SKIN DISEASE OINTMENT in block letters on a scrap of wrapping paper.

He slunk back behind the houses carrying three two-gallon cans and a length of rubber hose, which he hid behind the latrine. He came back to the trucks presently, ostentatiously buttoning his shorts.

In the darkness, early in the night, he came to the school-house; it may have been about ten o'clock. One of the Japanese soldiers was supposed to be on guard all night, but in the five weeks that they had been with this pair of guards the women had not shown the slightest inclination to escape, and their guards had long given up watching them at night. The Australian had made sure where they were, however, and when he had seen them squatting with the truck guards he came silently to the school.

At the open door he paused, and said quietly, "Which of you ladies was I talking to this afternoon? The one with the baby."

Jean was asleep; they woke her and she pulled up her sarong and slipped her top on, and came to the door. He had several little packages for her. "That's quinine," he said. "I can get more of that if you want it. I couldn't get Glauber's, but this is what the Chinese take for dysentery. It's all written in Chinese, but what he says it means is three of these leaves powdered up in warm water every four hours. That'll be for a grown-up person. If it's any good, keep the label and maybe you could get some more in a Chinese drug shop. I got this Zam-Buk for the skin, and there's more of that if you want it."

She took them gratefully from him. "That's marvellous," she said softly. "How much did it all cost?"

"That's all right," he said in his deliberate manner. "The Nips paid, but they don't know it."

She thanked him again. "What are you doing here?" she asked. "Where are you going with the trucks?"

"Kuantan," he said. "We should be back there tonight, but Ben Leggat—he's my cobber—he got the truck in bits so we had to give it away. Get down there tomorrow, or we might stretch it another day if it suits, though it'd be risky, I think." He told her that there were six of them driving six trucks for the Japanese; they drove regularly from Kuantan up country to a place upon the railway called Jerantut, a distance of about a hundred and thirty miles. They would drive up one day and load the truck with sleepers and railway lines taken up from the track, and drive back to Kuantan the next day, where the railway material was unloaded on to the quayside to be taken away by ship to some unknown destination. "Building another railway somewhere, I suppose," he said. A hundred and thirty miles is a long way to drive a heavily loaded truck in a day in tropical conditions, and they sometimes failed to reach Kuantan before dark; when that happened they spent the night in a village. Their absence would not be remarked particularly at Kuantan.

He had been taken somewhere in Johore, and had been driving trucks from Kuantan for about two months. "Better than being in a camp," he said.

She sat down on the top step of the three that led up to the school, and he squatted down before her on the ground. His manner of sitting intrigued her, because he sat down on one heel somewhat in the manner of a native, but with his left leg extended. "Are you a truck driver in Australia?" she asked.

"No bloody fear," he said. "I'm a ringer."

She asked, "What's a ringer?"

"A stockrider," he said. "I was born in Queensland out behind Cloncurry and my people, they're all Queenslanders. My dad, he came from London, from a place called Hammersmith. He used to drive a cab and so he knew about horses, and he came out to Queensland to work for Cobb and Co., and met Ma. But I've not been back to the Curry for some time. I was working in the Territory over to the west, on a station called Wollara. That's about a hundred and ten miles south-west of the Springs."

She smiled. "Where's the Springs, then?"

"Alice," he said. "Alice Springs. Right in the middle of Australia, half-way between Darwin and Adelaide."

She said, "I thought the middle of Australia was all desert."

He was concerned at her ignorance. "Oh my word," he said deliberately. "Alice is a bonza place. Plenty of water in Alice; people living there, they leave the sprinkler on all night, watering the lawn. That's right, they leave the sprinkler on all night. Course, the Territory's dry in some parts, but there's usually good feed along the creeks. Come to that, there's water all over if you look for it. You take a creek that only runs in the wet, now, say a couple of months in the year, or else not that. You get a sandy billabong, and you'll get water there by digging not a foot below the surface, like as not—even in the middle of the dry." His slow, even tones were strangely comforting. "You go to a place like that and you'll find little diggings all over in the sand, where the kangaroos and euros have dug for water. They know where to go. There's water all over in the outback, but you've got to know where to find it."

"What do you do at this place Wollara?" she asked. "Do you look after sheep?"

He shook his head. "You don't find sheep around the Alice region," he said. "It'd be too hot for them. Wollara is a cattle station."

"How many cattle have you got?"

"About eighteen thousand when I come away," he said. "It goes up and down, according to the wet, you know."

"Eighteen thousand? But how big is it?"

"Wollara? About two thousand seven hundred."

"Two thousand seven hundred acres," she said. "That's a big place."

He stared at her. "Not acres," he said. "Square miles. Wollara's two thousand seven hundred square miles."

She was startled. "But is that all one place—one farm, I mean?"

"It's one station," he replied. "One property."

"But however many of you does it take to run it?"

His mind ran lovingly around the well-remembered scene. "There's Mr. Duveen, Tommy Duveen—he's the manager, and then me—I'm the head stockman, or I was. Tommy said he'd keep a place for me when I got back. I'd like to get back to Wollara again, one day . . ." He mused a little. "We had three other ringers—whites," he said. "Then there was Happy, and Moonlight, and Nugget, and Snowy, and Tarmac . . ." He thought for a minute. "Nine boongs we had," he said. "That's all."

"Nine what?"

"Black boys—black stockriders. Abos."

"But that's only thirteen men," she said.

"That's right. Fourteen if you count Mr. Duveen."

"But can fourteen men look after all those cattle?" she asked.

"Oh yes," he said thoughtfully. "Wollara is an easy station, in a way, because it hasn't got any fences. It's fences make the work. We've got the Palmer River and the Levi Range to the north, and the sand country over to the west; the cattle don't go there. Then there's the Kernot Range to the south and Mount Ormerod and the Twins to the east. Fourteen men is all right for a station like that; it would be easier if we had more whites, but you can't get them. These bloody boongs, they're always going walkabout."

"What's that?" she asked.

"Walkabout? Why, an Abo ringer, he'll come up one day and he'll say, 'Boss, I go walkabout now.' You can't keep him. He'll leave the station and go wandering off just in a pair of pants and an old hat with a gun if he's got one, or a spear and a throwing stick, maybe, and he'll be away two or three months."

"But where does he go to?" she asked.

"Just travels. They go a long way on a walkabout—oh my word," he said. "Four or five hundred miles, maybe. Then when he's had enough, he'll come back to the station and join up for work again. But the trouble with the boongs is, you never know if they'll be there next week."

There was a short silence; they sat quietly in the tropic night together on the steps of the atap schoolhouse, exiles far from their homes. Over their heads the flying foxes swept in the moonlight with a dry rustling of leathery wings. "Eighteen thousand cattle . . ." she said thoughtfully.

"More or less," he said. "Get a good wet, and it'll maybe rise to twenty-one or twenty-two thousand. Then you get a dry year, and it'll go right down to twelve or thirteen thousnad. I reckon we lose about three thousand every year by drought."

"But can't you get them to water?"

He smiled slowly. "Not with fourteen men. There's enough cattle die of thirst each year in the Territory and Northern Queensland to feed the whole of England. Course, the horses make it worse on Wollara."

"Horses?"

"Oh my word," he said. "We've got about three thousand brumbies, but you can't do nothing with them—they're vermin. Wollara used to be a horse station years ago, selling horses to the Indian Army, but you can't sell horses now. We use a few, of course—maybe a hundred, with packhorses and that. You can't get rid of them except by shooting, and you'll never get a ringer to shoot horses. They eat the feed the cattle ought to get, and spoil it, too. Cattle don't like feeding where a horse has been."

She asked, "How big is Wollara—how long, and how wide?"

He said, "Oh, I'd say about ninety miles from east to west, and maybe forty-five to fifty, north to south, at the widest part. But it's a good station to manage, because the homestead is near the middle, so it's not so far in any one way. Over to the Kernot Range is the furthest; that's about sixty miles."

"Sixty miles from the homestead? That's where you live?"

"That's right."

"Are there any other homesteads on it?"

He stared at her. "There's only the one homestead on each station. Some have an outstation, a shack of some kind where the boys can leave blankets and maybe a little tucker, but not many."

"How long does it take you to get to the furthest point, then—to the Kernot Range?"

"Over to the Range? Oh well, to go there and come back might take about a week. That's with horses; in a utility you might do it in a day and a half. But horses are best, although they're a bit slow. You never take a packhorse faster 'n a walk, not if you can help it. It isn't like you see it on the movies, people galloping their horses everywhere—oh my word. You'd soon wear out a horse if you used him that way in the Territory."

They sat together for over an hour, talking quietly at the entrance to the schoolhouse. At the end the ringer got up from his strange posture on the ground, and said, "I mustn't stay any longer, case those Nips come back and start creating. My cobber, too—he'll be wondering what happened to me. I left him to boil up."

Jean got to her feet. "It's been terribly kind of you to get us these things. You don't know what they mean to us. Tell me, what's your name?"

"Joe Harman," he said. "Sergeant Harman—Ringer Harman, some of them call me." He hesitated. "Sorry I called you Mrs. Boong today," he said awkwardly. "It was a silly kind of joke."

She said, "My name's Jean Paget."

"That sounds like a Scotch name."

"It is," she said. "I'm not Scotch myself, but my mother came from Perth."

"My mother's family was Scotch," he said. "They came from Inverness."

She put out her hand. "Good night, Sergeant," she said. "It's been lovely talking to another white person."

He took her hand; there was great comfort for her in his masculine handshake. "Look, Mrs. Paget," he said. "I'll try if I can get the Nips to let your party ride down on the truck with us. If the little bastards won't wear it, then we'll have to give it away. In that case I'll see you on the road again before you get to Kuantan, and I'll make darn sure there's something crook with the truck. What else do you want?"

"Soap," she said. "Could you possibly get us soap?"

"Should be able to," he said.

"We've got no soap at all," she observed. "I've got a little gold locket that one of the women had, who died, a thing with a bit of hair in it. I was going to see if I could sell that here, and get some soap."

"Keep it," he said. "I'll see you get soap."

"We want that more than anything, now that you've got these medicines for us," she said.

"You'll have it." He hesitated, and then said, "Sorry I talked so much, boring you with the outback and all that. There's times when you get down a bit—can't make yourself believe you'll ever see it again."

"I wasn't bored," she said softly. "Good night, Sergeant."

"Good night."

In the morning Jean showed the women what she had got. "I heard you talking to him ever so long," Mrs. Price said. "Nice young man, I'd say."

"He's a very homesick young man," Jean said. "He loves talking about the cattle station he comes from."

"Homesick!" Mrs. Price said. "Aren't we all?"

The Australians had a smart argument with their guards that morning, who refused point blank to let the women ride down on the trucks. There was some reason in this from their point of view, because the weight of seventeen women and children added to two grossly overloaded trucks might well be the last straw that would bring final breakdown, in which case the guards themselves would have been lucky to escape with a flogging at the hands of their officer. Harman and Leggat had to put the back axle together again; they were finished and ready for the road about the middle of the morning.

Joe Harman said, "Keep that little bastard busy for a minute while I loose off the union." He indicated the Jap guard. Presently they started, Harman in the lead, dribbling a little petrol from a loosened pipe joint, unnoticed by the guard. It was just as well to have an alibi when they ran out of fuel, having parted with six gallons to the Chinaman.

From Maran to Kuantan is fifty-five miles. The women rested that day at Maran, and next day began the march down the tarmac road. They reached a village called Buan that night. Jean had looked for Joe Harman's truck all day expecting to see it returning; she was not to know that it had been stranded overnight at Pohoi, short of petrol, and was a day late in the return journey. They stayed next day at Buan in an atap shed; the women took turns with Jean watching for the truck. Their health already was somewhat improved. After the railway track and the jungle paths the tarmac road was easy walking, and the medicines were already having an effect. The country, too, was growing higher and healthier, and the more imaginative of them were already saying they could smell the sea. And finally their contact with the two Australians had had a marked effect on their morale.

They did not see Joe Harman's truck as it passed through. Instead, a Malay girl came to them in the evening with a brown paper parcel of six cakes of Lifebuoy soap; it was addressed to Mrs. Paget. Written on the parcel was a note which read,

Dear Lady,

I send some soap which is all that we can find just at present but I will get more later on. I am sorry not to see you but the Nip won't let us stop so I have given this to the Chinaman at Maran and he says he will get it to you. Look out for us on the way back and I will try and stop then.

JOE HARMAN.

The women were delighted. "Lifebuoy," said Mrs. Warner, sniffing it ecstatically. "You can just smell the carbolic in it! My dear, wherever do you think they got it?"

"I'd have two guesses," Jean replied. "Either they stole it, or they stole something to buy it with." In fact, the latter was correct. At Pohoi their Japanese guard had taken off his boots to wash his feet at the village well; he washed his feet for about thirty seconds and turned round, but the boots had vanished; it could not have been either of the Australians because they both appeared immediately from the other direction. The mystery was never cleared up. Ben Leggat, however, was most helpful and stole a pair from a sleeping Japanese that evening and gave them to their guard, who was so relieved that he gave Ben a dollar.

The next day the women marched to Berkapor. They were coming out into much better country now, a pleasant, relatively healthy part where the road wound round hillsides and was mostly shaded by the overhanging trees. That day for the first time they got coconuts. Mrs. Price had an old worn-out pair of slippers that had belonged to Mrs. Horsefall; she had carried them for weeks and had never really used them; they traded these at Berkapor as soon as they got in for milk coconuts, one for each member of the party, thinking that the vitamins contained in the fluid would be good for them. At Berkapor they were accommodated in a large atap copra shed beside the road, and just before dusk the two familiar trucks drew up in the village, driven by Ben Leggat and Joe Harman. As before, they were headed for the coast and loaded high with railway lines and sleepers.

Jean and several of the others walked across the road to meet them, with the Japanese sergeant; the Japanese guards fell into conversation together. Joe Harman turned to Jean. "We couldn't get loaded at Jerantut in time to make it down to Kuantan tonight," he said. "Ben's got a pig."

"A pig?" They crowded round Ben's truck. The corpse

was lying upon the top of the load, a black, long-nosed Oriental pig, somewhat mauled and already covered in flies. Somewhere near the Tekam River Ben, whose truck was in the lead, had found this pig upon the road and had chased it with the truck for a quarter of a mile. The Japanese guard beside him had fired six shots at it from his rifle and had missed it every time till with the seventh he had wounded it and so enabled Ben to run over it with one of the front wheels. They had stopped and Harman coming close behind them had stopped too, and the two Aussies and the Japanese guards had heaved the pig on to the load and got moving again before the infuriated Chinese storekeeper had caught up with them to claim his property. Harman said quietly to Jean, "We'll have to let the bloody Nips eat all they can and carry away a bit. Leave it to me; I'll see there's some for you."

That night the women got about thirty-five pounds of boiled pig meat, conveyed to them surreptitiously in several instalments. They made a fire of coconut shells behind the copra store and made a stew with their rice ration, and ate all of this that seemed prudent to them; at that there was enough meat left for the three meals that they would have before they took the road again. They sat about in the shade or at the roadside after they had finished, replete with the first really nourishing meal that they had had for months, and presently the Australians came across to talk to them.

Joe Harman came to Jean. "Sorry I couldn't send over more of that pig," he said in his slow Queensland drawl. "I had to let the bloody Nips have most of it."

She said, "It's been splendid, Joe. We've been eating and eating, and there's still lots left for tomorrow. I don't know when we last had such a meal."

"I'd say that's what you need," he observed. "There's not a lot of flesh on any of you, if I may say so."

He squatted down upon the ground beside the women, sitting on one heel in his peculiar way.

"I know we're pretty thin," Jean said. "But we're a darned sight better than we were. That Chinese stuff you got us as the substitute for Glauber's salts—that's doing the trick all right. It's stopping it."

"Fine," he said. "Maybe we could get some more of that in Kuantan."

"The pig was a godsend," she said. "That, and the fruit— we got some green coconuts today. We've been very lucky so far that we've had no beriberi, or that sort of thing."

"It's because we've had fresh rice," said Mrs. Frith unexpectedly. "Being in the country parts we've had fresh rice all through. It's old rice that gives you beriberi."

The Australian sat thoughtful, chewing a piece of stick. "Funny sort of a life for you ladies," he said at last. "Living in a place like this, and eating like the boongs. These Nips'll have something coming to them, when it's all added up."

He turned to Jean. "What were you all doing in Malaya?" he asked.

"Most of us were married," she said. "Our husbands had jobs here."

Mrs. Frith said, "My hubby's District Engineer on the railway. We had ever such a nice bungalow at Kajang."

Harman said, "All the husbands got interned separately, I suppose?"

"That's right," said Mrs. Price. "My Arthur's in Singapore. I heard about him when we was in Port Dickson. I think they're all in Singapore."

"All comfortable in a camp while you go walking round the country," he said.

"That's right," said Mrs. Frith. "Still, it's nice to know that they're all right, when all's said and done."

"It seems to me," said Harman, "the way they're kicking you around, they just don't know what they can do with you. It might not be too difficult for you to just stay in one place, as it might be this, and live till the war's over."

Mrs. Frith said, "That's what I've been thinking."

Jean said, "I know. I've thought of this ever since Mrs. Frith suggested it. The trouble is, the Japs feed us—or they make the village feed us. The village never gets paid. We'd have to earn our keep somehow, and I don't see how we could do it."

Harman said, "It was just an idea."

He said presently, "I believe I know where I could get a chicken or two. If I can I'll drop them off for you when we come up country, day after tomorrow."

Jean said, "We haven't paid you for the soap yet."

"Forget about it," he said slowly. "I didn't pay cash for it myself. I swapped it for a pair of Nip rubber boots." With slow, dry humour he told them about the boots. "You got the soap, the Nip got another pair of boots, and Ben got a dollar," he said. "Everybody's happy and satisfied."

Jean said, "Is that how you're going to get the chicken?"

"I'll get a chicken for you, one way or another," he said. "You ladies need feeding up."

She said, "Don't take any risks."

"You attend to your own business, Mrs. Boong," he said, "and take what you get. That's what you have to do when you're a prisoner, just take what you can get."

She smiled, and said, "All right." The fact that he had called her Mrs. Boong pleased her; it was a little tenuous bond between herself and this strange man that he should pull her leg about her sunburn, her native dress, and the baby that she carried on her hip like a Malay woman. The word *boong* put Australia into her mind, and the aboriginal stockriders, and she asked a question that had occurred to her, partly from curiosity and partly because she knew it pleased him to talk about his own country. "Tell me," she said, "is it very hot in Australia, the part you come from? Hotter than this?"

"It's hot," he said. "Oh my word, it can be hot when it tries. At Wollara it can go to a hundred and eighteen—that's a hot day, that is. But it's not like this heat here. It's a kind of a dry heat, so you don't sweat like you do here." He thought for a minute. "I got thrown once," he said, "breaking in a brumby to the saddle. I broke my thigh, and after it was set in the hospital they used to point a sort of lamp at it, a sunray lamp they called it, to tone up the muscles or something. Do you have those things in England?"

She nodded. "It's like that, is it?"

"That's right," he said. "It's a kind of a warm, dry heat, the sort that does you good and makes you thirsty for cold beer."

"What does the country look like?" she enquired. It pleased this man to talk about his own place and she wanted to please him; he had been so very kind to them.

"It's red," he said. "Red around Alice and where I come from, red earth and then, the mountains are all red. The Macdonnells and the Levis and the Kernots, great red ranges of bare hills against the blue sky. Evenings they go purple and all sorts of colours. After the wet there's green all over them. In the dry, parts of them go silvery white with the spinifex." He paused. "I suppose everybody likes his own place," he said quietly. "The country round about the Springs is my place. People come up on the 'Ghan from Adelaide and places in the south, and they say Alice is a lousy town. I only went to Adelaide once, and I thought that was lousy. The country round about the Springs is beautiful to me."

He mused. "Artists come up from the south and try and paint it in pictures," he said. "I only met one that ever got it right, and he was an Abo, an Abo called Albert out at Hermansburg. Somebody gave him a brush and some paints one time, and he started in and got it better than any of them, oh my word, he did. But he's an Abo, and he's painting his own place. I suppose that makes a difference."

He turned to Jean. "What's your place?" he asked. "Where do you come from?"

She said, "Southampton."

"Where the liners go to?"

"That's it," she said.

"What's it like there?" he asked.

She shifted the baby on her hip, and moved her feet in the sarong. "It's quiet, and cool, and happy," she said thoughtfully. "It's not particularly beautiful, although there's lovely country round about—the New Forest, and the Isle of Wight. It's my place, like the Springs is yours, and I shall go back there if I live through this time, because I love it so." She paused for a moment. "There was an ice rink there," she said. "I used to dance upon the ice, when I was a girl at school. One day I'll get back there and dance again."

"I've never seen an ice rink," said the man from Alice. "I've seen pictures of them, and on the movies."

She said, "It was such fun . . ."

Presently he got up to go; she walked across the road with him towards the trucks, the baby on her hip, as always. "I shan't be able to see you tomorrow," he said. "We start at dawn. But I'll be coming back up the road the day after."

"We shall be walking to Pohoi that day, I think," she said.

"I'll see if I can get you those chickens," he said.

She turned and faced him, standing beside her in the moonlit road, in all the noises of the tropic night. "Look, Joe," she said. "We don't want meat if it's going to mean trouble. It was grand of you to get that soap for us, but you did take a fearful risk, pinching that chap's boots."

"That's nothing," he said slowly. "You can run rings round these Nips when you learn how."

"You've done a lot for us," she said. "This pig, and the medicines, and the soap. It's made a world of difference to us in these last few days. I know you've taken risks to do these things. Do, please, be careful."

"Don't worry about me," he said. "I'll try and get the chickens, but if I find things getting hot I'll give it away. I won't go sticking out my neck."

"You'll promise that?" she asked.

"Don't worry about me," he said. "You've got enough

troubles on your own plate, my word. But we'll come out all right, so long as we just keep alive, that's all we got to do. Just keep alive another two years, till the war's over."

"You think that it will be so long as that?" she asked.

"Ben knows a lot more than I do about things like that," he said. "He thinks about two years." He grinned down at her. "You'd better have those chickens."

"I'll leave that with you," she said. "I'd never forgive myself if you got caught in anything, and bought it."

"I won't," he said. He put out his hand as if to take her own, and then dropped it again. "Good night, Mrs. Boong," he said.

She laughed. "I'll crack you with a coconut if you say Mrs. Boong again. Good night, Joe."

"Good night."

They did not see him next morning, though they heard the trucks go off. They rested that day at Berkapor, as was their custom, and the next day they marched on to Pohoi. The two trucks driven by Harman and Leggat passed them on the road about midday going up empty to Jerantut; each driver waved to the women as they passed, and they waved back. The Japanese guards seated beside the drivers scowled a little. No chickens dropped from the trucks and the trucks did not stop; in one way Jean was rather relieved. She knew something of the temper of these men by now, and she knew very well that they would stop at nothing, would be deterred by no risk, to get what they considered to be helpful for the women. No chickens meant no trouble, and she marched on for the rest of the day with an easy mind.

That evening, in the house that they had been put into at Pohoi, a little Malay boy came to Jean with a green canvas sack; he said that he had been sent by a Chinaman in Gambang. In the sack were five black cockerels, alive, with their feet tied. Poultry is usually transported in the East alive.

Their arrival put Jean in a difficulty, and she consulted with Mrs. Frith. It was impossible for them to kill, pluck and cook five cockerels without drawing the attention of their guards to what was going on, and the first thing that the guards would ask was, Where had the cockerels come from? If Jean had known the answer to that one herself it would have been easier to frame a lie. It would be possible, they thought, to say that they had bought them with money given to them by the Australians, but that was difficult if the sergeant wanted to know where they had bought them in Pohoi. It was unfortunate that Pohoi was a somewhat unfriendly village; it had been genuinely difficult for the village to evacuate a house for the women, and it was not to be expected that they would get much co-operation from the villagers in any deceit. Finally they decided to say that they had bought them with money given to them by the Australians, and that they had arranged at Berkapor for the poultry to be sent to them at Pohoi from a village called Limau, two or three miles off the road. It was a thin tale and one that would not stand up to a great deal of investigation, but they saw no reason why any investigation should take place.

They decided regretfully that they would have to part with one of the five cockerels to their guards; the gift of a chicken would make the sergeant sweet and involve him in the affair, rendering any serious investigation unlikely. Accordingly Jean took the sack and went to find the sergeant.

She bowed to him, to put him in a good temper. "Gunso," she said, "Good mishi tonight. We buy chickens." She opened the sack and showed him the fowls lying in the bottom. Then she reached down and pulled out one. "For you." She smiled at him with all the innocence that she could muster.

It was a great surprise to him. He had not known that they had so much money; they had never been able to buy anything but coconuts or bananas before, since he had been with them. "You buy?" he asked.

She nodded. "From Limau. Very good mishi for us all tonight."

"Where get money?" he enquired. Suspicion had not dawned, for they had never deceived him before; he was just curious.

For one fleeting moment Jean toyed with the idea of saying they had sold some jewellery, with a quick, intuitive feeling that it would be better not to mention the Australians. But she put the idea away; she must stick to the story that they had prepared and considered from all angles. "Man prisoner give us money for chicken," she said. "They say we too thin. Now we have good mishi tonight, Japanese and prisoner also."

He put up two fingers. "Two."

She went up in a sheet of flame. "One, not two, gunso," she said. "This is a present for you, because you have been kind and carried children, and allowed us to walk slowly. Five only, five." She showed him the sack, and he counted them carefully. It was only then that she took note of the fact that the birds were rather unusually large for the East, and jet black all over. "One for you, four for us."

He let the sack fall, and nodded; then he smiled at her, tucked the cockerel under his arm, and walked off with it towards the kitchen where his meal was in preparation.

That day there was a considerable row in progress at Kuantan. The local commanding officer was a Captain Sugamo, who was executed by the Allied War Crimes Tribunal in the year 1946 after trial for atrocities committed at Camp 302 on the Burma-Siam railway in the years 1943 and 1944: his duty in Kuantan at that time was to see to the evacuation of the railway material from the eastern railway in Malaya and to its shipment to Siam. He lived in the house formerly occupied by the District Commissioner of Kuantan, and the District Commissioner had kept a fine little flock of about twenty Black Leghorn fowls, specially imported from England in 1939. When Captain Sugamo woke up that morning, five of his twenty Black Leghorns were missing, with a green sack that had once held the mail for the District Commissioner, and was now used to store grain for the fowls.

Captain Sugamo was a very angry man. He called the Military Police and set them to work; their suspicion fell at once upon the Australian truck drivers who had a record for petty larceny unsurpassed in that district. Moreover, they had considerable opportunities, because the nature of their work allowed them a great deal of freedom; trucks had to be serviced and refuelled, often in the hours of darkness when it was difficult to ascertain exactly where each man might be. Their camp was searched that day for any sign of tell-tale feathers, or the sack, but nothing was discovered but a cache of tinned foods and cigarettes stolen from the quartermaster's store.

Captain Sugamo was not satisfied and he became more angry than ever. A question of face was now involved, because this theft from the commanding officer was a clear insult to his position, and so to the Imperial Japanese Army. He ordered a search of the entire town of Kuantan: on the following day every house was entered by troops working under the directions of the Military Police to look for signs of the black feathers or the green sack. It yielded no result.

Brooding over the insults levelled at his uniform, the captain ordered the barracks of the company of soldiers under his command to be searched. There was no result from that.

There remained one further avenue. Three of the trucks, driven by Australians, were up country on the road to or from Jerantut. Next day Sugamo dispatched a light truck up

the road manned by four men of his Military Police, to search
these trucks and to interrogate the drivers and the guards,
and anybody else who might have knowledge of the matter.
Between Pohoi and Blat they came upon a crowd of women
and children walking down the road loaded with bundles;
ahead of them marched a Japanese sergeant with his rifle
slung over one shoulder and a green sack over the other. The
truck stopped with a squeal of brakes.

For the next two hours Jean stuck to her story, that the
Australian had given her money and she had bought the
fowls from Limau. They put her through a sort of third
degree there on the road, with an insistent reiteration of
questions: when they felt that her attention was wandering
they slapped her face, kicked her shins, or stamped on her
bare feet with army boots. She stuck to it with desperate
resolution, knowing that it was a rotten story, knowing that
they disbelieved her, not knowing what else she could say.
At the end of that time a convoy of three trucks came down
the road; the driver of the second one, Joe Harman, was
recognized by the sergeant immediately, and brought before
Jean at the point of the bayonet. The sergeant of the Military Police said, "Is this man?"

Jean said desperately, "I've been telling them about the
four dollars you gave me to buy the chickens with, Joe, but
they won't believe me."

The military policeman said, "You steal chickens from
the shoko. Here is bag."

The ringer looked at the girl's bleeding face and at her
bleeding feet. "Leave her alone, you bloody mucking bastards," he said angrily in his slow Queensland drawl. "I stole
those mucking chickens, and I gave them to her. So what?"

Darkness was closing down in my London sitting-room,
the early darkness of a stormy afternoon. The rain still beat
upon the window. The girl sat staring into the fire, immersed
in her sad memories. "They crucified him," she said quietly.
"They took us all down to Kuantan, and they nailed his hands
to a tree, and beat him to death. They kept us there, and
made us look on while they did it."

Chapter 4

"MY DEAR," I said. "I am so very sorry."

She raised her head. "You don't have to be sorry," she replied. "It was one of those things that seem to happen in a war. It's a long time ago, now—nearly six years. And Captain Sugamo was hung—not for that, but for what he did upon the railway. It's all over and done with now, and nearly forgotten."

There was, of course, no women's camp in Kuantan, and Captain Sugamo was not the man to be bothered with a lot of women and children. The execution took place at midday at a tree that stood beside the recreation ground overlooking the tennis courts: as soon as the maimed, bleeding body hanging by its hands had ceased to twitch Captain Sugamo stood them in parade before him.

"You very bad people," he said. "No place here for you. I send you to Kota Bharu. You walk now."

They stumbled off without a word, in desperate hurry to get clear of that place of horror. The same sergeant that had escorted them from Gemas was sent with them, for he also was disgraced as having shared the chickens. It was as a punishment that he was ordered to continue with them, because all prisoners are disgraceful and dishonourable creatures in the eyes of the Japanese, and to guard them and escort them is an insulting and a menial job fit only for the lowest type of man. An honourable Japanese would kill himself rather than be taken prisoner. Perhaps to emphasize this point the private soldier was taken away, so that from Kuantan onwards the sergeant was their only guard.

So they took up their journey again, living from day to day. They left Kuantan about the middle of July. It is about two hundred miles from Kuantan to Kota Bharu: allowing for halts of several days for illness Jean anticipated it would take them two months at least to get there.

They got to Besarah on the first day: this is a fishing village on the sea, white white coral sand and palm trees at the head of the beach. It is a very lovely place but they slept little, for most of the children were awake and crying in the night with memories of the horror they had seen. They could not bear to stay so close to Kuantan and travelled on next day another short stage to Balok, another fishing village on another beach with more palm trees. Here they rested for a day.

Gradually they came to realize that they had entered a new land. The north-east coast of Malaya is a very lovely country, and comparatively healthy. It is beautiful with rocky headlands and long, sweeping, sandy beaches fringed with palm trees, and usually there is a fresh wind from the sea. Moreover there is an abundance of fresh fish in all the villages. For the first time since they left Panong the women had sufficient protein with their rice, and their health began to show an improvement at once. Most of them bathed in the warm sea at least once every day, and certain of the skin diseases that they suffered from began to heal with this salt water treatment, though not all. For the first time in months the children had sufficient energy to play.

They all improved, in fact, except the sergeant. The sergeant was suspicious of them now; he seldom carried a child or helped them in any way. He seemed to feel the reproofs that he had been given very much, and he had now no companion of his own race to talk to. He moped a great deal, sitting sullenly aloof from them in the evenings; once or twice Jean caught herself consciously trying to cheer him up, a queer reversal of the role of prisoner and guard. Upon this route they met very few Japanese. Occasionally they would find a detachment stationed in a river village or at an airstrip; when they came to such a unit the sergeant would smarten himself up and go and report to the officer in charge, who would usually come and inspect them. But there is very little industry between Kuantan and Kota Bharu and no town larger than a fishing village, nor was there any prospect of an enemy attack upon the eastern side of the Malay Peninsula. On several occasions a week passed without the women seeing any Japanese at all except the sergeant.

As they travelled slowly up the coast the condition of the women and the children altered greatly for the better. They were now a very different party to the helpless people who had started off from Panong nearly six months before. Death had ruthlessly eliminated the weakest members and reduced them to about half the original numbers, which made all problems of billeting and feeding in the villages far easier. They were infinitely more experienced by that time, too. They had learned to use the native remedies for malaria and dysentery, to clothe themselves and wash and sleep in the native manner; in consequence they now had far more leisure than when they had been fighting to maintain a western style of life in primitive conditions. The march of ten miles every other day was now no longer a great burden; in the intervening day they had more time for the children. Presently Mrs. Warner, who at one time had been an elementary school mistress, started a class for the children, and school became a regular institution on their day of rest.

Jean began to teach her baby, Robin Holland, how to walk. He was quite fit and healthy again, and getting quite a weight for her to carry, for he was now sixteen months old. She never burdened him with any clothes in that warm climate, and he crawled about naked in the shade of palm or casuarina trees, or in the sun upon the sand, like any Malay baby. He got nearly as brown as one, too.

In the weeks that followed they moved slowly northwards up the coast, through all the many fishing villages, Ular and Chendar and Kalong and Penunjok and Kemasik and many others. They had a little sickness and spent a few days here and there while various members of the party sweated out a fever, but they had no more deaths. The final horror at Kuantan was a matter that they never spoke about at all, each fearing to recall it to the memory of the others, but each was secretly of the opinion that it had changed their luck.

With Mrs. Frith this impression struck much deeper. She was a devout little woman who said her prayers morning and evening with the greatest regularity. It was Mrs. Frith who always knew when Sunday was: on that day she would read the Prayer Book and the Bible for an hour aloud to anyone who came to listen to her. If it was their rest day she would hold this service at eleven o'clock as near as she could guess it, because that was the correct time for Matins.

Mrs. Frith sought for the hand of God in everything that happened to them. Brooding over their experiences with this in mind, she was struck by certain similarities. She had read repeatedly about one Crucifixion; now there had been another. The Australian, in her mind, had had the power of healing, because the medicines he brought had cured her dysentery and Johnnie Horsefall's ringworm. It was beyond all doubt that they had been blessed in every way since his death for them. God had sent down His Son to earth in Palestine. What if He had done it again in Malaya?

Men and women who are in great and prolonged distress and forced into an entirely novel way of life, divorced entirely from their previous associations, frequently develop curious mental traits. Mrs. Frith did not thrust her views upon them, yet inevitably the matter that she was beginning to believe herself became known to the other women. It was received with incredulity at first, but as a matter that required the most deep and serious thought. Most of the women had been churchgoers when they got the chance, mostly of Low Church sects; deep in their hearts they had been longing for the help of God. As their physical health improved throughout these weeks, their capacity for religious thought increased, and, as the weeks went on, accurate memory of the Australian began to fade, and was replaced by an awed and roseate memory of the man he had not been. If this incredible event that Mrs. Frith believed could possibly be true, it meant indeed that they were in the hand of God; nothing could touch them then; they would win through and live through all their troubles and one day they would regain their homes, their husbands, and their western way of life. They marched on with renewed strength.

Jean did nothing to dispel these fancies which were evidently helpful to the women, but she was not herself impressed. She was the youngest of all of them, and the only one unmarried; she had formed a very different idea of Joe Harman. She knew him for a very human, very normal man; she had grown prettier, she knew, when he had come to talk to her, and more attractive. It had been a subconscious measure of defence that had led her to allow him to continue to refer to her as Mrs. Boong; if the baby on her hip had misled him into classing her with all the other married women, that was just as well. In those villages, in the hot tropic nights when they wore little clothing, in that place of extraordinary standards or no standards at all, she knew that anything might have happened between them if he had known that she was an unmarried girl, and it might well have happened very quickly. Her grief for him was more real and far deeper than that of the other women, and it was not in the least because she thought that he had been divine. She was entirely certain in her own mind that he wasn't.

Towards the end of August they were in a village called Kuala Telang about half-way between Kuantan and Kota Bharu. The Telang is a short, muddy river that wanders through a flat country of rice fields to the sea; the village stands on the south bank of the river just inside the sand bar at the mouth. It is a pretty place of palm and casuarina trees and long white beaches on which the rollers of the

South China Sea break in surf. The village lives upon the fishing and on the rice fields. About fifteen fishing boats operate from the river, big open sailing boats with strange, high, flat figureheads at bow and stern. There is a sort of village square with wood and palm-leaf native shops grouped round about it; behind this stands a godown for the rice beside the river bank. This godown was empty at the time, and it was here that the party was accommodated.

The Japanese sergeant fell ill with fever here, probably malaria. He had not been himself since Kuantan; he had been sullen and depressed, and he seemed to feel the lack of companionship very much. As the women had grown stronger so he had grown weaker, and this was strange to them at first, because he had never been ill before. At first they had been pleased and relieved that this queer, ugly, uncouth little man was in eclipse, but as he grew more unhappy they suffered a strange reversal of feeling. He had been with them for a long time and he had done what was possible within the limits of his duty to alleviate their lot; he had carried their children willingly and he had wept when children died. When it was obvious that he had fever they took turns at carrying his rifle and his tunic and his boots and his pack for him, so that they arrived in the village as a queer procession, Mrs. Warner leading the little yellow man clad only in his trousers stumbling along in a daze. He walked more comfortably barefoot. Behind them came the other women carrying all his equipment as well as their own burdens.

Jean found the headman, a man of about fifty called Mat Amin bin Taib, and explained the situation to him. "We are prisoners," she said, "marching from Kuantan to Kota Bharu, and this Japanese is our guard. He is ill with fever, and we must find a shady house for him to lie in. He has authority to sign chits in the name of the Imperial Japanese Army for our food and accommodation, and he will do this for you when he recovers; he will give you a paper. We must have a place to sleep ourselves, and food."

Mat Amin said, "I have no place where white mems would like to sleep."

Jean said, "We are not white mems any longer; we are prisoners and we are accustomed to living as your women live. All we need is a shelter and a floor to sleep on, and the use of cooking pots, and rice, and a little fish or meat and vegetables."

"You can have what we have ourselves," he said, "but it is strange to see mems living so."

He took the sergeant into his own house and produced a mattress stuffed with coconut fibre and a pillow of the same material; he had a mosquito net which was evidently his own and he offered this, but the women refused it because they knew the sergeant needed all the cooling breezes he could get. They made him take his trousers off and get into a sarong and lie down on the bed. They had no quinine left, but the headman produced a draught of his own concoction and they gave the sergeant some of this, and left him in the care of the headman's wife, and went to find their own quarters and food.

The fever was high all that night; in the morning when they came to see how he was getting on they did not like the look of him at all. He was still in a high fever and he was very much weaker than he had been; it seemed to them that he was giving up, and that was a bad sign. They took turns all that day to sit with him and bathe his face, and wash him; from time to time they talked to him to try to stimulate his interest, but without a great deal of success. In the evening Jean was sitting with him; he lay inert upon his back, sweating profusely; he did not answer anything she said.

Looking for something to attract his interest, she pulled his tunic to her and felt in the pocket for his paybook. She found a photograph in it, a photograph of a Japanese woman and four children standing by the entrance to a house. She said, "Your children, gunso?" and gave it to him. He took it without speaking and looked at it; then he gave it back to her and motioned to her to put it away again.

When she had laid the jacket down she looked at him and saw that tears were oozing from his eyes and falling down to mingle with the sweat beads on his cheeks. Very gently she wiped them away.

He grew weaker and weaker, and two days later he died in the night. There seemed no particular reason why he should have died, but the disgrace of Kuantan was heavy on him and he seemed to have lost interest and the will to live. They buried him that day in the Moslem cemetery outside the village, and most of them wept a little for him as an old and valued friend.

The death of the sergeant left them in a most unusual position, for they were now prisoners without a guard. They discussed it at some length that evening after the funeral. "I don't see why we shouldn't stay here, where we are," said Mrs. Frith. "It's a nice place, this is, as nice as any that we've come to. That's what He said, we ought to find a place where we'd be out of the way, and just live there."

Jean said, "I know. There's two things we'd have to settle though. First, the Japs are bound to find out sometime that we're living here, and then the headman will get into trouble for having allowed us to stay here without telling them. They'd probably kill him. You know what they are."

"Maybe they wouldn't find us, after all," said Mrs. Price.

"I don't believe Mat Amin is the man to take that risk," Jean said. "There isn't any reason why he should. If we stay he'll go straight to the Japanese and tell them that we're here." She paused. "The other thing is that we can't expect this village to go on feeding seventeen of us for ever just because we're white mems. They'll go and tell the Japs about us just to get rid of us."

Mrs. Frith said shrewdly, "We could grow our own food, perhaps. Half the paddy fields we walked by coming in haven't been planted this year."

Jean stared at her. "That's quite right—they haven't. I wonder why that is?"

"All the men must have gone to the war," said Mrs. Warner. "Working as coolies taking up that railway line, or something of that."

Jean said slowly, "What would you think of this? Suppose I go and tell Mat Amin that we'll work in the rice fields if he'll let us stay here? What would you think of that?"

Mrs. Price laughed. "Me, with my figure? Walking about in mud and water up to the knee planting them little seedlings in the mud, like you see the Malay girls doing?"

Jean said apologetically, "It was just a thought."

"And a very good one, too," said Mrs. Warner. "I wouldn't mind working in the paddy fields if we could stay here and live comfortable and settled."

Mrs. Frith said, "If we were growing rice like that, maybe they'd let us stay here—the Japs, I mean. After all, in that way we'd be doing something useful, instead of walking all over the country like a lot of whipped dogs with no home."

Next morning Jean went to the headman. She put her hands together in the praying gesture of greeting, and smiled at him, and said in Malay, "Mat Amin, why do we see the paddy fields not sown this year? We saw so many of them as we came to this place, not sown at all."

He said, "Most of the men, except the fishermen, are working for the army." He meant the Japanese Army.

"On the railway?"

"No. They are at Gong Kedak. They are making a long piece of land flat, and making roads, and covering the land they have made flat with tar and stones, so that aeroplanes can come down there."

"Are they coming back soon to plant paddy?"

"It is in the hand of God, but I do not think they will come back for many months. I have heard that after they have done this thing at Gong Kedak, there is another such place to be made at Machang, and another at Tan Yongmat. Once a man falls into the power of the Japanese it is not easy for him to escape and come back to his home."

"Who, then, will plant the paddy, and reap it?"

"The women will do what they can. Rice will be short next year, not here, because we shall not sell the paddy that we need to eat ourselves. We shall not have enough to sell to the Japanese. I do not know what they are going to eat, but it will not be rice."

Jean said, "Mat Amin, I have serious matters to discuss with you. If there were a man amongst us I would send him to talk for us, but there is no man. You will not be offended if I ask you to talk business with a woman, on behalf of women?" She now knew something of the right approach to a Mohammedan.

He bowed to her, and led her to his house. There was a small rickety verandah; they went up to this and sat down upon the floor facing each other. He was a level-eyed old man with close-cropped hair and a small, clipped moustache, naked to the waist and wearing a sarong; his face was firm, but not unkind. He called sharply to his wife within the house to bring out coffee.

Jean waited till the coffee appeared, making small talk for politeness; she knew the form after six months in the villages. It came in two thick glasses, without milk and sweet with sugar. She bowed to him, and lifted her glass and sipped, and set it down again. "We are in a difficulty," she said frankly. "Our guard is dead, and what now will become of us is in our own hands—and in yours. You know our story. We were taken prisoner at Panong, and since then we have walked many hundreds of miles to this place. No Japanese commander will receive us and put us in a camp and feed us and attend to us in illness, because each commander thinks that these things are the duty of the other; so they march us under guard from town to town. This has been going on now for more than six months, and in that time half of our party have died upon the road."

He inclined his head.

"Now that our gunso is dead," she said "what shall we do? If we go on until we find a Japanese officer and report to him, he will not want us; nobody in all this country wants us. They will not kill us quickly, as they might if we were men. They will get us out of the way by marching us on to some other place, perhaps into a country of swamps such as we have come through. So we shall grow ill again, and one by one we shall all die. That is what lies ahead of us, if we report now to the Japanese."

He replied, "It is written that the angels said, 'Every soul shall taste of death, and we will prove you with evil and with good for a trial of you, and unto us shall ye return.'"

She thought quickly; the words of the headman at Dilit came into her mind. She said, "It is also written, 'If ye be kind towards women and fear to wrong them, God is well acquainted with what ye do.'"

He eyed her steadily. "Where is that written?"

She said, "In the Fourth Surah."

"Are you of the Faith?" he asked incredulously.

She shook her head. "I do not want to deceive you. I am a Christian; we are all Christians. The headman of a village on our road was kind to us, and when I thanked him he said that to me. I do not know the Koran."

"You are a very clever woman," he said. "Tell me what you want."

"I want our party to stay here, in this village," she said, "and go to work in the paddy fields, as your women do." He stared at her, astonished. "This will be dangerous for you," she said, "we know that very well. If Japanese officers find us in this place before you have reported to them that we are here, they will be very angry. And so, I want you to do this. I want you to let us go to work at once with one or two of your women to show us what to do. We will work all day for our food alone and a place to sleep. When we have worked so for two weeks, I will go myself and find an officer and report to him, and tell him what we are doing. And you shall come with me, as headman of this village, and you shall tell the officer that more rice will be grown for the Japanese if we are allowed to continue working in the rice fields. These are the things I want."

"I have never heard of white mems working in the paddy fields," he said.

She asked, "Have you ever heard of white mems marching and dying as we have marched and died?"

He was silent.

"We are in your hands," she said. "If you say, 'Go upon your way and walk on to some other place,' then we must go, and going we must die. That will then be a matter between you and God. If you allow us to stay and cultivate your fields and live with you in peace and safety, you will get great honour when the English Tuans return to this country after their victory. Because they will win this war in the end; these Short Ones are in power now, but they cannot win against the Americans and all the free peoples of the world. One day the English Tuans will come back."

He said, "I shall be glad to see that day."

They sat in silence for a time, sipping the glasses of coffee. Presently the headman said, "This is a matter not to be decided lightly, for it concerns the whole village. I will think about it and I will talk it over with my brothers."

Jean went away, and that evening after the hour of evening prayer she saw a gathering of men squatting with the headman in front of his house; they were all old men, because there were very few young ones in Kuala Telang at that time, and young ones probably would not have been admitted to the conference in any case. Later that evening Mat Amin came to the godown and asked for Mem Paget; Jean came out to him, carrying the baby. She stood talking to him in the light of a small oil lamp.

"We have discussed this matter that we talked about," he said. "It is a strange thing, that white mems should work in our rice fields, and some of my brothers are afraid that the white Tuans will not understand when they come back, and that they will be angry saying we have made you work for us against your will."

Jean said, "We will give you a letter now, that you can show them if they should say that."

He shook his head. "It is not necessary. It is sufficient if you tell the Tuans when they come back that this thing was done because you wished it so."

She said, "That we will do."

They went to work next day. There were six married women in the party at that time, and Jean, and ten children including Jean's baby. The headman took them out to the fields with two Malay girls, Fatimah binti Darus and Raihana binti Hassan. He gave them seven small fields covered in weeds to start upon, an area that was easily within their power to manage. There was a roofed platform nearby in the fields for resting in the shade; they left the youngest children here and went to work.

The seven women were all fairly robust; the journey had eliminated the ones who would have been unable to stand agricultural work. Those who were left were women of determination and grit, with high morale and a good sense of humour. As soon as they became accustomed to the novelty of working ankle deep in mud and water they did not find the work exacting, and presently as they became accustomed to it they were seized with an ambition to show the village that white mems could do as much work as Malay women, or more.

Paddy is grown in little fields surrounded by a low wall of earth, so that water from a stream can be let into the field at will to turn it into a shallow pool. When the water is let out again the earth bottom is soft mud, and weeds can be pulled out by hand and the ground hoed and prepared for the seedlings. The seedlings are raised by scattering the rice in a similar nursery field, and they are then transplanted in rows into the muddy field. The field is then flooded again for a few days while the seedlings stand with their heads above the water in the hot sun, and the water is let out again for a few days to let the sun get to the roots. With alternating flood and dry in that hot climate the plants grow very quickly to about the height of wheat, with feathery ears of rice on top of the stalks. The rice is harvested by cutting off the ears with a little knife leaving the straw standing, and is taken in sacks to the village to be winnowed. Water buffaloes are then turned in to eat the straw and fertilize the ground and tramp it all about, and the ground is ready for sowing again to repeat the cycle. Two crops a year are normally got from the rice fields, and there is no rotation of crop.

Working in these fields is not unpleasant when you get accustomed to it. There are worse things to do in a very hot country than to put on a large conical sun hat of plaited palm leaves and take off most of your clothes, and play about with mud and water, damming and diverting little trickling streams. By the end of the fortnight the women had settled down to it and quite liked the work, and all the children loved it from the first. No Japanese came near the village in that time.

On the sixteenth day Jean started out with the headman, Mat Amin, to go and look for the Japanese; they carried the sergeant's rifle and equipment, and his uniform, and his paybook. There was a place called Kuala Rakit twenty-seven miles away where a Japanese detachment was stationed, and they went there.

They took two days to walk this distance, staying overnight at a place called Bukit Perah. They stayed with the headman there, Jean sleeping in the back quarters with the women. They went on next day and came to Kuala Rakit in the evening; it was a very large village, or small town. Here Mat Amin took her to see an official of the Malay administration at his house, Tungku Bentara Raja. Tungku Bentara was a little thin Malay who spoke excellent English; he was genuinely concerned at the story that he heard from Mat Amin and from Jean.

"I am very, very sorry," he said at last. "I cannot do much to help you directly, because the Japanese control everything we do. It is terrible that you should have to work in the rice fields."

"That's not terrible at all," Jean said. "As a matter of fact, we rather like it. We want to stay there, with Mat Amin here. If the Japanese have got a camp for women in this district I suppose they'll put us into that, but if they haven't, we don't want to go on marching all over Malaya. Half of us have died already doing that."

"You must stay with us tonight," he said. "Tomorrow I will have a talk with the Japanese Civil Administrator. There is no camp here for women, anyway."

That night Jean slept in a bed for the first time in nearly seven months. She did not care for it much; having grown used to sleeping on the floor she found it cooler to sleep so than to sleep on a mattress. She did not actually get out of bed and sleep upon the floor, but she came very near to it. The bath and shower, however, were a joy after the bath taken by holding a gourd full of water over her head, and she spent a long time washing.

In the morning she went with Tungku Bentara and Mat Amin to the Japanese Civil Administrator, and told her tale again. The Civil Administrator had been to the University of California and spoke first-class English; he was sympathetic, but declared that prisoners were nothing to do with him, being the concern of the Army. He went with them, however, to see the military commanding officer, a Colonel Matisaka, and Jean told her tale once more.

It was quite clear that Colonel Matisaka considered women prisoners to be a nuisance, and he had no intention whatsoever of diverting any portion of his force to guarding them. Left to himself he would probably have sent them marching on, but with Tungku Bentara and the Civil Administrator in his office and acquainted with the facts he could hardly do that. In the end he washed his hands of the whole thing and told the Civil Administrator to make what arrangements he thought best. The Civil Administrator told Bentara that the women could stay where they were for the time being, and Jean started back for Kuala Telang with Mat Amin.

They lived there for three years.

"It was three years wasted, just chopped out of one's life," she said. She raised her head and looked at me, hesitantly. "At least—I suppose it was. I know a lot about Malays, but that's not worth much here in England."

"You won't know if it was wasted until you come to the end of your life," I said. "Perhaps not then."

She nodded. "I suppose that's right." She took up the poker and began scraping the ash from the bars of the grate. "They were so very kind to us," she said. "They couldn't have been nicer, within the limits of what they are and what they've got. Fatimah, the girl who showed us what to do in the rice fields in those first weeks—she was a perfect dear. I got to know her very well indeed."

"Is that where you want to go back to?" I asked.

She nodded. "I would like to do something for them, now that I've got this money. We lived with them for three years, and they did everything for us. We'd all have died before the war was ended if they hadn't taken us in and let us stay with them. And now I've got so much, and they so very, very little . . ."

"Don't forget you haven't got as much as all that," I said. "Travelling to Malaya is a very expensive journey."

She smiled. "I know. What I want to do for them won't cost so very much—not more than fifty pounds, if that. We had to carry water in that village—that's the women's work —and it's a fearful job. You see, the river's tidal at the village so the water's brackish; you can use it for washing in or rinsing out your clothes, but drinking water has to be fetched from the spring, nearly a mile away. We used to go for it with gourds, two in each hand with a stick between them, morning and evening—a mile there and a mile back—four miles a day. Fatimah and the other girls didn't think about it; it's what the village has done always, generation after generation."

"That's why you want to dig a well?"

She nodded. "It's something I could do for them, for the

women—something that would make life easier for them, as they made life easier for us. A well right in the middle of the village, within a couple of hundred yards of every house. It's what they ought to have. I'm sure it wouldn't have to be more than about ten feet deep because there's water all about. The water level can't be more than about ten feet down, or fifteen feet at the most. I thought if I went back there and offered to engage a gang of well diggers to do this for them, it'd sort of wind things up. And after that I could enjoy this money with a clear conscience." She looked up at me again. "You don't think that's silly, do you?"

"No," I said. "I don't think that. The only thing is, I wish it wasn't quite so far away. Travelling there and back will make a very big hole in a year's income."

"I know that," she said. "If I run out of money, I'll take a job in Singapore or somewhere for a few months and save up a bit."

"As a matter of interest," I said, "why didn't you stay out there and get a job? You know the country so well."

She said, "I had a scunner of it, then—in 1945. We were all dying to get home. They sent three trucks for us from Kota Bharu, and we were taken to the airfield there and flown down to Singapore in a Dakota with an Australian crew. And there I met Bill Holland, and I had to tell him about Eileen, and Freddie and Jane." Her voice dropped. "All the family, except Robin; he was four years old by that time, and quite a sturdy little chap. They let me travel home with Bill and Robin, to look after Robin. He looked on me as his mother, of course."

She smiled a little. "Bill wanted to make it permanent," she said. "I couldn't do that. I couldn't have been the sort of wife he wanted."

I said nothing.

"When we landed, England was so green and beautiful," she said. "I wanted to forget about the war, and forget about the East, and grow to be an ordinary person again. I got this job with Pack and Levy and I've been there two years now— ladies' handbags and attaché cases for the luxury trade, nothing to do with wars or sickness or death. I've had a happy time there, on the whole."

She was very much alone when she got home. She had cabled to her mother directly she reached Singapore; there was a long delay, and then she got a cable in reply from her Aunt Agatha in Colwyn Bay, breaking to her the news that her mother was dead. Before she left Singapore she heard that her brother Donald had died upon the Burma-Siam railway. She must have felt very much alone in the world when she regained her freedom; it seemed to me that she had shown great strength of character in refusing an offer of marriage at that time. She landed at Liverpool, and went to stay for a few weeks with her Aunt Agatha at Colwyn Bay; then she went down to London to look for a job.

I asked her why she had not got in touch with her uncle, the old man at Ayr. "Quite honestly," she said, "I forgot all about him, or if I thought of him at all I thought he was dead, too. I only saw him once, that time when I was eleven years old, and he looked about dead then. It never entered my head that he would still be alive. Mother's estate was all wound up, and there were very few of her personal papers left, because they were all in the Pagets' house in Southhampton when that got blitzed. If I had thought about Uncle Douglas I wouldn't have known where he lived. . . ."

It was still pouring with rain. We decided to give up the idea of going out that afternoon, and to have tea in my flat. She went out into my little kitchen and began getting it, and I busied myself with laying the tea table and cutting bread and butter. When she came in with the tray, I asked. "When do you think of going to Malaya, then?"

She said, "I thought I'd book my passage for the end of May, and go on working at Pack and Levy up till then," she said. "That's about another six weeks. By then I'll have enough saved up to pay my passage out and home, and I'll still have about sixty pounds I saved out of my wages in this last two years." She had been into the cost of her journey, and had found a line of intermediate class cargo ships that took about a dozen passengers for a relatively modest fare to Singapore. "I think I'll have to fly to Kota Bharu from Singapore," she said. "Malayan Airways go to Kuantan and then to Kota Bharu. I don't know how I'll get from Kota Bharu to Kuala Telang, but I expect there'll be something."

She was quite capable of walking it, I thought; a journey through the heart of Malaya could mean little to her now. I had had the atlas out while she had been telling me her story to see where the places were, and I looked at it again now. "You could get off the aeroplane at Kuantan," I said. "It's shorter from there."

"I know," she said. "I know it's a bit shorter. But I couldn't bear to go back there again." There was distress in her voice.

To ease the situation I said idly, "It would take me years to learn how to remember these Malay names."

"It's all right when you know what they mean," she said. "They're just like English names. *Bharu* means New, and *Kota* means a fort. It's only Newcastle, in Malay."

She went on with her work at Perivale, and I went on with mine in Chancery Lane, but I was unable to get her story out of my mind. There is a man called Wright, a member of my club, who was in the Malayan Police and was a prisoner of the Japanese during their occupation of Malaya, I think in Changi gaol. I sat next to him at dinner one night, and I could not resist sounding him about it. "One of my clients told me an extraordinary story about Malaya the other day," I said. "She was one of a party of women that the Japanese refused to put into a camp."

He laid his knife down. "Not the party who were taken at Panong and marched across Malaya?"

"That was it," I said. "You know about them, do you?"

"Oh yes," he said. "It was a most extraordinary thing, as you say. The Japanese commanders marched them from place to place, till finally they were allowed to settle in a village on the east coast somewhere, and they lived there for the rest of the war. There was a very fine girl who was their leader; she spoke Malay fluently. She wasn't anybody notable; she'd been a shorthand-typist in an office in Kuala Lumpur. A very fine type."

I nodded. "She's my client."

"Is she! I always wondered what had happened to her. What's she doing now?"

I said dryly, "She's a shorthand-typist again, working in a handbag factory at Perivale."

"Really!" He ate a mouthful or two, and then he said, "I always thought that girl ought to have got a decoration of some sort. Unfortunately, there's nothing you can give to people like that. But if she hadn't been with them, all those women and children would have died. There was no one else in the party of that calibre at all."

"I understand that half of them did die," I said.

He nodded. "I believe that's true. She got them settled down and working in the rice fields in the end, and after that they were all right."

I saw Jean Paget from time to time in the six weeks before she left this country. She booked her passage to sail from London docks on June 2nd, and she gave notice to her firm to leave at the end of May. She told me that they were rather upset about it, and they offered her a ten-shilling rise at once; in view of that she had told Mr. Pack about her legacy, and he had accepted the inevitable.

I made arrangements for her income for the months of July and August and September to be available to her in Singapore, and I opened an account for her with the Chartered Bank for that purpose. As the time for her departure drew closer I became worried for her, not because I was afraid that she would overspend her income, but because I was afraid she would get into some difficulty due to her expenses being higher than she thought they would be. Nine hundred a year does not go very far in these days for a person travelling about the East.

I mentioned that to her about a week before she left. "Don't forget that you're a fairly wealthy woman now," I said. "You're quite right to live within your income and, indeed, I have to see you do. But don't forget that I have fairly wide discretionary powers under your uncle's will. If you get into any difficulty, or if you really need money, let me have a cable at once. As, for example, if you should get ill."

She smiled. "That's very sweet of you," she said. "But honestly, I think I'll be all right. I'm counting upon taking a job if I find I'm running short. After all, I haven't got to get back here to England by a given date, or anything like that."

I said, "Don't stay too long away."

She smiled. "I shan't, Mr. Strachan," she said. "There's nothing to keep me in Malaya once I've done this thing."

She was giving up her room in Ealing, of course, and she asked if she might leave a trunk and a suitcase in the boxroom of my flat till she came back to England. She brought them round the day before she sailed, and with them a pair of skating boots with skates attached, which wouldn't go into the trunk. She told me then that she was only taking one suitcase as her luggage.

"But what about your tropical kit?" I asked. "Have you had that sent on?"

She smiled. "I've got it with me in the suitcase," she said. "Fifty Paludrine tablets and a hundred Sulphatriads, some repellent, and my old sarong. I'm not going out to be a lady in Malaya."

She had nobody but me to go down to the docks with her to see her off; she was very much alone in the world, and friends she had who might have liked to come were all working in jobs, and couldn't get the time off. I drove her down in a taxi. She took her journey very much as a matter of course; she seemed to have made no more preparation for a voyage half-way round the world than a girl of my generation would have made for a week-end at Chislehurst. The ship was a new one and everything was bright and clean. When the steward opened the door of her cabin she stood back amazed, because he had arranged the flowers all round the little room, and there were plenty of them. "Oh, Noel, look!" she said. "Just look at all the flowers!" She turned to the steward. "Wherever did they come from? Not from the Company?"

"They come in three big boxes yesterday evening," he replied. "Make a nice show, don't they, Miss?"

She swung round on me. "I believe you sent them." And then she said, "Oh, how perfectly sweet of you!"

"English flowers," I said. "Just to remind you to come back to England soon." I must have had a premonition, even then, that she was never going to come back.

Before I could realize what she was doing, she had slipped an arm around my shoulders, and kissed me on the lips. "That's for the flowers, Noel," she said softly. "For the flowers, and for everything you've done for me." And I was so dumbfounded and confused that all I could find to say to her was, "I'll have another of those when you come back."

I didn't wait to see her ship go off, because partings are stupid things and best got over quickly. I went back in the taxi to my flat alone, and I remember that I stood for a long time at the window of my room watching the ornamented wall of the stables opposite and thinking of her fine new steamer going down the river past Gravesend and Tilbury, past Shoebury and the North Foreland, taking her away. And then I woke myself up and went and shifted her trunk and her suitcase to a corner of the boxroom by themselves, and I stood for some time with her boots and skates in my hand, personal things of hers, wondering where they had better go. Finally I took them to my bedroom and put them in the bottom of my wardrobe, because I should never have forgiven myself if they had been stolen. She was just such a girl as one would have liked to have for a daughter, but we never had a daughter at all.

She travelled across half the world in her tramp steamer and she wrote to me from most of the ports she called at, from Marseilles and Naples, from Alexandria and Aden, from Colombo, from Rangoon, and from Penang. Wright was always very interested in her because he had known about her in Malaya, and I got into the habit of carrying her latest letter about with me and telling him about her voyage and how she was getting on. He knew the British Adviser to the Raja at Kota Bharu quite well, a Mr. Wilson-Hays, and I got him to write out to Wilson-Hays by air mail telling him about Jean Paget and asking him to do what he could for her. He told me that that was rather necessary, because there was nowhere where a lady could stay in Kota Bharu except with one of the British people who were living there. We got a very friendly letter back from Wilson-Hays saying that he was expecting her, and I was able to get a letter out to her by air mail to meet her at the Chartered Bank telling her what we had done.

She only stayed one night in Singapore, and took the morning plane to Kota Bharu; the Dakota wandered about all over Malaya calling at various places, and put her down upon the airstrip at Kota Bharu early in the afternoon. She got out of the Dakota wearing the same light grey coat and skirt in which she had left London, and Wilson-Hays was there himself to meet the aeroplane, with his wife.

I met Wilson-Hayes at the United University Club a year later, when he was on leave. He was a tall, dark, quiet man with rather a long face. He said that she had been a little embarrassed to find that he had come to the airstrip to meet her personally; she did not seem to realize that she was quite a well-known person in that part of Malaya. Wilson-Hays knew all about her long before we wrote to him although, of course, he had heard nothing of her since the end of the war. He had sent word to Mat Amin when he got our letter to tell him that she was coming back to see them, and he had arranged to lend her his jeep with a driver to take her the hundred miles or so to Kuala Telang. I thought that very decent of him, and I told him so. He said that the prestige of the British was higher in the Kuala Telang district after the war was over than it was before, due solely to the presence of this girl and her party; he thought she'd earned the use of a jeep for a few days.

She stayed in the Residency two nights, and bought a few simple articles in the native shops. When she left in the jeep next morning she was wearing native clothes; she left her suitcase and most of her things with Mrs. Wilson-Hays. She took with her only what a native woman of good class would take; she wore a faded old blue and white chequered sarong with a white coatee. She wore sandals as a concession to the softness of her feet, and she carried a plain tan Chinese-type umbrella as a sunshade. She had done her hair up on top of her head in the native style with a large comb in the middle of

it. She carried a small palm-leaf basket, but Mrs. Wilson-
Hays told her husband there was very little in it; she took a
toothbrush but no toothpaste; she took a towel and a cake of
antiseptic soap and a few drugs. She took one change of
clothes, a new sarong and a flowered cotton top to match;
she took three small Woolworth brooches and two rings as
little presents for her friends, but she took no cosmetics.
That was about all she had.

"I thought her very wise to go like that," said Wilson-
Hays. "If she had gone dressed as an Englishwoman she'd
have made them embarrassed. Some of the English residents
were quite upset when they heard she'd gone off in native
dress—old school tie, and letting down the side, and all that
sort of thing. I must say, when I saw her go I thought it was
rather a good thing to do." He paused. "After all; it's how
she was dressed all through the war, and nobody talks about
her letting down the side then."

It is a long day in a jeep from Kota Bharu to Kuala Telang; the roads are very poor, and there are four main rivers
to be crossed which necessitate ferrying the jeep over in a
boat, apart from a large number of fords. It took her fourteen hours to cover the hundred miles, and it was dark when
they drove into Kuala Telang. There was a buzz of excitement as the jeep drove through the shadowy village, and
people came out of their houses doing up their sarongs; there
was a full moon that night, so that there was light enough to
see to drive. They stopped in front of the headman's house,
and she got out of the jeep a little wearily, and went to him,
and put her hands up in the praying gesture, and said in
Malay, "I have come back, Mat Amin, lest you should think
the white mems have forgotten all about you when their
need is past."

He said, "We have thought and talked about you ever
since you went." And then there were people thronging about
them, and she saw Fatimah approaching with a baby in her
arms and a toddler hanging on to her sarong, and she pushed
through the crowd and took her by the hand, and said, "It is
too long since we met." And there was Raihana, and Safirah
binti Yacob, and Safirah binti Taib, and little Ibrahim who
squinted, now grown into a young man, and his brother
Samat, and old Zubeidah, and Meriam, and many others some
of whom she did not know, because the men had come back
from the labour gangs soon after she left Malaya, and there
were a number of new faces.

Fatimah was married to a young man called Derahman

bin Ismail, and she brought him forward and presented him to the white mem; Jean bowed before him and wished that she had brought a shawl to pull over her face, as would have been polite when being introduced to a strange man. She put her hand up to her face, and said, "Excuse me that I have no veil." He bowed to her and said, "It is no matter," and Fatimah broke in and said, "He knows and everybody knows that the white mems never veiled their faces when they lived with us, because different people have different ways. Oh, Djeen, we are so happy that you have come back."

She made arrangements with Mat Amin for the accommodation of the driver, and then went with Fatimah to her husband's house. They asked if she had eaten, and she said no, and they made her a supper of rice and blachan, the highly spiced paste of ripe prawns and fish that the Malays preserve in an up-ended concrete drain pipe. And presently, tired out, she made a pillow of her palm-leaf bag and lay down on a mat as she had done a thousand times before, and loosened the sarong around her waist, and slept. It would not be entirely accurate to say that she slept well upon the floor after sleeping in a bed for three years. She woke many times throughout the night, and listened to the noises of the night, and watched the moonlight creep around the house, and she was happy.

She had a talk with Fatimah and Meriam and old Zubeidah next morning, squatting round the cooking pots behind the house out of the way of the men. "Every day that I have been away I have thought of this place," she said; it was not precisely true, but near enough. "I have thought of you all living and working as I lived and worked. I was working in England, working in an office at books in the way that women have to work in my country, because, as you know, I am a poor woman and I have had to work all my life to earn my living till I find a husband who suits me, and I am very particular." The woman laughed, and old Zubeidah said, "It is very strange that a woman should earn her living in that way."

Meriam said, "There is a woman of our people working in the bank at Kuala Rakit. I saw her through the window. She was doing something with her fingers on a machine, and it went click-click-click."

Jean nodded. "That is how I earn my living in my country, working a machine like that to make a printed letter for the Tuan. But recently my uncle died; he lived far away from me and I had only met him once, but he had no other relatives and I inherited his money, so that now I need not work unless

I want to." A murmur of appreciation went around the women. Two or three more had drifted up to enlarge the circle. "And now, having money of my own for the first time in my life, I thought more of you here in Kuala Telang than ever before, and of your kindness to us when we lived with you as prisoners. And it came to me that I should give a thank offering to this place, and that this thank offering should be a present from a woman to the women of Kuala Telang, nothing to do with the men."

There was a pleased and excited little buzz amongst the women who surrounded her. Old Zubeidah said, "It is true, the men get everything." One or two of the women looked shocked at this heresy.

"I have thought many times," Jean said, "that there should be a well in this place, so that you should not have to fetch fresh water from the spring morning and evening, but you could walk out of your houses only fifty paces at the most and there would be a well of fresh water with a bucket that you could go to and draw water at any time of the day whenever you had need of cool, fresh water." There was a little buzz of appreciation again. "There would be smooth stones around the well where you could sit and talk while the young men work the bucket for you. And close beside the well, I would have an atap house for washing clothes with long slabs of smooth stone or concrete arranged so that you could face each other while you wash, and talk, but all surrounded by an atap wall so that the men will not be able to see." The buzz rose to an excited clamour. "This is what I want to do, as a thank offering. I will engage a gang of well diggers, and they shall dig the well, and I will pay masons for the stonework round the top, and I will pay carpenters to build the washing house. But for the arrangement inside the house I shall want two or three women of experience to advise me how it should be devised, for the height of the slabs, for concrete pools or channels for the water, and so on. This is the gift of a woman for women, and in this thing the men shall do what women say."

There was a long clamour of discussion. Some of the women were doubtful if the men would ever allow such a thing, and some were doubtful whether it was not impious to wish to alter the arrangements that had satisfied their mothers and their grandmothers before them. But most were avid for the innovation if it could be achieved; once they were used to the idea they savoured it and turned it over, examining it in every detail and discussing where the well should be and where the wash house, and where the concrete pools should be, and where the drain. At the end of a couple of hours they had accepted the idea whole-heartedly, and Jean was satisfied that it would fill a real need, and that there was nothing that they would have preferred her to give.

That evening she sat opposite Mat Amin on the small verandah before his house, as she had sat so many times before when matters that concerned the women had to be discussed. She sipped her coffee. "I have come to talk with you," she said, "because I want to give a thank offering to this place, that people may remember when the white women came here, and you were kind to them."

He said, "The wife has been talking of nothing else all day, with other women. They say you want to make a well."

Jean said, "That is true. This is a thank offering from all the English mems to Kuala Telang, but because we are women it is fitting that it should be a present for the women of this place. When we lived here it was a great labour, morning and evening, to fetch water from the spring and I was sorry for your women when I thought of them, in England, fetching water all that way. That is why I want my thank offering to be a well in the middle of the village."

He said, "The spring was good enough for their mothers and their grandmothers before them. They will get ideas above their station in life if they have a well."

She said patiently, "They will have more energy to serve you faithfully and kindly if they have this well, Mat Amin. Do you remember Raihana binti Ismail who lost her baby when she was three months pregnant, carrying this water?" He was shocked that she should speak of such a thing, but English mems would speak of anything. "She was ill for a year after that, and I don't think she was any good to her husband ever again. If the women had had this well I want to give you as a thank offering, that accident would not have happened."

He said, "God disposes of the lives of women as well as those of men."

She smiled gently, "Do I have to remind you, Mat Amin, that it is written, 'Men's souls are naturally inclined to covetousness; but if ye be kind towards women and fear to wrong them, God is well acquainted with what ye do.' "

He laughed and slapped his thigh. "You said that to me many times when you lived here, whenever you wanted anything, but I have not heard it since."

"It would be kind to let the women have their well," she said.

He replied, still laughing, "I say this to you, Si-Jean; that when women want a thing as badly as they want this well that you have promised them, they usually get it. But this is a matter which concerns the village as a whole, and I must consult my brothers."

The men sat in conference next morning, squatting on their heels in the shade of the atap market house. Presently they sent for Jean and she squatted down with them a little to one side as is fitting for a woman, and they asked her where the well was to be put, and where the atap wash house. She said that everything was in their hands, but it would be convenient for the women if it was on the patch of ground in front of Chai San's shop, with the atap wash house west of it and pointing towards Ahmed's house. They all got up then and went to see the ground and discuss it from all angles, and all the women of the village stood around and watched their lords making this important decision, and Djeen talking with them almost as if she was an equal.

She did not hurry them; she had lived three years in this village and she knew the slowness of their mental processes, the caution with which all innovations were approached. It took them two days to make up their minds that the well would be a good thing to have, and that the Wrath of God would not descend upon them if they put the work in hand.

Well digging is a skilled craft, and there was one family only on the coast who could be entrusted with the work; they lived about five miles from Kuantan. Mat Amin dictated a letter for the Imam to write in the Jawi script, and then they took it into Kuala Rakit and posted it. Jean sent for five sacks of cement from Kota Bharu, and settled down to wait for several weeks while the situation developed.

She spent much of the time with the fishermen on their boats, or sitting on the beach and playing with the children. She taught them to build sand castles and to play Noughts and Crosses on a chequer drawn with the finger in the sand; she bathed and swam a good deal, and worked for a week in the rice fields at the time of harvest. She had lived so long with these people that she was patient about the passage of time; moreover, she had a use for time to consider what she was going to do with her life now that she had no further need to work. She waited there for three weeks in idleness, and she did not find it tedious.

The well diggers and the cement arrived about the same

time, and work commenced. The diggers were a family of an old grey-bearded father, Suleiman, and his two sons, Yacob and Hussein. They spent a day surveying the land and all the arguments for the site chosen for the well had to be gone over once again to satisfy these experts; when work finally commenced it was done quickly and well. The diggers worked from dawn till dusk, one at the bottom of the shaft and the other two disposing of the soil on top; they bricked it downwards from the top as they worked, supporting the brickwork upon stakes driven into the earth sides.

Old Suleiman, the father, was a mine of information to the village, for he travelled up and down the east coast of Malaya building and repairing wells, and so visited most villages from time to time. The men and women of Kuala Telang used to sit around watching the progress of the new well and gossiping with the old man, getting news of their acquaintances and relatives up and down the coast. Jean was sitting there one afternoon, and said to him, "You are from Kuantan?"

"From Batu Sawah," said the old man. "That is two hours' walk from Kuantan. Our home is there, but we are great travelers."

She was silent for a moment; then she said, "Do you remember the Japanese officer in charge at Kuantan in the first year of the war, Captain Sugamo?"

"Assuredly," the old man replied. "He is a very bad man, and we were glad when he went away. Captain Ichino who came after him was better."

Jean was surprised that he did not seem to know that Sugamo was dead; she had supposed that the War Crimes Commission would have taken evidence in Kuantan. She told him, "Captain Sugamo is dead now. He was sent to the Burma-Siam railway, and there he caused many atrocities, and many murders. But the Allies caught him when the war was over, and he was tried for murder, and executed in Penang."

"I am glad to hear it," the old man replied. "I will tell my sons." He called down the well with the news; it was discussed a little, and then the men went on with their work.

Jean asked, "Did he do many evil things in Kuantan?" There was one still hideously fresh in her mind, but she could not bring herself to speak of it directly.

Suleiman said, "Many people were tortured."

She nodded. "I saw one myself." It had to come out, and it did not matter what she said to this old man. "When we were starving and ill, a soldier who was a prisoner helped us. The Japanese caught him, and they crucified him with nails through his hands, and they beat him to death."

"I remember that," the old man said. "He was in hospital at Kuantan."

Jean stared at him. "Old man, when was he in hospital? He died."

"Perhaps there were two." He called down the well to Yacob. "The English soldier who was crucified and beaten at Kuantan in the first year of the war. The English mem knew him. Tell us, did that man die?"

Hussein broke in. "The one who was beaten was an Australian, not English. He was beaten because he stole chickens."

"Assuredly," the old man said. "It was for stealing the black chickens. But did he live or die?"

Yacob called up from the bottom of the well. "Captain Sugamo had him taken down that night; they pulled the nails out of his hands. He lived."

Chapter 5

IN KUANTAN, in the evening of that day in July 1942, a sergeant had come to Captain Sugamo in the District Commissioner's house, and had reported that the Australian was still alive. Captain Sugamo found this curious and interesting, and as there was still half an hour before his evening rice, he strolled down to the recreation ground to have a look.

The body still hung by its hands, facing the tree. Blood had drained from the blackened mess that was its back and had run down the legs to form a black pool on the ground, now dried and oxidized by the hot sun. A great mass of flies covered the body and the blood. But the man undoubtedly was still alive; when Captain Sugamo approached the face the eyes opened, and looked at him with recognition.

It is doubtful if the West can ever fully understand the working of a Japanese mind. When Captain Sugamo saw that the Australian recognized him from the threshold of death, he bowed reverently to the torn body, and he said with complete sincerity, "Is there anything that I can get for you before you die?"

The ringer said distinctly, "You bloody bastard. I'll have one of your black chickens and a bottle of beer."

Captain Sugamo stood looking at the wreck of the man nailed to the tree, and his face was completely expressionless. Presently he turned upon his heel and went back to his house. He called for his orderly as he went into the shade, and he told him to fetch a bottle of beer and a glass, but not to open the bottle.

The man protested that there was no beer. Captain Sugamo already knew that, but he sent his orderly to the town to visit all the Chinese eating houses to see if he could find a bottle of beer anywhere in Kuantan. In an hour the man came back; Captain Sugamo was sitting in exactly the same attitude as when he had gone out to find the beer. With considerable apprehension he informed his officer that there was no beer in all Kuantan. He was dismissed, and went away gladly.

Death to Captain Sugamo was a ritual. There had been an element of holiness in his approach to the Australian, and having offered in the hearing of his men to implement the last wishes of his victim he was personally dedicated to see that those last wishes were provided. If a bottle of beer had been available he would have sacrificed one of his remaining Black Leghorns and sent the cooked meat and the beer down to the dying body on the tree; he might even have carried the tray down himself. By doing so he would have set an example of chivalry and Bushido to the troops under his command. Unfortunately, it was impossible for him to provide the bottle of beer, and since the beer was missing and the soldier's dying wish could not be met in full, there was no point in sacrificing one of the remaining Black Leghorns. He could not carry out his own part in the ritual; he could not show Bushido by granting the man's dying wish. Therefore, the Australian could not be allowed to die, or he himself would be disgraced.

He called for his sergeant. When the man came, he ordered him to take a party with a stretcher to the recration ground. They were to pull the nails out and take the man down from the tree without injuring him any further, and put him face downwards on the stretcher, and take him to the hospital.

To Jean, the news that the Australian was still alive came like the opening of a door. She slipped away and went and sat in the shade of a casuarina tree at the head of the beach to consider this incredible fact. The sun glinted on the surf and the beach was so white, the sea so blue, that it was almost ecstasy to look at them. She felt as if she had suddenly come out of a dark tunnel that she had walked down for six years. She tried to pray, but she had never been religious and she didn't know how to put what she was feeling into a prayer. The best she could do was to recollect the words of a prayer that they had used at school sometimes. "Lighten our darkness, O Lord, and of Thy great mercy . . ." That was all she could remember, and she repeated it over and over to herself that afternoon. Her darkness had been lightened by the well diggers.

She went back that evening and spoke to Suleiman again about the matter, but neither he nor his sons could supply much further information. The Australian had been in the hospital at Kuantan for a long time, but how long they did not know. Yacob said that he had been there for a year but she soon found that he only meant, a very long time. Hussein said three months, and Suleiman did not know how long he had been there, but said that he was sent down on a ship to Singapore to a prison camp, and he was then walking with two sticks. She could not find out from them when that was.

So she had to leave it, and she stayed on in Kuala Telang till the well and wash house were completed. She had already started the carpenters upon the wash house after long consultations with the elder women, and the concrete work was now completed in the shuttering, and drying out. On the day that water was reached at the bottom of the well the carpenters began to erect the posts for the atap house, and the well and the house were finished about the same time. Two days were spent in bailing out the muddy water from the well till it ran clean, and then they had an opening ceremony when Jean washed her own sarong and all the women crowded into the wash house laughing, and the men stood round in a tolerant circle at a distance, wondering if they had been quite wise to allow anything that made the women laugh so much.

On the next day she sent a telegram by runner to Kuala Rakit to be dispatched to Wilson-Hays asking him to send the jeep for her, and a day or two later it arrived. She left in a flurry of shy good wishes with some moisture in her eyes; she was going back to her own place and her own people, but she was leaving three years of her life behind her, and that is never a very easy thing to do.

She got back to the Residency at Kota Bharu after dark that night, too tired to eat. Mrs. Wilson-Hays sent her up a

cup of tea and a little fruit to her bedroom, and she had a
long, warm bath, putting off her native clothes for the last
time. She lay on the bed in the cool, spacious room under
the mosquito net, rested and growing sleepy, and what she
thought about was Ringer Harman, and the red country he
had told her of round Alice Springs, and euros, and wild
horses.

She walked with Wilson-Hays in the garden of the Residency next morning after breakfast in the cool of the day.
She told him what she had done in Kuala Telang; he asked
her where she had got the idea of the wash house from. "It's
obvious that's what they need," she said. "Women don't like
washing their clothes in public, especially Moslem women."

He thought about it for a minute. "You've probably started
something," he remarked at last. "Every village will want
one now. Where did you get the plan of it—the arrangement
of the sinks and all that sort of thing?"

"We worked it out ourselves," she said. "They knew what
they wanted all right."

They strolled along by the river, brown and muddy and
half a mile wide, running its way down to the sea. As they
walked she told him about the Australian, because she could
talk freely about that now. She told him what had happened.
"His name was Joe Harman," she said, "and he came from a
place near Alice Springs. I would like to get in touch with
him again. Do you think I could find out anything about him
in Singapore?"

He shook his head. "I shouldn't think so, not now that
S.E.A.C. is disbanded. I shouldn't think there's any record
of prisoners of war in Singapore now."

"How would one find out about him, then?"

"You say he was an Australian?"

She nodded.

"I think you'd have to write to Canberra," he said. "They
ought to have a record of all prisoners there. I suppose you
don't happen to know his unit?"

She shook her head. "I'm afraid I don't."

"That might make it difficult, of course—there may be
several Joe Harmans. I should start off by writing to the
Minister for the Army—that's what they call him, the head
of the War Office. Just address your letter to the Minister
for the Army, Canberra, Australia. Something might come
of that. What you want is an address where you could write
to him, I suppose?"

Jean stared across the river at the rubber trees and coconut palms. "I suppose so. As a matter of fact, I've got an address of a sort. He used to work before the war on a cattle station called Wollara, near a place called Alice Springs. He said that they were keeping his job open for him there."

"If you've got that address," he observed, "I should write there. You're much more likely to find him that way than by writing to Canberra."

"I might do that," she said slowly. "I would like to see him again. You see, it was because of us that it all happened . . ."

It had been her intention to go back to Singapore and wait there for a boat to England; if she had to wait long for a cheap passage she intended to try to find a job for a few weeks or months. Malayan Airways called at Kota Bharu next day, and the Dakota landed at Kuantan on the way down to Singapore. She spoke to Wilson-Hays again that evening after dinner.

"Do you think there would be a hotel or anything at Kuantan if I stopped there for a day?" she asked.

He looked at her kindly. "Do you want to go back there?" he asked.

"I think I do," she said. "I'd like to go and see the people at the hospital and find out what I can."

He said, "You'd better stay with David and Joyce Bowen. Bowen is the District Commissioner; he'd be glad to put you up."

"I don't want to be a nuisance to people," she said. "Isn't there a rest house that I could stay in? After all, I know this country fairly well."

"That's why Bowen would like to meet you," he remarked. "You must realize that you're quite a well-known person in these parts. He would be very disappointed if you stayed at the rest house."

She looked at him in wonder. "Do people think of me like that? I only did what anybody could have done."

"That's as it may be," he replied. "The fact is, that you did it."

She flew on down to Kuantan next day. Someone must have told the crew of the aircraft about her, because the Malay stewardess came to her after half an hour and said, "We're just coming up to Kuala Telang, Miss Paget. Captain Philby wants to know if you would care to come forward to the cockpit and see it." So she went forward through the door and stood between the pilots; they brought the Dakota down to about seven hundred feet and circled the village; she could see the well and the new atap roof of the wash house, and she could see people standing gazing up at the machine, Fatimah and Zubeidah and Mat Amin. Then they straightened up and flew on down the coast, and Kuala Telang was left behind.

The Bowens met her at the airstrip, which is ten miles from the town of Kuantan; Wilson-Hays had sent them a signal that morning. They were a friendly, unsophisticated couple, and she had no difficulty in telling them a little about the Australian soldier who had been tortured when they were sitting in the D.C.'s house, where Captain Sugamo had sat so often, over a cup of tea. They said that Sister Frost was now in charge of the hospital, but it was doubtful if there was anybody now upon the staff who was there in 1942. They drove down after tea to see Sister Frost.

She received them in the Matron's room, very hygienic and smelling strongly of disinfectant. She was an English-woman about forty years of age. "There's nobody here now who was on the staff then," she said. "Nurses in a place like this—they're always leaving to get married. We never seem to keep them longer than about two years. I don't know what to suggest."

Bowen said, "What about Phyllis Williams? She was a nurse here, wasn't she?"

"Oh, her," the sister said disparagingly. "She was here for the first part of the war until she married that man. She might know something about it."

They left the hospital, and as they drove to find Phyllis Williams Mrs. Bowen enlightened Jean. "She's a Eurasian," she said. "Very dark, almost as dark as a Malay. She married a Chinese, a man called Bun Tai Lin who runs the cinema. What you'd call a mixed marriage, but they seem to get along all right. She's a Roman Catholic, of course." Jean never fathomed the "of course."

The Bun Tai Lins lived in a rickety wooden house up the hill overlooking the harbour. They could not get the car to the house, but left it in the road and walked up a short lane littered with garbage. They found Phyllis Williams at home, a merry-faced, brown woman with four children around her and evidently about to produce a fifth. She was glad to see them and took them into a shabby room, the chief decorations of which were a set of pewter beer mugs and a large oleograph of the King and Queen in coronation robes.

She spoke very good English. "Oh yes, I remember that poor boy," she said. "Joe Harman, that was his name. I nursed him for three or four months—he *was* in a state when he came in. We none of us thought he'd live. But he got over it. He must have led a very healthy life, because his flesh healed wonderfully. He said that he was like a dog, he healed so well."

She turned to Jean. "Are you the lady that was leading the party of women and children from Panong?" she asked. "I thought you must be. Fancy you coming here again! You know, he was always wanting to know about you and your party, if anybody knew the way you'd gone. And of course, we didn't know, and with that Captain Sugamo in the mood he was, nobody was going to go round asking questions to find out."

She turned to Jean. "I forget your name?"

"Paget. Jean Paget."

The Eurasian looked puzzled. "That wasn't it. I wonder now, was he talking about someone different? I can't remember now what he called her, but it wasn't that. I thought it would have been you."

"Mrs. Frith?"

She shook her head. "I'll remember presently."

She could not tell them very much more than Jean knew already. The Australian had been sent down to a prison camp in Singapore as soon as he was fit to travel; they heard no more of him. They thought that he would make a good recovery in the end, though it would be years before the muscles of his back got back their strength if, indeed, they ever would. She knew no more than that.

They left presently, and went down the garbage-strewn lane towards the car. When they were nearly at the bottom the woman called to them from the verandah. "I just remembered that name. Mrs. Boong. That's who he was always talking about, Mrs. Boong. Was that one of your party?"

Jean laughed, and called back to her, "That's what he used to call me!"

The woman was satisfied. "I thought it must have been you that he was always talking about."

On the way back to the D.C.'s house in the car, they passed the recreation ground. There were tennis nets rigged and one or two couples playing; there was a white young man playing a brown girl. The tree still stood overlooking the courts, and underneath it a couple of Malay women sat exactly where the feet of the tortured man had hung, on ground that had been soaked in blood, and gossiped while their children played around. It all looked very peaceful in the evening light.

Jean spent that night with the Bowens, and went on to Singapore next day in the Dakota. Wilson-Hays had advised her about hotels, and she stayed at the Adelphi opposite the Cathedral.

She wrote to me from there a couple of days later. It was a long letter, about eight pages long, written in ink smudged a little with the sweat that had formed on her hand as she wrote in that humid place. First she told me what had happened in Kuala Telang; she told me about the well diggers and that Joe Harman was still alive. And then she went on:

I've been puzzling over what I could do to get in touch with him again. You see, it was all because of us that it happened. He stole the chickens for us, and he must have known the sort of man that Captain Sugamo was, and the risk that he was taking. I must find out where he is living now, and if he's all right; I can't believe that he can be able to work as a stockrider after having been so terribly injured. I think he was a man who'd always fall upon his feet somehow or other if he was well enough, but I can't bear the thought that he might be still in hospital, perhaps, and likely to stay there for ever with his injuries.

I did think of writing to him at this place Wollara that he told me about, the cattle station that he worked on, somewhere near Alice Springs. But thinking it over, if he can't work he can't be there, and I don't suppose I'd ever get an answer to a letter from a place like that, or not for ages, anyway. I thought of writing to Canberra to try and find out something, but that's almost as bad. And this brings me to what I wanted to tell you when I started this letter, Noel, and I hope it won't be too much of a shock. I'm going on to Australia from here.

Don't think me absolutely crazy for doing this. The fare from here to Darwin costs sixty pounds by the Constellation, and you can get a bus from Darwin to Alice Springs; it takes two or three days but it ought to be much cheaper than flying. After paying the hotel bill here I shall still have about a hundred and seven pounds, not counting next month's money. I thought I'd go to Alice Springs and get to this place Wollara and find out about him there; someone in that district is bound to know what happened to him, and where he is now.

There are some merchant service officers staying here, very nice young men, and they tell me I can get a cabin on a merchant ship back to England probably from Townsville, that's on the east coast of Australia in Queensland, and if there isn't a ship there I'd certainly get one at Brisbane. I've been talking to a man in the Chartered Bank here in Raffles Place who is very helpful, and I've

arranged with him to transfer my next month's money to
the Bank of New South Wales in Alice Springs, and so
I'll have money to get me across to Townsville or Brisbane.
Write to me care of the Bank of New South Wales in
Alice Springs, because I know I'm going to feel a long
way from home when I get there.

I'm leaving here on Thursday by the Constellation, so
I'll be in Australia somewhere by the time you get this
letter. I have a feeling that I'm being a terrible nuisance to
you, Noel, but I'll have an awful lot to tell you when I get
back home. I don't think the trip home from Townsville
or Brisbane can take longer than three months at the outside, so I shall be home in England in time for Christmas
at the very latest.

I sat there reading and re-reading this, bitterly disappointed. I had been making plans for entertainments for her
when she came back, I suppose—in fact, I know I had been.
Old men who lead a somewhat empty life get rather stupid
over things like that. Lester Robinson came into my office
with a sheaf of papers in his hand as I was reading her letter for the third time; I laid the letter down. "My Paget
girl," I said. "You know—that Macfadden estate that we're
trustees for. She's not coming home after all. She's gone on
from Malaya to Australia."

He glanced at me, and I suppose the disappointment that
I felt showed in my face, because he said gently, "I told
you she was old enough to make a packet of trouble for us."
I looked up at him quickly to see what he meant by that, but
he began talking about an unadopted road in Colchester, and
the moment passed.

I went on with my work, but the black mood persisted
and it was with me when I reached the club that night. I
settled down after dinner in the library with a volume of
Horace because I thought the mental exercise required to
read the Latin would take my mind off things and put me in a
better frame of mind. But I had forgotten my Horace, I suppose, because a phrase I had not read or thought about for
forty years suddenly stared up at me from the page and
brought me up with a round turn,

—*Dulce ridentem Lalagen amabo,*
    Dulce loquentem.

It had been a part of my youth, that phrase, as I suppose
it is a part of the youth of many young men who have been
in love. I could not bear to go on reading Horace after that,

and I sat thinking of sweetly smiling, soft-spoken Lalage on her way to Alice Springs in a long-distance bus, until I broke away from morbid fancies and got up and put the book back in the shelf.

It must have been about a week after that that Derek Harris came into my room as the client went out. Derek is one of our two articled clerks, and one day I expect to make him a partner; a pleasant fresh-faced lad. He said, "Could you spare a few minutes for a stranger, sir?"

"What sort of stranger?" I enquired.

He said, "A man called Harman. He came about an hour ago without any appointment and asked to see you. Sergeant Gunning asked if I would see him as you were engaged, and I had a talk with him, but it's you that he wants to see. I understand that it's something to do with Miss Paget."

I knew now where I had heard that name before, but it was quite incredible. I asked, "What sort of a man is he?"

He grinned broadly. "Some sort of a colonial, I should think. Probably Australian. He's an outdoor type, anyway."

"Is he a reasonable person?"

"Oh, I think so, sir. He's some sort of a countryman, I should say."

It was all beginning to fit in, and yet it was incredible that an Australian stockrider should have found his way to my office in Chancery Lane. "Is his name Joseph, by any chance?" I asked.

"You know him, do you, sir? Joe Harman. Shall I ask him to come up?"

I nodded. "I'll see him now." Harris went down to fetch him, and I stood by my window looking out into the grey street, wondering what this visit meant and how it had come about, and how much of my client's business I could tell this man.

Harris showed him in, and I turned from the window to meet him.

He was a fair-haired man, about five feet ten in height. He was thickset but not fat; I judged him to be between thirty and thirty-five years old. His face was deeply tanned but his skin was clear; he had very bright blue eyes. He was not a handsome man; his face was too square and positive for that, but it was a simple and good-natured face. He walked towards me with a curious, stiff gait.

I shook hands with him. "Mr. Harman?" I said. "My name is Strachan. Do you want to see me?" And as I spoke, I was unable to resist the temptation to look down at his hand. There was a huge scar on the back of it.

He said a little awkwardly, "I don't want to keep you long." He was ill at ease and obviously embarrassed.

"Not at all," I said. "Sit down, Mr. Harman, and tell me what I can do for you." I put him in the client's chair before my desk and gave him a cigarette. He pulled from his pocket a tin box of wax matches of a style that was strange to me, and cracked one expertly with his thumbnail without burning himself. He was wearing a very readymade suit, quite new, and an unusually ornamental tie for London wear.

"I was wondering if you could tell me about Miss Jean Paget," he said. "Where she lives, or anything like that."

I smiled. "Miss Paget is a client of mine, Mr. Harman," I said. "You evidently know that. But a client's business is entirely confidential, you know. Are you a friend of hers?"

The question seemed to embarrass him still further. "Sort of," he replied. "We met once in the war, in Malaya that was. I'll have to tell you who I am, of course. I'm a Queenslander. I run a station in the Gulf Country, about twenty miles from Willstown." He spoke very slowly and deliberately, not from embarrassment but because that seemed to be his way. "I mean, the homestead is twenty miles from town, but one limb of the land runs down the creek to within five miles. Midhurst, that's the name of my station. Midhurst, Willstown, is the address."

I made a note upon my pad, and smiled at him again. "You're a long way from home, Mr. Harman," I said.

"Too right," he replied. "I don't know nobody in England except Miss Paget and a cobber I met in the prison camp who lives at a place called Gateshead in the north of England. I came here for a holiday, you might say, and I thought perhaps Miss Paget might be glad to know that I'm in England, but I don't know her address."

"Rather a long way to come for a holiday?" I observed.

He smiled a little sheepishly. "I struck it lucky. I won the Casket."

"The Casket?"

"The Golden Casket. Don't you have that here?"

I shook my head. "I'm afraid I've never heard of it."

"Oh my word," he said. "We couldn't get along without the Casket in Queensland. It's the State lottery that gets the money to build hospitals."

"I see," I said. "Did you win a prize in the lottery?"

"Oh my word," he repeated. "Did I win a prize. I won a

thousand pounds—not English pounds, of course, Australian pounds, but it's a thousand pounds to us. I always take a ticket in every Casket like everybody else because if you don't get a prize you get a hospital and there's times when that's more useful. You ought to see the hospital the Casket built at Willstown. Three wards it's got, with two beds in each, and two rooms for the sisters, and a separate house for the doctor, only we can't get a doctor to come yet because Willstown's a bit isolated, you see. We've got an X-ray apparatus there and a wireless so that the sister can call for the Cairns Ambulance—the aeroplane, you know. We couldn't do without the Casket."

I must say I was a little bit interested. "Does the Casket pay for the aeroplane, too?"

He shook his head. "You pay seven pounds ten a year to the Cairns Ambulance, each family, that is. Then if you get sick and have to go to Cairns the sister calls Cairns on the wireless and the aeroplane comes out to take you into Cairns to hospital. That's free, provided that you pay the seven pounds ten each year."

"How far are you from Cairns?"

"About three hundred miles."

I reverted to the business in hand. "Tell me, Mr. Harman," I said, "how did you get to know that I was Miss Paget's solicitor?"

"She told me in Malaya when we met, she lived in Southampton," he said. "I didn't know any address, so I went there and stayed in a hotel, because I thought maybe she'd like to know I was in England. I never saw a city that had been bombed before—oh my word. Well, then I looked in the telephone book and asked a lot of people but I couldn't find out nothing except she had an aunt that lived in Wales at a place called Colwyn Bay. So then I went to Colwyn Bay."

"You went right up there, did you?"

He nodded. "I think her aunt thought I was up to some crook game or other," he said simply. "She wouldn't tell me where she lived or anything. All she said was that you were her trustee, whatever that means. So I came here."

"When did you arrive in England?" I asked.

"Last Thursday. Five days ago."

"You landed at Southampton, did you?"

He shook his head. "I flew from Australia, by Quantas. You see, I got a good stockman looking after Midhurst for me, but I can't afford to be away so long. Jim Lennon's all right for a time, but I wouldn't want to be away from Midhurst more'n three months. You see, this is a slack time in the Gulf Country. We mustered in March this year on account of the late season and drove the stock down to Julia Creek in April—that's railhead, you know. I had about fourteen hundred stores I sold down to Rockhampton, for fattening. Well, after getting them on rail I had to get back up to Midhurst on account of the bore crew. I got Mrs. Spears—she's the owner of Midhurst—I got her to agree we sink a bore at Willow Creek, that's about twenty miles south-east of the homestead, to get water down at that end in the dry, and we got a bonza bore, we did. She's flowing over three thousand gallons a day; it's going to make a lot of difference down at that end. Well, that took up to about three weeks ago before I got that finished up, and I must be back at Midhurst by the end of October for getting in the stores and that before the wet begins at Christmas. So I thought that coming on this holiday I'd better fly."

Flying to England, I thought, must have made a considerable hole in his thousand pounds. "You came to London, then, and went straight down to Southampton?"

"That's right," he said.

"And from there you went up to North Wales. And from there you came here?"

"That's right."

I looked him in the eyes, and smiled. "You must want to see Miss Paget very much."

He met my gaze. "I do."

I leaned back in my chair. "I've got a disappointment for you, I'm afraid, Mr. Harman. Miss Paget is abroad."

He stared down at his hat for a moment. Then he raised his head. "Is she far away?" he asked. "I mean, is it France or anything like that, where I could get to see her?"

I shook my head. "She's travelling in the East."

He said quietly, "I see."

I couldn't help liking and respecting this man. It was perfectly obvious that he had come twelve thousand miles or so mainly to find Jean Paget, and now he wasn't going to find her. It was bad luck, to say the least of it, and he was taking it well. I felt that I wanted a little time to consider this affair.

"The most that I can do for you," I said, "is to forward a letter. I can do that, if you care to write one, and I'll send it to her by air mail. But I'm afraid that you may have to wait a month or so before you get an answer."

He brightened. "I'd like to do that. I never thought that after coming all this way I'd find that she'd gone walkabout."

He thought for a minute. "What address should I put upon the letter?"

"I can't give you my client's address, Mr. Harman," I said. "What I suggest that you should do is to write her a letter and bring it in to me here tomorrow morning. I will send it on with a short covering note explaining how it came into my hands. Then if she wants to see you she will get in touch with you herself."

"You don't think she'll want to see me?" he said heavily.

I smiled. "I didn't say anything of the sort, Mr. Harman. I'm quite sure that when she hears you've been in England looking for her she will write to you. What I'm saying is that I have her interests to consider, and I'm not going to give her address to anyone who comes into this office and cares to ask for it." I paused. "There's one thing that you'd better know," I said. "Miss Paget is a fairly wealthy woman. Women who have command of a good deal of money are apt to be troubled by touts. I'm not saying that you're a tout or that you're after her money. I *am* saying that you must write to her first of all, and then let her decide if she wants to meet you. If you're a friend of hers you'll see that that's reasonable."

He stared at me. "I never knew that she had money. She told me she was just a typist in an office."

"That's quite true," I said. "She inherited some money recently."

He was silent.

"Suppose you come back tomorrow morning, Mr. Harman," I said. I glanced at my engagement diary. "Say, twelve o'clock tomorrow morning. Write her a letter saying whatever it is you want to say, and bring it here then. I will forward it to her tomorrow evening."

"All right," he said. He got up and I got up with him. "Where are you staying, Mr. Harman?" I asked.

"At the Kingsway Palace Hotel."

"All right, Mr. Harman," I said. "I shall expect you tomorrow morning, at twelve o'clock."

I spent most of that evening wondering if I had done the right thing in refusing Mr. Harman the address. I thought ruefully that Jean would have been very angry if she had known I had done such a thing, especially when she was looking for him all over Australia. At the same time, what I had done would not delay a letter from him reaching her, and there was no sense in putting all her cards upon the table for him to see just at present. One thing that puzzled me a little was, why had he suddenly awoken to the fact that he wanted to meet Jean Paget again, after six years? A question or two upon that point seemed to be in order, and I prepared a small interrogation for him when he came to see me with his letter.

Twelve o'clock next morning came, and he didn't turn up for his appointment. I waited in for him till one o'clock, and then I went to lunch.

By three o'clock I was a little bit concerned. The initiative had passed into his hands. If he should vanish into thin air now and never come back to see me again, Jean Paget would be very cross with me, and rightly so. Between clients I put in a telephone call to the Kingsway Palace Hotel and asked to speak to Mr. Joseph Harman. The answer was that Mr. Harman had gone out after breakfast, and had left no message at the desk. I left one for him, asking him to ring me as soon as he came in.

He did not ring that day.

At half past ten that night I rang the hotel again, but I was told that Mr. Harman was not in.

At eight o'clock next morning I rang again. They told me that Mr. Harman had not checked out and his luggage was still in his room, but that he had not slept in the room that night.

As soon as I got in to the office I sent for Derek Harris. "Harris," I said. "I want you to try and find that man Harman. He's an Australian." I told him briefly what had happened. "I should try the hotel again, and if you draw a blank, ring round the various police courts. I think I may have given him some rather unwelcome news, and it's quite possible he's been out on a blind."

He came back in a quarter of an hour. "You must have second sight, sir," he said. "He's coming up at Bow Street this morning, drunk and disorderly. They had him in the cooler for the night."

"He's a friend of Miss Paget's," I said. "Get along down to Bow Street, Harris, and make yourself known to him. Which court is he coming up in?"

"Mr. Horler's."

I glanced at my watch. "Get along down there right away. Stay with Harman and pay the fine if he hasn't got any money. Then give me a ring, and if it's all in order take him in a taxi to my flat. I'll meet you there."

There was nothing on my desk that day that could not be postponed or handled by Lester. I got back to my flat in time to catch my charwoman at work and tell her to make up the spare room bed. I told her I should want food in the flat for three or four meals, and I gave her money and sent her out to buy whatever food she could get off the ration.

Harris arrived with Harman half an hour later, and the Australian looked a little bit the worse for wear. He was cheerful and sober after his night in the cells, but he had lost one shoe and he had lost his collar stud and his hat. I met him in the hall. "Morning, Mr. Harman," I said. "I thought perhaps you'd rather come round here and clean up. You'd better not go back to the hotel looking like that."

He looked me in the eyes. "I've been on the grog," he said.

"So I see. The water's hot for a bath if you want one, and there's a razor in the bathroom." I took him and showed him the geography of the house. "You can use this room." I looked him up and down, smiling. "I'll get you a clean shirt and collar. You can try a pair of my shoes; if they're too small I'll send out for a pair."

He wagged his head. "I dunno why you want to do this for me. I'll be all right."

"You'll be righter when you've had a bath and a shave," I said. "Miss Paget would never forgive me if I let a friend of hers go wandering about the streets like that."

He looked at me curiously, but I left him and went back to the sitting-room. Harris was waiting for me there. "Thanks, Derek," I said. "There was a fine, I suppose?"

"Forty shillings," he said. "I paid it."

I gave him the money. "He was cleaned out?"

"He's got four and fourpence halfpenny," he replied. "He thinks he had about seventy pounds, but he's not sure."

"It doesn't seem to worry him," I said.

He laughed. "I don't think it does. He seems quite cheerful over it."

I sent Harris back to the office and settled down to write a few letters while Harman was in the bath. He came into the sitting-room presently looking a bit sheepish, and again I noticed the curious, stiff gait with which he walked. "I dunno what to say," he said in his slow way. "Those jokers I was with got all the money I had on me so Mr. Harris had to pay the fine. But I got some more. I got a thing called a letter of credit that the bank in Brisbane gave me. I can get some money on that and pay him back."

"That's all right," I said. "Have you had any breakfast?"

"No."

"Want any?"

"Well, I dunno. Maybe I'll get something round at the hotel."

"You don't have to do that," I said. "My woman's here still; she'll get you some breakfast." I went out and organized this, and then I came back and found him standing by the window. "You didn't come back with that letter," I observed.

"I changed my mind," he said. "I'm going to give it away."

"Give it away?"

"That's right," he said. "I won't be writing any letter."

"That seems rather a pity," I said quietly.

"Maybe. I had a good long think about it, and I won't be writing any letter. I decided that. That's why I didn't come back at the time you said."

"As you like," I said. "Perhaps you'd like to tell me a bit more about it when you've had some breakfast."

I left him to his breakfast and went on with my letters. My woman took it to the dining-room and he went in there to eat it; a quarter of an hour later he came back to me in the sitting-room.

"I'd better be getting along now," he said awkwardly. "Will it be all right if I come round later in the day and leave these shoes with the woman?"

I got up and offered him a cigarette. "Will you tell me a bit more about yourself before you go?" I asked. "You see, I shall be writing to Miss Paget in a day or two, and she's sure to want to know all about you."

He stared at me, cigarette in hand. "You're going to write and tell her I've been here?"

"Of course."

He stood silent for a moment, and then said in his slow Queensland way, "It would be better to forget about it, Mr. Strachan. Just don't say nothing at all."

I struck a match and lit his cigarette for him. "Is this because I told you about her inheritance?"

"You mean, the money?"

"Yes."

He grinned. "I wouldn't mind about her having money, same as any man. No, it's Willstown."

That was rather less intelligible than Greek to me, of course. I said, "Look, Joe, it won't hurt you to sit down for a few minutes and tell me one or two things." I called him Joe because I thought that it might make him loosen up.

"I dunno as there's much to tell," he said sheepishly.

"Sit down, anyway." I thought for a moment, and then I said, "I'm right in thinking that you met Miss Paget first in the war?"

"That's right," he said.

"That was in Malaya, when you were both prisoners?"

"That's right."

"Some time in 1942?"

"That's right."

"And you've never met her since, nor written to her?"

"That's right."

"Well, what I don't understand is this," I said. "Why do you want to meet her now so very badly? After all, it's six years since you met her. Why the sudden urge to get in touch with her now?" It was still vaguely in my mind that he had somehow heard about her money.

He looked up at me, grinning. "I thought she was a married woman."

I stared at him. "I see. . . . When did you find out that she wasn't married?"

"I only found out that this May. I met the pilot that had flown her out from some place in Malaya called Kota Bharu. At Julia Creek, that was."

He had driven his fourteen hundred cattle down from Midhurst station to Julia Creek with Jim Lennon and two Abo stockriders to help. From Midhurst to Julia Creek is about three hundred miles by way of the Norman River, the Saxby River and the Flinders River. They left Midhurst at the end of March and got the herd to railhead at Julia Creek on the third of May, moving them at the rate of about ten miles a day. The beasts were corralled in the stockyards of the railway, and they set to work to load them into trains; this took about three days.

During this time Jim and Joe lived in the Post Office Hotel at Julia Creek. It was very hot and they were working fourteen hours a day to load the cattle into trucks; whenever they were not working they were standing in the bar of the hotel drinking hugely at the cold Australian light beer that does no harm to people sweating freely at hard manual work. One evening while they were standing so two dapper men in uniform came into the bar and shouted a couple of rounds; these were the pilots of a Trans-Australian Air Line Dakota which had stopped there for the night with an oil leak in the starboard engine.

Joe Harman found himself next to the chief pilot. Joe was wearing an old green linen sun hat that had once belonged to the American Army, a cotton singlet, a pair of dirty khaki shorts, and boots without socks; his appearance contrasted strangely with the neatness of the airman, but the pilot was accustomed to the outback. They fell into conversation about the war and soon discovered they had both served in Malaya. Joe showed the scars upon his hands and the pilots examined them with interest; he told them how he had been nailed up to be beaten, and they shouted another grog for him.

"The funniest do I ever struck," said the chief pilot presently, "was a party of women and children that never got into a prison camp at all. They spent most of the war in a Malay village working in the paddy fields."

Joe said quickly, "Where was that in Malaya? I met that party."

The pilot said, "It was somewhere between Kuantan and Kota Bharu. When we got back they were taken in trucks to Kota Bharu, and I flew them down to Singapore. All English, they were, but they looked just like Malays. All the women were in native clothes, and brown as anything."

Joe said, "Was there a Mrs. Paget with them then?" It was vastly important to him to hear if Jean had survived the war.

The pilot said, "There was a *Miss* Paget. She was the hell of a fine girl; she was their leader."

Joe said, "Mrs. A dark-haired girl, with a baby."

The pilot said, "That's right—a dark-haired girl. She had a little boy about four years old that she was looking after, but it wasn't hers. It belonged to one of the other women, one who died. I know that, because she was the only unmarried girl among the lot of them, and she was their leader. Just a typist in Kuala Lumpur before the war. Miss Jean Paget."

Joe stared at him. "I thought she was a married woman."

"She wasn't married. I know she wasn't, because the Japs had taken all their wedding rings so they had to be sorted out and that was quite easy, because they were all Mrs. So and So except this one girl, and she was Miss Jean Paget."

"That's right," the ringer said slowly. "Jean was her name."

He left the bar presently, and went out to the verandah and stood looking up at the stars. Presently he left the pub and strolled towards the stockyards; he found a gate to lean upon and stood there for a long time in the night, thinking things over. He told me a little about what he had been thinking, that morning in my London flat.

"She was a bonza girl," he said simply. "If ever I got married it would have to be with somebody like her."

I smiled. "I see," I said. "That's why you came to England?"

"That's right," he said simply. He had ridden back with Jim Lennon and the Abo stockriders to Midhurst, a journey that took them about ten days, leading their string of fifteen packhorses; since they had started mustering on the station in February he had been in the saddle almost continuously for three months. "Then there was the bore to see to," he said. "I'd made such a point of that with Mrs. Spears that I couldn't hardly leave before that was finished, but then I got away and I went into Cairns one Wednesday with John Duffy on the Milk Run"—I found out later that he meant the weekly Dakota air mail service—"and so down to Brisbane. And from Brisbane I came here."

"What about the Golden Casket?" I enquired.

He said a little awkwardly, "I didn't tell you right about that. I *did* win the Casket, but not this year. I won it in 1946, the year after I got back to Queensland. I won a thousand pounds then, like I said."

"I see," I observed. "You hadn't spent it?"

He shook his head. "I was saving it, in case some day I got to have a station of my own, or do a deal with cattle, or something."

"How much do you think you've got left now?"

He said, "There's five hundred pounds of our money on the letter of credit, and I suppose that's all I've got. Four hundred pounds of yours. There's my pay as manager goes into the bank at Willstown each month, of course."

I sat smoking for a time in silence, and I couldn't help being sorry for this man. Since he had met Jean Paget six years previously he had held the image of her in his mind hoping to find somebody a little like her. When he had heard that she was not a married woman he had drawn the whole of his small savings and hurried expensively half across the world to England, hoping to find her and to find that she was still unmarried. It was a gambler's action, but his whole life had probably been made up of gambles; it could hardly be otherwise in the outback. Clearly he thought little of his money if it could buy a chance for him of marrying Jean Paget.

It was ironical to think that she was at that moment busy looking for him in his own country. I did not feel that I was quite prepared to tell him that.

"I still don't quite understand why you've given up the

idea of writing to Miss Paget," I said at last. "You said something about Willstown."

"Yes." There was a pause, and then he said in his slow way, "I thought a lot about things after I left you, Mr. Strachan. Maybe I'd have done better to have done some thinking before ever I left Midhurst. I told you, I got none of them high-falutin ideas about not marrying a girl with money. So long as she was the right girl, I'd be tickled to death if she had money, same as any man. But there's more to it than that."

He paused again. "I come from the outback," he said slowly. "Running a cattle station is the only work I know, and it's where I like to be. I couldn't make out in any of the big cities, Brisbane or Sydney. I couldn't make out even in Cairns for very long, and anyway, there'd be no work there I could do. I never got a lot of schooling, living on a station like we did. I don't say that I won't make money. I can run a station better'n most ringers, and I seem to do all right with selling the stock too. I'll hope to get a station of my own one day, and there's plenty of station owners finish up with fifty thousand pounds. But if I get that far, it'll be by staying in the outback and doing what I'm cut out for. And I tell you, Mr. Strachan, the outback is a crook place for a woman."

"In what way?" I asked quietly. We were really getting down to something now.

He smiled a little wryly. "Take Willstown, as an example. There's no radio station to listen to, only the short wave stuff from Brisbane and that comes and goes with static. There's no shop where you can buy fruit or fresh vegetables. The sister says that it's because of that so many of the old folk get this pellagra. There's no fresh milk. There's no dress shop, only what a woman can get in Bill Duncan's Store along with the dried peas and Jeyes Fluid and that. There's no ice cream in Willstown. There's nowhere that a woman can buy a paper or a magazine or a book, and there's no doctor because we can't get one to come to Willstown. There's no telephone. There's no swimming pool where a girl could sit around in a pretty bathing dress, although it can be hot there, oh my word. There's no other young women. I don't believe there's more'n five women in the district between the age of seventeen and forty; as soon as they're old enough to leave home they're off out of it, and down to the city. To get to Cairns to do a bit of shopping you can either fly, which costs money, or you can drive for four days in a jeep, and after that you'll find the jeep needs a new set of tyres." He paused. "It's a grand country for a man to live and work in, and good money, too. But it's a crook place for a woman."

"I see," I said. "Are all the outback towns like that?"

"Most of them," he said. "You get the bigger ones, like the Curry, they're better, of course. But Camooweal and Normanton and Burketown and Croydon and Georgetown—they're all just the same as Willstown." He paused for a moment in thought. "There's only one good one for a woman," he said. "Alice Springs. Alice is a bonza place, oh my word. A girl's got everything in Alice—two picture houses, shops for everything, fruit, ice cream, fresh milk, Eddie Maclean's swimming pool, plenty of girls and young married women in the place, and nice houses to live in. Alice is a bonza town," he said, "but that's the only one."

"Why is that?" I asked. "What makes Alice different to the others?"

He scratched his head. "I dunno," he said. "It's just that it's got bigger, I suppose."

I left that one. "What you mean is that if you got Miss Paget to agree to marry you, she wouldn't have a very happy life in Willstown."

He nodded. "That's right," he said, and there was pain in his eyes. "It all seemed sort of different when I met her in Malaya. You see, she was a prisoner and she hadn't got nothing, and I hadn't got nothing either, so there was a pair of us. When I got to know there was a chance she wouldn't be married I was so much in a hurry to get over here I didn't stop to think about the outback, or if I did I thought of her as someone who'd got nothing so she'd be all right in Willstown. See what I mean?" He looked at me appealingly. "But then I come to England and I see Southampton and the sort of way people live there, bombed and muggered up although it is, and I been in London and I been in Colwyn Bay. Then when you told me she'd come into money I got thinking about how she would be living and the sort of things that she'd be used to and she wouldn't get in Willstown, and then I thought I'd acted a bit hasty. I never know it to work, for a girl to come straight out from England to the outback. And for a girl with money of her own, it'd be worse still." He paused, and grinned at me. "So I went out on the grog."

In all the circumstances, it now seemed to me that he had taken a very reasonable line of action, but it was a pity it had cost him seventy pounds. "Look, Joe," I said. "We want to think about this thing a bit. I think I'll have to write and tell Miss Paget that I've met you. You see, she thought you were dead."

He stared at me. "You knew about me, then?"

"Not very much," I said. "I know that you stole chickens for her, and the Japs nailed you up and beat you. She thought you died.

"I bloody nearly did," he said, grinning. "She told you that, did she?"

I nodded. "It's been a very deep grief to her," I said quietly. "You wouldn't want her to go on like that? You see, she thinks it was her fault."

"It wasn't her fault at all," he said in his slow way. "She told me not to stick my neck out, and I went and bought it. It wasn't her fault at all."

"I think you ought to write to her," I repeated.

There was a long pause.

"I dunno what in hell I'd say to her if I did," he muttered.

There was no point in going on agonizing about it. I got up. "Look, Joe," I said. "Take a bit of time to think it over. When have you got to be back in Australia?"

"I wouldn't be doing right by Mrs. Spears unless I get back on the station by the end of October," he said. "I don't want to serve her a crook deal."

"That gives you two and a half months," I said. "How much did your airline ticket cost you when you came here?"

"Three hundred and twenty-five pounds," he said.

"And you've got five hundred pounds left, on your letter of credit."

"That's right."

"Do you want to go back by air, or would you rather go by sea? I could find out about sea passages for you, if you like. I think it would cost about eighty pounds on a tramp steamer, but you'd have to leave pretty soon—within a fortnight, say."

"There don't seem to be much point in staying here," he said a little wearily. "There wouldn't be no chance that she'll be coming back to England?"

"Not in that time, I'm afraid."

"I'd better go back by sea, and save what's left of the money."

"I think that's wise," I said. "I'll get my office on to finding out about the passages. In the meantime, why don't you move in here? You're welcome to use that spare room till you go, and it will be cheaper for you than living in the hotel."

"Wouldn't I be in your way?"

"Not in the least," I said. "I'm out most of the day, and I'd be very glad for you to stay here if you'd like to."

He agreed to that, and I asked him what he wanted most to see in England in his brief visit. He wanted to see No. 19 Acacia Road, Hammersmith, where his father had been born. He wanted to see a live broadcast of Much Binding in the Marsh which he listened to on short wave from Brisbane when the static permitted. ("They've got a bonza radio at Alice," he said wistfully. "A local station, right in the town.") He wanted to see all he could of thoroughbred horses and thoroughbred cattle. He was interested in saddlery, but he didn't think that we had much to teach them about that.

There was no difficulty about Hammersmith, of course; I put him in a bus that afternoon, and went in to my office to deal with my neglected work. Apart from the clients who came to see me, I had plenty to think about. Whether Jean Paget chose to marry this man when she met him was entirely her own affair, but it was quite a possibility that she would do so. Whatever one might think about the suitability of such a match, there was no denying that Joe Harman had some very solid virtues; he seemed to be hard-working, thrifty if one excepts the great extravagance of flying half across the world to look for the girl he loved, and likely to make a success of his life; quite certainly he was a kind man who would make a good husband.

There was another aspect of the matter which was worth investigation. Whether she knew it or not, Jean Paget had Australia in her ancestry. She had never mentioned her grandfather, James Macfadden, to me and it seemed quite possible that she had never thought about him much. And yet, he was the original source of her money, and apparently he had made it in Australia before coming home to England to break his neck while riding in a point to point in Yorkshire. It would be interesting, I thought, to find out a little more about James Macfadden. Had he made his money on an outback cattle station, too? Had he been just such another as Joe Harman?

I sent my girl that afternoon to bring me the Macfadden box, and I sat looking through the old deeds and wills after my last client had gone. The only clue I found was in the Will of James Macfadden dated September 18th 1903, which began, "I, James Nelson Macfadden of Lowdale Manor, Kirkby Moorside in the County of Yorkshire, and of Hall's Creek in Western Australia, do hereby revoke all former wills . . . etc." I knew nothing of Hall's Creek at that time, but I noted the name for future investigation. That is all there was.

I got Marcus Fernie on the telephone that afternoon at his office at the B.B.C. and asked if I could have a ticket for Much Binding in the Marsh. I had to tell him something about Joe Harman in order to get it because there seemed to be considerable competition, and he came back at once with a demand that Harman should be interviewed for the programme In Town Tonight. I said I'd see him about that, and he promised to send over the ticket. Then I got on to old Sir Dennis Frampton who has a herd of pedigree Herefords at his place down by Taunton and told him about Joe Harman, and he very kindly invited him down for a couple of nights.

I got back to my flat about seven o'clock; I had arranged for dinner there. Joe Harman was there, and he had been to the bank and the hotel, and he had brought his suit-case round to my spare room. I asked if he had found his father's house at Hammersmith.

"I found it," he said. "Oh my word, I did."

"Pretty bad?"

He grinned. "That's putting it mild. We got some slums in Australia, but nothing like that. Dad did all right for himself when he come away from that and out to Queensland."

I offered him a glass of sherry, but he preferred a beer; I went and got him a bottle. "When did your father leave this country?" I enquired.

"1904," he said. "He went out to the Curry, to Cobb and Co. They used to run the stage coaches, before motors came. He must have been about fifteen then. He fought in the first war with the Aussies at Gallipoli."

"He's dead now, is he?"

"Aye," he said. "He died in 1940, soon after I joined the Army." He paused. "Mother's still alive. She lives with my sister Amy at the Curry."

"Tell me," I said, "do you know a place called Hall's Creek?"

"Where the gold was? Over by Wyndham, in West Australia?"

"That will be the place," I said. "There are gold mines there, are there?"

"I don't think they work it now," he said. "There was a lot of gold there in the nineties, like in Queensland, in the Gulf Country. I've never been to Hall's Creek, but I've always thought that it would be like Croydon. There was a lot of gold at Croydon, oh my word. It lasted for about ten years, and then they had to go so deep for it, it didn't pay any longer. Croydon had thirty thousand people one time, so they say. Now it's got two hundred. It's the same at Normanton and Burketown—Willstown's the same. All gold towns at one time, they were."

"You never heard of anybody called Macfadden over at Hall's Creek, did you?"

He shook his head. "I never heard the name."

I told him I was getting a ticket for Much Binding in the Marsh, and that they wanted him to broadcast on Saturday night. He agreed diffidently to do this; when the time came I listened in and thought he did it surprisingly well. The announcer shepherded him along quite skilfully, and Harman spoke for about six or seven minutes about Midhurst cattle station and the country down below the Gulf of Carpentaria that he called the Gulf Country. Marcus Fernie took the trouble to ring me up next day to tell me how well it had gone. "I only wish we could get more chaps like him now and then," he said. "It makes a difference when you hear the real McCoy."

I put him on the train on Sunday down to Taunton to see Sir Dennis Frampton's cows. He had not much time left, because a ship of the Shaw Savill line was leaving on the following Friday morning for New Zealand and Australia, and I had managed to get him a cheap berth on that. He came back on the Wednesday full of what he had seen. "He's got a bonza herd there, oh my word," he said. "I learned more about raising up the quality of stock there in two days than I'd have learned in ten years in the Gulf Country. Of course, you couldn't do the things that he does on a station like Midhurst, but I got plenty to think about."

"You mean, about breeding?"

"We don't breed for quality at all in the Gulf," he said. "Not like you set about it here in England. All we do is go out and shoot the scrub bulls when you see them so you keep the best ones breeding. I'd like to see a herd of pedigree stock out there, like he's got. I never see such beasts outside a show."

After dinner I had a word with him about Miss Paget. "I shall write to her in a day or two and give her your address," I said. "I know that she'll be very sorry to have missed you, and I should think you'd find a letter from her waiting for you at Midhurst when you get there. In fact, I know you will, because I shall write air mail, and she's certain to write air mail to you."

He brightened considerably at the thought. "I don't think I'll write to her from here," he said. "If you're going to do that I'll wait and write when I hear from her. I'm glad I didn't meet her over here, in a way. It's probably all turning out for the best."

It was on the tip of my tongue to tell him then that she was in Australia, but I refrained. I had written to her in Alice Springs the day before Joe Harman had come to me, and I was expecting a letter from her any day now, because she used to write once a week, very regularly. If necessary, I could cable her to tell her his address in order that she might not leave Australia without seeing him, but there was no reason to lay all her cards before him at this stage.

I saw him off at the docks two days later, as I had seen Jean Paget a few months before. As I turned to go down the gangway he said gruffly, "Thank you for doing so much for me, Mr. Strachan. I'll be writing from Midhurst." And he shook my hand with a grip that made me wince, for all the injury his hand had suffered.

I turned to go down the gangway. "That's all right, Joe. You'll find a letter from Miss Paget when you get back home. You might even find more than that."

I had a reason for that last remark, because I had a letter from her in my pocket that had come by that day's post, and it was postmarked Willstown.

Chapter 6

WHEN Jean Paget stepped down the gangway from the Constellation on to Darwin airport she was wildly and unreasonably happy. It is a fact, I think, that till that time she had never really recovered from the war. She had come to England when she was repatriated and she had done her job efficiently and well with Pack and Levy for two years or so, but she had done it in the manner of a woman of fifty. She lived, but she had very little zest for life. Deep in the background of her mind remained the tragedy of Kuantan, killing her youth. She had only been speaking the truth when she had told me once that she felt about seventy years old.

She landed at about eight-fifteen at night, after dark; as she was getting off the plane at Darwin, Quantas had booked a room for her at the Darwin Hotel. She stepped on to the concrete and was marshalled to the Customs office in the hangar; at the foot of the gangway there were three young men who scrutinized her carefully. At the time she took them for officials of the airport. It was only later that she found out that they were reporters on the staff of various Australian newspapers engaged in what must surely be the worst assignment in all journalism, meeting every aeroplane that lands on Darwin airport in the hope of finding a Prime Minister on board, or a woman with two heads.

One of them came up to her as soon as she was through the Customs; there had been nothing to make a story in this load of passengers. A happy-looking girl was a small dividend, however. He said, "Miss Paget? The stewardess tells me that you're getting off here and you're staying at the Darwin Hotel. Can I give you a lift into town? My name is Stuart Hopkinson; I represent the Sydney *Monitor* up here."

She said, "That's terribly kind of you, Mr. Hopkinson. I don't want to take you out of your way, though."

He said, "I'm staying there myself." He had a small Vauxhall parked outside the hangar; he took her suitcase and put it in the back seat and they got in, chatting about the Constellation and the journey from Singapore. And presently, as they drove past the remains of Vestey's meat works, he said, "You're English, aren't you, Miss Paget?" She agreed. "Would you like to tell me why you're visiting Australia?"

She laughed. "Not very much, Mr. Hopkinson. It's only something personal—it wouldn't make a story. Is this where I get out and walk?"

"You don't have to do that," he said. "It was just a thought. I haven't filed a story for a week."

"Would it help if I said that I thought Darwin was just wonderful? 'London Typist thinks Darwin wonderful'?"

"We can't go panning London, not in the *Monitor*. Is that what you are, a typist?"

She nodded.

"Come out to get married?"

"I don't think so."

He sighed. "I'm afraid you're not much good to me for a story."

"Tell me, Mr. Hopkinson," she said. "How do the buses go from here to Alice Springs? I want to go down there, and I haven't got much money, so I thought I'd go by bus. That's possible, isn't it?"

"Sure," he said. "One went this morning. You'll have to wait till Monday now; they don't run over the week-end."

"How long does it take?"

"Two days. You start on Monday, stop at Daly Waters Monday night, and get in late on Tuesday. It's not too bad a journey, but it can be hot, you know."

He put her down at the hotel and carried her bag into the lobby for her. She was lucky in that overcrowded place to get a room to herself, a room with a balcony overlooking the harbour. It was hot in Darwin, with a damp enervating heat that brought her out in streams of perspiration at the slightest movement. This was no novelty to her because she was accustomed to the tropics; she bolted the door and took off her clothes and had a shower, and washed some things in the hand basin, and lay down to sleep with a bare minimum of covering.

She woke early next morning and lay for some time in the cool of the dawn considering her position. It was imperative to her that she should find Joe Harman and talk to him; at the same time the meeting with Mr. Hopkinson had warned her that there were certain difficulties ahead. However pleasant these young men might be, their duty was to get a story for the paper, and she had no desire whatever to figure in the headlines, as she certainly would do if the truth of her intentions became known. "Girl flies from Britain to seek soldier crucified for her. . . ." It would be far easier if she were a man.

However, she wasn't. She set to work to invent a story for herself, and finally decided that she was going out to Adelaide to stay with her sister who was married to a man called Holmes who worked in the Post Office; that seemed a fairly safe one. She was travelling by way of Darwin and Alice Springs because a second cousin called Joe Harman was supposed to be working there but hadn't written home for nine years, and her uncle wanted to know if he was still alive. From Alice she would take the train down to Adelaide.

It didn't quite explain why she had come to Darwin in a Constellation, except that there is no other way to get to Darwin. Lying on her bed and cogitating this it seemed a pretty waterproof tale; when she got up and went downstairs for breakfast she decided to try it out on Stuart Hopkinson. She got her chance that morning as he showed her the way to the bus booking office; she let it out in little artistic snippets over half an hour of conversation, and the representative of the Sydney *Monitor* swallowed it without question so that she became a little ashamed of herself.

He took her into a milk bar and stood her a Coca-Cola. "Joe Harman . . ." he said. "What was he doing at Alice nine years ago?"

She sucked her straw. "He was a cowboy on a cattle farm," she said innocently, and hoped she wasn't overdoing it.

"A stockrider? Do you remember the name of the station?"

"Wollara," she said. "That's the name, Wollara. That's near Alice Springs, isn't it?"

"I don't know," he said. "I'll try and find out."

He came back to her after lunch with Hal Porter of the Adelaide *Herald*. "Wollara's a good long way from Alice Springs," said Mr. Porter. "The homestead must be nearly a hundred and twenty miles away. You mean Tommy Duveen's place?"

"I think that's it," she said. "Is there a bus there from Alice Springs?"

"There's no bus or any way of getting there except to drive there in a truck or a utility."

Hopkinson said, "It's on one of Eddie Maclean's rounds, isn't it?"

"Now you mention it, I think it is." Porter turned to Jean. "Maclean Airways run around most of those stations once a week, delivering the mail," he said. "You may find that you could get there by plane. If so, that's much the easiest."

Her ideas about reporters had been moulded by the cinema; it was a surprise to her to find that in real life they could be kind and helpful people with good manners. She thanked them with sincere gratitude, and they took her out for a run round Darwin in a car. She exclaimed at the marvellous, white sand beaches and the azure blue of the sea, and suggested that a bathing party might be a good thing.

"There's one or two objections," Mr. Porter said. "One is the sharks. They'll take you if you go out more than knee-deep. Another is the alligators. Then there's the stone fish —he lies on the beach and looks just like a stone until you tread on him, and then he squirts about a pint of poison into you. The Portuguese Men of War aren't so good, either. But the thing that really puts me off is Coral Ear."

"What's that?"

"A sort of growth inside your head that comes from getting this fine coral sand into your ear."

Jean came to the conclusion that perhaps she wouldn't bathe in Darwin after all.

She got her bathe, however, because on Sunday they drove her forty miles or so southwards down the one road to a place called Berry Springs, a deep water hole in a river where the bathing was good. The reporters eyed her curiously when she appeared in her two-piece costume because the weeks that she had spent in native clothes in Kuala Telang had left her body tanned with sunburn in unusual places. It was the first mistake that she had made, and for the first time a dim suspicion crossed their minds that this girl held a story for them if they could only get it out of her.

"Joe Harman . . ." said Hal Porter thoughtfully to Stuart Hopkinson. "I'm sure I've heard that name before somewhere, but I can't place it."

As they drove back from the bathe the reporters told her about Darwin, and the picture that they painted was a gloomy one. "Everything that happens here goes crook," Hal Porter said. "The meat works has been closed for years because of labour troubles—they got so many strikes they had to close it down. The railway was intended to go south to Alice and join up with the one from Alice down to Adelaide —go from north to south of the continent. It might have been some good if it had done that, but it got as far as Birdum and then stopped. God knows what it does now. This road has just about put the railway out of business— what business it ever had. There used to be an ice factory, but that's closed down." He paused. "Everywhere you go round here you'll see ruins of things that have been tried and failed."

"Why is that?" Jean asked. "It's not a bad place, this. It's got a marvellous harbour."

"Of course it has. It ought to be a great big port, this place—a port like Singapore. It's the only town of any size at all on the north coast. I don't know. I've been up here too long. It gives me the willies."

Stuart Hopkinson said cynically, "It's got outbackitis." He smiled at Jean. "You'll see a lot of this in Australia, specially in the north."

She asked, "Is Alice Springs like this?" It was so very different to the glowing recollections of Alice that Joe Harman had poured out to her, six years before.

"Oh, well," said Hopkinson, "Alice is different. Alice is all right."

"Why is it different?" she asked.

"I don't really know. It's railhead, of course, for shipping cattle down to Adelaide—that's one thing. But it's a go-ahead place is Alice; all sorts of things go on there. I wish to God the *Monitor'd* send me there instead of here."

She said good-bye to her two friends that night, and started at dawn next morning in the bus for Alice Springs. The bus was a big, modern Bedford, heavily streamlined; it towed a trailer carrying goods and luggage. It was comfortable enough although not air conditioned; it cruised down the wide, empty tarmac road at fifty miles an hour, hour after hour, manned by ex-naval crew.

As far as Katherine, where the bus stopped for lunch, the country was well wooded with rather stunted eucalyptus trees, which Jean discovered were called gums. Between these trees were open meadows of wild land, ungrazed, unused, and uninhabited. She discussed this country with a fellow traveller, a bank inspector on his way to Tennant Creek, and she was told that all this coastal belt was useless for farming for some reason that she could not understand. After Katherine the country gradually became more arid, the trees more scattered and desiccated, till by the evening they were running through a country that was near to desert.

At dusk they stopped for the night at a place called Daly Waters. Daly Waters, she discovered, was a hotel, a post office, a large aerodrome, and nothing else whatsoever. The hotel was a rambling collection of single-storey wooden huts or dormitories for men and for women, strange to Jean but comfortable enough. She strolled outside before tea, in the dusk, and looked around. In front of the hotel three young men were squatting on their heels with one leg extended in the peculiar attitude that Joe Harman had used; they wore a sort of jodhpur trouser and elastic-sided boots with a very thin sole, and they were playing cards upon the ground, intent upon their game. She realized that she was looking at her first ringers.

She studied them with interest; that was how Joe Harman would have looked before he joined the Army. She resisted an absurd temptation to go up to one of them and ask if they knew anything about him.

The bus started at dawn next day, and drove on southwards down the tarmac road, past Milners Lagoon and Newcastle Waters and Muckety Bore to Tennant Creek. As they went the vegetation grew sparser and the sun grew hotter, till by the time they stopped at Tennant Creek for a meal and a rest the country had become pure sand desert. They went on after an hour, driving at fifty to fifty-five miles an hour down the scorching road past tiny places of two or three houses dignified with a name, Wauchope and Barrow Creek and Aileron. Towards evening they found themselves running towards the Macdonnell Ranges, lines of bare red hills against the pale blue sky, and at about dusk they ran slowly into Alice Springs and drew up at the Talbot Arms Hotel.

Jean went into the hotel and got a room opening on to a balcony, the hotel being a bungalow-type building with a single storey, as practically every other building in Alice Springs. Tea was served immediately after they arrived, and she had already learned that in Australian country hotels unless you are punctual for your meals you will get nothing. She changed her dress and strolled out in the town after tea, walking very slowly down the broad suburban roads, examining the town.

She found it as Joe Harman had described it to her, a pleasant place with plenty of young people in it. In spite of its tropical surroundings and the bungalow nature of the houses there was a faint suggestion of an English suburb in Alice Springs which made her feel at home. There were the houses standing each in a small garden fenced around or bordered by a hedge for privacy; the streets were laid out in the way of English streets with shade trees planted along the curbs. Shutting her eyes to the Macdonnell Ranges, she could almost imagine she was back in Bassett as a child. She could now see well what everybody meant by saying Alice was a bonza place. She knew that she could build a happy life for herself in this town, living in one of these suburban houses, with two or three children, perhaps.

She found her way back to the main street and strolled up it looking at the shops. It was quite true; this town had everything a reasonable girl could want—a hair dressing saloon, a good dress shop or two, two picture houses . . . She turned into the milk bar at about nine o'clock and bought herself an ice cream soda. If this was the outback, she thought, there were a great many worse places.

Next morning, after breakfast, she went and found the manageress, a Mrs. Driver, in the hotel office. She said, "I want to try and get in touch with a second cousin of mine, who hasn't written home for ten years." She told her story about being on her way from London to Adelaide to stay with her sister. "I told my uncle that I'd come this way and stop in Alice Springs and try and find out something about Joe."

Mrs. Driver was interested. "What's his name?"

"Joe Harman."

"Joe Harman! Worked out at Wollara?"

"That's right," Jean said. "Do you know if he's there still?"

The woman shook her head. "He used to come in 'ere a lot just after the war, but he was only here about six months. I only came here in the war; I don't know about before that. He was a prisoner of the Japs, he was. They treated him terribly. Came back with scars on his hands where they'd put nails right through, crucified him, or something."

Jean expressed surprise and horror. "Do you know where he is now?"

"I don't know, I'm sure. Maybe one of the boys would know."

Old Art Foster, the general handyman who had lived in Alice Springs for thirty years, said, "Joe Harman? He went back to Queensland where he come from. He was at Wollara for about six months after the war, and then he got a job as station manager at some place up in the Gulf Country."

Jean asked, "You don't know his address?"

"I don't. Tommy Duveen would know it, out at Wollara."

"Does he come into town much?"

"Aye, he was in town on Friday. He comes about once every three or four weeks."

Jean asked innocently. "I suppose Joe Harman took his family with him when he went to Queensland. They aren't living here still, are they?"

The old man stared at her. "I never heard Joe Harman had a family. He wasn't married, not so far as I know."

She said defensively, "My uncle back in England thinks he's married."

"I never heard nothing of a wife," the old man said.

Jean thought about this for a minute, and then said to Mrs. Driver, "Is there a telephone at Wollara? I mean, if Mr. Duveen knows his address, I'd like to ring him up and get it."

"There isn't any telephone," she said. "They'll be speaking on the radio schedule morning and evening from Wollara, of course." There was an extensive radio network operated by the flying doctor service from the hospital; morning and evening an operator at the hospital sat down to call up forty or fifty stations on the radio telephone to transmit messages, pass news, and generally ascertain that all was well. The station housewife operated the other end. "Mrs. Duveen is sure to be on the air tonight because her sister Amy is in hospital here for a baby and Edith'll want to know if it's come off yet. If you write out a telegram and take it down to Mr. Taylor at the hospital, he'll pass it to them tonight."

Jean went back to her room and wrote out a suitable cable and took it down to the hospital to Mr. Taylor, who agreed to pass it to Wollara. "Come back at about eight o'clock, and I may have the answer if they know the address right off; if they've got to look it up they'll probably transmit it on the schedule tomorrow morning." That freed her for the remainder of the day, and she went back to the milk bar for another ice cream.

In the milk bar she made a friend, a girl called Rose Sawyer. Miss Sawyer was about eighteen and had an Aberdeen terrier on a lead; she worked in the dress shop in the afternoons. She was very interested to hear that Jean came from England, and they talked about England for a time. "How do you like Alice?" she asked presently, and there was a touch of conventional scorn in her tone.

"I like it," Jean said candidly. "I've seen many worse places. I should think you could have a pretty good time here."

The girl said, "Well, I like it all right. We were in Newcastle before, and then Daddy got the job of being manager here and we all thought it would be awful. All my friends said these outback places were just terrible. I thought I wouldn't be able to stick it, but I've been here fifteen months now and it's not so bad."

"Alice is better than most, isn't it?"

"That's what they say—I haven't been in any of the others. Of course, all this has come quite recently. There weren't any of these shops before the war, they say."

Jean learned a little of the history of the town and she was surprised at the rapidity of its growth. In 1928 it was about three houses and a pub; that was the year when the railway reached it from Oodnadatta. The flying doctor service started about 1930 and small hospitals were placed about in the surrounding districts. The sisters married furiously, and Jean learned that most of the oldest families were those of these sisters. By 1939 the population was about three hundred; when the war came the town became a military staging point. After the war the population had risen to about seven hundred and fifty in 1945, and when Jean was there it was about twelve hundred. "All these new houses and shops going up," Miss Sawyer said. "People seem to be coming in here all the time now."

She suggested that Jean should come swimming in the late afternoon. "Mrs. Maclean's got a lovely swimming pool, just out by the aerodrome," she said. "I'll ring her up and ask if I can bring you."

She called for Jean that afternoon at five o'clock and Jean joined the swimming party at the pool; sitting and basking in the evening sun and looking at the gaunt line of Mount Ertwa, she became absorbed into the social life of Alice Springs. Most of the girls and married women were under thirty; she found them kindly, hospitable people, well educated and avid for news of England. They spoke quite naturally of England as "home" though none of them had ever been there; each of them cherished the ambition that one day she would be able to go "home" for a trip. By the end of the evening Jean was in a humble frame of mind; these pleasant people knew so much about her country, and she knew so very little about theirs.

She strolled down to the hospital in the cool night, after tea. Mrs. Duveen had not been able to give Joe Harman's address off-hand, but she confirmed that he was managing a station somewhere in the Gulf Country. She would ask her husband and send a message on the morning schedule.

That night Jean thought a good deal about what she would do when she did get the address. It was clear now that her first apprehensions were unfounded; Joe Harman had made a good recovery from his injuries, and was able to carry on his work in the outback. She was amazed that this could be so, but the man was tough. Though there was no compelling need for her to find him now, she felt that it would be impossible to leave Australia without seeing him again; too much had passed between them. She did not fear embarrassment when she met him. She felt that she could tell him the truth frankly; that she had heard of his survival and had come to satisfy herself that he was quite all right. If anything should happen after that, well, that would be just one of those things.

She drifted into sleep, smiling a little.

She went down to the hospital in the morning after the radio schedule, and learned that Joe Harman was the manager of Midhurst station, near Willstown. She had never heard of Willstown before; Mr. Taylor obligingly got out a map of Australia designed to show the various radio facilities and frequencies of the outback stations, and showed her Willstown at the mouth of the Gilbert River on the Gulf of Carpentaria.

"What sort of a place is it?" she asked him. "Is it a place like this?"

He laughed. "It's a fair cow up there." He studied the map. "It's got an airstrip, anyway. I don't suppose it's got much else. I've never been there, and I've never heard of anyone who had."

"I'm going there," she said. "I've got to see Joe Harman, after coming all this way."

"It's likely to be rough living," he said. "Oh my word."

"Would there be a hotel?"

"Oh, there'll be a hotel. They've got to have their grog."

She left the hospital and went thoughtfully to the milk bar; as she ordered her ice cream soda it occurred to her that it might be a long time before she had another. When she had finished her soda she walked up the street a little way and turned into the magazine and book shop, and bought a map of Australia and a bus time-table and an airline time-table. Then she went back to the milk bar and had another ice cream soda while she studied this literature.

Presently Rose Sawyer came into the milk bar with her dog. Jean said, "I've found out where Joe Harman lives. Now I've got to find out how to get there. There doesn't seem to be a bus going that way at all."

They studied the time-tables together. "It's going to be much easiest to fly," said Rose. "That's how everybody goes, these days. It's more expensive, but it may not be in the long run because you've got so many meals and hotels if you try and go by land. I should take the Maclean service to Cloncurry, next Monday."

It meant staying a few days more in Alice Springs, but it seemed the best thing to do. "You could come and stay with us," said Rose. "Daddy and Mummy would love to have somebody from England. It's not very nice in the hotel, is it? I've never been in there, of course."

"It's a bit beery," said Jean. She was already aware of the strict Australian code, that makes it impossible for a woman to go into a bar. "I would like to do that, if you're sure it wouldn't be a lot of trouble."

"We'd love to have you. It's so seldom one can talk to anyone that comes from England." They walked round to the Sawyers' house; on the way they met Mrs. Maclean, fair-haired and youthful, pushing her pram. They stopped, and Jean said, "I've got to go to Willstown in the Gulf Country to see Joe Harman. Can I get a seat on your plane on Monday, as far as Cloncurry?"

"I should think you could. I'm just going to the office; I'll tell them to put you down for Monday. Shall I ask them to arrange the passage for you from Cloncurry on to Willstown? I think you can get there direct from the Curry, but they'll find out that and make the booking if you want."

"That's awfully good of you," said Jean. "I would like them to do that."

"Okay. Coming down to the pool this evening?"

"Yes, please."

They went on to the Sawyer house, a pleasant bungalow with a rambler rose climbing over it, standing in a small garden full of English flowers, with a sprinkler playing on the lawn. Mrs. Sawyer was grey-haired and practical; she made Jean welcome. "Much better for you to be here with us than in that nasty place," she said, with all of an Australian woman's aversion to hotels. "It'll be nice having you, Miss Paget. Rose was telling us about you yesterday. It's nice to meet somebody from home."

She went back to the hotel to pack her suitcase, and on the way she stopped at the Post Office. She spent a quarter of an hour sucking the end of a pencil, trying to word a telegram to Joe Harman to tell him that she was coming to see him. Finally she said,

HEARD OF YOUR RECOVERY FROM KUANTAN ATROC-
ITY QUITE RECENTLY PERFECTLY DELIGHTED STOP
I AM IN AUSTRALIA NOW AND COMING UP TO WILLS-
TOWN TO SEE YOU NEXT WEEK.

                                        JEAN PAGET.

She took her suitcase round to the Sawyers' house in a taxi and settled in with them. She stayed with these kind people for four days. On the third day she could not bear to go on lying to them; she told Rose and her mother what had happened in Malaya, and why she was looking for Joe Harman. She begged them not to spread the story; she was terribly afraid that it would get into the papers. They agreed to this, but asked her to tell her story again to Mr. Sawyer when he came back from the office.

Mr. Sawyer had a lot to say that interested her that evening. "Joe Harman may be on to a good thing up there," he said. "The Gulf Country's not much just at present, but he's a young man, and things can happen very quickly in Australia. This town was nothing twenty years ago, and look at it now! The Gulf's got one thing in its favour, and that's rain. We get about six or seven inches a year here—about a quarter of what London gets. Up where Joe Harman is they probably get thirty inches—more than England does. That's bound to tell in the long run, you know."

He sucked at his pipe. "Mind you," he said. "It's not much good to them, that rainfall, because it all comes in two months and runs off into the sea. It's not spread out all the year round, like yours is in England. But I met a chap from home last year, and he said most of your water would run off into the sea, in England, if you hadn't got a weir every three miles or so on every river. That's what Australia hasn't got around to yet—water conservation on the stations. They're going a little at it, but not much."

In the days she spent with the Sawyers, Jean inevitably heard about Rose Sawyer's love life, which was not so far very serious. It chiefly centred round a Mr. Billy Wakeling, who built roads when he could get a road to build. "He did awfully well in the war," she told Jean. "He was a captain when he was twenty-three. But he's nothing to compare with your Joe Harman. He hasn't been crucified for me yet. . . ,"

"I'm not in love with Joe Harman," Jean said with some dignity. "I just want to know that he's all right."

Rose was still looking round for work that would suit her. "I like a shop," she said. "I couldn't ever learn shorthand, like you do. I like a shop all right, but I don't know that the dress shop is much catch. I can never tell what suits a person till I see it on, so I don't think I'll ever be a dress designer. I'd like to run a milk bar, that's what I'd like to do. I think it must be ever such fun, running a milk bar. . . ."

Jean visited Mr. Sawyer at the bank in his professional capacity, and arranged for him to transfer to Willstown any credits that might come for her account after she had gone. She left Alice Springs on Monday morning with regret, and the Sawyers and Macleans were sorry to see her go.

She flew all that day in a Dragonfly, and it was a very instructive day for her. The machine did not go directly to Cloncurry, but zigzagged to and fro across the wastes of Central Australia, depositing small bags of mail at cattle stations and picking up stockriders and mounted policemen to drop them off after a hundred or a hundred and fifty miles. They landed eight or ten times in the course of the day, at Ammaroo and Hatches Creek and Kurundi and Rockhampton Downs and many other stations; at each place they would get out of the plane and drink a cup of tea and gossip with the station manager or owner, and get back into the plane and go on their way. By the end of the day Jean Paget knew exactly what the homestead of a cattle station looked like, and she was beginning to have a very good idea of what went on there.

They got to Cloncurry at dusk, a fairly extensive town on a railway that ran eastward to the sea at Townsville. Here she was in Queensland, and she heard for the first time the slow, deliberate speech of the Queenslander that reminded her of Joe Harman at once. She was driven into town in a very old open car and deposited at the Post Office Hotel; she got a bedroom but tea was over, and she had to go down the wide, dusty main street to a café for her evening meal. Cloncurry, she found, had none of the clean glamour of Alice Springs; it was a town redolent of cattle, with wide streets through which to drive the herds down to the stock-yards, many hotels, and a few shops. All the houses were of wood with red-painted corrugated-iron roofs; the hotels were of two stories, but very few of the other houses were more than bungalows.

She had to spend a day here, because the air service to Normanton and Willstown ran weekly on a Wednesday. She went out after breakfast while the air was still cool and walked up the huge main street for half a mile till she came to the end of the town, and she walked down it a quarter of a mile till she came to the other end. Then she went and had a look at the railway station, and, having seen the aerodrome, with that she had exhausted the sights of Cloncurry. She looked in at a shop that sold toys and newspapers, but they were sold out of all reading matter except a few dressmaking journals; as the day was starting to warm up she went back to the hotel. She managed to borrow a copy of the *Australian Women's Weekly* from the manageress of the hotel and took it up to her room, and took off most of her clothes and lay down on her bed to sweat it out during the heat of the day. Most of the other citizens of Cloncurry seemed to be doing the same thing.

She revived shortly before tea and had a shower, and went out to the café for an ice cream soda. Stupefied by the heavy meal of roast beef and plum pudding that the Queens-landers call "tea," she sat in a deck chair for a little in the dusk of the verandah, and went to bed again at about eight o'clock.

She was called before dawn, and was out at the aerodrome with the first light. The aircraft this time was a vintage Dra-gon, which wandered round the cattle stations as on the previous flight, Canobie and Wandoola and Milgarra. About midday, after four or five landings, they came to the sea, a desolate, marshy coast, and shortly after that they put down at Normanton. Half an hour later they were in the air again for Constance Downs station; they had a cup of tea here and a chat with the manager's wife, and took off on the last leg to Willstown.

They got there about the middle of the afternoon, and Jean got a bird's-eye view of the place as they circled for a landing. The country was well wooded with gum trees and fairly green; the Gilbert River ran into the sea about three miles below the town. There was deep, permanent water in it as far up as Willstown and beyond, because she could see a wooden jetty, and the river ran inland out of sight into the heat haze with water in it as far as she could see. All the other watercourses, however, seemed to be dry.

The town itself consisted of about thirty buildings, very widely scattered on two enormous intersecting streets or areas of land, for the streets were not paved. Only one building, which she later learned to be the hotel, was of two stories. From the town dirt tracks ran out into the country in various directions. That was all that one could see of Willstown, that and a magnificent aerodrome put there in the war for defence purposes, with three enormous tarmac runways each a mile long.

They landed upon one of these huge runways, and taxied towards a truck parked at the runway intersection, this truck was loaded with two barrels of petrol and a semi-rotary pump for refuelling. The pilot said to Jean as he came down the cabin, "You're getting off here, Miss Paget? Is anyone meeting you?"

She shook her head. "I want to see a man who's living in this district, on one of the stations. I'll have to go to the hotel, I think."

"Who is it? Al Burns, the Shell agent out there on the truck, he knows everybody here."

She said, "Oh, that's a good idea. I want to see Mr. Joe Harman. He's manager of Midhurst station."

They got out of the aeroplane together. "Morning, Al," the pilot said. "She'll take about forty gallons. I'll have a look at the oil in a minute. Is Joe Harman in town?"

"Joe Harman?" said the man in the truck. He was a lean, dark-haired man of forty or so. "Joe Harman's in England. Went there for a holiday."

Jean blinked, and tried to collect her thoughts. She had

been prepared to hear that Harman was out on his property or even that he was away in Cairns or Townsville, but it was absurd to be told that he was in England. She was staggered for a moment, and then she wanted to laugh. She realized that the men were looking at her curiously. "I sent him a telegram to say that I was coming," she said foolishly. "I suppose he didn't get that."

"Couldn't have done," said Al Burns slowly. "When did you send it?"

"About four or five days ago, from Alice Springs."

"Oh no, he wouldn't have got that. Jim Lennon might have it, out at Midhurst station."

"That's dinky-die, is it?" the pilot asked. "He's gone to England?"

"Went about a month ago," the man said. "Jim Lennon said the other night that he'd be back about the end of October."

The pilot turned to Jean. "What will you do, Miss Paget? Do you want to stay here now? It's not much of a place, you know."

She bit her lip in thought. "When will you be taking off?" she asked. "You're going back to Cloncurry?"

"That's right," he replied. "We're going back to Normanton tonight and night-stopping there, and back to the Curry tomorrow morning. I'm going into town now while Al fills her up. Take off in about half an hour."

Cloncurry was the last place that she wanted to go back to. "I'll have to think about this," she said. "I'll have to stay in Australia, till I've seen Joe Harman. Cairns is a nice place to stay, isn't it?"

"Oh, Cairns is a bonza town," he said. "Townsville, too. If you've got to wait six or eight weeks you don't want to wait here, Miss Paget."

"How could I get to Cairns?" she asked.

"Well," he said. "You could come back with me to Cloncurry and then go by train to Townsville and up to Cairns. I don't quite know how long that would take in the train—it must be between six and seven hundred miles. Or you could wait here till next Wednesday, today week, and go by the Dakota straight to Cairns in about two and a half hours."

"How long would the train take, from Cloncurry to Cairns?"

"Oh, I don't know about that. I don't think they go every day from Townsville to Cairns, but I'm not really sure. I think you'd have to allow three days." He paused. "Of course, the best way would be to fly from Cloncurry to Townsville and then fly up to Cairns."

"I know." She was getting very sensitive to the cost of flying these vast distances, but the alternative of three days in an outback train in sweltering heat was almost unbearable. "It'd be much cheaper to stay here and go by the Dakota next week, wouldn't it?"

The pilot said, "Oh much. From here to Cairns would cost you ten pounds fifteen shillings. Flying back to Cloncurry and then on to Townsville and Cairns would be about thirty pounds."

"I suppose the hotel here is quite cheap?"

"About twelve and six a day, I should think." He turned to the Shell agent, busy with the fuel. "Al, how much does Mrs. Connor charge?"

"Ten and six."

Jean did a rapid mental calculation; by staying in this place and waiting for the Dakota in a week's time she would save sixteen pounds. "I think I'll stay here," she said. "It's much cheaper than going back with you. I'll stay here and see Jim Lennon and wait for the Dakota next week."

"You know what it's going to be like, Miss Paget?"

"Like the Post Office Hotel at Cloncurry?"

"It's a bit more primitive than that. The whatnot's out in the back yard."

She laughed. "Will I have to lock myself in my room and take a revolver to bed with me?"

He was a little shocked. "Oh, you'll find it quite respectable. But, well, you may find it a little primitive, you know."

"I expect I'll survive."

By that time another truck had appeared, a lorry with a couple of men in it; they stared at Jean curiously. The pilot took her suitcase and put it in the back; the driver helped her up into the cab beside him. It was a relief to get out of the blazing sunshine into the shade again.

The driver said, "Staying in Willstown?"

"I wanted to see Joe Harman, but they say he's away. I'm staying here till next week if Mrs. Connor can have me, and going on to Cairns in the Dakota."

He looked at her curiously. "Joe Harman's gone to England. You're English, aren't you?"

The truck moved off down the wide tarmac runway. "That's right," she replied.

He beamed at her. "My mother and my dad, they both came from England. My dad, he was born in Lewisham, that's part of London, I think, and my mother, she came from Hull." He paused. "My name's Small," he said. "Sam Small, like the chap with the musket."

The truck left the runway and began bumping and swaying over the earth track leading to the town. Dust rose into the cab, the engine roared, and blue fumes enveloped them; every item of the structure creaked and rattled. "Why did Joe Harman go to England?" she shouted above the din. "What did he go for?"

"Just took a fancy, I think," Mrs. Small replied. "He won the Casket couple of years back." This was Greek to her. "There's not a lot to do upon the stations, this time of the year."

She shouted, "Do you know if there's a room vacant at the hotel?"

"Oh, aye, there'll be a room for you. You just out from England?"

"Yes."

"What's the rationing like at home, now?"

She shouted her information to him as the truck bumped and swayed across the landscape to the town. A wooden shack appeared on one side of the truck, and fifty yards on there was another on the left; there was another some distance ahead, and they were in the main street. They drew up in front of a two-storied building with a faded signboard on the first-floor verandah, AUSTRALIAN HOTEL. "This is it," said Mr. Small. "Come on in, and I'll find Mrs. Connor."

The Australian Hotel was a fair-sized building with about ten small bedrooms opening on to the top-floor verandah. It had wooden floors and wooden doors; the whole of the rest of it was built of corrugated iron on a wood framework. Jean was accustomed by that time to the universal corrugated-iron roofs, but a corrugated-iron wall to her bedroom was a novelty.

She waited on the upstairs verandah while Mr. Small went to find Mrs. Connor; the verandah had one or two beds on it. When the landlady appeared she was evidently only just awake; she was a tall, grey-haired, determined woman of about fifty.

Jean said, "Good afternoon. My name's Jean Paget, and I've got to stop here till next week. Have you got a room?"

The woman looked her up and down. "Well, I don't know, I'm sure. You travelling alone?"

"Yes. I really came to see Joe Harman, but they tell me he's away. I'm going on to Cairns."

"You just missed the Cairns aeroplane."

"I know. They say I'll have to wait a week for the next one."

"That's right." The woman looked around. "Well, I don't know. You see, the men sleep out on this balcony, often as not. That wouldn't be very nice for you."

Sam Small said, "What about the two back rooms, Ma?"

"Aye, she could go there." She turned to Jean. "It's on the back balcony, looks out over the yard. You'll see the boys all going to the gents, but I can't help that."

Jean said, "I expect I'll survive that."

"You been in outback towns before?"

She shook her head. "I've only just come out from England."

"Is that so! What's it like in England now? Do you get enough to eat?"

Jean said her piece again.

"I got a sister married to an Englishman," the woman said. "Living at a place called Goole. I send her home a parcel every month."

She took Jean and showed her the room. It was clean and with a good mosquito net; it was small, but the passage door was opposite the double window opening on to the balcony, giving a clear draught through. "Nobody don't come along this balcony, except Annie—she's the maid. She sleeps in this other room, and if you hear any goings on at night I hope you'll let me know. I got my eye upon that girl." She reverted to the ventilation. "You leave your door open a chink, prop your case against it so that no one can't come barging in by mistake, and have the windows open, and you'll get a nice draught through. I never had no difficulty sleeping in this place."

She glanced down at Jean's hand. "You ain't married?"

"No."

"Well, there'll be every ringer in this district coming into town to have a look at you. You'd better be prepared for that."

Jean laughed. "I will."

"You a friend of Joe Harman, then?"

"I met him in the war," Jean said. "In Singapore, when we were both waiting for a passage home." It was nearer to the truth than her last lie, anyway. "Then as I was in Australia I sent him a telegram to say I'd come and see him. I didn't get an answer so I came here anyway. But he's gone walkabout."

The woman smiled. "You picked up some Aussie slang."

"Joe Harman taught me that one, when I met him in the war."

Sam Small brought up her suitcase; she thanked him, and he turned away, embarrassed. She went into her room and changed her damp clothes for dry ones, and went along to the bathroom and had a shower, and was ready for tea at half past six when the bell echoed through the corrugated-iron building.

She found her way down to the dining-room. Three or four men were seated there already who looked at her curiously; a well-developed girl of sixteen whom she came to know as Annie indicated a separate small table laid for one. "Roast beef, roast lamb, roast pork, roast turkey," she said. "Tea or coffee?"

It was sweltering hot still. Flies were everywhere in the dining-room; they lighted on Jean's face, her lips, her hands. "Roast turkey," she said; time enough to try for a light meal tomorrow, when she knew the form. "Tea."

A plate was brought to her heaped high with meat and vegetables, hot and greasy and already an attraction for the flies. Tea came, with milk out of a tin; the potatoes seemed to be fresh, but the carrots and the turnips were evidently tinned. She thought philosophically that the flies would probably result in dysentery but she knew what to do about that; she had plenty of sulphatriad to see her through the week. She ate about a quarter of the huge plate of food and drank two cups of tea; then she was defeated.

She got outside into the open air as soon as possible, escaping from the flies. On the downstairs verandah three feet above the level of the ground there were two or three deck chairs, a little distance from the entrance to the bar. She had seen nowhere else in the hotel where she could sit and she already knew enough about Australian conventions not to go near the bar; she went and sat down in one of these chairs wondering if by doing so she was offending against local manners.

She lit a cigarette and sat there smoking, looking at the scene. It was evening but the sun was still strong; the dusty great expanse that served as a street was flooded with a golden light. On the opposite side of the road, more than a hundred yards away, there was a fairly extensive single-storey building that had been built on to from time to time; this was labelled—Wm. Duncan, General Merchant. There was no sign of any other shop in the town. Outside Mr. Duncan's establishment three coloured Abo stockriders were gossiping together; one held the bridle of a horse. They were big, well-set-up young men, very like Negroes in appearance and, like Negroes, they seemed to have plenty to laugh about.

Further along the other side of the great street a six-inch pipe rose vertically from the ground to a height of about eight feet. A fountain of water gushed from the top of this pipe and this water seemed to be boiling hot, because a cloud of steam surrounded the fountain, and the stream running away into the background was steaming along its length. A quarter of a mile away a small hut was built across the course of the stream so that the stream ran into the hut and out the other side, but Jean had yet to discover the purpose of this edifice.

A low murmur of voices reached her from the bar; from time to time a man passed her and went in through the open door. She saw no women in the place.

Presently a young man, passing by upon the road, smiled at her and said, "Good evening." She smiled back at him, and said, "Good evening."

He checked immediately, and she knew that she had started something. He said, "I saw you come in with Sam Small this afternoon. Came in the aeroplane, didn't you?"

He was a clean-looking young yokel; he walked with the typical swaying gait of the ringer, and he wore the green jodhpurs and the elastic-sided boots that marked his calling. It was no good trying to be stand-offish. "That's right," she said. "I came up from Cloncurry. Tell me, is that water natural?"

He looked where she was pointing. "Natural? That's a bore. Never seen one before?"

She shook her head. "I've only just come out from England."

"From England? Oh my word." He spoke in the slow manner of the outback. "What's it like in England? Do you get enough to eat?"

She said her piece again. "My dad came from England," he said. "From a place called Wolverhampton. Is that near where you live?"

"About two hundred miles," she replied.

"Oh, quite close. You'll know the family then. Fletcher is the name. I'm Pete Fletcher."

She explained to Pete that there were quite a lot of people in England, and reverted to the subject of the bore. "Does all the water that you get from bores come up hot like that?"

"Too right," he said. "It's mineral, too—you couldn't drink that water. There's gas comes up with it as well. I'll light it for you if you'd like to see." He explained that it would make a flame five or six feet high. "Wait till it gets a bit darker, and I'll light it for you then."

She said that that was terribly kind of him, and he looked embarrassed. Al Burns, the Shell agent and truck repairer, came by and stopped to join them. "Got fixed up all right, Miss Paget?"

"Yes, thank you. I'm staying here till Wednesday and then going on to Cairns."

"Good-oh. We don't see too many strange faces, here in Willstown."

"I was asking Pete here about the bore. Pete, do the cattle drink that water?"

The boy laughed. "When they can't get nothing sweeter they'll drink that. You'll see that they won't touch it in the wet, but then in the dry you'll see them drinking it all right."

"Some bores they won't touch," said Al. He was rolling himself a cigarette. "They sunk a bore on Invergordon, that's a station between here and Normanton—over to the south a bit. They had to go down close on three thousand feet before they got the water and did it cost them something, oh my word. The bore crew, they were there close on three months. Then when they got the water it was stinking with the minerals and the cattle wouldn't touch it, not even in the dry. What's more, it wouldn't grow grass, either."

Two more men had drifted up and joined the little gathering about her chair. "Tell me," she said, "why is this town so spread out? Why aren't the houses closer together?"

One of the newcomers, a man of forty that she later learned to know as Tim Whelan, a carpenter, said, "There was houses all along here once. I got a photograph of this town in 1905. I'll bring it and show you tomorrow."

"Were there more people living here then?"

Al Burns said, "Oh my word. This was one of the gold towns, Miss Paget. Maybe you wouldn't know about that, but there was thirty thousand people living here one time."

The other newcomer said, "Eight thousand. I saw that in a book."

Al Burns said stubbornly, "My dad always said there was thirty thousand when he come here first."

It was evidently an old argument. Jean asked, "How many are there now?"

"Oh, I dunno." Al turned to the others. "How many would you say now, Tim?" To Jean, aside, he said, "He builds the coffins so he ought to know."

"A hundred and fifty," said Mr. Whelan.

Sam Small had joined them on the verandah. "There's not a hundred and fifty living in Willstown now. There's not more than a hundred and twenty." He paused. "Living here in the town, not the stations, of course. Living right here in the town, not counting boongs."

A slow wrangle developed, so they set to work to count them; Jean sat amused while the evening light faded and the census was taken. The result was a hundred and forty-six, and by the time that that had been determined she had heard the name and occupation of most people in the town.

"Were there gold mines here?" she asked.

"That's right," said Mr. Small. "They had claims by the hundred one time, all up and down these creeks, oh my word. There were seventeen hotels here, seventeen."

Somebody else said, "Steamers used to come here from Brisbane in those days—all around Cape York and right up the river to the landing stage. I never see them myself, but that's what my old man told me."

Jean asked. "What happened? Did the gold come to an end?"

"Aye. They got the stuff out of the creeks and the surface reefs, the stuff that was easy got. Then when they had to go deep and use a lot of machinery and that, it didn't pay. It's the same in all these towns. Croydon was the same, and Normanton."

"They say they're going to start the mine in Croydon—open it again," said somebody.

"They been talking like that ever since I can remember."

Jean asked, "But what happened to the houses? Did the people go away?"

"The houses just fell down, or were pulled down to patch up others," Al told her. "The people didn't stay here when the gold was done—they couldn't. There's only the cattle stations here now."

The talk developed among the men, with Jean throwing in an occasional remark or question. "Ghost towns," somebody said. "That's what they called the Gulf towns in a book that I read once. Ghost towns. That's because they're ghosts of what they were once, when the gold was on."

"It didn't last for long," somebody said. The year "1893 was the year that the first gold here was found, and there wasn't many people still living here in 1905."

Jean sat while the men talked, trying to visualize this derelict little place as a town with eight thousand inhabitants, or thirty thousand; a place with seventeen hotels and houses thickly clustered in the angles of the streets. Whoever had planned the layout had dreamed a great dream; with people streaming in to take up claims and the population doubling itself every few days, the planner had had some excuse for dreaming of a New York of the Gulf of Carpentaria. Now all that remained was a network of rectangular tracks where once there had been streets of wooden houses; odd buildings alone remained among this network to show what had been the dream.

As the light faded Pete and Al went out and lit the bore for Jean. They struck half a dozen matches and got it to light; a flame shot upwards from it and lit up the whole town, playing and flickering amongst the water and the steam till finally it was extinguished by a vomit of water. They lit it again, and Jean admired it duly; it was clear that this was the one entertainment that the town provided, and they were doing their best to give her a good time. "It's wonderful," she said. "I've never seen anything like that in England."

They were duly modest. "Most towns around here have a bore like that, that you can light," they said.

She was tired with her day of flying; at nine o'clock she excused herself from their company and they all wished her good night. She drew Al Burns a little to one side before she went. "Al," she said. "I'd like to see Jim Lennon—he's the man at Midhurst, isn't he? I'd like to see him before I go on Wednesday. Will he be coming into town?"

"Saturday he might be in," Al said. "I'd say that he'd be in here Saturday for his grog. If I hear of anybody going out that way I'll send him word and say that you're in town, and want to see him."

"Do they work a radio schedule at Midhurst?"

He shook his head "It's too close in town, it wouldn't be worth it. If anyone gets sick or has an accident they can get him into town here in an hour or so, and the sister has a radio at the hospital." He paused. "There'll be someone going out that way in the next day or so. If not, and if Jim Lennon doesn't come in on Saturday, I'll run you out there in the truck on Sunday."

"That's awfully kind of you," she said. "I don't want to put you to that trouble."

"It's no trouble," he said. "Make a bit of a change."

She went up to bed. The hotel was lit by electric light made in the back yard by an oil engine and generator set that thumped steadily outside her room till she heard the bar close at ten o'clock; at five past ten the engine stopped and all the lights went out. Willstown slept.

She was roused at five o'clock with the first light with the sounds of people getting up and washing; she lay dozing listening to the early morning sounds. Breakfast was not till half past seven; she got up and had a shower and was punctual in the dining-room. She found that the standard breakfast in Willstown was half a pound of steak with two fried eggs on top of it; she surprised Annie very much by asking for one fried egg and no steak. "Breakfast is steak and eggs," Annie explained patiently to this queer Englishwoman.

"I know it is," said Jean. "But I don't want the steak."

"Well, you don't have to eat it." The girl was obviously puzzled.

"Could I have just one fried egg, and no steak?" asked Jean.

"You mean, just one fried egg on a plate by itself?"

"That's right."

Food conservation in Willstown was evidently quite a new idea. "I'll ask Mrs. Connor," said Annie. She came back from the kitchen with a steak with two fried eggs on top. "We've only got the one breakfast," she explained. Jean gave up the struggle.

She ventured out to the kitchen after breakfast and found Mrs. Connor. "I've got a few things to wash," she said. "Could I use your wash tub, do you think? And—have you got an iron?"

"Annie'll do them for you," Mrs. Connor said, "Just give them to her."

Jean had no intention of trusting her clothes to Annie. "She's got a lot of work to do," she said, "and I've got nothing. I'll do them myself if I can borrow the tub."

"Good-oh."

Jean spent the morning washing and ironing in the back ground-floor verandah just outside the kitchen; in that dry, torrid place clothes hung out on a line were dry in ten minutes. In the kitchen the temperature must have been close on a hundred and twenty Fahrenheit; Jean made quick rushes in there to fetch her irons from the stove, and wondered at the fortitude of women who cooked three hot meals a day in such conditions. Annie came presently and stood around on the back verandah, furtively examining Jean's washing.

She picked up a carton of soap flakes. "How much of this do you put in the water?"

Jean said, "I think it's an ounce to a gallon of water, isn't it? I used to know. I put in just a bit. It tells you on the packet."

The girl turned the packet over in her hands, scrutinizing it. "Where it says, DIRECTIONS FOR USE," said Jean.

From the door behind her Mrs. Connor said, "Annie don't read very well."

The girl said, "I can read."

"Oh, can you? Well then, read us out what's written on that packet."

The girl put the carton down. "I ain't had much practice lately. I could read all right when I was at school."

To ease the situation Jean said, "All you do is just go on putting in the soap flakes till the water lathers properly. It's different with different sorts of water, because of the hardness."

"I use ordinary soap," said Annie. "It don't come up so well as this."

Presently the girl said, "Are you a nurse?"

Jean shook her head. "I'm a typist."

"Oh, I thought you might be a nurse. Most women that come to Willstown are nurses. They don't stay here long. Six months, and then they've had enough."

There was a pause. "If you'd been a nurse," the girl said, "I'd have asked you for some medicine. I've been feeling ever so ill lately just after getting up. I was sick this morning."

"That's bad," said Jean cautiously. There did not seem to be much else to say.

"I think I'll go up to the hospital," said Annie, "and ask Sister Douglas for some medicine."

"I should do that," said Jean.

In the course of the day she met most of the notable citizens of Willstown. She walked across to the store to try to buy some cigarettes, but only succeeded in buying a tin of tobacco and a packet of papers. While she was chatting to Mr. Bill Duncan in the store and examining the piece of quartz with gold in it that he showed her, Miss Kenroy came in, the school-teacher. Half an hour later, as Jean was walking back across the road to the hotel, Al Burns met her and wanted to introduce her to Mr. Carter, the Shire Clerk.

She slept most of the afternoon upon her bed, in common

with the rest of Willstown; when the day cooled off she came down to the lower verandah and sat there in a deck chair, as she had the previous evening. She had not long to wait before the ringers found her; they came one by one, diffidently, unsure of themselves before this English girl, and yet unable to keep away. She had a little circle of them squatting with her on the verandah presently.

She got them to talk about themselves; it seemed the best way to put them at their ease. "It's all right here," said one. "It's good cattle country; more rain here than what you get down further south. But I'm off out of it next year. My brother, he's down at Rockhampton working on the railway. He said he'd get me in the gang if I went down and joined him."

Jean asked, "Is it better pay down there?"

"Well, no. I don't think it's so good. We get five pounds seventeen and six here—that's all found, of course. That's for an ordinary stockrider."

She was surprised. "That's not bad pay, is it? For a single man?"

Pete Fletcher said, "The pay's all right. Trouble is this place. There's nothing to do here."

"Do you get a cinema here ever?"

"There's a chap supposed to come here every fortnight and show films in the Shire Hall—that building over there." She saw a low, barn-like wooden structure. "He hasn't been for a month, but he's coming next week, Mr. Carter says."

"What about dances?" Jean asked.

There was a cynical laugh. "They try it sometimes, but it's a crook place for a dance. Not enough girls."

Peter Fletcher said, "There's about fifty of us stockriders come into Willstown, Miss Paget, and there's two unmarried girls to dance with, Doris Nash and Susie Anderson. That's between the age of seventeen and twenty-two, say. Not counting the kids and the married women."

One of the ringers laughed sourly. "Susie's more than twenty-two."

Jean asked, "But what happens to all the girls? There must be more than that round here?"

"They all go to the cities for a job," said somebody. "There's nothing for a girl to do in Willstown. They go to Townsville and Rockhampton—Brisbane, too."

Pete Fletcher said, "That's where I'm going, Brisbane."

Jean said, "Don't you like it on a cattle station, then?"

She was thinking of Joe Harman and his love for the outback.

"Oh, the station's all right," said Pete. He hesitated, uncertain how to put what he felt to this Englishwoman without incautiously using a rude word. "I mean," he said, "a fellow's got a right to have a girl and marry, like anybody else."

She stared at him. "It's really like that, is it?"

"It's a fair cow," said somebody. "It's a fair cow up here. No kidding, lady. It's two unmarried girls for fifty men in Willstown. A fellow hasn't got a chance of marrying up here."

Somebody else explained to her, "You see, Miss Paget, if a girl's a normal girl and got her head screwed on right—say, like it might be you—you wouldn't stay here. Soon as you were old enough to go away from home you'd be off to some place where you could get a job and make your own living, not have to depend on your folks all the time. My word, you would. The only girls that stay in Willstown are the ones who are a bit stupid and couldn't make out in any other place, or else ones who feel they've got to stay and look after the old folks."

Somebody else said, "That kind take the old folks with them down to the city. Like Elsie Freeman."

Jean laughed. "You mean, that if you stay in Willstown you'll finish up by marrying a girl who's not so hot."

They looked over their shoulders, embarrassed. "Well, a fellow wants to look around a bit . . ."

"Who's going to run the stations if you all go down to the cities, looking round a bit?" Jean said.

"That's the manager's headache," said Pete. "I've got headaches of my own."

That evening shortly before tea a utility drove up, a battered old Chevrolet with a cab front and an open, truck-like body behind. It was driven by a man of about fifty with lean, sensitive features. Beside him sat a brown girl of twenty or twenty-five with a smooth skin and a serene face; she was not pure Abo, but probably a quarter white. She wore a bright red dress, and she carried a kitten which was evidently a great amusement and interest to her. They passed into the hotel, the man carrying their bags; evidently they were staying for the night. At tea time Jean saw them in the dining-room sitting with the men at the other table, but they were keeping very much to themselves.

Jean asked Mrs. Connor who they were, after tea. "That's Eddie Page," she said. "He's manager of a station called

Carlisle about a hundred miles out. The lubra's his wife; they've come in to buy stores."

"Real wife?" asked Jean.

"Oh yes, he married her properly. One of the Bush Brothers was round that way last year, Brother Copeland, and he married them. They come in here from time to time. I must say, she never makes any trouble. She can't read or write, of course, and she doesn't speak much. Always got a kitten or a puppy along with her; that's what she likes."

The picture of the man's sensitive, intelligent face came incongruously into Jean's mind. "I wonder what made him do that?"

Mrs. Connor shrugged her shoulders. "Got lonely, I suppose."

That night, when Jean went up to her bedroom, she saw a figure standing by the rail of the balcony that overlooked the back yard. There were two bedrooms only that opened on that balcony, her own and Annie's. In the dim light as she was going in at her window, she said, "Good night, Annie."

The girl came towards her. "I been feeling awful bad," she muttered. "Mind if I ask you something, Miss Paget?"

Jean stopped. "Of course, Annie. What's the matter?"

"Do you know how to get rid of a baby, Miss Paget?"

Jean had been prepared for that one by the morning's conversation; a deep pity for the child welled up in her. "I'm terribly sorry, Annie, but I don't. I don't think it's a very good thing to do, you know."

"I went up to Sister Douglas and she said that's what's the matter with me. Pa'll beat the daylights out of me when he hears."

Jean took her hand, and drew her into the bedroom. "Come in here and tell me about it."

Annie said, "I know there's things you can do like eating something or riding on a horse or something like that. I thought perhaps you might have had to do it, and you'd know."

"I've never had to do it, Annie. I don't know. Why don't you ask him to marry you and have it normally?"

The girl said, "I don't know how you'd tell which one it was. They'd all say it was one of the others, wouldn't they?"

It was a problem that Jean had never had to face. "I suppose they would."

"I think I'll ask my sister Bessie. She might know. She had two kids afore getting married."

It did not look as if Bessie's knowledge had been very useful to her. Jean asked, "Wouldn't the sister do anything to help you?"

"All she did was call me a wicked girl. That don't help much. Suppose I am a wicked girl. There's nothing else to do in a crook place like this."

Jean did what she could to comfort her with words, but words were little good to Annie. Her interests were not moral, but practical. "Pa will be mad as anything when he gets to know about it," she said apprehensively. "He'll beat the daylights out o' me."

There was nothing Jean could do to help the girl, and presently they went to bed. Jean lay awake for a long time beset by human suffering.

She continued for the next two days in Willstown, sitting on the verandah and talking to the ringers, and visiting the various establishments in the town. Miss Kenroy took her and showed her the school. Sister Douglas showed her the hospital. Mr. Carter showed her the Shire Hall with the pathetically few books that constituted the public library; Mr. Watkins showed her the bank, which was full of flies, and Sergeant Haines showed her the Police Station. By the end of the week she was beginning to know a good deal about Willstown.

Jim Lennon came into town on Saturday, as predicted, for his grog. He came in an International utility that Jean learned was the property of Joe Harman, an outsize in motor cars with a truck body behind the front seat, furnished with tanks for seventy gallons of petrol and fifty gallons of water. Mr. Lennon was a lean, bronzed, taciturn man.

"I got an air mail letter yesterday," he said with the deliberation of the Queenslander. "Joe's starting on his way back from England in a ship. He said he'd be here about the middle of October, so he thought."

"I see," said Jean. "I want to see him before I go back to England. I've arranged to fly to Cairns on Wednesday and wait there for him."

"Aye. There's not much for you to do, I don't suppose, waiting round here. I'd say come out and live at Midhurst, but there's less to do there."

"What's Joe been doing in England, Mr. Lennon? Did he tell you what he was going for?"

The stockrider laughed. "I didn't even know he was going. All I knew was he was going down to Brisbane. Then I got a letter that he'd gone to England. *I* don't know why he went. He did say in this letter I got yesterday he'd seen a bonza herd of Herefords, belonging to a Sir Dennis Frampton. Maybe he's having bulls shipped out to raise the quality of the stock. He didn't tell me nothing."

She gave him her address as the Strand Hotel in Cairns, and asked him to let her know when he got accurate news of Joe's arrival.

That evening as she was sitting in her deck chair on the verandah, Al Burns brought a bashful, bearded old man to her; he had disengaged the old man from the bar with some difficulty. He was carrying a sack. "Miss Paget," he said, "want you to meet Jeff Pocock." Jean got up and shook hands. "Thought you'd like to meet Jeff," Al said cheerfully. "Jeff's the best alligator hunter in all Queensland. Aren't you, Jeff?"

The old man wagged his head. "I been hunting 'gators since I was a boy," he said. "I reckon I know 'gators by this time."

Al said, "He's got an alligator skin to show you, Miss Paget." To the old man he said, "Show her your skin, Jeff. I bet she's never seen a skin like that in England."

Jeff Pocock took the sack and opened it, and took out a small alligator skin rolled up. "Course," he said, "I cleaned and trimmed and tanned this one myself. Mostly we just salt them and sell 'em to the tannery like that." He unrolled the skin before her on the floor of the verandah. "Pretty markings, ain't they? I bet you never seen a skin like that in England."

The sight of it brought back nostalgic memories to Jean of red buses on the Great West Road at Perivale, and Pack and Levy Ltd, and rows of girls sitting at the work benches making up alligator-skin shoes and alligator-skin handbags and alligator-skin dressing cases. She laughed. "I've seen hundreds of them in England," she replied. "This is one thing I really know about. I used to work in a factory that made these skins up into handbags and dressing cases." She picked up the skin and handled it. "Ours were harder than this, I think. You've done the curing very well, Jeff."

Two or three other men had drifted up; her story was repeated back and forth in other words, and she told them all about Pack and Levy Ltd. They were very interested; none of them knew much about the skins after they had left the Gulf Country. "I know as they make shoes of them," said Jeff. "I never see a pair."

A vague idea was forming in Jean's mind. "How many of these do you get a year?" she asked.

"I turned in eighty-two last year," the old man said. "Course that's a little 'un. They mostly run about thirty to thirty-six inch—width of skin, that is. That's a 'gator about eleven foot long."

Jean said, "Will you sell me this one, Jeff?"

"What do you want it for?"

She laughed. "I want to make myself a pair of shoes out of it." She paused. "That's if Tim Whelan can make up a pair of lasts for me."

He looked embarrassed. "I don't want nothing for it," he said gruffly. "I'll give it to you."

She argued with him for a little while, and then accepted gracefully. "We'll want a bit of calf skin for the soles," she said, "and some thicker stuff for building up the heels."

She fondled the skin in her hands. "It's beautifully soft," she said. "I'll show you what to do with this."

Chapter 7

JEAN made that pair of shoes working upon the dressing table of her bedroom; to be more exact, she made three pairs before she got a pair that she could wear.

She started off upon Tim Whelan. Tim had made lasts for shoes from time to time, working for various cobblers; the outback woodworker must turn his hand to anything. Jean lent him one of her shoes and lent him her foot to measure in his carpenter's shop, and he made a pair of lasts for her in mulga wood in a couple of days. She asked Pete Fletcher about leather for the soles and heels, and he produced some pieces of tanned cow skin which were about the right thickness for the soles, and a piece of bull's skin for building up the heels. The lining was a major difficulty at first till somebody suggested a young wallaby skin. Pete Fletcher went out and shot the wallaby and skinned it, and the tanning was carried out by a committee of Pete Fletcher and Al Burns and Don Duncan, working in the back of Bill Duncan's store. The business of this pair of shoes assumed such an importance in the life of Willstown that Jean put off her trip to Cairns for a week, and then another week.

The wallaby skin for the lining was not ready, so Jean made up the first pair with a white satin lining that she bought in the store. She knew every process of shoe-making intimately from the point of view of an onlooker, and from the office end, but she had never done it herself before, and the first pair of shoes were terrible. They were shoes of a sort, but they pinched her toes and the heels were too large by a quarter of an inch, and they hurt her instep. The satin lining was not a success, and the whole job was messy with the streaming perspiration of her fingers. Still, they were shoes, and wearable by anyone whose feet happened to be that shape.

She could not show shoes like that to the men downstairs, and so she set to work to make another pair. She got Tim to alter the lasts for her, bought another knife and a small carborundum stone from the store, and started again. For fixative she was using small tubes of Durofix, also from the store.

In all this work, Annie took a great interest. She used to come and sit and watch Jean working as she trimmed and filed the soles or stretched the wet alligator hides carefully upon the lasts. "I do think you're clever to be able to do that," she said. "They're almost as good as you could buy in a shop."

The second pair were better. They fitted Jean moderately well, but the wallaby skin lining was uneven and lumpy, and the whole job was still messy and finger-marked with sweat. Undaunted, she began upon a third pair. This time she used portions of the wallaby skin that were of even thickness, having no means of trimming the skin down, and when it came to the final assembly of the shoes she worked in the early morning when the perspiration of her hands was least. The final result was quite a creditable shoe with rather an ugly-coloured lining, but a shoe that she could have worn anywhere.

She took the three pairs downstairs and showed them to Al Burns on the verandah; Al fetched two or three of the other men, and Mrs. Connor came to have a look at them. "That's what happens to the alligator skins in England," Jean said. "They make them up into shoes like that. Pretty, aren't they?"

One of the men said, "You made them yourself, Miss Paget?"

She laughed. "Ask Mrs. Connor. She knows the mess I've been making in the bedroom."

The man turned the shoe over in his hand. "Oh my word," he said slowly. "It's as good as you'd buy in a shop."

Jean shook her head. "It's not," she said. "It's not really." She pointed out the defects to him. "I haven't got the proper brads or the proper fixative. And the whole thing's messy, too. I just made it up to show you what they do with all these skins that Jeff brings in."

"I bet you could sell that in Cairns," the man said stubbornly. "Oh my word, you could."

Sam Small said, "How much does a pair of shoes like that cost in England?"

"In a shop?" She thought for a minute. "About four pounds fifteen shillings, I should say. I know the manufacturer gets about forty-five bob, but then there's purchase tax and retailer's commission to go on." She paused. "Of course, you can pay much more than that for a really good shoe. People pay up to ten pounds in some shops."

"Ten pounds for a pair of shoes like that? Oh my word."

Jeff was out of town up the river visiting his traps, so she could not show him the shoes that day. She left them with the men to take into the bar and talk over, and she went to have a bath. She had discovered how to have a bath in Willstown by that time; Annie had showed her. The Australian Hotel had a cold shower for ladies, which was usually a very hot shower because the tank stood in the sun. But if you wanted to wallow in hot water, there was another technique altogether.

Where the water from the bore ran off in a hot stream, a small wooden hut had been constructed spanning the stream, at such a distance from the bore that the temperature was just right for a bath. A rough concrete pool had been constructed here large enough for two bodies to lie in side by side; you took your towel and soap and went to the hut and locked yourself in and bathed in the warm, saline water flowing through the pool. The salts in the water made this bath unusually refreshing.

Jean lay in the warm water, locked in the little hut alone; the sunlight came in through little chinks in the woodwork and played on the water as she lay. Since she had seen Jeff Pocock's alligator skin the idea of making shoes had been in her mind. From the time that she had first met me and learned of her inheritance she had been puzzled, and at times distressed, by the problem of what she was going to do with her life. She had no background of education or environment that would have enabled her to take gracefully to a life of ease. She was a business girl, accustomed to industry. She had given up her work with Pack and Levy as was only natural when she inherited nine hundred a year, but she had found nothing yet to fill the gap left in her life. Subconsciously she had been searching, questing, for the last six months, seeking to find something that she could work at. The only work she really knew about was fancy leather goods, alligator shoes and handbags and attaché cases. She did know a little bit about the business of making and selling those.

She lay in the warm, medicated water, thinking deeply. Suppose a little workshop with about five girls in it, and a small tannery outside. Two hand presses and a rotary polisher; that meant a supply of electric current. A small motor generator set, unless perhaps she could buy current from the hotel. An air conditioner to keep the workshop cool and keep the girls' hands from sweating as they worked. It was imperative that the finished shoes should be virgin clean.

Could such a set-up pay? She lay calculating in her bath. She had discovered that Jeff Pocock got about seventy shillings for an average alligator skin, uncured. She knew that Pack and Levy paid about a hundred and eighty shillings for cured skins. It did not seem to her that it could cost more than twenty shillings to trim and tan an alligator skin, and her figures were in Australian money, too. The skins should be much cheaper than in England. Labour, too, would be cheaper; girl labour in Willstown would be cheaper than girl labour in Perivale. But then there would be the cost of shipping the shoes to England, and an agent's fees.

She wondered if Pack and Levy would sell for her. She knew that Mr. Pack had been lukewarm for a long time about the manufacturing side of the business. They did sell other people's products, too—those handbags made by that French firm, Ducros Frères. Pack and Levy sold those, although they made handbags themselves . . .

The major problem was not the business, she thought. In Willstown both labour and materials were cheap; the business end of it might well be all right. But could she train the sort of girl that she could get in Willstown to turn out first-class quality work, capable of being sold in Bond Street shops? That was the real problem.

She lay for a long time in her warm, medicated bath, thinking very deeply.

That evening as she was sitting in her deck chair on the verandah, Sam Small came to her. "Miss Paget," he said. "Mind if we have a talk?"

"Of course, Sam," she said.

"I been thinking about that pair of shoes you made," he said. "I been wondering if you could teach our Judy."

"How old is Judy, Sam?"

"Fifteen," he said. "Sixteen next November."

"Do you want her to learn shoe-making?"

He said, "I been thinking that anyone who could make a dinkum pair of ladies' shoes like that, they could sell them in Cairns in the shops. You see, Judy's getting to an age when she's got to do some work, and there ain't nothing here a girl can do to make a living. She'll have to go into the cities, like the other girls. Well, that's a crook deal for her mother, Miss Paget. We've only got the one girl—three boys and one girl, that's our litter. It'll be a crook deal for her mother if Judy goes to Brisbane, like the other girls. And I thought this shoe-making, well, maybe it would be a thing that she could do at home. After all," he said, "it looks like we've got everything you need to do it with, right here in Willstown."

"Not buckles," Jean said thoughtfully. "We'd have to do something about buckles." She was speaking half to herself.

She thought for a minute. "It wouldn't work like that, Sam," she said. "You think that pair of shoes are wonderful, but they aren't. They're a rotten pair of shoes. You couldn't sell a pair like that in England, not to the sort of people who buy shoes like that. I don't think you could sell them in any first-class shop, even in Cairns."

"They look all right to me," he said stubbornly.

She shook her head. "They aren't. I've been in this business, Sam—I know what a shoe ought to look like. I'm not saying that we can't turn out a decent shoe in Willstown; I'd rather like to try. But to get the job right it'll need machinery, and proper benches and hand tools, and proper materials. I see your point about Judy, and I'd like to see her with a job here in Willstown. But it's too big a thing for her to tackle on her own."

He looked at her keenly. "Was you thinking of a factory or something?"

"I don't know. Suppose somebody started something of the sort here. How many girls would you get to work regular hours, morning and afternoon—say for five pounds a week?"

"Here in Willstown?"

"That's right."

"How young would you let them start?"

She thought for a minute. "When they leave school, I suppose. That's fourteen, isn't it?"

"You wouldn't pay a girl of fourteen five pounds a week?"

"No. Work them up to that when they got skilled."

He considered the matter. "I think you'd get six or seven round about sixteen or seventeen, Miss Paget. Then there'd be more coming on from school."

She turned to another aspect of the matter. "Sam, what would it cost to put up a hut for a workshop?"

"How big?"

She looked around. "About as long as from here to the end of the verandah, and about half as wide."

"That's thirty foot by fifteen wide. You mean a wooden hut, like it might be an army hut, with an iron roof, and windows all along?"

"That's the sort of thing."

He calculated slowly in his head. "About two hundred pounds."

"I think I'd want it to have a double roof and a verandah, like that house that Sergeant Haines lives in. It's got to be cool."

"Ah, that puts up the cost. A house like that'd cost you close upon four hundred, with a verandah all around."

"How long would that take to build?"

"Oh, I dunno. Have to get the timber up from Normanton. Tim Whelan and his boys'd put that up in a couple of months, I'd say."

There would be extra buildings needed for the tanning and the dyeing of the hides. "Tell me, Sam," she said. "Would people here like something of that sort started? Or would they think it just a bit of nonsense?"

"You mean, if it kept the girls here in the town, earning money?"

"That's right."

"Oh my word," he said. "Would they like it. They'd like anything that kept the girls at home, so long as they was happy and got work to do." He paused thoughtfully. "It isn't natural the way the girls go off a thousand miles from home in this country," he said slowly. "That's what Ma and I was saying the other night. It isn't natural."

They sat in silence for a time. "Takes a bit of thinking about, Sam," she said at last.

When the Dakota came next Wednesday she left Willstown for Cairns. She took two days to get there because that was the unhurried way of the Dakota; they left Willstown in the afternoon and called at various cattle stations with the mail and correspondence lessons for the children from the school at Cairns, at Dunbar and Miranda and Vanrook.

With the last of the light they put down at Normanton for the night, and drove into the town in a truck.

The hotel at Normanton was similar to the hotel at Willstown, but rather larger. Jean had tea with the pilot, a man called Mackenzie; after tea she sat with him on the verandah. She asked him if anyone made shoes in Normanton. "I don't think so," he said. He called out to an acquaintance. "Ted, does anyone make shoes round here?"

Ted shook his head. "Buy 'em from Burns Philp," he said. "Want a pair of shoes mended?"

Jean said, "No—I was just curious. They all come from the cities, do they?"

"That's right." Ted rolled himself a cigarette. "My wife's sister, she works in a shoe factory down at Rockhampton. That's where a lot of the shoes come from. Manning Cooper, at Rockhampton. That's where Burns Philp get 'em from."

Jean asked, "Was your wife's sister born round here?"

"Croydon," he said. "Their dad used to keep a hotel at Croydon, but he give up; there wasn't work for two. Mrs. Bridson's is the only one there now."

"She's not married?"

"Who? Elsie Peters?"

"That's the one who works at Manning Cooper, is it?"

"No, she's not married. Got to be a charge hand now, with a lot of girls under her."

When he had moved on Jean asked the pilot, "Who is that?"

"Him? Ted Horner. He runs the garage here." She noted the name for future reference.

They flew on to Cairns early the next morning; she drove into the town and went to the Strand Hotel. Cairns, she found, was a prosperous town of about twenty thousand people, situated rather beautifully on an inlet of the sea. There were several streets of shops, wide avenues with flower beds down the middle of the road; the buildings were all wood and most had iron roofs. It looked rather like the cinema pictures she had seen of American towns in the Deep South, with its wide board sidewalks shaded by verandahs to enable you to look into the shop windows in the shade, but it was almost agressively English in its loyalties. She liked Cairns from the start.

She wrote to me from there. She had written to me twice from Willstown, and at the Strand Hotel she found a letter from me waiting for her that had been there for some days, on account of her delays. She wrote,

Strand Hotel,
Cairns,
North Queensland.

My Dear Noel,

I got your letter of the 24th when I arrived here yesterday, and you will have got my two from Willstown by this time. I wish I had a typewriter because this is going to be a long letter. I think I'll have to get a portable soon in order to keep copies of my letters—not to you, but I'm getting involved a bit in business out here.

First of all, thank you so very much for telling me what you did about Joe Harman. You've evidently been very nice to him and, as you know, that's being nice to me. I can't get over what you say about him rushing off to England and spending all that money, just to see me again. But people out here are like that, I think. I could say an awful lot of rude things about Australians by this time, but I can say this, too. The people that I've met in the outback have all been like Joe Harman, very simple, very genuine, and very true.

And now, about Willstown. I don't know if Joe Harman will still be so keen on marrying me when he sees me; six years is a long time, and people change. I don't know if I'll be keen on marrying him. But if we were to want to marry, what he told you about Willstown is absolutely right.

It's just terrible there, Noel. There are some places in the outback where one could live a full and happy life. Alice Springs is a grand little town. But Willstown's not one of them. Noel, it's absolutely the bottom. There's nothing for a woman there at all except the wash tub. I know that one ought to be able to get along without such things as radio and lipstick and ice cream and pretty clothes. I think I *can* get along all right without them—I did in Malaya. But when it comes to no fresh milk and no fresh vegetables or fruit, it's a bit thick. I think that what Joe told you was absolutely right. I don't think any girl could come straight out from England and live happily in Willstown. I don't think I could.

And yet, Noel, I wouldn't want to see Joe try and change his way of life. He's a first-class station manager, and he'll do very well. I asked all sorts of people about the way Midhurst is run, and it's good. I don't say it couldn't be better if he travelled a bit more widely and saw what other cattle breeders do, but relative to the other stations in the Gulf Country, Midhurst is pretty good and getting better every year. The last manager let it run down, so they tell me, but Joe's done a good job in the two years that he's been there. I wouldn't want to see Joe try and make his life anywhere else, just because he'd married a rich wife who couldn't or wouldn't live in Willstown, where his work is.

Of course, you'll probably say that he could get another station near a better town, perhaps near Alice. I'm not sure that that would be very easy; I've thought a lot about that one. But if it was possible, I wouldn't like it much. Midhurst is in good country with more rainfall than in England; for a life's work it seems to me that the Gulf Country is a far better prospect than anything round Alice. I wouldn't like to think that he'd left good land and gone to bad land, just because of me. That wouldn't be a very good start for a station manager's wife.

Noel, do you think I could have five thousand pounds of my capital? I'm going to take the advice you always shove at me, and not do anything in a hurry. If when I meet Joe Harman he still wants to marry me, and if I want to marry him, I'm going to wait a bit if I can get him to agree. I'd like to work in Willstown for a year or so myself before committing myself to live there for ever. I want to see if I could ever get to adapt myself to the place, or if it's hopeless. I don't want to think that. I would like to find it possible to live in the Gulf Country even though I was brought up in England, because they are such very, very decent people living there.

I want to try and start a tiny workshop, making shoes and handbags out of alligator skins. I told you about that in my last letter. It's work I know about, and all the materials are there to hand in the Gulf Country, except the metal parts. I've written a long letter this morning to Mr. Pack to ask him if he would sell for me in England if the stuff is good enough, and to let me know the maximum price that he could give for shoes delivered at Perivale. And I've asked him to make me out a list of the things I'd want for a workshop employing up to ten girls, and what they cost; things like a press and a polisher with the heads for it, and a Knighton No. 6 sewing machine.

The sewing machine is a heavy duty one for leather and that's the most expensive single item. I should think the lot, including £400 for a building to work in, would cost about a thousand pounds. But I'm afraid that's not the whole story. If I'm going to start a workshop for girls, they've got to have something to spend their wages on. I want to start a shop to sell the sort of things that women want.

Not a big shop, just a little one. I want it to be a sort of ice cream parlour with a few chromium-plated chairs and glass-topped tables. I want to sell fruit there and fresh vegetables; if I can't get them any other way I'll have them flown in from Cairns. There's plenty of money in the outback for that. I want to sell fresh milk there, too; Joe will have to play and keep a few milking cows. I want to sell sweets, and just a few little things like lipstick and powder and face cream and magazines.

The big expense here is the refrigerators and freezers, of course. I think we'd have to allow five hundred pounds for those, and then there's the building and the furniture—say £1200 the lot. That makes, say, £2500 for capital expenditure. If I have five thousand of my capital, I should be able to stock the shop and the workshop and employ five or six girls for a year without selling anything at all, and by that time the income should be coming in, I think. If it isn't, well that's just too bad and I shall have lost my money.

I want to do this, Noel. Apart from Joe Harman and me, they're decent people in Willstown, and they've got so very little. I'd like to work there for a year as a sort of self-discipline and to keep from running to seed now that I've got all this money. I think I'd want to do this even if there wasn't any Joe Harman in the background at all, but I shan't make up my mind or take any definite step until I've had a talk with him.

So what I want is five thousand pounds, please, Noel. May I have it if I want to go ahead with this?

JEAN.

I got this letter five days later by the air mail. I marked the passages about her money with a red pencil, and wrote a little note upon the top, and sent it in to Lester for him to read. I went into his office later in the day. "You read that letter from the Paget girl?" I asked.

He took it up from the desk before him. "Yes. I've just been looking at the will. Did you draft that discretionary clause yourself?"

"I did."

He smiled. "I think it's a masterpiece. It covers us all right, if you think she ought to have this money."

"It's about nine per cent of her capital," I said. "For a commercial venture that she intends to work at whole time, herself."

"The testator didn't know her, did he?"

I shook my head.

"She's twenty-seven years old?"

"That is correct."

"I think that we might let her have it," he said. "It would be very extreme to do the other thing, to withhold it. We've got ample latitude under your discretionary clause to let her have it, and she seems to be a responsible person."

"I'd like to think it over for a day or so," I said. "It seems to me to be a very small amount of capital for what she wants to do."

I put her letter on one side for a couple of days because I never like to take any action in a hurry. After a period of reflection it seemed to me that I would be carrying out the wishes of the late Mr. Douglas Macfadden if I exerted myself to see that Jean Paget did not lose her money in this venture, and I picked up my telephone and rang up Mr. Pack of Pack and Levy Ltd.

I said, "Mr. Pack, this is Strachan, of Owen, Dalhousie, and Peters. I believe you've had a letter from a client of mine, Miss Jean Paget."

"Aye, that's right," he said. "You're her solicitor, are you? The one that's her trustee?"

"That is correct," I said. "I've had a letter from her, too. I was thinking it might be a good thing if we got together, Mr. Pack, and had a talk about it."

"Well, that suits me," he replied. "She asked for a list of what she'd want to start up in a small way. I got a list together, but I haven't got all the f.o.b. prices in yet."

I made an appointment with him for the following Friday when he expected to be in London on other business. He came to see me then at my office. He was a small, fat, cheerful man, very much of a works manager. He brought with him a brown paper parcel.

"Afore we start," he said, "these come in this morning." He untied the parcel on my desk and produced a pair of alligator-skin shoes. I picked one up curiously.

"What are these?" I asked.

"They're what she made herself at this place Willstown," he said. "Did she tell you about that?"

I shook my head, and examined them with fresh interest. "Did she make these herself, with her own hands?"

"Made 'em with her own hands in her hotel bedroom, so she said," he replied.

I turned one over. "Are they any good?"

"Depends on how you look at it," he observed. "For selling in the trade they're bloody awful. Look at this, and this, and this." He pointed out the various irregularities and crudities. "They're not even the same. But she knows that. If you take them as a pair of shoes made by a typist that hadn't ever made a shoe before, working on her bed with no equipment, well, they're bloody marvellous."

I laid down the shoe and offered him a cigarette. "She told you what she wants to do?"

He told me what he had heard from her, and I told him some of what she had written to me; we talked for a quarter of an hour. At the end of that time I asked him, "What do you really think about her proposition, Mr. Pack?"

"I don't think she can do it," he said flatly. "Not the way she's thinking of. I don't think she knows enough about the shoe business to make a go of it."

I must say, I was disappointed, but it was as well to have the facts. "I see," I said quietly.

"You see," he explained, "she hasn't got the experience. She's a good girl, Mr. Strachan, and she's got a good business head. But she's got no experience of making shoes to sell, and she's got no experience of keeping girls in order 'n making them bloody well work for their money. It's not even as if she was in her own country. These Australian country girls she writes about, they're just like so many foreigners to her. They may be willing, but they've never seen a factory before—they won't have the idea at all. She's got to learn her own job and teach them theirs at the same time. Well, she can't do it."

"I see," I said again.

"I'd like to help her," said the little man, "but she'll have to change her ideas a bit. She's on to a good wheeze, if she can put it over. I must say, when I read her letter where it says that she's paying seventy shillings for an alligator skin uncured, you could have knocked me down with a feather. Australian shillings, too—fifty-six bob of our money. Here have I been paying a hundred and seventy, hundred and eighty shillings for a cured skin, all these years, and thinking I was getting 'em cheap at that! I said to Mr. Levy, I said, couple of bloody mugs, we are."

"What can you suggest to help her?" I asked.

"What I thought was this," he said. "If she could pay the passage of a forewoman out and home, I'd let her have a girl out of my shop, say for the first year. I got a girl that's getting restless—well, a woman she is, thirty-five if she's a day. She's a married woman but she isn't living with her husband—hasn't been for a long time. She was a sergeant in the A.T.S. in the war, out in Egypt some of the time, so she knows about a hot country. Aggie Topp, the name is. You wouldn't get girls playing up in any shop with Aggie Topp in charge."

"Does Miss Paget know her?" I enquired.

"Oh, aye, Jean knows Aggie. And Aggie knows Jean. Matter of fact, Aggie come in yesterday and handed in her notice. I handed it back to her and jollied her along, you know. She does that every two or three months, getting restless, like I said. But I asked her then, how would she like to go out to Australia for a year to work with Miss Paget. She said she'd go anywhere to get away from standing in a queue for the bloody rations. She'd go out for a year, if Jean wants her. They all liked Jean."

I said, "Can you spare her?"

"She won't stay long, anyway," he said. "I don't want to lose her and perhaps I won't. If she gets a trip out to Australia and sees that other places aren't so good as England, then maybe she'll come back and settle down with us again. Get it out of her system."

We talked about this for a time. The woman's passages and pay while travelling would tot up to about three hundred pounds, but it seemed cheap to me if it would help the venture through the early stages. For the rest of it, Mr. Pack thought Jean's estimates of capital were on the low side, but not excessively so. "You can't afford much mechanization in the quality shoe trade," he said. "You got to keep changing the style all the time."

About the style, he suggested that they airmailed a sample to Willstown from time to time for Jean's party to copy. He was quite willing to do the selling for her. "Mind, I don't know if she'll be able to make a go of it upon the prices we can sell at," he said. "I'll tell her what we can buy at, and it's up to her. But I'd like to give this thing a spin, I must say. Manufacturing's getting so bloody difficult in this country with controls and that, one feels like trying something different."

I thanked him very sincerely, and he went away. I wrote all this out to Jean Paget by air mail, and I believe Mr. Pack wrote to her by the same mail. She did not get these letters for some days after their arrival, because she had gone down to Rockhampton to look for the girl Elsie Peters who worked in the shoe factory there. She went economically by train, a slow, hot journey of some seven hundred miles; till then she had not realized how vast and sparsely populated a state Queensland was. The aeroplanes had dwarfed it for her; fifty-one hours in the train to Rockhampton expanded it again.

She found Elsie Peters, and the meeting was a complete fiasco. It only lasted about ten minutes. They met in a café close outside the works; as soon as Jean broached the subject of a job in the Gulf Country, Elsie told her she could save her breath. It might be a good thing, she conceded, to start something in the Gulf Country, but not for her. Wild horses would not drag her back again.

Jean came away from the café relieved in one way, and yet depressed. She would not have wanted anybody in that frame of mind, but she had been counting rather heavily on this unknown woman. She was very conscious of her own lack of managerial experience; as the venture became closer difficulties loomed up which had not been quite so obvious at the birth of the idea. She spent a depressed evening in the hotel, and flew back to Cairns next day in revolt at the long train journey; she found the air fare very little more expensive.

She found our letters waiting for her at the Strand Hotel when she got back there, and her spirits revived again. She remembered the gaunt, stern Aggie very well; if Aggie was prepared to come to Queensland for a year that really was something. I think she was beginning to feel very much alone and amongst strangers while she was waiting in Cairns for Joe Harman.

She wrote temporizing letters to us, for she would not make her mind up about anything until she had seen Harman. She told me later that the three weeks that she spent in Cairns living at the Strand Hotel after she came back from Rockhampton were the worst time of her life. Each morning she woke up in the cold light of dawn convinced that she was making a colossal fool of herself, that she could never settle down in this outlandish country, that she and Harman would have nothing in common and that it would be much better not to meet him at all. The wise course was to take the next plane down to Sydney and get a cheap passage to England, where she belonged. By noon some rough Australian kindness from a waitress or the manageress had sown a seed of doubt in the smooth bed of her resolution, that grew like a weed throughout the afternoon; by evening she knew that if she left that country and that place she would be running away from things that might be well worth having, things that she might never find again her whole life through. So she would go to bed resolved to be patient, and in the morning the whole cycle would start off again.

She knew the name of Harman's ship, of course, from my letters, and she had no difficulty in finding out when it docked at Brisbane. A few discreet enquiries showed her that he must pass through Cairns to get to Willstown, and convinced her that he would have to wait for several days in Cairns because his ship docked in Brisbane on a Monday and the weekly plane into the Gulf Country left at dawn on Tuesday; he could never make that connection. She had found out in Willstown that he stayed at the Strand Hotel in Cairns, and so she waited there for him.

She wrote to him care of the shipping line at Brisbane, and she had some difficulty with that letter. Finally she said,

> Dear Joe,
>
> I got a letter from Mr. Strachan telling me that you had been to see him while you were in England, and that you were sorry to have missed me. Funnily enough, I have been in Australia for some weeks, and I will wait at Cairns here so that we can have a talk before you go on to Willstown.
>
> Don't let's talk too much about Malaya when we meet. We both know what happened; let's try and forget about it.
>
> Will you let me know your movements—when you'll be coming up to Cairns? I do want to meet you again.
>
> Yours sincerely,
JEAN PAGET.

She got a telegram on Tuesday morning to tell her he was staying to see Mrs. Spears, the owner of Midhurst, and he would be flying up to Cairns on Thursday. She went to meet him at the aerodrome, feeling absurdly like a girl of seventeen keeping her first date.

I think Joe Harman was in a position of some difficulty as the Dakota drew near to Cairns. For six years he had carried the image of this girl in his heart, but, in sober fact, he didn't in the least know what she looked like. The girl that he remembered had long black hair done in a pigtail down her back with the end tied up with a bit of string, like a Chinese woman. She was a very sunburnt girl, almost as brown as a Malay. She wore a tattered, faded, blouse-like top part with a cheap cotton sarong underneath; she walked on bare feet which were very brown and usually dirty, and she habitually carried a baby on her hip. He did not really think that she would look like that at Cairns, and he was troubled and distressed by the fact that he probably wouldn't be able to recognize her again. It was unfortunate that the inner light in her, the quality that made her what he called a bonza girl, didn't show on the surface.

Something of his difficulty was apparent to Jean; she had wondered if he would know her while she was making herself pretty for him in her room, and had decided that he probably wouldn't. She had no such difficulty herself for he would have changed less than she, and anyway he carried stigmata upon his hands if there were any doubt. She stood waiting for him by the white rails bounding the tarmac as the Dakota taxied in in the hot sun.

She recognized him as he came out of the machine, fair-haired, blue-eyed, and broad-shouldered. He was looking anxiously about; his gaze fell on her, rested a minute, and passed on. She watched him, wondering if she was looking very old, and saw him start to walk towards the airline office with his curious, stiff gait. A little shaft of pain struck her; that was Kuantan, and it had left its mark on him. With her intellect she had known that this must be so, but seeing it for the first time was painful, all the same.

She left the rails, and walked quickly across the tarmac to him, and said, "Joe!" He stopped and stared at her incredulously. He had been looking for a stranger, but it was unbelievable to him that this smart, pretty girl in a light summer frock was the tragic, ragged figure that he had last seen on the road in Malaya, sunburnt, dirty, bullied by the Japanese soldiers, with blood upon her face where they had hit her, with blood upon her feet. Then he saw a characteristic turn of her head and memories came flooding back on him; it was Mrs. Boong again, the Mrs. Boong he had remembered all those years.

It was not in him to be able to express what he was feeling. He grinned a little sheepishly, and said, "Hullo, Miss Paget."

She took his hand impulsively, and said, "Oh, Joe!" He pressed her hand and looked down into her eyes, and then he said, "Where are you staying? How long are you here for?"

She said, "I'm staying in the Strand Hotel."

"Why, that's where I'm staying," he said. "I always go there."

"I know," she said. "Mrs. Smythe told me."

There was much here that he did not understand, but first things came first. "Wait while I get my luggage," he said. "We can drive in together."

"I've got a taxi waiting," she said. "Don't let's go in the bus."

In the taxi as they drove into the town she asked him, "How was Mr. Strachan, Joe?"

"He was fine," he said. "I stayed with him quite a long time, in his flat."

"Did you!" She had not known that part of it because I had not told her; I had told her the bare minimum about him since it was obvious that they were going to meet. "How long were you in England, Joe?"

"About three weeks."

She did not ask him why he went because she knew that already, and it was hardly a matter to be entered on behind the taxi driver. He forestalled her, however, by asking, "What have you been doing in Australia, Miss Paget?"

She temporized. "Didn't you know I was here?"

He shook his head. "All I knew was what Mr. Strachan said, that you were travelling in the East. You could have knocked me down with a feather when I got your letter at Brisbane. Oh my word, you could. Tell me, what are you doing in Cairns?"

A little smile played around her mouth. "What were you doing in England?"

He was silent, not knowing what to say to that. He had no lie ready. They were running through the outskirts of the town, past the churches. "We've got a good bit of explaining to do, Joe," she said. "Let's leave it till you've got your room at the hotel, and then we'll find somewhere to talk."

They sat in silence till they got to the hotel. Jean had a bedroom opening on to a verandah that looked out over the sea to the wild, jungle-covered hills behind Cape Grafton; they arranged to meet there when he had had a wash. She knew something of Australian habits by that time. "What about a beer or two?" she asked.

He grinned. "Good-oh."

She asked Doris the waitress to get four beers, three for Joe and one for her; large quantities of cold liquid were necessary in that torrid place. It was symbolic of Australia, she felt, that they should hold their first sentimental conversation with the assistance of four bottles of beer.

She dragged two deck chairs into a patch of shade outside her room; the beer and Joe arrived about the same time. When the waitress had gone and they were alone, she said quietly, "Let me have a good look at you, Joe."

He stood before her, examining her beauty; he had not dreamed when he had met her in Malaya that she was a girl like this. "You've not changed," she said. "Does the back trouble you?"

"Not much," he said. "It doesn't hinder me riding, thank

the Lord, but I can't lift heavy weights. They told me in the hospital I won't ever be able to lift heavy weights again, and I'd better not try."

She nodded, and took one of his hands in hers. He stood beside her while she turned it over in her own, and looked at the great scars upon the palm and on the back. "What about these, Joe?"

"They're all right," he said. "I can grip anything—start up a truck, or anything."

She turned to the table. "Have a beer." She handed him a glass. "You must be thirsty. Three of these are for you."

"Good-oh." He took a glass and sank half of it. They sat down together in the deck chairs. "Tell me what happened to you," he asked. "I know you said not to talk about Malaya. It was a fair cow, that place. I don't want to remember about it any more. But I do want to know what happened to you—after Kuantan."

She sipped her beer. "We went on," she said. "Captain Sugamo sent us on the same day, after—after that. We went on up the east coast with just the sergeant in charge of us. I was sorry for the sergeant, Joe, because he was very much in disgrace, because of what happened. He never got over it, and then he got fever and gave up. He died at a place called Kuala Telang, about half way between Kuantan and Kota Bharu. That was about a month later."

"He was the only Nip guarding you?" he asked.

She nodded.

"Well, what did you do then?"

She raised her head. "They let us stay there all the war," she said. "We just lived in the village, working in the paddy fields till the war was over."

"You mean, paddling about in the water, planting the rice, like the Malays?"

"That's right," she said.

"Oh my word," he breathed.

She said, "It wasn't a bad life. I'd rather have been there than in a camp, I think—once we got settled down. We were all fairly healthy when the war ended, and we were able to make a little school and teach the children something. We taught some of the Malay children, too."

"I did hear a bit about that," he said thoughtfully. "I heard from a pilot on the airline, down at Julia Creek."

She stared at him. "How did he know about us?"

"He was the pilot of the aeroplane that flew you out, in 1945," he replied. "He said that you got taken in trucks to

Kota Bharu. He flew you from Kota Bharu to Singapore. He's working for T.A.A. now, on the route from Townsville to Mount Isa. That goes through Julia Creek. I met him there this last May, when I was down there putting stock on to the train."

"I remember," she said slowly. "It was an Australian Dakota that flew us out. Was he a thin, fair-haired boy?"

"That'd be the one."

She thought for a minute. "What did he tell you, Joe?"

"Just what I said. He said he'd flown you down to Singapore."

"What did he tell you about me?" She looked at him, and there was laughter in her eyes.

He grinned sheepishly, and said nothing.

"Come on, Joe," she said. "Have another beer, and let's get this straight."

"All right," he said. He took a glass and held it in his hand, but did not drink. "He said you were a single woman, Mrs. Boong. I always thought the lot of you was married."

"They all were, except me. Is that why you went rushing off to England?"

He met her eyes. "That's right."

"Oh, Joe! What a waste of money, when here we are in Cairns!"

He laughed with her, and took a long drink of beer. "Well, how was I to know that you'd be turning up in Cairns?" He thought for a minute. "What are you doing here, anyway?" he asked. "You haven't told me that."

She was embarrassed in her turn. "I came into some money," she said. "I think Noel Strachan told you about that."

"That's right," he said kindly.

"I didn't know what to do with myself then," she said. "I didn't want to go on working as a typist in a London suburb any more. And then I got the idea into my head that I wanted to do something for the village where we lived for those three years, Kuala Telang. I wanted to give them a well."

"A well?" he asked.

Sitting there with a glass of beer in her hand she told him about Kuala Telang, and about her friends there, and the wash house, and the well. Then she came to the difficult bit. "The well diggers came from Kuantan," she said. "I thought that you were dead, Joe. We all did."

He grinned. "I bloody nearly was."

"The well diggers told me that you weren't," she said.

"They told me that you'd been put into the hospital, and you'd recovered."

"That's right," he said. "I tried to find out what had happened to you, but they didn't know, or if they knew they wouldn't say. I reckon they were all scared stiff of that Sugamo."

She nodded. "I went to Kuantan. It's very peaceful there now. People playing tennis on the tennis courts, and sitting gossiping under that ghastly tree. They told me at the hospital that you'd asked about us." She smiled. "Mrs. Boong."

He grinned. "But did you come on to Australia from there?"

She nodded. "Yes."

"What for?"

"Well," she said awkwardly, "I wanted to see if you were all right. I thought perhaps you might be still in hospital or something."

"Is that dinky-die?" he asked. "You came on to Australia because of me?"

"In a way," she said. "Don't let it put ideas into your head."

He grinned. "I'd have done the same if you'd have been an Abo."

"Well, you're a fine one to talk about me wasting money," he said. "We'd have met all right if you'd have stayed in England."

She said indignantly, "Well, how was I to know that you'd be turning up in England, and as fit as a flea?"

They sat drinking their beer for a time. "How did you get here?" he asked. "Where did you come to first?"

She said, "I knew you used to work at Wollara and I thought they'd know about you there. So I flew from Singapore to Darwin, and went down to Alice on the bus."

"Oh my word. You went to Alice Springs? Did you go out to Wollara and see Tommy Duveen?"

She shook her head. "I stayed about a week in Alice, and I got your address at Midhurst from Mr. Duveen over the radio, from the hospital. So then I flew up to Willstown—I sent you a wire at Midhurst to say I was coming. But they told me there, of course, that you were in England."

He stared at her. "Is that dinky-die? You've been to Willstown?"

She nodded. "I was there three weeks."

"Three weeks!" He stared at her. "Where did you stay?"

"With Mrs. Connor, in the hotel."

"But why three weeks? Three hours would have been enough for most people."

"I had to stay somewhere," she said. "If you go running off to England, people who want to see you have to hang around. You'll probably find the Australian Hotel's full of them when you get back."

He grinned. "My word, I will. What did you do all the time?"

"Sat around and talked to Al Burns and Pete Fletcher and Sam Small, and all the rest."

"You must have created a riot." He paused, thinking deeply about this new aspect of the matter. "Did you go out to Midhurst?"

She shook her head. "I stayed in Willstown all the time. I met Jim Lennon, though."

The bell rang downstairs for tea. "We'd better go down, Joe," she said. "They don't like it if you're late."

"I know." He picked up his glass to drain it, but sat with it in his hand, untouched. At last he said, "What did you think of Willstown, Miss Paget?"

She smiled. "Look, Joe, forget about Miss Paget. You can call me Mrs. Boong or you can call me Jean, but if you go on with Miss Paget I'll go home tomorrow."

He smiled slightly. "All right, Mrs. Boong. What did you think of Willstown?"

"We'll be late for tea, Joe, if we start on that."

"Tell me," he said.

She smiled at him with her eyes. "I thought it was an awful place, Joe," she said quietly. "I can't see how anyone can bear to live there." She laid her hand upon his arm. "I want to talk to you about it, but we must go and have tea now."

He got up from his chair, and set the glass down. "Too right," he said heavily. "It's a crook kind of a place for a woman."

They went down to tea and sat at a table together, Joe deep in gloom. When they had ordered, Jean said, "Joe, how long have you got? When have you got to be back at Midhurst?"

He raised his head and grinned. "When I'm ready to go back," he said. "I been away so long a few days more won't make any difference." He paused. "What about you?"

"I only came here to see if you were all right, Joe," she said. "I suppose I'll go down to Brisbane and start looking for a boat home next week."

Their food came, roast beef for Joe, cold ham and salad

for Jean. "What have you been doing since you came to Cairns?" he asked presently. "Been out to the Reef?"

She shook her head. "I went down to Rockhampton once, and I went on one of the White Tours up to the Tableland, and stayed a night in Atherton. I've not been anywhere else."

"Oh my word," he said. "You can't go home without seeing the Great Barrier Reef." He paused, and then he said, "Would you like to go out to Green Island for the week-end?"

She cocked an eye at him. "What's Green Island like?"

"It's just a coral island on the reef," he explained. "A little round one, about half a mile across. There's a restaurant on it and little sort of bedroom huts where you can stay, in among the trees. It's a bonza little place if you like bathing. Wear your bathers all the day."

Jean thought the little bedroom huts among the trees wanted checking up on, but the suggestion certainly had its points. They knew so little about each other; they had so much to learn, so much to talk about. Whatever else might happen if she spent a week-end in her bathing dress with Joe Harman on a coral island, they would certainly come back from it knowing more about each other than they would learn under the restraints of Cairns.

"I'd like to do that, Joe," she said. "How would we get there?"

He beamed with pleasure, and she was glad for him. "I'll slip out after tea and find Ernie," he said. "He's probably in the bar at Hides. He's got a boat, and he'll run us out there tomorrow; it'll take about three hours. We'd better start about eight o'clock, before the sun gets hot. Then I'd ask him to come out and fetch us on Monday, say."

"All right," she agreed. "But look, Joe—this is to be Dutch treat." He did not understand that term. "I mean, you pay the boat one way and I'll pay it the other, and we both pay our own bills." He objected strenuously. "If we don't do that, Joe, I won't come," she said. "I'll think you're plotting to do me a bit of no good."

He grinned. "Too right." And then he said, "All right, Mrs. Boong, we'll each pay our own whack."

He went out after tea and came back to her on the verandah half an hour later; he had found Ernie and arranged the boat, and he had bought a large basket of fruit to take with them. In the quick dusk and the darkness they sat together for some hours, talking of everything but Willstown. She learned a lot about his early life on the various stations, and about his relations in and around Cloncurry, about his war service, and about Midhurst. "It's got a bonza rainfall, Midhurst has," he said. "We got thirty-four inches in the last wet; down at Alice it's a good year if you get ten inches. I've been asking Mrs. Spears if we couldn't build a couple of dams at the head of the creeks to hold back some of the water—one across the head of Kangaroo Creek and one on the Dry Gum."

"Did she agree?"

"She'll pay for them," he said. "Trouble is, of course, to get the labour. You can't get chaps to come and work in the outback. It's a fair cow."

"Why is that?" she asked. She had a very good idea, herself, but she wanted to hear his views.

"I don't know," he said. "They all want to go and work in the towns."

She did not pursue the subject; there was time enough for that. They talked of pleasant, unimportant things; she found that he was very anxious to get back to Midhurst to see his horses and his dogs. "I got a bitch called Lily," he said. "Her mother was a blue cattle dog and she got mated by a dingo, so Lily's half a dingo. She's a bonza dog. Well, I mated her with another blue cattle dog before I come away and she'll have had the litter now, so they'll be quarter dingo. A cross between dingo and cattle dog makes a grand dog, but you've got to get the dingo strain weak or they aren't reliable. I had a quarter dingo dog before the war at Wollara, and he was grand."

He told her that he had about sixty saddle- and packhorses on the station, but they did not seem to be as close to his heart as his dogs. "A dog comes into the homestead and sits around with you in the evenings," he said, and she could picture the long, lonely nights that were his normal life. "You couldn't get along in the outback without dogs."

At ten o'clock they went to bed, prepared for an early start in the morning. They stood together in the darkness by the entrance to her room for a moment. "Have I changed much, Joe?" she asked.

He grinned. "I wouldn't have known you again."

"I didn't think you would. Six years is a long time."

"You haven't changed at all, really," he said. "You're the same person underneath."

"I think I am," she said slowly. "After the war I felt like an old woman, Joe. After Kuantan, I didn't think I'd ever enjoy anything again." She smiled. "Like a week-end at Green Island."

"There's nothing to do there, you know," he said. "You bathe and go out in a glass-bottomed boat to see the coral and the fishes."

"I know. It's going to be such fun."

They left next morning in Ernie's fishing boat, a motor launch with a canopy. For two hours they chugged out over a smooth sea, trolling a line behind and catching two large, brilliantly coloured horse mackerel. Green Island appeared after an hour as the tops of coconut palms visible above the horizon; as they drew near the little circular island appeared, fringed round completely with a white coral beach. There was a long landing stage built out over the shallow water of the reef; they landed and walked down this together, pausing to look at the scarlet and blue fishes playing round the coral heads below.

There were no other visitors staying on the island and they got two of the little bedroom huts in among the trees; these huts had open sides to let the breeze blow through, with an occasional curtain for privacy. They bathed at once and met upon the beach; Jean had a new white two-piece costume and was flattered at the reception that it got. "It's pretty as a picture," he said. "Oh my word."

She laughed. "There's not enough of it to fill a picture frame, Joe."

"Too right," he said. "But there aren't any wowsers here."

"I'll have to look out I don't get burnt," she said. "I bet I'm the whitest white woman that ever bathed here."

"You are in parts," he observed. He stood looking at her, reluctant to take his eyes off her beauty. "You've been out in the sun up top, though."

Her shoulders and her arms were tanned; there was a hard line above her breasts, brown above and white below. "That's where I was wearing a sarong in Malaya," she said. "While they were building the well. In the village we used to wear the sarong up high, under the arms. It's beautifully cool like that, and yet it protects most of you from sunburn. And it's reasonably decent, too."

"Have you got it here?" he asked.

She nodded. "I'm going to put it on presently."

As they turned to go into the water she saw his back for the first time, lined and puckered and distorted with enormous scars. Deep pity for him welled up in her at the sight; this man had been hurt enough for her already. She must not hurt him any more. He glanced back at her and said, "We'd better not go in more than about knee-deep. There's plenty of sharks round here." And then he looked at her more closely, and said, "What's the matter?"

She laughed quickly. "It's the sun," she said. "It's making my eyes water. I ought to have brought my dark glasses."

"I'll go and get them. Where are they?"

"I don't want them, really." She threw herself forward in a shallow dive over the sand in about two feet of water and rolled over on her back, flirting the water from her face. "It's marvellous," she said. He flung himself forward, wallowed for a little, and sat beside her on the coral sand in the warm sea. "Tell me, Joe," she said. "Do sharks really come in close like this?"

"They'll take you in water that's only waist deep," he said. "Oh my word, they will. I don't know if there are any here just now. Trouble is, you never can tell. Didn't you have sharks in Malaya?"

"I think there were," she said. "The villagers never went out more than about knee-deep, so we didn't. There were crocodiles in the river, too." She laughed. "Taking it all in all, there's nothing to beat a good swimming pool in a hot country."

They rolled over in the blue, translucent water; the sun came shimmering through the ripples and made silvery lights upon the coral sand around them. "I've never bathed in a swimming pool," he said. "They make them with a shallow end, do they? Where you can sit, like this?"

"Of course. They have a shallow and a deep end, with diving boards at the deep end. Don't they have swimming pools here, in Australia?"

"Oh my word. They have them down in places like Sydney and Melbourne. I've heard of station owners having them upon their land, too. But places like Cairns and Townsville and Mackay, they're on the sea, so they don't need a pool."

"Mrs. Maclean's got a pool at Alice Springs," she said.

"I know. They only made it a year or two ago. I've never seen it."

She rolled over on her back, and watched a seagull soaring in the thermals from the island. "You could have a pool at Willstown," she said. "You've got all the water in the world, from the bore, running to waste right in the middle of the town. You could make a lovely swimming pool right opposite the hotel."

"That water isn't running to waste," he observed. "Oh my word. The cattle drink that, in the dry."

"It wouldn't hurt the cattle if we borrowed it first and

used it for a swimming pool," she said. "It'd taste all the sweeter."

"Might taste sweeter if you swam in it," he concurred. "I don't know about me."

He would not let her stay in the water more than a quarter of an hour. "You'll burn," he said. "Midday, like this, you can burn just as easy in the sea as on the land. You want to be careful, with a skin as white as yours." They went up from the beach into the shade of the trees and sat smoking for a time; then they went back to their huts to put on a little more covering for lunch. Australian hotels, she had discovered, are very particular about dress at meal times; in Cairns even on the hottest day of summer a man without a jacket and tie would not be served in the dining-room, nor would a woman in slacks.

Harman had arranged a light lunch for her, cold meat and fruit; she was touched by the care that he was taking to make her week-end a success. While struggling to eat a mango decently she asked, "Joe, why don't places like Willstown have more fresh fruit? Won't it grow?"

"Mangoes grow all right," he said. "We've got three or four mango trees at Midhurst. Aren't there any in the town? I'd have thought there must be."

"I don't believe there are. I never saw any fruit in the hotel, or anywhere on sale."

"Oh, well, maybe you wouldn't. People don't seem to bother much about it. Some places have every shade tree a mango tree. Cooktown, in the early summer you drive over them, all along the road."

"Don't the people like fresh fruit and vegetables? I mean, they get all sorts of skin diseases through not having them."

"It's too hot for the old folks to work in gardens, like in other places," he said. "There aren't enough people in the country to grow things like that. We can't even get men to work as ringers on the stations—we have to use two-thirds boongs as stockriders, or more. There just aren't enough people. They won't come to the outback."

She said thoughtfully, "There were plenty of fresh vegetables at Alice Springs."

"Ah, yes," he replied. "Alice is different. Alice is a bonza little town."

They slept on their beds in the heat of the day after lunch and bathed again before tea; in the cool of the evening they went out to the end of the jetty and fished. They caught some sand snappers and three or four brilliant red and blue fish which were poisonous to eat and had to be handled with a glove because they stung; then tiring of this rather unprofitable sport they rolled up their lines and sat and watched the sunset over the heights of the Atherton Tableland on the horizon. "It's a funny thing," Jean said. "You go to a new country, and you expect everything to be different, and then you find there's such a lot that stays the same. That sunset looks just like it does in England, on a fine summer evening."

"Do you see much that's like England here?" he asked.

She smiled. "Not on Green Island, and not much in Willstown. But in Cairns—a lot. Vauxhall and Austin motor cars parked in the streets, and politicians telling people to buy British, and the North British Insurance Company, and Tattersalls, and bank clerks in the hotel listening to Itma. Even the newsboys selling papers in the street—'Read all about it.' Listening to them with your eyes shut, they sound just the same. They used to shout exactly like that when I lived in Ealing."

"Ealing's the place near London where you lived when you were working, isn't it?"

"That's right. It's a part of London, really—a suburb."

"Are you going to live there again when you go home?"

"I don't know," she said slowly. "I don't know what I'm going to do, Joe."

In the evening light, sitting together on the jetty and watching the sunset over the calm water, she had expected him to follow up this opening, and she was disappointed that he did not do so. She had expected more than this of him, and that she didn't get it was beginning to distress her. She had expected to spend the whole week-end on the defensive, in repelling boarders, so to speak, but so far things had worked out very differently. Joe Harman's behaviour towards her had been above reproach; he had not tried to kiss her or even to make opportunities of touching her. But for the fact that he had been to England for no other purpose than to look for her, she might have thought he wasn't interested in her at all. By the end of the day she was becoming seriously worried about his restraint. She had caused him enough pain already.

It was no better when they went to bed. She would have liked to have been kissed, in the quiet darkness under the palm trees, but Joe didn't do it. They said good night in the most orderly way, not even shaking hands, and they retired to their own huts with perfect decorum. Jean lay awake for some time, restless and troubled. She had taken it for granted

that they would arrive at some emotional conclusion at
Green Island, but if things went on as they were going they
would leave on Monday with nothing settled at all. If that
happened, she would have to go down to Brisbane and go
home; there would be no excuse for doing anything else. The
thought was almost unbearable.

She knew that her English ways were strange to him; he
could not know how very willing she was to adapt herself
to his Queensland life. Perhaps, too, her money stood between them. She did not think that so sincere and genuine a
man would have any scruples about marrying a girl with
money, but it might well make him shy of her. She had a
feeling that there was a difference between herself, a strange,
wealthy, English girl, and an Australian girl from Cairns. If
Joe Harman had been so much interested in a girl from
Cairns, Jean thought, she would have been in bed with him
by then; whereas she herself had not even been kissed.

She lay awake for a long time.

Things were not better the next day. They bathed in the
cool of the morning in that marvellous translucent sea; they
walked out upon the reef at low tide to see the coloured
coral; they paddled about in a glass-bottomed boat to see
the coloured fishes, and a good six inches separated them
all the time. By tea time they were finding that they had exhausted their light conversation; the restraint was heavy
upon both of them, and there were long awkward pauses when
neither of them seemed to know what to say.

In the evening light they decided to walk round the island
on the beach. She left him at the door of her hut, and said,
"Give me a couple of minutes, Joe. I don't want to go round
the beach in this frock." She pulled one of the curtains for
privacy; as she changed she thought that they had only one
more day, and so much to settle that they had not started on.
She would get nowhere without taking a bit of a risk, and it
was worth it for Joe.

In the half light he turned as she came out of the hut, and
he was back in the Malay scene of six years ago. She was
wearing the same old faded cotton sarøng or one very like it,
held up in a roll under her arms; her brown shoulders and
her brown arms were bare. She was barefooted, and her hair
hung down in a long plait, tied at the end with a bit of string,
as it had been in Malaya. She was no longer the strange
English girl with money; she was Mrs. Boong again, the Mrs.
Boong he had remembered all those years. She came to him

rather shyly and put both hands on his shoulders, and said, "Is this better, Joe?"

She could never remember very clearly what happened in the next five minutes. She was standing locked in his arms as he kissed her face and her neck and her shoulders hungrily while his hands fondled her body; in the tumult of feelings that swept over her she knew that this man wanted her as nobody had ever wanted her before. She stood unresisting in his arms; it never entered her head to struggle or to try to get away. But presently, when she had breath to speak, she said, "Oh, Joe! They'll see us from the house!"

The next thing that she realized was that they were in her bedroom hut. She never knew how they got there, but thinking of it afterwards she came to the conclusion that he must have picked her up and carried her. And now a new confusion came to her. A sarong held up by a tight roll above the breasts will stay in place all day if given proper usage but it does not stand up very well to energetic manhandling; she could feel that it was getting loose and falling, and she had no other garment on at all.

Standing in his arms still unresisting, smothered by his kisses, she thought, This is it. And then she thought, It had to happen sometime, and I'm glad it's Joe. And then she thought, It's not his fault; I brought this on myself. And then she thought, I must sit down on something, or I'll be stark naked, and at that she escaped backwards from his arms and sat down on the bed.

He followed her down, laughing, and her eyes laughed back at him as she tried to hold her sarong up with her left hand to hide her bosom. Then she was in his arms again and he was hindering her. And then he said quite simply, "Do you mind?"

She reached her right arm round his shoulders, and said quietly, "Dear Joe. Not if you've got to. If you *can* wait till we're married, I'd much rather, but whatever you do now, I'll love you just the same."

He looked down into her eyes. "Say that again."

She drew his head down to her and kissed him. "Dear Joe. Of course I'm in love with you. What do you think I came to Australia for?"

"Will you marry me?"

"Of course I'll marry you." She looked up at him with fondness and with laughter in her eyes. "Anyone looking at us now would say we were married already."

He grinned; he was holding her more gently now. "I don't know what you must think of me."

"Shall I tell you?" She took one of his wounded hands in hers and fondled the great scars. "I think you're the man I want to marry and have children by." It did not seem to matter now that the sarong had fallen to her waist. "I'd rather wait a few months and get our lives arranged a little first, Joe. Marriage is a big thing, and there are things that ought to be done first, before we marry. But if you say we can't wait, then I'll marry you tomorrow, or tonight."

He drew her to him gently, and kissed her finger-tips. "I can wait. I've waited six years for this, and I can wait a bit longer."

She said softly, "Poor Joe. I'll try and make it easy, and not tantalize you. I oughtn't to have done this." She freed herself from his arms and pulled up the sarong and rolled it round. "Just get outside a minute, and I'll put on some more clothes."

He said, "You don't need to do that. I won't do anything, except perhaps kiss you now and then. Stay that way for tonight, as if it was Malaya."

"Just for tonight," she said. They went out presently and stood upon the beach in the bright moonlight, holding each other close. "I never knew a man could be so happy," he said once.

Half an hour later she said, "Joe, we're both tired now, and it's time for bed. We've got an awful lot to talk about, but we'll talk better in the morning. There's just one thing I want to say tonight. If you ever feel you can't bear waiting any longer, you'll tell me, won't you? If you come to me like that, I promise we'll get married right away, or sooner than that."

He said gently, "I can wait a long time for you, after this."

"Dear Joe. I won't keep you waiting any more than I can help."

She was so tired that when she got into her hut she did not light the candle, but fell upon her bed and loosened her sarong, Malay fashion, and slept almost at once. She woke with the first light of dawn and lay reflecting upon what had happened, absurdly happy; at last, she felt, things were going to go right between them. She got up as the sun rose and peered cautiously over to Joe's hut and the restaurant building. There was no sign of any movement anywhere, so she put on her bathing dress and went down to the sea and had a bathe. Lying in the shallow water as the sun rose she discovered a number of bruises on her person, and reflected on the narrowness of her escape from a fate worse than death.

She went back very quietly to her hut and put on a frock. Then she went over to the restaurant. It stood open but there was nobody about; she put the kettle on the oil stove and made a pot of tea. Carrying a cup she went to Joe's hut and peered in cautiously.

He was lying on the bed asleep in a pair of shorts; she stood there for some minutes, watching him as he slept. The troubled lines had vanished from his face and he was sleeping easily and quietly, like a little boy; the scars upon his back stood out with an appalling and contrasting ferocity. She stood watching him for a time with fondness in her eyes, knowing that she would see him so most of the mornings of her life to come, and the thought pleased her.

She moved a little and put down the cup, and when she looked at him again he had opened his eyes, and he was looking at her. "Morning, Joe," she said, wondering if she ought to be running like a rabbit. "I've made you a cup of tea."

He leaned up on one arm. "Tell me," he said. "Did what I think happened last night really happen?"

"I think so, Joe," she said. "I think it must have done. I've got bruises all over me."

He stretched out one hand. "Come here, and let me give you a kiss."

She retreated. "Not on your life. I'll give you a kiss when you've got up and had a bathe and got some clothes on."

He laughed. "Aren't you going to bathe?"

"I've bathed," she said. "Ive been up and pottering about for an hour, while you've been sleeping. I'll come down and watch you."

He asked, "Did you sleep all right?"

She nodded. "Like a log."

"So did I." They smiled with mutual understanding. "Give me a minute, and I'll come down to the beach."

She sat on the sand and chatted to him while he bathed. Then he came out and went to shave, and presently appeared in a clean shirt and a clean pair of khaki drill slacks, and she came into his arms and gave him his kiss. Then, as there was no sign yet of breakfast, they sat very close together on the beach in the cool morning breeze, talking and talking and talking. They had no difficulty in finding things to talk of now, and even their silences were intimate.

After breakfast, as they sat smoking cigarettes over a last cup of coffee, he said, "I've been thinking. I'm going to give up Midhurst, soon as Mrs. Spears can find another manager." She listened in consternation; what was coming now? "If we could get a grazing farm for fattening, in back of Adelaide, at Mallala or Hamley Bridge or Balaklava or some place like that, that's on the railway down from Alice Springs and not too far from the abattoir, that's what I'd like to do. I think we might be able to find a place like that only about fifty miles from the city, so as we could get in any time."

She sat in silence for a minute; this needed careful handling. "Why do you want to do that, Joe? What's wrong with Midhurst?"

"It's too far from anywhere," he said. "All right for a single man, perhaps, but not for a married couple. Now Adelaide's a bonza city. I'm a Queenslander, but I like Adelaide better than Brisbane. I haven't seen Sydney or Melbourne, but Adelaide's a bonza city, oh my word. It's got streets and streets of shops, and trams, and cinemas, and dance halls, and it's a pretty place, too, with hills behind and vineyards growing grapes to make the wine. We could have a bonza time if we got a farm near Adelaide."

"But, Joe," she said, "is that the sort of work you want to do? Just buying store cattle from the outback and fattening them? It sounds awfully dull to me. Are you fed up with the outback?"

He ground his cigarette out on the floor beneath his heel. "There's places that suit single men and places that suit married people," he said. "You've got to make a change or two when you get married."

They had the breakfast table between them, separating them much too far for their new-found intimacy; she could not deal with so serious a matter as this without touching him. "Let's go outside," she said. So they went out and found a patch of sandy grass at the head of the beach in the shade, and sat down there together. "I don't think that's right, Joe," she said slowly. "I don't think you ought to leave the outback just because we're getting married."

He smiled at her. "The Gulf Country's no place for a woman," he said. "Not unless she's been brought up and raised in the outback, and sometimes not then. I've seen some married people out from England try it, and I've never known it work. The life's too different, too hard."

She said slowly, "I know it's very different, and very hard. I've lived in Willstown for three weeks, Joe, and so I know a bit about it." She took his hand and fondled the great scars between her own two hands. "I know what you're afraid of. You're afraid that a girl straight out from England, a girl like me, will be unhappy in the outback, Joe. You're afraid that I'll get restless and start making excuses to go and stay in the city, for the dentist, or for shopping, and things like that. You're afraid that if we start at Midhurst you'll be trying me too hard, and that our marriage will go wrong."

She raised her eyes and looked at him. "That's what you're afraid of, isn't it, Joe?"

He met her eyes. "Too right," he said. "A man hasn't got a right to try and make an English girl live in a crook place like Willstown."

She smiled. "It isn't only English girls, Joe. Australian girls, girls born in Willstown, they run a thousand miles to get away from it."

He grinned. "That's right. If they can't stand it, how could you?"

"I don't know that I could," she said thoughtfully. One had to be honest. "Are all the towns in the Gulf Country the same?"

He nodded. "Normanton's a bit bigger; it's got three pubs instead of one, and it's got a church."

There was a long silence. "I'm afraid of things, too," she said at last.

He took her hand; he could not bear that she should be afraid of anything in the new life before them. She had been brave enough last night. "What's that?" he asked gently.

She said, "I'm afraid of changing your job." She paused. "I can't believe that that would ever work out properly, that a man should change his work because his wife couldn't stand conditions that he could. You've been used to a property about two thousand square miles big, Joe, going off for three weeks at a time with packhorses and never going off your own land. What would a man like you do on a thousand acres?"

He grinned weakly; she had put her finger on the spot. "Get accustomed to it pretty soon, I should think."

"I know you'd do it," she said quietly. "You might even learn to do it reasonably well. But it could never satisfy you after the Gulf Country, and cinemas won't fill the gap, or streets of shops, or dance halls. And sometimes when we squabble—we shall squabble, Joe—you'll think about your old life in the Gulf Country, and how you had to give it up, because of me. And I shall know you're thinking that and

blaming it on me, and that will be between us all the time.
That's what I'm afraid of, Joe. I think we ought to stay up
in the Gulf Country, where your work is."

"You just said you couldn't stand Willstown," he objected.
"Burketown and Croydon—well, they're just the same."

"I know," she said thoughtfully. "I'm not being very reasonable, am I? First I say I couldn't stand living in a place
like that, and then I say that you oughtn't to think of living
anywhere else."

"That's right." He was puzzled and distressed. "We've got
to try and work it out some way to find what suits us both."

"There's only one way to do that, Joe."

"What's that?"

She smiled at him. "We'll have to do something about
Willstown."

Chapter 8

THEY spent that day in a curious mixture of love-making
and economic discussion. "You can't tell me that a country
with three times the rainfall of the Territory can't support a
town as good as Alice," she said once. "I know Alice has a
railway. Willstown's got rain, and I know which I'd rather
have for raising cattle. If you go on doing that, Joe, I'll go
off and sit by myself. We aren't married yet." She removed
his hand and kissed it.

"Rain's not the only thing you want for raising cattle," he
said. "The better the feed, or course, the more calves live
through the dry and the more you've got to sell. But there's
a lot more to it than that, oh my word."

"Tell me, Joe." She had his hand in a firm grip.

"One thing," he said, "you've got to keep that water when
you've got it. It's true enough that Midhurst gets a lot of rainfall, but it's all gone in a flash. We get rain from the middle
of December till the end of February, and you'll see the
creeks all running full in flood. But three weeks later, by the
end of March, they'll all be dry again, and the country as dry
as ever."

"Is that what you want to build the dams for, at Kangaroo
Creek and Dry Gum Creek?"

"That's right," he said. "I want to make a start with building little kind of barrages to hold back the water. Do a bit each year, starting at the head of each creek and working down. Get a little pool held back every two or three miles all down the creeks till they run out into the Gilbert. They wouldn't hold the water right through the dry, of course; the sun's too strong. But you could add a lot of feed to Midhurst if you had a lot of little dams like that. Oh my word, you could."

She released his hand. "How big is Midhurst, Joe?"

"Eleven hundred square miles."

"How many cattle does it carry?"

"About nine thousand. Ought to carry more than that, but it's dry up at the top end. Very dry."

"Suppose you could get all the little dams that you're imagining. How many would it carry then?"

He thought for a minute. "I don't see why it shouldn't carry double what's on it now. That'd be about sixteen to the mile. With a rainfall like we've got you should be able to do that."

"You sold fourteen hundred head this year, didn't you?"

"That's right."

"How much a head?"

"Four pound sixteen."

She grabbed his hand again, and held it imprisoned. "I'm trying to think, Joe. If you doubled the stock on the station you'd have another fourteen hundred to sell each year. That's —that's between six and seven thousand pounds a year more to sell. You'd be selling twelve or thirteen thousand pounds' worth every year then, Joe. It'd be worth spending a bit of capital on dams to get that rise in turnover, wouldn't it?"

He looked at her with a new respect. "Well, that's the way I worked it out. I told Mrs. Spears, I said, I want to keep a permanent gang of three men and a few Abos on this. Do a bit each year, working down from the top. Spend about fifteen hundred a year, you might say. There'd be less profit the first year, but after that it should rise steadily to nearly double. That's what I told her."

"She agreed, did she?"

"She agreed to spend the money. But that's only the start of it, the easy part. It may be years before I get the men."

She looked at him incredulously. "Years?"

"Too right," he said heavily. "It's all very well to think of things like that, but it's another thing to do them. Might be five years before I get the work in hand. You see, there's only three of us on Midhurst—whites, that is—me and Jim

Lennon, and Dave Hope. We've got to find three more who'll work out all the week up country, forty miles from the homestead, working with a pick and shovel mostly, and responsible enough to get on by themselves with only just a visit once a week or once a fortnight. Well, you can't get men like that. There are fewer people in the Gulf Country every year. If it wasn't for the Abo stockriders, the boongs, I don't know what we'd do."

"Are there really only three of you—whites—running Midhurst?"

He put his arm around her shoulders. "When you come it'll be four."

She thought it would be five or six soon after that, but she refrained from saying so. "How many would you like to have?"

"You mean with eighteen thousand head of cattle, some time in the future?" She nodded. "I could use twenty on a station like that," he said. "That wouldn't be too many, not if you were running tame bulls in a paddock, to improve the stock. There'd be fences and stockyards and all sorts of things to make. I could use twenty white ringers, and some other hands besides."

She said slowly, "Pete Fletcher said that there were fifty ringers coming into Willstown, using it as their town."

"That's about right," he said.

"If all the stations developed like you say," she observed, "that means seven times as many ringers, because there are only three of you now. Three or four hundred ringers in the district, all with wives and families, and shops for them, and pubs, and garages, and radio, and cinemas. There's room here for a town of two or three thousand people, Joe."

He smiled. "You'll be making it as big as Brisbane next."

She said severely, "Joe. There was an old girl in our party in Malaya called Mrs. Frith. She thought you must be Jesus Christ, because you'd been crucified. I tried to tell her that you weren't. If she saw what you're doing now she'd probably believe me."

They talked about Mrs. Frith for a time, and then reverted to more mundane matters. "Joe," she said, "listen to me. Would you think it very stupid if I said I wanted to start a business in Willstown?"

He stared at her. "A business? What sort of business could you do in Willstown?"

"Do you know what I was doing in England?" she enquired.

"Shorthand-typing, wasn't it?" he asked.

She took his hand and smoothed it between her own. "There's such a lot that you don't know about me," she said. "So much to tell you." She started in to tell him about Pack and Levy, and Mr. Pack, and about alligator-skin shoes, and Aggie Topp. Half an hour later she said, "That's what I want to do, Joe. Do you think it's crazy?"

"I don't know." And then, quite unexpectedly, he said, "I took a walk down Bond Street, looking in the shops."

She turned to him surprised. "Did you, Joe?"

He nodded. "I asked Mr. Strachan what I ought to see in London and he asked me how much history I knew and I told him that I never got much schooling. So then he said to go and see St. Paul's and Westminster Abbey, and then he said to take the bus to Piccadilly Circus and walk up Regent Street and along Oxford Street and down Bond Street and back along Piccadilly; he said I'd see all the best shops that way."

She nodded. It seemed very far away from Green Island, and the whisper of the coconut palms overhead in the sea breeze.

"I saw a lot of alligator-skin shoes," he said. "Sort of dressing cases, too." He turned to her. "It was interesting seeing those, and wondering if they were skins that old Jeff Pocock trapped. Made me feel quite at home. Beautifully done up, they were. But the prices—oh my word. Most of them hadn't got no labels, but there was one, just a little alligator-skin case with silvery things in it, for a lady. A hundred guineas, that one was."

She was excited. "Joe, I bet that was made by Pack and Levy. We did all that sort of work."

"You weren't thinking you could make that sort of stuff in Willstown?"

"Not cases, Joe. Just shoes—shoes to start with, anyway. A little workshop with six or seven girls making alligator-skin shoes. It won't cost very much, Joe—not more than I can afford to lose if it goes wrong. But I don't know—perhaps it won't go wrong. If it worked out all right, and if it paid, it'd be a good thing for the town."

"Six or seven girls all earning money at a job in Willstown?" he said thoughtfully. "You wouldn't keep them six weeks. They'd all be married—oh my word, they would."

She laughed. "Then I'd have to find six or seven more." She got up. "Let's go and bathe. It'll be too hot if we don't bathe soon."

They went and changed and lay in the clean, silvery water on the coral sand. "Look at those bruises," she said. "You great bully. Hit somebody your own size." And presently she said, "I've got another shock for you. You won't drown if I tell you now? I want to start an ice cream parlour."

"Oh my word."

"I'm going to pay these girls a lot of money, Joe," she said seriously. "I've got to get some of it back."

He looked at her, uncertain if she were laughing or not. "An ice cream parlour in Willstown?" he said. "It'll never pay."

"You wait till you see what I charge for an ice cream," she said. "Not only ice cream, Joe—fruit and vegetables, quick-frozen stuff, and women's magazines, and cosmetics, and all the little bits of things that women want. I've got a very pretty girl who wants to come and run it for me, a girl called Rose Sawyer who lives in Alice Springs."

He said slowly, "If you've got a girl like that to run it, the women won't be able to get in the shop. It'll be full of ringers."

"That's all right," she said, "so long as they buy ice cream." She turned to him. "Joe, did you ever spend a Sunday in Alice Springs?"

He shook his head. "I don't think I ever did. Not since before the war, anyway."

"I know why that is, too," she said. "The pubs are shut."

He grinned. "Too right."

"The pub's shut in Willstown, too, on Sundays."

"The bar's shut," he said. "You can usually get it out of Ma Connor, round the back."

She rolled over in the water. "I'll have to tip off Sergeant Haines, Joe. Sunday's the best day of all for the ice cream parlour at Alice. All the men who are in the bar all the week come along with their wives and kids on Sunday to the ice cream parlour and put down ice cream sodas and Coca-Cola. That place does a roaring trade on Sundays."

"It would," he said thoughtfully. "There'd be nothing else to do."

They got out of the sea presently and went and sat in the shade; he would not let her stay in long for fear of sunburn. When they were smoking together under the trees, he said, "It's going to cost a hell of a lot of money, all this you want to do. Three or four thousand pounds, I'd say, or more than that."

"I've got enough," she said.

He turned to her. "Mr. Strachan told me you were a wealthy woman," he said quietly. "It worried me, that did, till I got used to the idea. How much have you got? Don't tell me if you'd rather not say, but if I knew about how much I'd be able to help you more."

"Of course," she said. Nothing would come between them now, after last night. "Mr. Strachan says I've got about fifty-three thousand pounds. It's all in trust for me until I'm thirty-five, though. If I want to spend capital before then, I've got to ask him."

"Oh my word."

"It is a lot of money, isn't it?" she said. "I'm glad that it's in trust for me in a way, because I wouldn't in the least know what to do with it. And Noel has been such a dear." She paused. "I want to do something useful with it," she said. "I don't know anything about real business. The only thing I know about at all is what Pack and Levy made. I thought if we could start a little workshop of that sort, and a shop where women could get things they like—well, even if it didn't pay very well, it'd be using money the way money ought to be used, in places like Willstown."

He bent and kissed her. "There's another thing, Joe," she said. "I don't know, but I've got a sort of feeling that there's more to it than just employing a few girls. You say the ringers are all leaving the Gulf Country, and men won't come to the outback. Well, of course they won't if they can't get a girl. And all the girls go because they can't get a job. For every girl I make a job for, I believe you'll get a man to work at Midhurst. Don't you think that's true?"

"I don't know." He stared out over the sea to the dim blue line of the Tableland. "It'd certainly help to have a flock of girls around. It can be lonely in the outback, oh my word."

A poignant realization of the solitude struck her. The long nights alone in the homestead, when "you couldn't get along in the outback without dogs." The sensitive, intelligent face of the manager of Carlisle, Eddie Page, who had married his illiterate, inarticulate lubra. She turned to him with quick understanding and sympathy. "I feel an awful pig asking you to wait," she said. He took her hand and squeezed it. "I do want to try and start this business before we get married, Joe," she said. She smiled at him. "You know, you're a pretty energetic lover. I don't believe you'll waste much time starting a family."

He grinned. "I won't go quicker than you want to."

"I want to have them, too." She pulled his head down to

her and kissed him. "But that means I'll only have six months for business after we get married, and then I'll have to begin thinking of other things. Joe, when do you start mustering?"

"After the wet," he said. "It was March this year because of the late season, but normally we'd start mustering about the middle of February."

"How long does the muster go on for?"

"About three weeks or a month. After that there's the branding of the calves, and driving the stock down to Julia Creek."

"Could we get married after the mustering, Joe? Say early in April?"

"Of course."

She said thoughtfully, "That would mean that I'd have nearly a year from now, to get it to the stage when I could leave the business for a month or two while we start your family. I think that's fair enough. If it couldn't run without me for a month by then the whole thing wouldn't be much good, and we'd better pack it up."

He said, "I'll be around, of course."

She laughed. "Handing out ice creams and selling lipsticks to young girls. I won't ask you to do that, Joe."

He thought about this programme. "Jim could drive the stores alone down to Julia Creek," he said, "while we're getting married. I'd send Bourneville and some of the other boongs with him. Then we could drive down in the utility and catch him up about the time he got there, and put them on the train. Have it as a kind of honeymoon."

She smiled. "I like your idea of a honeymoon." He grinned. "Is there anything to do in Julia Creek, Joe, except drink beer?"

"Oh my word," he said. "There's plenty to do in Julia Creek."

"What is there to do there?"

"Put fifteen hundred cattle into railway trucks." He grinned at her. "There's not many English girls get a chance of a honeymoon like that," he said.

They went and changed for lunch, and over lunch he said, "About this tanning and dressing the alligator skins. I'd give that away." He was very much against attempting to do that in Willstown; it was messy work, unsuitable for girls, and no men were available to do it. He told her that there was a tannery in Cairns who could dress any skins she sent them. "A joker called Gordon runs it," he said. "He was over in the Gulf Country last year. We could go and see him to-morrow afternoon, if you like."

"Would he have any white kid basils, do you think?"

"Might do. If not he'll probably get them."

With his knowledge of station management he was a great help to her with suggestions for the workshop. "I'd make it good and big, while you're at it," he said. "It's the transport of the wood to Willstown that's going to cost the money." He thought for a minute. "There's three of you new girls coming in to live in Willstown, if all goes right," he said. "You and this Rose Sawyer and this Aggie Topp. Why don't you make your workshop building a bit bigger and have three bed-sitting-rooms at the end, walled off from the rest of it and with a separate entrance? Then you wouldn't have to live in the hotel and you'd be all comfortable by your-selves. Then if the business grows you can pull down the wall and throw it all in to one." This seemed to her to be a very good idea indeed.

They got a paper and pencil after lunch and jotted down a few essential things to do in Cairns when they got back there, and orders to be placed. Then they retired to their own huts and slept in the heat of the day. She was roused by Joe calling her outside her hut. "Come on and bathe," he was saying. "It's nearly five o'clock."

She pulled the sheet over quickly. "I won't be a minute. Have you been looking in?"

"I wouldn't do a thing like that."

"I wish I could believe you." She pulled the curtain across and put on her bathing dress, and joined him on the beach. And lying with him in the warm blue and silvery water on the sand, she said, "Joe, do you want us to be engaged, with a ring and everything?"

"You'd like that, wouldn't you?"

She shook her head. "Not unless it would prevent you worrying. I'll marry you early in April, Joe—that's dinkum." He smiled. "But for the present, I believe we'd get on better if we weren't officially engaged." She turned to him. "You see, when we get back to Willstown I'll be doing some pretty odd things, things that Willstown people will think crazy. Some of them may be, because there'll probably be some mistakes. I don't want you to have to be mixed up in it, just because we're engaged. You've got a position to keep up."

"Wouldn't it help if people thought I was with you in whatever you're doing?"

She smiled, and rolled over and kissed him. "You're all

salt. It wouldn't help if you get in a fight every Saturday night in the bar because somebody says something rude about your fiancée." He grinned. "They will, you know. They're bound to think I'm crackers."

They got out of the water presently and sat in the shade of the trees, talking and talking about the future. "Joe," she said once, "what do I do if a boong comes into the ice cream parlour and wants a soda? A boong stockrider? Do I serve him in the same place, or has he got to have a different shop?"

He scratched his head. "I dunno that it's ever happened in Willstown. They go into Bill Duncan's store. I don't think you could serve them in an ice cream parlour, with a white girl behind the counter."

She said firmly, "Then I'll have to have another parlour for them with a black girl in it. There's such a lot of them, Joe—we can't cut them out. We'll have two parlours, with the freezes and the kitchen between." She drew a little diagram on the white sand with her forefinger. "Like this."

"Oh my word," he said. "You're going to start some talk in Willstown."

She nodded. "I know. That's why I don't want us to be engaged till just before we're married."

In the evening as they kissed good night between their bedroom huts, she said, "We won't be able to do this in Willstown. I'll remember this Green Island all my life, Joe."

He grinned. "Come back here in April, if you like. Before Julia Creek."

They left next morning, when Ernie came for them with his motor boat, and landed at Cairns early in the afternoon. They took their bags to the hotel, and then went straight to see Mr. Gordon at the tannery, and spent an hour with him discussing alligator skins and other shoe materials. He advised them to dismiss the idea of kid for linings. "Anything that can be done with kid we'll do for you with wallaby," he said. "You've got any amount of wallaby out there, and it's as good as kid—texture, appearance, bleaching, glazing—anything you like." Harman arranged to send him half a dozen skins for sample treatment by the next lorry. "Be a good thing to keep down some of these wallabies," he said. "They eat an awful lot of feed out on the station. Too many of them altogether."

They spent the rest of the afternoon shopping and ordering, and got back to the hotel at dusk, tired out, having booked their passages to Willstown upon the morning plane.

Jean said, "There's one thing I must do tonight, Joe, before leaving Cairns. I must write to Noel Strachan and tell him what's happened."

In the warm, scented night of early summer by the Queensland Sea, she sat down on the verandah after tea and wrote me a long letter. Joe Harman sat beside her as she wrote, smoking quietly, at peace.

She was very good about writing, and she still is; she still writes every week. I got that letter early in November; I remember it so well. It was a foggy, dark morning with a light rain or drizzle falling. I had to have the electric light on for breakfast, and the Palace stables on the other side of the road were hardly visible. In the street below the taxis went past with a wet swish of mud and water on the wet wood blocks.

It was a long letter from a very happy girl, telling me about her love. I was delighted at the news, of course. I sat reading it with my breakfast before me, and then I read it through again, and then I read it a third time. When I woke up to realities my coffee was cold and the fried egg had frozen to the dish in front of me in cold, congealed fat, but I was too absorbed in her news to want it. I went into my bedroom to put my shoes and coat on for the office, and as I opened the wardrobe to get my coat I saw her boots and skates, that I had been keeping for her till she came back for them. Old men get rather silly, sometimes, and I must say that that rather dashed me for a moment, because she wouldn't be coming back for them. She wouldn't be coming back to England ever again.

I went to the front door, and my charwoman was in the flat, just coming out of the dining-room. "Such good news, Mrs. Chambers," I said. "Do you remember Miss Paget, who used to come here sometimes? She's got engaged to be married, to an Australian, out in Queensland."

"Oh, I am glad," she said. "Such a nice lady, she was."

"Yes, wasn't she?" I repeated. "Such a nice lady."

She said, "You didn't eat your breakfast, sir. Was everything all right?"

"Yes, quite all right, thanks, Mrs. Chambers," I said. "I didn't want anything this morning."

It was cold and raw out in the street, one of those yellow foggy mornings with a reeking chill that makes you cough. I walked on towards the office in a dream, thinking about wallabies and laughing black stockriders, about blue water running over the white coral sands, about Jean Paget and the trouble she had had with her sarong in that hot country where all clothes are a burden. Then there was a fierce, rending squeal right on top of me, and a heavy blow on my right arm so that I staggered and nearly fell, and I was in the middle of Pall Mall with a taxi broadside on across the road beside me. I didn't know where I was for a moment, and then I heard the white-faced driver saying, "For Christ's sake. You can think yourself bloody lucky that you're still alive."

"I'm sorry," I said. "I wasn't looking where I was going."

"Stepping out into the road like that," he said angrily. "Ought to have more sense, at your age. Did I hit you?"

A little crowd was starting to collect. "Only my arm," I said. I moved it, and it worked all right. "It's nothing."

"Well, that's a bloody miracle," he said. "Look out where you're going to next time." He put his gear in, straightened up his taxi, and drove on; I walked on to the office.

The girl brought in the letters for me to go through, as usual, but I put them on one side in favour of another letter that I had in my breast pocket. I had a client or two that morning, I suppose; I usually have, and I suppose I gave them some advice, but my mind was twelve thousand miles away. Lester Robinson came in once with some business or other and I said to him, "You remember my Paget girl—the heir to that Macfadden estate? She's got herself engaged to be married to an Australian. He seems to be a very good chap."

He grunted. "I forget. Does that terminate our trust?"

"No," I said. "That goes on for some time to come. Till she's thirty-five."

"Pity," he said. "It's made a lot of work for you, that trust has. It'll be a good thing when it's all wound up."

"It's been no trouble, really," I said. By the end of the day I think I knew her letter by heart although it was eight quarto pages long, but I took it with me to the club. I had a glass of sherry in the bar and told Moore about her engagement because he knew something about her story, and after dinner we sat down to a couple of rubbers of bridge, Dennison and Strickland and Callaghan, the four of us who play together every evening, and I told them about her.

I got up from the table at about eleven o'clock, and went into the library for a final cigarette before going back across the park to my flat. The big room was empty but for Wright, who had been in the Malay Police and knew her story. I

212

dropped down into a chair beside him, and remarked, "You know that girl, Jean Paget? I think I've spoken to you about her once or twice before."

He smiled. "You have."

"She's got herself engaged to be married," I told him. "To the manager of a cattle station, in Northern Queensland."

"Indeed?" he said. "What's he like?"

"I've met him," I replied. "He's a very good chap. She's very much in love with him. I think they're going to be very happy."

"Is she coming back to England before getting married?" he asked.

I sat staring at the rows of books upon the wall, the gold-embossed carving at the corner of the ceiling. "No," I said. "I don't think she's ever coming back to England, ever again."

He was silent.

"It's too far," I said. "I think she'll make her life in Queensland now."

There was a long pause. "After all, there's no reason why she should come back to England," I said at last. "There's nothing for her to come back for. She's got no ties in this country."

And then he said a very foolish thing. He meant it well enough, but it was a stupid thing to say. I got up and left him and went home to my dark, empty flat, and I avoided meeting him for some time after that. I was seventy-three years old that autumn, old enough to be her grandfather. I couldn't possibly have been in love with her myself.

Chapter 9

IN THE months of November and December that year Jean Paget worked harder than she had ever worked before.

Rose Sawyer joined her in Willstown within a fortnight, and Aggie Topp sailed early in November. I got Mr. Pack to send Aggie to see me before she left. She was a gaunt, rather prim woman, but I could see at once that Pack had been quite right; if anyone could make girls work this woman could. I gave her her ticket and a typed sheet of instructions telling her how she would get by air from Sydney to Willstown, and then I talked to her about the job.

"You know, it's very, very rough," I said. "It's rough, and it's hot, and Miss Paget is having to start absolutely from nothing. She's got plenty of money, but it's going to be hard, all the time. You understand that, Mrs. Topp?"

She said, "I've had two letters from Miss Paget, and she sent a photograph of the place, the main street. It don't look up to much, I must say."

"You're quite happy to go out there, are you?"

She said, "Oh, well, I've been in rough places before. It's only for a year to start with, anyway." And then she said, "I always liked Miss Paget."

I had another matter to fix up with Aggie Topp. Jean was very anxious to get hold of an air-conditioning unit, a thing about the size of a small refrigerator which stood in the room and took hot air into itself and pumped it out cold into the room; it seemed to her important to have this to prevent the girls' hands from sweating as they worked and marking the delicate leathers of the shoes. She had not been able to get hold of one in Australia and had cabled me, and I had found a firm that made them and got hold of one with a good deal of difficulty and some small payments on the side. Derek Harris is rather good at that sort of negotiation. I had it in our office standing at the foot of the stairs and I showed it to Mrs. Topp, and arranged for her to take it out with her to Syndney. From Sydney it would have to be flown up with her to Cairns and Willstown at some considerable expense, but it seemed to me to be worth it since it was then the hottest time of the year.

This was the biggest commission that I got from Jean and was my own main contribution to the venture; the remainder of her cables were concerned with little bits of things that were no trouble. Aggie Topp took out with her a good deal of stuff from Pack and Levy, too; three cases full of tools and lasts and formers and all sort of things, the bill for which came to about a hundred and forty-six pounds, which I paid for Jean in England.

Joe Harman helped her to get the buildings started on the day that they arrived in Willstown. They had a meeting with Tim Whelan and his two sons, in the carpenter's shop amongst the coffins. They had already placed orders for two lorry loads of lumber in Cairns. The men stood or sat squatting, ringer fashion, on the floor with papers on the floor before them, planning the layout of the buildings; the workshop with its three-bedroom annexe was to be built first, and after that the ice cream parlour next to it, leaving room for the expansion of the workshop one way and of the ice cream parlour the other way. There were no great difficulties of expansion in the built-up area of Willstown.

They sent Tim Whelan presently to find Mr. Carter, the Shire Clerk, to pass the plans of the new buildings and to grant a lease of the site in the main street. "It'll be all right there," he said thoughtfully. "There was a whole row of houses there in 1905—I've got a photograph. But nobody ever paid rent for that land in my time." Jean asked what rent would be required for the area she wanted, a difficult matter to decide in view of the fact that no plans existed and the area that she wanted was quite uncertain. "This is a town borough," Mr. Carter said. "You don't lease land upon an acreage basis in a town borough. If you're going to develop the land by building, then I'd say about a shilling a year for each hundred foot of frontage. It's in the main street, you see. If you wanted it for chickens or anything like that I'd have to charge five shillings."

They adjourned to the bar of the hotel to seal the contracts; Jean sat on the steps outside with a lemonade, as was fitting for a lady with a reputation to preserve in Willstown.

She went to Brisbane a week later, flying to Cairns and flying on the same day down to Brisbane. She stayed there for three days and came back, having ordered an electric generating set, a very large refrigerator, two deep freezes, a stainless steel counter, eight glass-topped tables, thirty-two chairs, two sink units, and a mass of minor shop-fittings, glasses, plates, cutlery, and furnishings as well as a good deal of electrical fittings and cable. She made arrangements with the firms for all this stuff to be crated and consigned to Forsayth; in Cairns she made arrangements for the truck transport of these goods from Forsayth to Willstown. I had arranged the necessary credits for her and she was able to pay cash for everything.

She came back to Willstown a week later having made tentative arrangements for supplies of stock for her ice cream parlour, and found the framework of the workshop already erected; a wooden building goes up very quickly. The matter was a nine-days' wonder in Willstown and old men used to stand around wondering at this midsummer madness of an English girl, a stranger to the Gulf Country, who proposed to make shoes there and send them all the way to England to be sold. They were too kindly to be rude to her or to laugh at such an eccentricity, but an aura of disbelief surrounded the whole venture and made her feel very much alone in those first weeks.

She visited Midhurst at a very early stage, one Sunday when no work was going on upon her building. Joe Harman drove in to fetch her in his big utility at dawn one day, and took her back to Midhurst in time for breakfast. As soon as they were out of sight of the town they stopped for five minutes to kiss and talk.

Presently they disentangled and went on. Jean was accustomed by this time to the idea that no road in this country had a metalled surface. She had not been beyond the town hitherto; very soon she discovered that a road was where the car drove across country. The land was parched and dry with the heat of summer, covered with thin tufts of scorched grass. It was a wooded land, covered thinly with spindly, distorted eucalyptus gum trees averaging twenty to thirty feet in height; these trees were fairly widely spaced so that it was possible for a car or truck driven across country to find a way between them. This was the road, and when the surface of the earth became too deeply pitted and potholed with traffic the cars and trucks would deviate and choose another course. These tracks followed the same general direction, coming together at the fords where creeks, now dry and stony, had to be crossed, and fanning out again upon the other side.

Once in the twenty miles she saw half a dozen cattle, that stampeded wildly at the noise of the utility as it bounced and rocketed over the uneven ground. She asked Joe what on earth the cattle found to eat; the ground seemed to her to be completely barren. "They get along," he said. "There's plenty here for them to eat, my word. This dry stuff in the tussocks, why, it's just the same as hay." He told her that there was a water hole a little way from their track. "They never go more than three or four miles from water," he said. "Horses, now— you'll find them grazing up to twenty miles from a drink."

Once she exclaimed at three brown, furry forms bounding away among the trees. "Oh, Joe—kangaroos!"

He corrected her. "Wallabies. We don't get any 'roos up in these parts."

She stared after the flying forms, entranced. "What's the difference between a wallaby and a kangaroo, Joe?"

"A wallaby's smaller," he said. "A big, buck kangaroo, he'll stand up to six feet high, but a wallaby's not more than four. A kangaroo, he's got a face like a deer. A wallaby, he's got a face like a rabbit, or a rat. I got a little wallaby to show you at the homestead."

"A wild one?"

"He's a tame one now. He'll get wild as he grows older; then he'll go off to his own folks." He told her that when they had shot the wallabies to send the sample skins to Cairns for her they had shot a doe with a joey, and rather than leave the small defenceless creature to die they had taken it home to rear. "I like a wallaby about the place," he said.

They came to Midhurst presently. A fence of two wire strands tacked to the trees, with an occasional post in the wider gaps, crossed their path, with an iron gate; beyond the gate the track became the semblance of a road. She got out of the utility and opened the gate and he drove through. "This is the home paddock," he said. "For horses, mostly." She could see horses standing underneath the trees, lean riding horses, swishing long black tails. "I've got about three square miles fenced off like this around the house."

The road swung round, and she saw Midhurst homestead. It was prettily situated on a low hill above the bend of a creek; this creek was not running, but there were still pools of water held along its length. "Of course, you're seeing it at the worst time of year," he said, and she became aware of his anxiety. "It's a lovely little river in the winter, oh my word. But even in the worst part of the dry, like now, there's always water there."

The homestead was a fairly large building that stood high off the ground on posts, so that you climbed eight feet up a flight of steps to reach the verandah and the one floor of the house. It was built of wood and had the inevitable corrugated-iron roof. Four rooms, three bedrooms and one sitting-room, were surrounded on all four sides by a verandah twelve feet deep; masses of ferns and greenery of all sorts stood in pots and on stands on this verandah at the outer edge and killed most of the direct rays of the sun. There was a kitchen annexe at one end and a bathroom annexe at the other; the toilet was a little hut over a pit in the paddock, some distance from the house. Most of the life of the building evidently went on in the verandah and the rooms seemed to be little used; in the verandah were Joe's bed and his mosquito net, and several cane easy chairs, and the dining-room table and chairs. Suspended from the rafters was a large canvas water bag cooling in the draught, with an enamelled mug hung from it by a string.

Five or six dogs greeted them noisily as the utility came to a standstill before the steps. Joe brushed them aside, but pointed out a large blue and yellow bitch like no dog Jean had ever seen before. "That's Lily," he said fondly. "She had a bonza litter, oh my word."

He took her up into the coolness of the verandah; she turned to him. "Oh, Joe, this is nice!"

"Like it?" Puppies were surging about them, grovelling and licking their hands; odd-shaped yellow and blue puppies. Along the verandah a small animal stood erect behind a chair, peering at them around the corner. He took the puppies one by one and dropped them into a wire-netting enclosure in one corner. "I let them out this morning before driving in," he said. "They'll be big enough to go down in the yard pretty soon."

"Joe, who fixed up these plants? Did you?"

He shook his head. "Mrs. Spears did that, when she used to live here. I keep them going. The lubras water them, morning and evening." He told her that he had three Abo women, wives of three of his stockriders, who shared the domestic duties of the homestead and cooked for him.

He looked around. "There's the joey somewhere." They found the little wallaby lolloping about on the other side of the verandah; it stood like a little kangaroo about eighteen inches high, and had no fear of them. Jean stooped beside it and it nibbled at her fingers. "What do you feed it on, Joe?"

"Bread and milk. It's doing fine on that."

"Don't the puppies hurt it?"

"They chase it now and then, but it can kick all right. A full-grown wallaby can kill a dog. Rip him right up." He paused, watching her caress the little creature, thinking how lovely she was. "It's all in fun," he said. "They get along all right. By and by when he gets bigger and the dogs are bigger he'll get angry with them, and then he'll go off into the bush."

A fat, middle-aged lubra, a black golliwog of a woman, laid the table and presently appeared with two plates of the inevitable steak with two eggs on the top, and a pot of strong tea. Jean had become accustomed to the outback breakfast by this time but this steak was tougher than most; she made mental notes to look into the Midhurst cooking as she struggled with it. In the end she gave up and sat back laughing. "I'm sorry, Joe," she said. "It's because I'm English, I suppose."

He was very much concerned. "Have a couple more fried eggs. You haven't eaten anything."

"I've eaten six times as much as I ever ate in England for breakfast, Joe. Who does the cooking?"

"Palmolive did this," he said. "It's her day. Mary cooks much better, but it's her day off."

"Who are they, Joe?"

"I've got a ringer called Moonshine," he said. "Palmolive's his gin. My boss Abo, he's called Bourneville; he's a bonza boy. Mary's his gin. Mary cooks all right."

"Tell me, Joe," she said, "do you ever get any indigestion?"

He grinned. "Not very often. Just now and then."

"You won't mind if I reorganize the cooking a bit when I come in?"

"Not so long as you don't do it all yourself," he said.

"You wouldn't like me to do that?"

He shook his head. "I'd rather see you keep time for the things you want to do, the shoes, and the ice cream parlour, and that."

She touched his hand. "I want to keep time for you."

He took her out before the heat of the day and showed her the establishment. Although the property covered over a thousand square miles, there were no more buildings round the homestead than she had seen on a four-hundred-acre farm in England. There were three or four cottages of two rooms at the most, for stockriders; there were two small bunk houses for unmarried ringers, white and black. There was a shed housing the truck and the utility and a mass of oddments of machinery. There was a stable for about six horses, which was empty, and a saddle room, and a butcher's room. There was a diesel engine that drove an electric generator and pumped water from the creek. That was about all.

Once he said, "Can you ride a horse?"

She shook her head. "I'm afraid not, Joe. Ordinary people don't ride horses much in England."

"Oh my word," he said. "You should be able to do that."

"Could I learn?"

"Too right."

He put his fingers in his mouth like a schoolboy and blew a shrill whistle; a black head came poking out of the window of a single-room cottage. "Bourneville," he called. "Get out and bring in Auntie and Robin, 'n saddle up. I'll be down to help you in a minute."

He turned to her, surveying her cotton frock. "I dunno about your things. Could you get into a pair of my strides, or would you rather not?"

She laughed. "Oh, Joe, they'd go round me twice!"

"I wasn't always as fat as this," he said. "I got a pair I used to wear before the war, I can't get into now. It doesn't matter if they don't fit right; we'll only be walking the horses so you'll see what it feels like."

He took her up into the homestead and produced a clean man's shirt and a faded pair of jodhpurs and a belt for her; she took them from him laughing, and went into his spare room and put them on, with a pair of his elastic-sided, thin-soled riding boots that were far too big for her. It gave her a queer feeling of possession to be dressed all in his clothes. She walked gingerly down into the yard with the feeling that everything was likely to fall off her, as it had done on another memorable occasion.

He helped her up into the saddle; once astride the patient, fourteen-year-old Auntie the feeling of insecurity left her. They adjusted her stirrups and showed her how to set her foot; once she was fairly settled she felt very safe. She knew little about horses or saddlery at that time, but this saddle was like no saddle she had ever seen in England, even in a picture. It rose up in an arch high behind her seat and high in front of her, so that she was seated as in a hammock. There was a great horn that projected above each of her thighs and another one under each thigh, so that she was as if clamped into place. "I don't believe that any one could fall off from a saddle like this," she said.

"You aren't meant to fall off," he replied.

They walked the horses out of the yard and down the track to the creek; as they went he showed her how to hold the reins and how to use her heels. He took her up the creek for about a mile and then by a wide circuit through the bush, winding beneath the trees so far as possible to seek the shade. Once she saw four scurrying black forms vanishing among the trees and he told her that these were wild pig, and once in a wide stretch of water covered with water lilies there was a violent swirl of water as an alligator dived away from them. She saw several wallabies bounding away before their horses.

They returned to the homestead after an hour or so. Although they had walked the horses all the way Jean was drenched with sweat under the hot sun, and she had a raging thirst. In the verandah she drank several mugs of water, and then she went into the bathroom and had a shower, and changed back into her own cool clothes.

They lunched in the verandah on steak and bread and jam, a repeat of breakfast without the eggs. "Palmolive hasn't got much imagination in the matter of tucker," he said apologetically.

"She's looking very tired," Jean said. "Great black circles under her eyes. Give her the afternoon off, Joe. I'll make tea for you."

He offered her the use of the spare room bed to sleep on after lunch, but they had seen so little of each other in the last fortnight that the time seemed too precious to waste in sleep. "Let's sit out here," she said. "If I should go to sleep, Joe, it'll be just one of those things." So they pulled two of the long cane chairs to the corner of the verandah where there might be a little breeze, and sat together close, so that they could touch hands. "It's not always as hot as this," he said, still anxious for her approval of the place. "Just these two months are the bad ones. By January it'll be beginning to cool off, when the rain gets properly under way."

"It's not too bad," she said. "I remember times when it was quite as hot as this in Malaya."

She led him on to tell her about his work on the station; having seen a little of the terrain that morning she felt she could appreciate what he told her better now. "There's not a lot to do this time of year," he said. "I like to get up to the top end of the station once a fortnight, if I can, in case of duffers. Make a cache or two of tucker up there, too, this time of year, and shoot the worst of the scrub bulls you see around."

"What's a duffer, Joe?"

"Why, cattle duffers—cattle thieves. We've not had much of it this year. Sometimes the drovers coming down to Julia Creek from the Cape stations—they pick up a few as they go through the property and put them with the herd. It means faking the brands, of course, and there's the police at Julia to keep an eye open for fresh-branded beasts as they go on the train. They caught a joker at it two years ago and he got six months. We've not had much since then. Poddy dodging, now—well, that's another matter."

"What's poddy dodging, Joe?" She was beginning to grow sleepy, but she wanted to know all she could.

"Why, a poddy's a cleanskin, a calf born since the last

muster that hasn't been branded. Some of these jokers, even your best friends, they'll come on to your station and round up the poddys and drive them off on to their own land, and then there's nothing to say they're yours. That's poddy dodging, that is. It's a fair cow. Of course, there's always cattle crossing the boundaries because there aren't any fences, so it's a bit of a mix-up generally when you come to muster. But I've been on stations where there weren't hardly any poddys there at all when we come to muster. All the jokers on the other stations had got them."

She said, "But do the poddys just stay on the new land? Don't they want to go back to mother?"

He glanced at her, appreciating the question. "That's right —they would if you let them. They'd go straight back to their own herd on their own land, even if it was fifty miles. But what these jokers do is this. They build a little corral on their land in some place where no one wouldn't ever think to look, and they drive your poddys into it. Then they leave them there for four or five days without food or water—don't give them nothing at all. Well, if you do that to a poddy he goes sort of silly and forgets about the herd, and mother. All he wants is a drink of water, same as you or I. Then you let him out and let him drink his fill at a water hole. He's had such a thirst he won't leave that water hole for months. He forgets all about his own place, and just stays in his new home."

Her eyes closed, and she slept. When she woke up the sun was lower in the sky, and Joe had left her. She got up and sponged her face in the bathroom, and saw him outside working on the engine of the truck. She tidied herself up, looked at her watch, and went to investigate the kitchen.

Primitive was the word, she thought. There was a woodburning hearth which mercifully was out, and a wick-burning oil stove; this was the cooking equipment. There was a small kerosene refrigerator. Masses of cooked meat were stored in a wire-gauze meat safe with nearly as many flies inside it as there were outside. The utensils were old-fashioned and dirty and few in number; it was a nightmare of a kitchen. Jean felt that the right course would be to burn it down and start again, and she wondered if this could be done without burning down the house as well. There was little in the store cupboard but staple foods such as flour and salt and soap.

She put on a kettle to boil for tea and looked around for something to cook, other than meat. Eggs were plentiful at Midhurst and she found some stale cheese; she went and consulted Joe, and then came back and made him a cheese omelette with eight eggs. He cleaned his hands and came and watched her while she did it. "Oh my word," he said. "Where did you learn cooking?"

"In Ealing," she said, and it all seemed very far away; the grey skies, the big red buses, and the clamour of the Underground. "I had a sort of little kitchenette with an electric cooker. I always used to cook myself a two-course evening meal."

He grinned awkwardly. "Afraid you won't find many electric cookers in the outback."

She touched his hand. "I know that, Joe. But there are lots of things that could be done here to make it a bit easier." As they ate their tea they talked about the kitchen and the house. "It's just the kitchen that needs altering," she said. "The rest of it is lovely."

"I'll get a toilet fixed up in the house before you come," he promised her. "It's all right for me going out there, but it's not nice for you."

She laughed. "I don't mind that, so long as you keep up the supplies of *The Saturday Evening Post*." He grinned, but she found him set upon this alteration. "Some places have a septic tank and everything," he said. "They put one in at Augustus when the Duke and Duchess stayed there. I reckon that we'll have to wait a while for that."

They ate their tea out on the verandah as the sun went down, and sat looking out over the creek and the bush, smoking and talking quietly. "What are you doing next week?" she asked. "Will you be in town, Joe?"

He nodded. "I'll be in on Thursday, or Friday at the latest. I'm going up to the top end tomorrow for a couple of days, just see what's going on."

She smiled. "Looking after the poddys?"

He grinned. "That's right. It's a bit difficult this time of year, in the dry, because the tracks don't show so good. I got a boy called Nugget on the station now, and he's a bonza tracker, oh my word. I'm taking him up with me. I've got a kind of feeling that Don Curtis, up on Windermere station, he's been at my poddys."

"What would you do if you found tracks, then, Joe? Tracks leading off your land and on to his?"

He grinned. "Go after them and find 'em and drive 'em back," he said. "Hope Don doesn't come along while we're doing it."

He drove her into Willstown at about nine o'clock that

night; they halted for a while outside the town to say good night in proper style. She lay against his shoulder with his arm around her, listening to the noises of the bush, the croaking of the frogs, the sound of crickets, and the crying of a night bird. "It's a lovely place you live in, Joe," she said. "It just wants a new kitchen, that's all. Don't ever worry about me not liking it."

He kissed her. "It'll be all ready for you when you come."

"April," she said. "Early in April, Joe."

She started up the shoe workshop in the first week of December, three or four days after Aggie Topp arrived. To start with she had five girls, Judy Small and her friend Lois Strang, and Annie, whose figure was beginning to deteriorate and who had been sacked from the hotel, and two fifteen-year-olds who had recently left school. For cleanliness and to mark the fact that they were working in a regular job she put everyone into a green overall coat in the workshop, and gave them a mirror on the wall so that they could see what they looked like.

From the first days she found that the fifteen-year-olds were the best employees. Girls straight from school were used to the discipline of regular hours of work; she seldom got the girls from outback homes to settle down to it so well as the younger ones. The monotony was irksome to the older girls who had left school for some years, or who had never been to school at all. She tried to help them by ordering an automatic-changing gramophone from Cairns, with a supply of records; the music certainly intrigued and amused the whole of Willstown and may have helped the older girls a little, but not much. The big attraction of the workshop was the air conditioner.

The air conditioner was the best recruiting agent of the lot. In that torrid summer heat which ranged between a hundred and a hundred and ten degrees at midday, she managed to keep the temperature of the workshop down to about seventy degrees, at which the girls could work without their hands sweating. For the girls it meant that they got respite from the heat of the day, and music to listen to, and the novelty of a clean green overall to wear, and money in their pockets at the end of the week. The workshop was popular from the first, and Jean never had any difficulty in getting as many recruits for it as she could handle. For the early months, however, she was content with five.

She spent a hectic fortnight after the workshop opened getting the ice cream parlour furnished and stocked. She was resolved to have this open by Christmas Day, and she achieved her aim by opening on December 20th. On Joe's advice she only opened half of it at first, leaving the parlour for the Abos till it was established that they wanted ice cream. This saved her the wages of a coloured girl and the expense of furnishing. In fact, it was not for nearly a year that the demand arose and Abo ringers started hanging round the kitchen door to buy an ice cream soda. She opened the coloured annexe in the following September.

She stood with Joe outside in the blazing sunlit street on that first afternoon, looking at what she had done. The workshop and the ice cream parlour stood more or less side by side on the main street. The windows of the workshop were closed to keep the cool air in, but they could hear the girls singing as they worked over the shoes. Christmas was near, and they were singing carols—*Holy Night*, and *Good King Wenceslas*, and *See Amid the Winter Snow*. The shirt was sticking to Jean's back and she shifted her shoulders to get a little air inside. "Well, there it all is," she said. "Now we've got to see if we can make it pay."

"Come on and I'll buy you a soda," he said. "That'll help." They went in and bought a soda from Rose Sawyer behind the counter. "This part of it'll pay," he said. "I don't know about the shoes, but this should do all right. I was talking to George Connor up at the hotel. He's getting very worried about his bar, with you starting up."

"I don't see why he's got anything to worry about," she said. "I'm not going to sell beer."

"You're going to sell drinks to ringers," he remarked. "If you had a bar instead of this, wouldn't it rile you?"

She laughed. "I suppose it would. I can't see myself putting the bar out of business, Joe."

"I can see you doing all right, all the same." As they sat at the little chromium glass-topped table, Pete Fletcher came in shyly and sidled up to the bar and ordered an ice cream, and began chatting with Rose Sawyer. Joe said, "Poor old George Connor." They laughed together, and then he said, "I bet you don't keep Rose six months."

Jean had seen a good deal of Rose Sawyer in the last month. "I'll take you," she said. "Bet you a quid she's still there in a year from now, Joe." They shook hands on it according to the custom of the place. "If she is," he said, "it'll be a miracle."

Now that the businesses were started, she was very tired; she felt slack and listless in the great heat, drained of all energy. She would have liked to go out with Joe to Mid-hurst that evening and live quietly there for a day or two, sleeping and riding and playing with the little wallaby. A cautionary instinct warned her not to offend against the rural code of morals by an indiscretion of that sort; if she was to make a success of what she had set out to do for women in that place her own behaviour would have to be above reproach. No mothers in the outback, she knew, would care to let their daughters work for her if it were known that she was spending nights alone at Midhurst with Joe Harman; no married man would care to bring his wife and daughters to an ice cream parlour run by a loose woman of that sort.

It was a Wednesday, but Sunday was no longer an off day for Jean since it was likely to be the biggest day of all for the ice cream and soft drinks. She arranged with Joe that he should call for her at the hotel soon after dawn and take her out to Midhurst for the day. She said good-bye to him and went to her room as soon as work stopped in the workshop, pausing only to see the girls from the workshop sampling the ice cream parlour. She went and lay down on her bed, exhausted and too tired to eat that night; it was refreshingly cool in the workshop building, for the air conditioner had been on all day. She took off her clothes and put on her pyjamas, and slept in the coolness; she slept so for twelve hours.

She had been out to Midhurst several times since that first visit, and had fitted herself out with a small pair of ringer's trousers in Bill Duncan's store for riding, with a pair of elastic-sided ringer's riding boots to match. She met Joe in the early morning with a little bundle of riding things under her arm, and got into the utility with him. As usual they drove a little way out of town and stopped for an exchange of mutual esteem; as he held her he asked, "How are you feeling this morning?"

She smiled. "I'm better now, Joe. It was the reaction, I suppose—getting it finished and open. I went to bed just after leaving you and slept right through. Twelve solid hours. I'm feeling fine."

"Take things very easy today," he said.

She stroked his hair. "Dear Joe. It's going to be much easier from now on."

"This bloody weather'll break soon," he said. "We'll get rain starting within the week, and after that it'll begin to get cool."

They drove on presently. "Joe," she said. "I had an awful row this week with the Bank Manager—Mr. Watkins. Did you hear about it?"

He grinned. "I did hear something," he admitted. "What really happened?"

"It was the flies," she said. "It was so hot on Friday, and I was so tired. I went into that miserable little bank to cash the wages cheque and you know how full of flies it always is. I had to wait a few minutes and the flies started crawling all over me, in my hair and in my mouth and in my eyes. I was sweating, I suppose. I lost my temper, Joe. I oughtn't to have done that."

"It's a crook place, that bank is," he observed. "There's no reason why it should have all those flies. What did you say?"

"Everything," she said simply. "I told him I was closing my account because I couldn't stand his bloody flies. I said I was going to bank in Cairns and get the cash in by Dakota every week. I said I was going to write to his head office in Sydney and tell them why I'd done it, and I said I was going to write to the Bank of New South Wales and offer my account to them if they'd start up a branch here with no flies. I said I used a D.D.T. spray and I didn't get flies in my workshop and I wasn't going to have them in my bank. I said he ought to be setting an example to Willstown instead of . . ." She stopped.

"Instead of what?" he asked.

She said weakly, "I forget what I did say."

He stared straight ahead at the track. "I did hear in the bar you told him he ought to set an example instead of sitting on his arse and scratching."

"Oh, Joe, I couldn't have said that!"

He grinned. "That's what they're saying that you told him, in Willstown."

"Oh. . . ." They drove on in silence for a time. "I'll go in on Friday and apologize," she said. "It's no good making quarrels in a place like this."

"I don't see why you should apologize," he objected. "It's up to him to apologize to you. After all, you're the customer." He paused. "I'd go in there on Friday and see how he's getting on," he advised. "I know he got ten gallons of D.D.T. spray on Saturday because Al Burns told me."

When they got to Midhurst he made her go at once and sit in a long chair at the corner of the verandah with a glass of lemon squash made with cold water from the refrigerator.

He would not let her move for breakfast, but brought her a cup of tea and a boiled egg and some bread and butter on a tray. She sat there, relaxed, with the fatigue soaking out of her, content to have him gently fussing over her. When the day grew hot he suggested that she take the spare bedroom and lie down upon the bed leaving the double doors open at each end of the room to get the draught through; he promised, grinning, not to look if he passed along the verandah. She took him at his word and took off most of her clothes in the spare room and lay down on the bed and slept through the midday heat.

When she woke up it was nearly four o'clock and she was cool and rested and at ease. She lay for a while wondering if he had looked; then she got up and slipped her frock on and went to the shower, and stood for a long time under the warm stream of water. She came to him presently on the verandah, fresh and rested and full of fondness for him in his generosity, and found him squatting on the floor mending a bridle with palm, needle, and waxed thread. She stooped and kissed him, and said, "Thanks for everything, Joe. I had a lovely sleep." And then she said, "Can we go riding after tea?"

"Still a bit hot," he said. "Think that's a good thing?"

"I'd like to," she said. "I want to be able to sit on a horse properly."

He said, "You did all right last time." She had been promoted from the fourteen-year-old Auntie to the more energetic Sally and she was gradually learning how to trot. She found that trotting in that climate made her sweat more than the horse and made it difficult for her to sit down next day, but the exercise, she knew, was good for her. Starting at her age, she would never be a very good rider, but she was determined to achieve the ability to do it as a means of locomotion in that country.

They rode for an hour and a half that evening, coming back to Midhurst in the early dusk. He would not let her stay out longer than that, though she wanted to. "I'm not a bit tired now," she said. "I believe I'm getting the hang of this, Joe. It's much easier on Sally than it was on Auntie."

"Aye," he said. "The better the horse the less tiring for the rider, long as you can manage him."

"I'd like to come with you one day up to the top end," she said. "I suppose it'll have to be after we're married."

He grinned. "Plenty of wowsers back in Willstown to talk about it, if you came before."

"Do I ride well enough for that?"

"Oh, aye," he said. "Take it easy and you'd get along all right on Sally. I never travel more than twenty miles in the day, not unless there's some special reason."

He drove her into Willstown in the utility, and as they kissed good night he said he would be in during the following week. She went to bed that night rested and content, refreshed by her quiet day.

She went to the bank on Friday and cashed the wages cheque as usual; she found that the walls were in the process of being distempered and there was not a fly in the place. Mr. Watkins was distant in his manner and ignored her; Len James, the young bank clerk, gave her her money with a broad grin and a wink. She saw Len again on Saturday afternoon, when he brought in Doris Nash for an ice cream soda. He grinned at her, and said, "You wouldn't know the bank, Miss Paget."

"I was in there yesterday," she said."You're having it all distempered."

"That's right," he said. "You started something."

"Is he very sore?" she asked.

"Not really," the boy said. "He's been wanting to decorate for a long time, but he's been scared of what the head office would say. There's not a lot of turnover in a place like this, you know. Well, now he's doing it."

"I'm sorry I was rude," she said. "If you get a chance, tell him I said that."

"I will," he promised her. "I'm glad you were. Haven't had such a laugh for years. I don't like flies, either."

On that first Sunday she worked steadily in the ice cream parlour with Rose Sawyer from nine in the morning till ten o'clock at night. They sold a hundred and eighty-two ice creams at a shilling each and three hundred and forty-one soft drinks at sixpence. Dead tired, Jean counted the money in the till at the end of the day. "Seventeen pounds thirteen shillings," she said. She stared at Rose in wonder. "That doesn't seem so bad for a town with a hundred and forty-six people, all told. How much is that a head?"

"About two and six, isn't it?"

"Do you think it's going to go on like this?"

"I don't see why not. Lots of people didn't come in today. Most of them came in two or three times. Judy must have had about ten bob's worth."

"She can't keep that up," Jean said. "She'll be sick, and we'll get a recession. Come on and let's go to bed."

She opened the ice cream parlour after lunch on Christmas Day and took twenty pounds in the afternoon and evening. She had the gramophone from the workshop in the parlour that evening playing dance music so that the little wooden shack that was her ice cream parlour streamed out music and light into the dark wastes of the main street, and seemed to the inhabitants just like a bit of Manly Beach dropped down in Willstown. Old, withered women that Jean had never seen before came in that night with equally old men to have an ice cream soda, drawn by the lights and by the music. Although the parlour was still full of people she closed punctually at ten o'clock, thinking it better as a start to stick to the bar closing time and not introduce the complication of late hours and night life into a rural community.

The workshop went fairly steadily under Aggie Topp and they dispatched two packing cases of shoes to Forsayth just after Christmas to be sent by rail to Brisbane and by ship to England. She had already sent a few early samples of their work to Pack and Levy by air mail.

On Boxing Day the rain came. They had had one or two short showers before, but that day the clouds massed high in great peaks of cumulo nimbus that spread and covered the whole sky so that it grew dark. Then down it came, a steady, vertical torrent of rain that went on and on, unending. At first the conditions became worse, with no less heat and very high humidity; in the workshop the girls sweated freely even at seventy degrees, and Aggie Topp had to postpone the finishing operations and concentrate on the earlier, less delicate stages of the manufacture of shoes.

Jean went with Joe to Midhurst for a day soon after the New Year; as usual he called for her just after dawn. This time it was a grey dawn of hot, streaming rain; she scuttled quickly from the door of her room into the cab of the utility. By that time she was getting used to being wet through to the skin, and drying, and getting wet again; the water as it fell was nearly blood temperature and the chance of a chill was slight. She said as she got into the car, "What are the creeks like, Joe?"

"Coming up," he said. "Nothing to worry over yet." A time would come when for a few weeks he would be unable to reach Willstown from Midhurst in the utility, and would have to ride in if they were to meet at all. He had been stocking up with foodstuffs for the homestead in the last week or two. There were two creeks between Willstown and Midhurst, wide bottoms of sand and boulders that she knew as hot, arid places in the dry. Now they were wide streams of yellow, muddy water, rather terrifying to her. At the first one she said, "Can we get through that, Joe?"

"That's all right," he said. "It's only a foot deep. You see that tree there with the overhanging branch? When that branch gets covered, at the fork, it's a bit deep then."

They drove the utility ploughing through the water and emerged the other side; they forded the second creek in the same way, leaping from boulder to boulder, and went on to Midhurst. They got there as usual in time for breakfast. It was still streaming rain down in a steady torrent, too wet for any outdoor activity. They set to work after breakfast to plan out the new kitchen and the toilet he had set his heart on.

In Cairns that morning, four hundred miles to the east of them, Miss Jacqueline Bacon tripped delicately down the pavement in the rain from her home to the Cairns Ambulance and Fire Station. She wore a blue raincoat and she carried an umbrella. She hurried in between the fire engines, and shook the rain from her umbrella. She said to one of the firemen on duty, "My, isn't it wet?"

He sucked his empty pipe and stared out at the rain. "Fine weather for ducks."

She went into her little office off the main hall where the gleaming fire engines stood and glanced at the clock; she had still three minutes to go. The room was furnished with a table and with a microphone and a writing pad, and two tall metal cabinets of wireless gear; a set stood on the table before her pad. She turned three switches for the apparatus to warm up and took off her wet coat and her hat. Then she found her pencil and drew the pad to her, and a card with a long list of call signs and stations on it. She sat down and began her daily work.

She turned a switch on the face of the cabinet before her and said, "Eight Baker Tare, Eight Baker Tare, this is Eight Queen Charlie calling Eight Baker Tare. Eight Baker Tare, Eight Baker Tare, this is Eight Queen Charlie calling Eight Baker Tare. Eight Baker Tare, if you are receiving Eight Queen Charlie will you please come in. Over to you. Over." She turned the switch.

From the speaker in the set before her came a woman's voice. "Eight Queen Charlie, Eight Queen Charlie, this is Eight Baker Tare. Can you hear me, Jackie?"

Miss Bacon turned the switch and said, "Eight Baker

Tare this is Eight Queen Charlie. I'm receiving you quite well, about strength four. What's the weather like with you, Mrs. Corbett? Over to you. Over."

"Oh my dear," the loudspeaker said, "It's coming down in torrents here. We're having a lovely rain; Jim says we've really got it at last. I do believe it's getting cooler already. Over to you."

"Eight Baker Tare," said Miss Bacon, "this is Eight Queen Charlie. We're having a lovely rain here, too. I have nothing for you, Mrs. Corbett, but if you should have anybody going into Georgetown, will you pass word to Mrs. Cutter that her son Ronnie came up on the train from Mackay last night and he's coming on by train to Forsayth. He'll be there on Thursday morning, so he should be home on Thursday night. Is this Roger, Mrs. Corbett? Over to you. Over."

The loudspeaker said, "That's Roger, Jackie. One of the boys or Jim will be in Georgetown later on today, and I'll see Mrs. Cutter gets that message. Over."

"Eight Baker Tare," said Miss Bacon, "this is Eight Queen Charlie. Roger, Mrs. Corbett. I must sign off now. Listening out. Eight Easy Victor, Eight Easy Victor, this is Eight Queen Charlie calling Eight Easy Victor. Eight Easy Victor, this is Eight Queen Charlie calling Eight Easy Victor. If you are receiving me, Mrs. Marshall, will you please come in. Over to you. Over."

There was silence. Miss Bacon went on calling Eight Easy Victor for a minute, but Mrs. Marshall, she knew, was in the habit of feeding the hens at the time of the morning schedule and more usually came in in the evening. She made her statutory number of calls and went on to the next. "Eight Nan How, this is Eight Queen Charlie," and repeated herself. "If you are receiving me, Eight Nan How, will you please come in. Over to you. Over."

A man's voice said, "Eight Queen Charlie, this is Eight Nan How. Over."

Miss Bacon said, "Eight Nan How, this is Eight Queen Charlie. I have a telegram for you, Mr. Gosling. Have you got a pencil and paper? I can wait just one minute. Only one minute, mind. Call me when you're ready. Over."

She waited till he called her back, and then said, "Eight Nan How, this is Eight Queen Charlie. Your telegram is from Townsville and it reads, Molly had son seven last night eight pounds four ounces both doing fine. And the signature is, Bert. Have you got that, Mr. Gosling? Over to you. Over."

The speaker said, "I got that. It's another boy. Over."

Miss Bacon said, "I am *so* glad it's all gone off all right. Give Molly my love when you write, won't you, Mr. Gosling? Have you got anything else for me? Over."

The speaker said, "I'll think out a reply to this, Jackie, and give it to you on the evening schedule. Over to you. Over."

She said, "Okay, Mr. Gosling, I'll take it then. Now I must sign off from you. Eight Item Yoke, Eight Item Yoke, this is Eight Queen Charlie calling Eight Item Yoke." She went on with her work.

Twenty minutes later she was still at it. "Eight Able George, Eight Able George, this is Eight Queen Charlie calling Eight Able George. Eight Able George, if you are receiving Eight Queen Charlie will you come in now. Over."

The answer came in a sobbing torrent of words, rather impeded by the static of three hundred miles. "Oh, Jackie, I'm so glad you've come. We're in such trouble here. Don's horse came back last night. I heard the horse come in about two o'clock in the morning and I thought, that's funny, because Don never travels at night because of the trees, you know. And then I thought, that's funny, because there was only one horse and he had Samson with him so I got up to look and I couldn't see the horse, my dear, so I got a torch and put my coat on and went out in the rain and, my dear, there it was, Don's horse, Jubilee, saddled and everything, and Don wasn't there, and I'm so frightened." The voice dissolved into a torrent of sobs.

Miss Bacon sat motionless before the microphone, one hand on the transmitter switch, listening to the carrier wave and the low sobbing at the other end, clearly distinguishable through the static. There was nothing to be done until Helen Curtis recovered herself and remembered to switch over to Receive. She glanced quickly at the list before her; she hesitated, and then left her chair and opened the door, and called to the fireman on duty. "Fred, ring up Mr. Barnes and ask him to come down if he can. Something's happened at Windermere."

She went back to her chair, and now a heterodyne squeal shrilled out, drowning the sobbing as some sympathetic, foolish woman came in on the same wave saying something unintelligible. She sat patiently waiting for the air to clear; until they remembered their routines she could do nothing for them. The heterodyne stopped and Helen Curtis was still sobbing at the microphone three hundred miles away, beneath the coloured picture of the King and Queen in coronation robes and the picture of their daughter's wedding group that stood upon the set. Then she said, "Jackie, Jackie, are you there? Oh, I forgot. Over."

Miss Bacon turned her switch and said, "All right, Helen, this is Jackie here. Look, everybody, this is Eight Queen Charlie talking to Eight Able George. Will everybody please keep off the air and not transmit. You can stay listening in, but not transmit. I'll call you if you can do anything. Mrs. Curtis, I've sent Fred to telephone to Mr. Barnes to get him to come down. Now sit down quietly and tell me what happened and I'll take it down. Remember your routine and switch over when you want me to answer. It's going to be all right, Helen. Just tell me quietly what happened. Over to you. Over."

The speaker said, "Oh, Jackie, it *is* good to hear you. I've got nobody here except the boongs. Dave's on holiday and Pete's in Normanton. What happened was this. Don went up to the Disappointment Creek part of the station three days ago and he took Samson with him and he said he'd be away two days. I wasn't worried when they didn't get back because the rain, you know, and I thought they'd have to go around because the creeks would be up. And then last night Don's horse came back alone, and no sign of Samson. Samson's our new Abo stockrider. I've got a very good tracker here called Johnnie Walker, and Johnnie went out at dawn to track the horse back. But he came back an hour ago and it wasn't any good because the rain had washed the tracks out; he could only follow it about three miles and then he lost it, and now I don't know what to do." There was a pause, and then she said, "Oh, over."

Miss Bacon's pad was covered with rough notes. She turned her switch and said, "This is Jackie, Helen. Tell me, what stations are north and south of you? Over."

"It's Carlisle north of us, Jackie—that's Eddie Page. It's Midhurst to the south, and Pelican to the east. Midhurst is Joe Harman and Pelican, Len Driver. I don't think Midhurst's got a radio, though. Over."

Miss Bacon said, "All right, Helen, I'll call some of them. Stay listening in, because Mr. Barnes will want to speak to you when he comes. Now I'm going over to Carlisle. I have telegrams for Eight Dog Sugar and for Eight Jig William, and I will give them as soon as I'm free. Eight Charlie Peter,

Eight Charlie Peter, this is Eight Queen Charlie. If you are receiving me, Eight Charlie Peter, will you come in. Over."

She turned her switch and heard the measured tones of Eddie Page, and sighed with relief. "Eight Queen Charlie, this is Eight Charlie Peter. I heard all that, Jackie. I've got Fred Dawson here, and we'll get down to Windermere soon as we can. Tell Helen we'll be with her in about four hours and see what we can do. Will you be keeping a listening watch? Over."

She said, "That's fine, Mr. Page. We shall be on watch here till this is squared up listening every hour, from the hour till ten minutes past the hour. Is this Roger? Over."

He said, "Okay, Jackie, that's Roger. I'll sign off now and go and saddle up. You won't be able to raise me any more; Olive can't work it. Out."

She called Pelican next, but got no answer, so she called Eight Love Mike, the Willstown Mounted Police Station, and got Sergeant Haines at once. He said, "Okay, Jackie, I've heard all of that. I'm sending Phil Duncan and one of my trackers, and we'll see if any of the boys can come along. I'll see that someone goes round by Midhurst and tells Joe Harman. Tell Mr. Barnes that Constable Duncan will be at Windermere about three or four this afternoon. Your listening watch is Roger. Good girl, Jackie. Out."

Drama or no drama, the day's work still remained to be done. Miss Bacon said, "Eight Dog Sugar, this is Eight Queen Charlie calling Eight Dog Sugar. I have a telegram for Eight Dog Sugar. If you are receiving Eight Queen Charlie will you please come in. Over." She went on with her work.

At Midhurst Jean was measuring up the kitchen with Joe Harman and making a plan on a writing pad, when they heard a horse approaching about noon. It was still raining, though less fiercely than before. They went to the other side of the house and saw Pete Fletcher handing his horse over to Moonshine; he came up to the verandah. He was wearing his broad ringer's hat and he was soaked to the skin; his boots squelched as he climbed the steps.

He said, "Did you hear the radio?"

"No. What's that?"

"Some kind of trouble up on Windermere," the boy said. "Don Curtis went up with an Abo ringer to the top end of his station three days ago. Now the horse is back without him."

"Tracked the horse back?" Joe asked at once.

"Tried that, but it didn't work. Tracks all washed out." The boy sat down on the edge of the verandah and began taking off his boots to tip the water out of them; a little pool formed round him. "Jackie Bacon, the girl on the Cairns radio, she got the news on the morning schedule. She called Sergeant Haines, and he sent Phil Duncan to Windermere. Phil's on his way there now, with Al Burns. I said I'd come round this way and tell you. Eddie Page is on his way to Windermere from Carlisle, with Fred Dawson."

Joe asked, "Who was the Abo ringer he had with him?"

"Chap called Samson from the Mitchell River. He's been with Don about a month."

"Do they know where on the station he was going to?"

"Up by Disappointment Creek."

"For Christ's sake," Joe said. "Then I know what he's been up to." Jean, looking at him, saw his mouth set in a hard line.

"What's that?" asked Pete.

"He's been at my poddys again," said Joe. "The mugger's got a poddy corral up there."

"How do you know that?" asked Pete.

"Found the sod," said Joe. "I'll tell you where it is. You know where Disappointment Creek runs into the Fish River?" The boy nodded. "Well, from there you go up Disappointment Creek about four miles and you'll come to an island and a little bit of a creek running in from the north just by it. Well, go on past that about a mile and you'll see a lot of thick bush north of the creek with a little bare hill behind. You can't mistake it. The poddy corral's round the back of that thick bush, just under the bare hill. If you get up on that hill—it's only about fifty feet high—you'll see the poddy corral to the south of you." He paused. "If you're going on a search party I'd start off with that."

"Thanks, Joe," Pete said. "I'll tell them at Windermere."

"Aye, you'd better. I don't suppose Mrs. Curtis knows anything about it."

Jean had been hesitant to break in on a discussion about things that she knew nothing of, but now she said, "How did you get to know about it, Joe?"

He turned to her. "I was up at the top end just after Christmas with Bourneville, and I thought poddys were a bit scarcer than they ought to be. So then Bourneville got to tracking and the rain hadn't hardly begun then, so it was easy. The Cartwright River makes the station boundary just there, and we followed the tracks across and on to Windermere. Two horses there were, with a lot of poddys. We found

the corral like I said, and there they were; been there two
or three days. I let 'em out, of course, and drove them back.
Had a cow of a job to get them past the first water, oh my
word."

Pete asked, "How many were there, Joe?"

"Forty-seven."

"All cleanskins?"

"Oh yes." Joe was rather shocked at the implied suggestion. "Don wouldn't go and do a thing like that," he
said.

The boy put on his boots and got up. "What'll you do, Joe?
Come along with me?"

"I don't think so," Joe replied slowly. "I think I'll get up to
the top end of my station, where he got those poddys from.
Maybe he's been after some more, and had his accident up
there. That's south of the Cartwright River, and east of the
new bore we made. If I can't see any trace of him on my
land, then I'll follow the way he drove those poddys to his
corral. Maybe I'll meet you around there somewhere, tomorrow or the next day."

Pete nodded. "I'll tell Phil."

"Tell him I'll be taking Bourneville with me, and I'll start
as soon as I've run Miss Paget here back into town in the
utility."

Forty miles in the utility in those wet conditions would
take the best part of three hours. Jean said, "Joe, don't
bother about me. I'll stay here till you come back. You get
off at once."

He hesitated. "I may be away for days."

"Well then, I'll ride into town on Sally. One of the boongs
can come with me and bring Sally back."

"You could do that," he said slowly. "Moonshine will be
here, and he could go with you. I'll be taking Bourneville
along with me."

"Well then," she said, "that's perfectly all right. What time's
Dave coming back?"

"Should be back this afternoon," he said. He turned to
Pete. "I've got Jim Lennon on holiday, and Dave's off visiting a girl, one of the nurses down at Normanton. But he'll be
back today."

Jean said, "I'll stay here till Dave comes, in case anything
crops up, Joe."

He smiled at her. "Well, that would be a help. I don't like
leaving the place with just the boongs. I'll tell Moonshine

he's to take you into town any time you want to go." He
turned to Pete. "Want another horse?"

"I don't think so. 'Bout thirty miles to Windermere from
here?"

"That's right. Cross over the river here, you know, and
you'll find a track that leads there all the way. It's not been
used much lately. If you miss it, go north to the Gilbert and
follow up a mile or two and you'll find a little hut Jeff Pocock uses when he's hunting 'gators. There's a shallow about
two miles up from that where you can get across. Go north
from there about ten miles and you'll find their track from
the homestead to Willstown. You can't mistake that."

"Okay."

"What about some tucker?"

The boy shook his head. "Think I'll get on my way."

They went down into the yard and saw him saddle up
and ride away. The rain had practically stopped, but the
clouds were heavy and black overhead. Joe turned to her.
"Sorry about this," he said quietly. "It's spoilt our day. You're
sure you don't mind riding in with Moonshine?"

"Of course not," she said. "You must get away at once."

She hurried in to galvanize Palmolive to prepare some
lunch and food for them to take with them; down in the
yard the men were saddling up. They took their riding horses
and one pack horse with them, loaded with a tent and camp-
ing gear. She was distressed at the meagre quantity and poor
quality of the food Joe seemed to think it necessary to take
with them. He took a hunk of horrible black, overcooked
meat out of the meat safe and dropped it into a sack with
three loaves of bread; he took a couple of handfuls of tea in
an old cocoa tin and a couple of handfuls of sugar in another.
That was the whole of his provision for a journey of in-
definite length. She did not interfere, seeing that he was
absorbed in his preparations and not wanting to fuss him,
but she stored up the knowledge for her future information.

He kissed her good-bye on the verandah and she went
down with him to the yard. "Look after yourself, Joe," she
said.

He grinned. "See you in Willstown next week." Then he
was trotting out of the gate with Bourneville by his side and
the pack horse behind on a lead, and she was left alone at
Midhurst with the boongs.

It began to rain again, and she went up into the verandah.
It was very quiet and empty now that Joe was gone, and
Palmolive had retired to her own place. The rain made a

steady drumming on the iron roof. It occurred to her that the whole business might be over. Don Curtis might have turned up at Windermere and Joe's journey might be so much wasted effort. It was absurd that Midhurst had not got a radio transmitter. It was true enough that they were only twenty miles from the hospital and so would hardly need it for their own accidents, but in a case like this it was both difficult and trying not to know what was going on. She made up her mind to have a transmitter at Midhurst when they were married. A cattle station without one in these days was a back number.

She had never been alone in Midhurst before. She wandered through from room to room, slowly, deep in thought, and the wallaby lolloped after her; from time to time she dropped her hand to caress it, and it nibbled her fingers. She spent a long time in his room, touching and fingering the rough gear and clothes that were essentially Joe. He had so few things. Yet it was in this room he had dreamed and planned that fantastic journey to England in search of her, that journey that had ended in Noel Strachan's office in Chancery Lane. Chancery Lane seemed very far away.

At about three o'clock Dave Hope arrived. He came riding from Willstown through the rain as Pete Fletcher had come in the morning; he had got a lift up on a truck from Normanton. He had heard all about the Windermere affair in Willstown which he had left shortly before noon, and he could add further information from the radio. He told her that the Abo ringer, Samson, had returned to the homestead.

"Seems they were looking for some poddys," he said, "somewhere up at the Disappointment Creek end of the station. They separated and one went one way, one the other, for some reason; they left the camp standing and were going to meet back in the evening. Don didn't turn up that evening and of course the Abo couldn't track him in the dark. When the morning came the whole place was swimming in water, and he couldn't track him at all. That's how it seems to be."

They talked about it for some time on the verandah. Somewhere thirty or forty miles from them a man must be lying injured on the ground; he might be anywhere within a circle thirty miles in diameter. He might be lying under a bush and very probably by that time he would be unconscious; looking for him would be like looking for a needle in a bundle of hay.

"You'd better go and help, Dave," Jean said at last.

"There's nothing to do here. I'll stay here and look after things."

He was a little doubtful. "What did Mr. Harman say I was to do?"

"He didn't say anything. I said I'd stay here till you got back. He doesn't want the station left without anyone at all, except the boongs. I'll stay here, Dave, till somebody else comes. You go and join them over at Windermere. That's the best thing you can do."

"It certainly seems crook to stay here doing nothing," he admitted.

She got him off in the late afternoon with about two hours of daylight left. He knew Windermere station well, and was quite happy about finishing his journey in the dark. Left to herself, Jean went on with the plan of the kitchen she would have liked to see built, with a view to getting Joe to pull the old one down completely and start again from scratch. Presently Palmolive came in and cooked eggs for her tea, and fed the various animals, and watered the verandah plants.

When Palmolive had gone away, she was alone in Midhurst for the night, with only the puppies and the wallaby for company. Somewhere out in the darkness and the rain Joe Harman would be pushing on towards the top end of the property, horses and men soaked through, picking their way cautiously through the darkness. She could do nothing to help them, nothing but sit and wait.

She learned a lot that evening. She learned a little of the fortitude that a wife on a cattle station must develop, even, she thought a little grimly, a wife with fifty-three thousand pounds. She learned that a radio transmitting and receiving set was almost indispensable to such a wife; even on that first evening she would have liked to exchange a word or two with Jackie Bacon in Cairns. She learned how much a lonely person turns to animals, and queerly the memory of Olive came into her mind, the brown Abo girl who could not bear to be separated from her kitten even on a visit to the Willstown hotel. By the time she went to bed she understood Olive a bit better.

She went to bed about nine. There were one or two old British and American magazines about the place, tattered, much read stories about a different world. She took one of these and tried to read it in bed, but the fiction failed to satisfy her or to quell her anxieties. The rain stopped, and started, and then stopped again, and presently she slept.

She slept lightly and woke many times, and dozed again. She woke before dawn to the sound of a horse in the yard. She got up at once and put her frock on and went out on the verandah, and switched on the light, and called, "Who's that?"

A man came forward into the light at the foot of the steps, and said, "It's me, Missy, Bourneville. Missa Hope, him come back?"

He spoke with a thick accent; she could not understand what he was saying. She said, "Come up here, Bourneville. What is it?"

He came up to her in the verandah. He was a man of about fifty years of age, very black, with a seamed, wrinkled face and greying hair. He said again, "Missa Hope, him come back?"

She understood this time. "He's gone over to Windermere. He came back here, and went on to Windermere. What's happened to Mr. Harman, Bourneville?"

He said, "Missa Harman, him up top end. Him find Missa Curtis, him leg broken. Missa Harman, him send me back fetch Missa Hope, him drive utility up top end, bring Missa Curtis down."

She was angry with herself that she could not fully understand what he was saying. The fault lay within herself; a woman of the Gulf Country would understand this man at once, and it was terribly important that she should understand. She said quietly, "I'm sorry, Bourneville. Say that again slowly."

She got it at the second repetition. "Mr. Hope's not here," she said. "He's gone to Windermere."

He was silent for a time. Then he said, "No white feller here, drive utility?"

She shook her head. "Can you drive the utility, Bourneville?"

"No, Missy."

"Can any of the other Abos drive the utility?"

"No, Missy."

The thought came to her that she could drive it up to them herself, with Bourneville as a guide, but it was not a thing to be undertaken lightly. She had never owned a car, and though she had driven cars belonging to various young men from time to time and knew the movements, her total driving experience did not exceed five hours. Again, she was angry and humiliated by her own incompetence.

She lit a cigarette and thought deeply. It would benefit

nobody if she attempted to drive the utility and crashed it. It was a very big vechicle, larger than any ordinary car and much bigger than anything she had ever driven before. The alternative would be to send Bourneville riding on to Willstown, perhaps to the police station; they would send a truck or a utility out with a driver who would go on to the top end. The return journey to Willstown was forty miles. It would mean at least six hours' delay before the truck could arrive at Midhurst ready to start for the top end.

She asked, "How far away is Mr. Harman, Bourneville?"

He thought. "Four mile past bore."

Joe had once told her that the new bore was twenty-two miles from the homestead; that made the scene of the accident twenty-six miles away. She said, "What's the track like? Can the utility get there?"

"Him bonza track in dry far as bore," he said. She nodded; this was likely enough because the bore had only been made a few months and there must have been trucks going up to it. It would probably be possible to get along it even in this rain. Already the sky was getting grey; full daylight was not far away.

She asked, "Are there any creeks to cross?"

He held up three fingers. "Tree."

"Are they deep? Can the utility go through?"

"Yes, Missy. Creeks not too deep."

If Bourneville rode a horse beside the utility to guide her, she thought that she could make it. It was worth trying, anyway; the worst that could happen would be that she would get it stuck and have to send Bourneville back to Willstown with a note for them to send up somebody more competent. So long as he had his horse there was no risk of any great delay. She said, "All right, Bourneville, I'll drive the utility. You come up with me on your horse."

"Get fresh horse, Missy. Him tired."

"All right, get a fresh horse." Bourneville must be tired too, but she was too unaccustomed to these seamed black faces to be able to detect fatigue. "You get some tucker," she said. "I get tucker, too. We'll start in half an hour."

He went off, and she put the kettle on for a cup of tea and then went and changed into her riding shirt and breeches. There was an old tin trunk in Joe's room which she had discovered the night before; it was half full of bandages and splints and various medicines. Being of tin, she thought, it would be waterproof, and she filled it up with blankets and some tins of food from the store cupboard, and a small sack of flour. That was all she could think of for provision in case she got stuck half-way and had to spend a night or two in the utility.

She had a cup of tea and a small meal of meat and bread and jam; then she went down to the yard and examined the utility. The huge petrol tank had twenty gallons in it, and the sump was full of oil. She filled the radiator from the water butt and filled the water bag suspended from the lamp bracket. Then she sat in it; to her relief the gears were clearly marked. She switched it on and pressed the starter and jiggeted the accelerator, and was both alarmed and pleased when the engine started. Very gingerly she put it in reverse and drove it out into the yard.

They put the trunk into the back and started off, Bourneville riding ahead of her to show her the way. Partly because of Bourneville on his horse and partly because she thoroughly distrusted her own competence, she never got it into top gear all the way, and never exceeded ten miles an hour. She drove through each of the three creeks along the line that Bourneville showed her, following the agitated, plunging horse as he forced it through the yellow water swirling about its legs. Once the water rose above the floorboards of the cab and she was very frightened. But she kept the utility going and the designer had anticipated such usage and had placed the ignition system above the cylinders, and it came through bounding from rock to rock with water pouring out of every hole and cranny.

Four miles beyond the bore Joe Harman sat at the mouth of his small tent. It was pitched in a clearing in a thick patch of bush in the bottom of a little valley. A heavy log stockade or corral had been built in this clearing and stood immediately behind the tent; the movable logs that formed a gate had been pulled down and the corral was empty. Joe had built a fire before the tent, and he was boiling up in a billy over it.

A man lay inside upon a bed of brushwood covered with a waterproof sheet, with a blanket over him. Joe turned his head, and said, "What happened, Don? Did they rush you when you got the pole down?"

From the tent the man said, "My bloody oath. They pushed the pole back on to me and knocked me down. Then about six of them ran over me."

Joe said, "Serve you bloody well right. Teach you to go muggering about on other people's land."

There was a pause. Then he said, "How many of mine did you get last year, Don?"

" 'Bout three hundred."

Mr. Harman laughed. "I got three hundred and fifty of yours."

From the tent Mr. Curtis said a very rude word.

Chapter 10

JEAN drove the utility slowly up to the tent with Bourneville riding beside her; she took out the gear and stopped it with a sigh of relief. Joe came to her as she sat there. "What's happened to Dave?" he asked. "Didn't he come back?"

She told him what had happened. "I thought I'd better have a go at driving it up myself," she said. "I've only driven a car about three times before. I don't think I've done it any good, Joe."

He stepped back. "Looks all right," he said. "Did you hit anything?"

"I didn't hit anything. I couldn't get the gears in sometimes and it made an awful noise."

"Do they work still?"

"Oh, I think so."

"That's all right, then. What were the creeks like?"

"Pretty high," she said. "It came over the floor of the cab."

He grunted. "Get along back soon as we can. I wish this bloody rain'd stop."

She asked, "Is Mr. Curtis here, Joe?"

He nodded. "In the tent."

"What's wrong?"

"Got his leg bust," he said. "Compound fracture—that's what you call it when the bone's sticking out, isn't it? I think he's got a broken ankle, too."

She pursed her lips. "I brought up that trunk with your splints and things."

He asked, "Do you know about breaks? Ever been a nurse or anything like that?"

She shook her head. "I've not."

"I've had a look at it and washed it," he said. "I set it well as I could, but it's a mess. I made a sort of a long splint this morning and tied it all down on that. We'll get him down to hospital, soon as we can. It's been done two days."

They set to work to strike camp. They removed the tent from over the injured man and he saw Jean for the first time. "Hullo, Miss Paget," he said. "You don't remember me. I saw you in Willstown, day you arrived."

She smiled at him. "You'll be back there in a little while. In the hospital."

Once as she worked she turned to Joe with a puzzled expression. "Whose land are we on, Joe?"

"Midhurst," he said. "Why?"

She glanced at the corral. "What's that for?"

"That?" he said. "Oh, that's just a place we put the cattle in sometimes, for branding and that."

She said no more, but went on with her work; once or twice a little smile played round her lips. They worked a blanket underneath the brushwood bed as the man lay upon the ground, and lowered the tail board of the utility; then, with infinite care and great labour they lifted him on his bed into the body of the truck. The man was white and sweating when they had done and a little blood was showing on his lip where he had bitten it, but there was nothing else that they could do to ease his pain.

They started off at about nine o'clock, Joe driving the utility, Jean riding in the back with the injured man, and Bourneville following behind, riding and leading the two horses. They passed the bore and went on for about five miles till they came to the creeks. The water was considerably higher than when Jean had crossed a couple of hours earlier.

They crossed the first without difficulty, though the water was in the cab of the utility and only just below the floor of the truck body on which the sick man lay. They came through that one and went on. At the second creek the water was higher. Joe stopped on the edge and consulted with Jean and Bourneville about the crossing they had made before. It seemed shallower fifty yards above the point where Jean had crossed; Joe sent Bourneville into the water on his horse to sound the crossing. It looked good enough, so he drove the utility into the water.

It grew deep quickly, and he accelerated to keep her going. The bottom, under the swirling yellow flood, was very rough; the big car went forward leaping from boulder to boulder under the water. Then she came down heavily on something with a crunch of metal, and stopped dead.

Joe said, "Jesus," and pressed the starter, but the engine

was immovable. Oil began to appear on the eddying yellow surface of the water and slide away downstream in black and yellow tails. He stared at it in consternation.

Jean said, "What's happened, Joe?"

"I've cracked the bloody sump," he said shortly.

He got down into the water from the cab, feeling his way gingerly; it was well above his knees, close on waist deep. He called Bourneville and made Jean pass him a coil of rope from the back of the truck. The utility was only about ten yards from the bank. They made a sort of tandem harness for the three horses with lariats that they carried at the pommel of the riding saddles, and harnessed this team to the back axle of the utility, groping and spluttering under the water to do so. In ten minutes the vehicle was on dry land; a performance that left Jean awed by its efficiency.

She got down from the back and went to Joe, who was lying on his back under the front axle. She stooped down with him to look; the cast iron sump was crushed and splintered. "Say it, Joe," she said quietly.

He grinned at her, and said, "It's a fair mugger." He picked the broken pieces of cast iron from the hole, and got out from underneath. He went and got the starting handle from the cab and turned the engine carefully. He sighed with relief. "Crankshaft's all right," he said. "It's only just the sump."

He stood in deep thought for a minute, starting handle in his hand; the rain poured down upon them steadily. She asked, "Where do we go from here, Joe?"

"I could patch that," he said, "good enough to get her home. But then we haven't got any oil. It's no good going down to fetch the truck the way these creeks are rising." He stood watching the water for a minute or two. "Never get the truck through by the time it got here," he said finally. "There's only one thing for it now. He'll have to be flown out."

The country round about was covered with rocks and trees. "Is there anywhere an aeroplane can land here?" she asked.

"I know one place it might," he said. "Five hundred yards, they want, and then a good approach."

He took his horse and went off to the south; by the river they unpacked the tent and arranged it over Don Curtis to keep the rain off him. The wounded man said faintly once, "Joe Harman's a clumsy mugger with a car. He's a good poddy dodger, though." Jean laughed. "Pair of criminals, the two of you," she said. "I'm going to have a word with Mrs. Curtis."

"Don't do it," he said. "She don't know nothing about this."

She said, "Lie still, and don't talk. Joe's gone off to find a place where the aeroplane can land to fly you out."

"Hope he makes a better job of it than he did driving this bloody truck," said Mr. Curtis.

Joe came back in a quarter of an hour. "Think we can make something of it," he said. "It's only about a mile away." With Bourneville he harnessed up the tandem team of three horses to the front axle of the truck, and with Jean at the wheel they set off through the bush, steering and manoeuvring between the trees.

They came presently to an open space, a long grassy sward with low bushes dotted about on it. It was more than five hundred yards long, but there were trees at each end. It would be possible to make an airstrip there. "Clear off some of these bushes," Joe said, "and fell some of those trees. I've seen them use a lot worse places than this."

An axe and a spade were part of the equipment of the utility; they had tools enough. Their labour was quite inadequate for the work. "We'll have to get the boys up from Midhurst," he said. "Everyone that's there. And get a message down to Willstown about the aeroplane."

She said, "I'll ride down with Bourneville to the homestead, Joe. Then he can bring the boys back, and I'll go on to Willstown."

He stared at her. "You can't ride that far."

"How far is it?"

"Forty miles, to Willstown."

"I can get to Midhurst, anyway," she said. "If I can't go on I'll send Moonshine in with a note to Sergeant Haines. He's the best man to tell, isn't he?"

"That's right. If you do this, there's to be no riding alone. If you go on from Midhurst to town, you've got to take Moonshine or one of the other boys with you. I won't have you trying to cross them creeks alone, on a horse."

She touched his arm. "All right, Joe. I'll take someone with me." She paused. "We could get on the radio from Willstown," she said. "We could get some people over from Windermere to help you then, couldn't we?"

"That's right," he said. "It would be better if we had a radio at Midhurst." He paused. "There's one thing that they'll all want to know," he said, "and that's where this place is. We're about six miles west-south-west of the new bore. Can you remember that?"

"I've got that, Joe," she said. "Six miles west-south-west of the new bore." She paused. "What are you going to do?" she asked.

"I'll make camp here." He looked around. I'll pitch the tent over the back of the utility," he said. "We don't want to shift him again if we can help it, not until we get a stretcher. After that I'll start and fell some of those trees for the approach."

"What about your back?" she asked.

"That'll be all right."

She thought of swinging a two-handed axe to fell a tree. "Have you done that, Joe?"

"No, but it'll be all right."

She said, "If you're going to cut down trees I'll take back what I said about not riding alone. I'll send Moonshine up with the other boongs to help you here."

"You're not to do that," he said. "It's not safe for you crossing them creeks."

"It's not safe for you to swing an axe," she said. "It won't help if you go and ruin your back up here, Joe." She touched his arm again. "Let's both be sensible," she said. "The work you'll do in cutting down those trees alone is only what the boongs will do in an hour when they get here. Don't take risks, Joe."

He smiled at her. "All right. But you're not to ride alone."

"I'll promise that," she said.

It was about half past ten when they put her up on Joe's horse Robin. Robin was a much bigger horse than she had ridden before, and she was rather afraid of him. He was little, if any, wider for her to straddle than the horses she was used to, and Joe's saddle was much better than the casual saddles she had been using up till then; it was soft and worn and supple with much use and yet efficient and in very good repair. When they got the stirrups adjusted for her legs she found herself fairly comfortable.

She started off with Bourneville at a slow trot through the trees, and so began a feat of endurance which she was to look back upon with awe for years to come. She found the horse docile, responsive, and energetic; moreover, he had a very easy gait when trotting. At the same time, the bald fact remained that she had only been on a horse six times before, and never for more than an hour and a half at a time.

The rain had stopped for the moment, and they came to the creek and waded through the tumbling yellow water, Bourneville close beside her. They came through that one and went on, walking and trotting alternately. After an hour they came to the second creek and found it very deep; Bourneville made her take her feet out of the stirrups and be prepared to swim, holding to the horse's mane. That was not necessary and they came through to the other side in good order, and then the creeks were over.

"Too deep for the utility," she said.

"Yes, Missy. Him too deep now."

No creeks now lay between them and Midhurst; it remained only for them to ride. The rain began again and soaked her to the skin, mingling with the sweat streaming off her. Very soon the wet strides began to chafe her legs and thighs; she could feel the soreness growing, but there was nothing to be done about that. She had said that she would ride, and ride she would.

She found, on the good going that was before them now, that she could get along faster than Bourneville. She was on a much better horse, and a horse that was fresh whereas he had ridden his from Midhurst with the utility. Frequently she had to slow to a walk for him when Robin would have trotted on, and these walks helped her, easing her fatigue.

They came to Midhurst homestead at about half past two. By that time she had a raging thirst, and she was getting very tired. Moonshine and one or two of the other boys ran out and took her bridle and helped her down from Robin; she could not manage the stretch from the stirrup to the ground. She said, "Bourneville, tell Moonshine to saddle up and come with me to Willstown. I'm going to have a cup of tea and some tucker, and then we'll start. You take all the boys back to Mr. Harman. That okay?"

He said, "Yes, Missy." It struck her that if she was tired he must be exhausted; he had been in the saddle continuously for twenty-three hours. She looked at the seamed black face and said, "Can you make it, Bourneville? Are you very tired?"

He grinned. "Me not tired, Missy. Go back to Missa Harman with the boys after tucker." He went away shouting, "Palmolive, Palmolive. You go longa kitchen, make tea and tucker for Missy. You go longa kitchen quick."

She sat down wearily upon the chair in the verandah, and in a very short time Palmolive appeared with a pot of tea and two fried eggs upon a steak that was almost uneatable. She ate the eggs and a corner of the steak and drank six huge cups of tea. She did not dare to change her clothes or examine her sores; once started on that sort of thing, she knew, she would never get going again. She finished eating and called out for Moonshine and went down into the yard. The black stockriders, saddling their own horses and making up the bundles for the packhorses in the rain, put her up into the saddle and she was off again for Willstown with Moonshine by her side.

The short rest had stiffened her, and it needed all her courage to face the twenty miles that lay ahead. Every muscle in her body was stretched and aching. Her legs ceased to function much to hold her in the saddle, but the big horns above and below her thighs came into play and held her in place.

They crossed the creeks, now too deep for a car, and rode on. They were following the car track, and the going was good. She was the laggard now, because Moonshine's horse was fresh and Robin was tiring. She rode the last ten miles in a daze, walking and trotting wearily; for the last five miles the black stockrider rode close by her side to try and catch her if she fell. But she didn't fall. She rode into Willstown in the darkness at about seven o'clock, a very tired girl on a very tired horse with a black ringer riding beside her. She rode past the hotel and past the ice cream parlour with its lights streaming out into the street, and came to a stand outside Sergeant Haines' police station and house. She had been about eight hours in the saddle.

Moonshine dismounted and held Robin's head. She summoned a last effort and got her right leg back over the saddle, and slithered down on to the ground. She could not stand at first without holding on to something, and she held on to Robin's saddle. Then Sergeant Haines was there.

"Why, Miss Paget," he said in the slow Queensland way, "where have you come from?"

"From Joe Harman," she said. "He's got Don Curtis up at the top end of Midhurst with a broken leg. Look, tell Moonshine what he can do with these horses, and then help me inside, and I'll tell you."

He told Moonshine to take the horses round to the police corral and to bed down for the night with the police trackers in the bunk house; then he turned to Jean. "Come on in the house," he said. "Here, take my arm. How far have you ridden?"

"Forty miles," she said, and even in her fatigue there was a touch of pride in the achievement. "Joe Harman's up there now with Mr. Curtis. All the Midhurst stockriders have gone up there to make an airstrip. It's the only way to get him out, Joe says. You can't get through the creeks with a utility."

He took her in and sat her down in his mosquito-wired verandah, and Mrs. Haines brought out a cup of tea. He glanced at the clock and settled down to listen to her in slow time; he had missed the listening watch of seven o'clock on the Cairns Ambulance radio, and now there was three quarters of an hour to wait before he could take any action. "Six miles west-south-west of the new bore," he said thoughtfully. "I know, there's open country round about that part. I'll get on to the radio presently, and get the plane out in the morning."

"Joe thought if you got on the radio some ringers might go out from Windermere and help him make the strip," she said. "He's talking about cutting down some trees. I don't want him to do that, because of his back."

He nodded. "I'll be getting Windermere at the same time." And then he said, "I never knew you were a rider, Miss Paget."

"I'm not," she said. "I've been on a horse six times before."

He smiled, and then said, "Oh my word. Are you sore?"

She got up wearily. "I'm going home to bed," she said, and caught hold of the back of the chair. "If I stay here any longer I won't be able to walk at all."

"Stay where you are," he said. "I'll get out the utility and run you to the hospital."

"I don't want to go to the hospital."

"I don't care if you want to go or not," he said, "but that's where you're going. You'll be better off there for tonight, and Sister Douglas, she's got everything you'll want."

Half an hour later she was bathed and in a hospital bed with penicillin ointment on various parts of her anatomy, feeling like a very small child. Back in his office Sergeant Haines sat down before his transmitter.

"Eight Queen Charlie, Eight Queen Charlie," he said, "this is Eight Love Mike calling Eight Queen Charlie. Eight Queen Charlie, if you are receiving Eight Love Mike will you please come in. Over to you. Over."

He turned his switch, and the speaker on top of the set said in a girl's voice, "Eight Love Mike, this is Eight Queen Charlie answering, receiving you strength three. Pass your message. Over."

He said, "Eight Queen Charlie, we've got Don Curtis. Joe Harman found him up at the top end of Midhurst. His injuries are compound fracture of the left leg two and a half days old, probably left ankle broken in addition. Position of the camp is six miles west-south-west of Harman's new bore. Tell me now if this is Roger. Over."

The girl's voice from the speaker said, "Oh, I *am* glad—we've all been so worried at this end. That is Roger, but I will repeat." She repeated. "Over to you. Over."

He said, "Okay, Jackie. Now take a message for Mr. Barnes. Message reads, Request ambulance aircraft at Willstown soon as possible prepared for bush landing. Just read that back to me. Over."

She read it back to him.

"Okay, Jackie," he said. "Now call Windermere for me and let me speak to them. Over."

She said, "Eight Able George, Eight Able George, this is Eight Queen Charlie calling Eight Able George. If you are receiving me, Eight Able George, please come in. Over to you. Over."

A tremulous woman's voice said in thirty speakers in thirty homesteads, "Eight queen Charlie, this is Eight Able George. I've heard all that, Jackie. Isn't it marvellous the way prayer gets answered? Oh my dear, I'm that relieved I don't know what to say. I'm sure we all ought to go down on our bended knees tonight and thank God for His mercy. I'm sure we all ought to do that. Oh—over."

Miss Bacon turned her switch. "I'm sure we'll all thank God tonight, Helen. Now Sergeant Haines is waiting to speak to you. You stay listening with your switch on to Receive, Helen. Eight Love Mike, will you come in now? Over."

In Willstown Sergeant Haines said, "Eight Love Mike calling Eight Able George. Mrs. Curtis, you've heard Joe Harman's with your husband up at the top end of Midhurst. He's got to make an airstrip for the ambulance to land on, and he's taken all his stockriders up there. Will you send everyone you have upon your station to help make this airstrip? I'll give you the position. If you have a pencil and a bit of paper write this down." He paused. "The place where Joe Harman is making the strip is six miles west-south-west of his new bore. Six miles west-south-west of his new bore. I want you to send every man you've got there to help him, and pass that message to Constable Duncan if he's with you. Is that Roger, Mrs. Curtis? Over."

The tremulous voice said, "That's Roger, sergeant. Six miles west-south-west of Joe's new bore. I've got that written down. Eddie Page is here, and I'm expecting Phil Duncan to come back tonight. I'll send everybody up there. Isn't it marvellous what God can do for us? When I think of all

His mercies to us suffering sinners I could go down on my bended knees and cry." There was a pause, and then she said, "Oh, I keep on forgetting. Over."

He turned his switch and said, "It's not only God you've got to thank, Mrs. Curtis." He was very well aware that most of the housewives in a hundred thousand square miles of the Gulf Country would be listening in to this conversation, and one good turn deserved another. "Miss Paget rode forty miles down from the top end of Midhurst to bring this message about Don. You know Jean Paget, the English girl that's started the shoe workshop and the ice cream shop? She was out at Midhurst spending the day when we heard Don was missing, and she rode in forty miles to tell me where this airstrip was to be. She's only been astride a horse six times before, and the poor girl's so sore she can't stand. Sister Douglas has her in the hospital for a good rest. She'll be all right in a day or two. Over."

She said, "Oh my word. I don't know what to say to thank her. Give her my very dearest love, and I do hope she'll be better soon." There was a pause, and then she said, "I've been so troubled in my mind about that ice cream parlour. It didn't seem right to have a thing like that in Willstown, and opening it on Sundays and Christmas Day and all. I couldn't find nothing in the Bible either for or against it, and I've been perplexed. But now it seems God has that under His hand like everything else. I do think it's wonderful. Over."

"That's right," said Sergeant Haines non-committally. He had been uncertain about the shop closing hours himself and had written to his head office for guidance; it was a good long time since he had been in a district where there was a shop to close. "Now I must sign off, Mrs. Curtis. Eight Queen Charlie, this is Eight Love Mike. It's okay here if you want to close down your listening watch for tonight, Jackie. I'd like to have a listening watch in daylight hours tomorrow, from seven o'clock on. Is this Roger? Over."

Miss Bacon said, "That is Roger, sergeant. I'll tell Mr. Barnes. If you have nothing more for me, I shall close down. Over."

"Nothing more, Jackie. Good night. Out."

"Good night, sergeant. Out."

Miss Bacon switched off her sets thankfully. There was no proper organization for a twenty-four-hour listening watch at the Cairns Ambulance; in an emergency such as this everybody had to muscle in and lend a hand. She had been on duty the previous day from eight in the morning till midnight, and from eight o'clock that morning till then; Mr. Barnes had taken the night watch and was preparing to do so again. She thought, ruefully, that she had missed Humphrey Bogart and Lauren Bacall; the show would be half over. But there was still one more night, and with any luck this flap would be over and she could see it tomorrow. She went to telephone to Mr. Barnes.

Mr. Barnes telephoned to Mr. Smythe of Australian National Airways, and Mr. Smythe telephoned to his reserve pilot, Captain Jimmie Cope. Mr. Cope said, "Hell, I hope it's better in the morning than it was today. We'd never have got over the Tableland today. Better say take off at six, I suppose. I'll be along at the hangar then."

When he got to the aerodrome at dawn the old Dragon, surely the best aircraft ever built for ambulance work in the outback, was running up both engines. The clouds hung low at about five hundred feet, shrouding the hill immediately behind the aerodrome; it was raining a little. Willstown lay about four hundred miles to the west-north-west; the first seventy miles of this course lay over the Atherton Tableland with mountains up to three thousand five hundred feet in height. With no radio navigational aids he would have to fly visually all the way, scraping along between the clouds and the tree tops as best he could.

He said a sour word or two to the control officer and took off down the runway with an ambulance orderly on board. Once in the air it was worse than ever. He flew at three hundred feet up the Barron River towards the mountains, hoping to find a break in the low cloud that would enable him to get up on to the Tableland through the Kuranda Gap. The grey vapour closed around him and the sides of the jungle-covered gorge drew very near his wings. There was no sign of a break ahead. He edged over to the starboard side and made a tight, dicey turn round in the gorge with about a hundred feet to spare, and headed back for the coast. He lifted his microphone and said, "Cairns Tower, this is Victor How Able Mike Baker. I can't make it by Kuranda. I'm going up to Cooktown by the coast, and try it from there. Tell Cooktown I'll be landing there in about an hour, and I'll want twenty gallons of seventy-three octane."

He flew on up the tropical Queensland coast at about three hundred feet, and came to Cooktown an hour later. Cooktown is a pretty little town of about three hundred people, but it was grey and rainswept when he got there. He landed on the aerodrome and refuelled. "I'm going to try and make Willstown from here," he said. "There's not much high stuff on the way. If it gets too bad I shall come back. I'll be on a direct course from here to Willstown." He said that in case a search party should be necessary.

He took off again immediately the refueling was finished and flew inland on a compass course. In the whole of that flight he was never more than two hundred feet above the tree tops. He scraped over the Great Dividing Range, petering out up in this northern latitude, with about fifty feet to spare, always on the point of turning back, always seeing a faint break ahead that made it necessary to go on. Behind him the orderly sat gripping his seat, only too well aware of danger in the flight and impotent to do anything about it. For three hours they flew like that, and then as they neared the Gulf of Carpentaria the pilot started picking up the landmarks that he knew, a river bend, a burnt patch of the bush, a curving sandy waste like a banana. He came to Willstown and flew round the few houses at a hundred feet to tell them he was there, and landed on the airstrip. He taxied in to where the truck was standing waiting for him; he was strained and tired. It was still raining.

He held a little conference with Sergeant Haines and Sister Douglas and Al Burns beside the truck. "I'll have a crack at flying him back here," he said. "If it's no better this afternoon he'll have to spend the night in hospital here. I can't fly him to Cairns in this weather. It'll probably be better by tomorrow." They gave him a freehand pencil map which the sergeant had prepared for him, showing him the creeks and Midhurst homestead, and the new bore, and the probable position of the airstrip, and he took off again. That was at about eleven o'clock.

Following this map he found the place without much difficulty. It was clear where they meant him to land, because trees had been felled upon a line he was to come in on, and bushes had been cleared for a short distance on what seemed to be a grassy meadow. He could see about ten men working or standing looking up at him; he could see a utility parked with a tent over it. He circled round under the low cloud, considering the risks. The runway that they had prepared was pitifully short, even for a Dragon. Time was also short, however; the man had had his compound fracture three days now. Sepsis and gangrene and all sorts of things would be setting in; he must not delay. He bit his lip and lined the Dragon up with the runway for a trial approach.

He came in as slowly as he dared over the trees, missing them by no more than five feet, motoring in with careful graduations of the throttles. Over the cut trees he throttled back and stuffed her down towards the grass, hoping it was smooth. He could . . . he couldn't, he could never stop her in time. With wheels no more than two feet from the ground he jammed the throttles forward, held her level for a moment, and climbed away.

He turned to the orderly behind him as he circled low under the clouds, keeping the airstrip in sight. "Got a pencil and paper? Write this." He thought for a moment. " 'Sorry I can't make it. Strip must be about a hundred yards longer, or a hundred and fifty if you can manage it. I will come back at four o'clock this afternoon.' " They put this in a message bag with coloured streamers flying from it, and flew over, and dropped it on the middle of the strip.

Back at the Willstown airfield he told them what had happened. "They've not had time to make it long enough," the sergeant said. "You'll find it'll be all right this afternoon." He drove the pilot in to the hotel and Al Burns took him to the bar, but the pilot would drink nothing but lemonade till the difficult flying of the afternoon was over.

He lunched at the hotel and strolled into the ice cream parlour after lunch. It was new since he had last been in Willstown, and he stared around him with amused wonder. He ordered an ice; Rose Sawyer told him briskly to be quick and eat it, because she was shutting up. He asked if she closed every afternoon and was told that she was going up to see Miss Paget at the hospital. Then, of course, he heard all about her ride.

At four o'clock he was back over the airstrip at the top end of Midhurst; the rain had stopped and he was able to approach at about eight hundred feet. He circled once and had a good look; they had made the strip much longer and he would have no difficulty now. He came in and touched down at the near end; the Dragon bounced on the uneven ground and landed again, and rolled bumping and swaying to a standstill.

He stopped the engines and got out; they took a stretcher from the cabin and the orderly began the business of getting Don Curtis on to the stretcher and into the cabin, helped by the ringers. The pilot lit a cigarette and gave one to Joe Harman.

Joe asked, "Did you hear anything about Miss Paget, down in Willstown?"

The pilot said, "She's in the hospital. Nothing much wrong, they say; just tired and sore. She must be quite a girl."

Joe said, "Too right. If you see anyone from the hospital, leave a message for Miss Paget, will you? Tell her I'll be in town tomorrow afternoon."

"I'll do that," said the pilot. "I'll be staying there tonight. It's too late now to get to Cairns; I can't do night flying in this weather, not in this thing."

The loading was completed now. He got into his seat; the orderly swung the propellers, and they taxied back to the far end of the track. It was short, but he could make it. He opened out and took off down the runway, and cleared the trees at the far end with about fifteen feet to spare. Half an hour later he was on the ground at Willstown, helping to transfer the stretcher to the truck that was to take Don Curtis to the hospital.

In hospital that afternoon Jean Paget showed Rose Sawyer the more accessible of her wounds, great chafed raw places six inches long. "Honourable scars," Rose said. "Pity you can't show them."

"It's because everything was so wet," Jean said. "But I'm going to have a proper pair of riding breeches made, I think. Ringers' strides are for ringers' skins."

"I'd never want to get up on a horse again if it'd done that to me."

"It's going to be some time before I can," said Jean.

Presently Rose said, "Tell me, Jean. Do you think there'd be any work up here for a contractor?"

Jean stared at her. "What sort of a contractor?"

"Making roads and things like that. Buildings, too."

"Is this Billy Wakeling, from Alice?"

Rose nodded. "He wrote to me," she said carelessly. For the bunch of seven letters that arrived by the Dakota regularly every Wednesday, this seemed to Jean to be an understatement. "You know, his father's a contractor in Newcastle—he's got graders and bulldozers and steam shovels and all sorts of things like that. He started Billy off in Alice after the war because he said Alice was expanding and expanding places meant work for contractors. But Billy says he's fed up with Alice."

"He's coming up here for a visit as soon as the wet's over," she added artlessly.

"He won't get any roads or buildings to contract for here,"

Jean observed. "There's nobody to pay for them. I know what does want doing though. Joe Harman wants some little dams built up on Midhurst. I don't know if that's in his line."

"I should think it might be," Rose said slowly. "After all, it's shifting muck, and that's what Billy does. He'd do it with a bulldozer in the dry, wouldn't he?"

"I haven't the least idea," said Jean. "Can he get hold of a bulldozer?"

"His old man's got about forty down at Newcastle," Rose said. "I should think he could spare one for Billy."

"They're only little dams," said Jean.

"Well, everything's got to start. I don't think Billy expects a contract like the Sydney Harbour Bridge, not in the first year."

Jean asked, "Could you scoop out a hole for a swimming pool with a bulldozer?"

"I should think so. Yes, I'm sure you could. I went out with him once and watched one working. He let me drive it; it was awful fun. You'd scoop it out first with a bulldozer, and then you'd put up wooden stuff that they call shuttering and make the concrete sides."

"Could he do all that, too?"

"Oh, Billy can do that. Why, do you want a swimming pool?"

Jean stared at the white painted wall. "It was just an idea. A nice, big pool just by the bore, with diving boards and everything, big enough for everybody to get into and have fun. You see, you've got the water there, right in the main street. You'd have a wooden thing they call a cooling tower and run the water through that to cool it off before it went into the pool. Have a lawn of grass by it, where people could lie and sunbathe if they want to. An old man taking the cash at the gate, a bob a bathe . . ."

Rose stared at her. "You've got it all worked out. Are you thinking of doing that, Jean?"

"I don't know. It would be fun to have it, and I believe it'd pay like anything. Mixed bathing, of course."

Rose laughed. "Have all the wowsers in the place looking over the rails to see what was going on."

"Charge them sixpence for that," said Jean. She turned to Rose. "Ask Billy to get hold of plans and things," she said, "and tell us what it would cost when he comes up after the wet. I don't believe that there's a swimming pool in the whole Gulf Country. It would be fun to have one."

"I'll ask him. Anything else?"

Jean stretched in her bed. "A nice hairdressing saloon and beauty parlour," she said, "with a pretty French brunette in it who really knew her stuff, and could make one look like Rita Hayworth. That's what I want, sometimes. But I don't think that's in Billy's line."

"It had better not be," said Rose.

Jean got up next day and left the hospital, and walked awkwardly to the workshop. There was an air mail letter from Mr. Pack about the air freight consignment of shoes that he had received from them. His enthusiasm was temperate; he pointed out a number of defects and crudities which would require correction in production batches; most of these they were aware of and had attended to. He finished up by saying he would try and shift them, which, knowing Mr. Pack, Jean and Aggie Topp interpreted as praise.

"He'll like the next lot better," Aggie said. And then she said, "I had two girls come along for jobs while you were away. One was Fred Dawson's daughter; he's the chief stockman or something on a station called Carlisle. She's fifteen; her mother brought her in. She's a bit young, but she'd be all right. The other was a girl of nineteen who's been working in the store at Normanton. I didn't like her so much."

"I don't want to take on anyone else until that first batch of shoes have been sold," said Jean. "If Mrs. Dawson comes in again, tell her that we'll let her know about the kid after the wet. I'd like to have her if I can. I don't think we want the other one, do we?"

"I don't think so. Bit of a slut, she was."

They talked about the details of the business for an hour. "We haven't got the overalls back yet," said Aggie. "I went and saw Mrs. Harrison, but her back's bad again. We'll have to find someone else." They issued the girls with a clean overall each week to work in, and the washing of these overalls was something of a problem to them.

"What we want," said Jean, "is one of those Home Laundry things, and do them ourselves. We could run it off the generating set . . . Of course, it needs hot water." She thought for a minute. "Think about that one," she said. "Hire it out, do people's washing for them. Anyway, see if you can find another Mrs. Harrison for the time being."

Aggie said, "Everybody's talking about your ride, Miss Paget."

"Are they?"

She nodded. "Even that girl from Normanton, she knew about it, too."

"How on earth did she get to hear?"

"It's these little wireless sets they have upon the cattle stations," Aggie said. "The boys here were telling me, they all listen in to what everybody else is saying—telegrams and everything. They've got nothing else to do. You can't keep anything secret in this country." And then she said, "I heard the aeroplane go off this morning. Was the man very bad?"

"Not too good," said Jean. "Sister thinks they'll be able to save the leg. We ought to have a doctor here, of course."

"There's not enough work to keep a doctor occupied in a place like this," said Aggie. "Where did they fly him to?"

"Cairns. There's a good hospital in Cairns." She turned to the door, and paused. "Aggie," she said, "how do you think a swimming pool would go in Willstown? Would people use it?"

Joe Harman rode into the town that afternoon with Pete Fletcher. He put his horse into the stable behind the Australian Hotel and came to find Jean; he was wet and dirty in his riding clothes because the creeks were up, and though he had started spick and span from Midhurst as befits a man going into town to see his girl, he had had to swim one of the two creeks on the way holding to the mane and saddle of his horse, which had rather spoilt the sartorial effect. He was half dry when he got to Willstown; he combed his hair and emptied out his boots, and went to the ice cream parlour to ask Rose where Jean was.

He found her in her bedroom, writing a long letter to me. He tapped on the door and she came out to him. "We can't talk here, Joe. I'll never hear the last of it if you come in. Let's go and have an ice cream in the parlour." It was borne in on her that this was literally the only place in Willstown where young men and young women could meet reputably to talk; the alternative, in the wet, would be to go into the stable or a barn. They picked a table by the wall; she looked around her at the rectangular walls and the adjacent tables with discontent. "This won't do at all," she said. "I'll have some sort of booths made, little corners where people can talk privately."

"What'll you have?" he asked.

"I'll have a banana split," she said. "I want feeding up. I don't know if you know it, but I've been very ill. Don't pay, Joe—have it on the house."

He grinned. "Think I'm the kind of man to take a girl out and let her shout?"

"If you're feeling like that, I'll have two. The bananas will be going bad by tomorrow." She was getting fruit flown in by the Dakota every Wednesday, and she had little difficulty in selling the small quantities she got at prices that would pay for the air freight. Her trouble was that usually she could not keep it for a week.

He came back with the ices and sat down with her. "Now, Joe," she said, "what about the poddy corral?"

He grinned sheepishly, and looked over his shoulder. "That's crook," he said. "There's no poddy corral on Midhurst."

"There's something damn like one," she said, laughing. "Come clean, Joe. What happened to Don Curtis, anyway?"

"He was moseying about on my land where he hadn't got no right to be," Joe said carefully. "He found that corral where I'd got some poddys—my own poddys, mind you. I'd put 'em in there to consider things a bit, because they'd been wandering. Well, Don went to steal them off me, and he took down the top bar, but they were pretty wild, those poddys were; they hadn't had no water for about four days except the rain. Far as I can make out they pushed the second bar out on top of him when he went to loose it, and knocked him over on his back with the pole on top, and then they all ran over him and bust his leg. They ran out on the horse, too; Don had hitched his horse by the rein to something or other, and these poddys, they come charging down on to the horse and he bust the rein and he went too. So there Don was, and serve him bloody well right for going where he hadn't got no business to be."

"Whose poddys were they, really, Joe?"

"Mine," he replied firmly.

She smiled. "Where had they been wandering?"

He grinned. "Windermere. But they were my poddys. He pinched 'em off me. You heard me telling Pete he's got a poddy corral there."

"Were these poddys that you had in your corral the same ones that you let out of his corral?" she asked. It seemed to be getting just a little bit involved.

"Most of 'em," he said. "There might have been one or two with them that we picked up as damages, you might say." He paused. "Things get a bit mixed up sometimes," he observed.

"Where are the poddys now?" she asked. "The ones that Don let out?"

"They'll be on Midhurst," he said. "They'll be somewhere

round about the bore, I'd say. They won't stir from the first water that they find, not even in the wet."

She ate a little of her banana split in silence. Then she said, "Well anyway, you're not to go after any of his poddys while he's in hospital, Joe. That's not fair. He'll come out of hospital and find there's not a poddy left."

"I wouldn't do a thing like that."

"I bet you would. I don't know how this game is played, Joe, but I'm quite sure that's against the rules."

He grinned. "All right. But he'll be after mine as soon as he gets back. That's sure as anything."

"Why can't you let each other's poddys alone?"

"I'll let his alone, but he won't let mine alone. You see," he said simply, "I got about fifty more of his last year than he got of mine."

This conversation, Jean felt, was not getting them anywhere; where poddys were concerned Joe's moral standards seemed to be extremely low. She changed the subject, and said, "Joe, about those little dams you were talking about on Green Island. Have you got anyone to build them for you yet?"

He shook his head. "It's no good thinking about those until the dry."

"Could a bulldozer build them?"

"Oh my word," he said. "If anybody had a bulldozer he'd build the lot inside a month. But there's no bulldozer this side of the Curry."

"There might be one," she said. She told him about Rose Sawyer and Billy Wakeling. "He's coming up to see her anyway," she said, "and she says he's looking for that sort of work to do up here. I suppose he's turning into Rose's steady. You'd better take him out to Midhurst when he comes, and have a talk to him."

"My word," he said. "If we had a joker with a bulldozer in Willstown it'd make a lot of difference to the stations."

"It'd make a lot of difference in Willstown," she observed. "Joe, if we had a really decent swimming pool just by the bore, with little cabins to change in and green lawns to sunbathe on, and diving boards, and an old man in charge to mow the grass and keep it clean and nice—would people use it, Joe? If we charged, say, a bob a bathe?"

They discussed the swimming pool for some time, and came to the conclusion that it could never pay upon the basis of a town with a hundred and fifty people. "It's just a question of how fast this town is going to grow," he said. "A swimming pool is just another thing to make it grow. There's not a town in the whole Gulf Country that's got a pool."

"The ice cream parlour's paying, definitely," Jean said. "If we can keep up the quality, I feel we're home on that one. I'd like to try the swimming pool next, I think, if I can get the money for it out of Noel Strachan."

He smiled, in curious wonder. "What comes after the swimming pool?"

She stared out at the wet, miry expanse of earth that was the street. "They'll get their hair wet in the swimming pool, so we'll have to have a beauty parlour," she said. "I think that's the next thing. And after that, an open-air cinema. And after that, a battery of Home Laundries for the wet wash, and after that a decent dress shop." She turned to him. "Don't laugh, Joe. I know it sounds crackers, but just look at the results. I start an ice cream parlour and put Rose in it, and young Wakeling comes after her with a bulldozer, so you get your dams built."

"You're a bit ahead of the game," he said. "They aren't built yet."

"They will be soon."

He glanced around the ice cream palour. "If everything you want to do works out like this," he said slowly, "you'll have a town as good as Alice Springs in no time."

"That's what I want to have," she said. "A town like Alice."

Chapter 11

ALL THAT happened nearly three years ago.

I cannot deny that in that time her letters have been a great interest to me, perhaps the greatest interest in my rather barren life. I think that after the affair of Mr. Curtis and the poddy dodging she became more closely integrated into the life of the Gulf Country than she had been before, because even before her marriage there was a subtle change in her letters. She ceased to write as an Englishwoman living in a strange, hard, foreign land; she gradually began to write about the people as if she was one of them, about the place as if it was her place. That may be merely my fancy, of course, or it may be that I made such a study of her letters, reading and re-reading them and filing them carefully away in a special set of folders that I keep in my flat, that I found subtleties of meaning in them that a more casual reader would not have noticed.

She married Joe Harman in April after the mustering, as she had promised him. They were married by a travelling Church of England priest, one of the Bush Brothers who had been, queerly enough, a curate at St. John's in Kingston-on-Thames, not ten miles from where I used to live in Wimbledon. There was, of course, no church in Willstown at that time though one is to be built next year; they were married in the Shire Hall, and all the countryside came to the wedding. They had their honeymoon, or part of it, on Green Island, and I suppose she took her sarong with her, though she did not tell me that.

In the first two years of her married life she made considerable inroads into her capital. She was very good about it; she always started off one thing and got it trading smoothly before starting on another, after the first effort when she started both the ice cream parlour and the workshop together. She used to send me accounts of her ventures, too, prepared for her by a young man called Len James who worked in the Bank. But all the same, she asked me for three or four thousand pounds every six months or so, till by the time her second son was born, the one that she called Noel after me, she had had over eighteen thousand pounds for her various local businesses. Although they all seemed to be making profits Lester and I were growing, by that time, a little concerned about our duty as trustees, broad though our terms of reference under the Macfadden will might be. Our duty was to keep her capital intact and hand it over to her when she was thirty-five, and I began to worry sometimes about the chances of a slump or some unknown disaster in Australia which would extinguish the thirty per cent of her inheritance that we had let her have. Too many eggs seemed to be going into one basket, and her investments, laudable though they might be, could hardly be classed as trustee stocks.

The climax came in February, when she wrote me a long letter from the hospital at Willstown, soon after she had given birth to Noel. She asked me if I would be one of his godfathers, and of course that pleased me very much although there was very little prospect that I should live long enough to discharge my duties by him. Wakeling was to be the second godfather, and as he had married Rose Sawyer about six months previously and seemed to be settled in the district I felt that she would not be injuring her child by giving him an elderly godfather who lived on the other side of the world. I made a corresponding alteration to my will immediately, of course.

She went on in the same letter to discuss affairs at Midhurst. "You know, Joe's only manager at present," she wrote. "He's done awfully well; there were about eight thousand head of cattle on the place when he went there, but now there are twelve or thirteen thousand. We shall be selling over two thousand head this year, too many to send down to Julia in one herd, so Joe's got to make two trips. It looks as if there'll be a steady increase for the next few years, because each year in the dry Bill Wakeling builds a couple more dams for us so we get more and more feed each year."

She went on to tell me about Mrs. Spears, the owner. "She left the Gulf Country after her husband died about ten years ago," she said, "and now she lives in Brisbane. Joe and I went down and stayed a couple of nights with her last October; I didn't tell you about it then because I wanted to think it over and we had to find out if we could get a loan, too."

She told me that Mrs. Spears was getting very old, and she wanted to realize a part of the considerable capital that she had locked up in Midhurst; probably she wanted to give it away during her life time to avoid death duties. "She asked if we could buy a half share in the station," she said. "She would give us an option to buy the other half at a valuation at the time of her death, whenever that might be. It means finding about thirty thousand pounds; that's about the value of half the stock. The land is rented from the State, of course, and there's seventeen years to go upon the present lease; it means an alteration to the lease to put Joe's name into it jointly with hers."

She told me that they had been to the bank. The bank would advance two-thirds of the thirty thousand pounds that they would have to find. "They sent an inspector up who knows the cattle business, and he came out to Midhurst," she wrote. "Joe's got a good name in the Gulf Country and I think he thought that we were doing all right with the property. That leaves us with ten thousand pounds to find in cash, and that's what I wanted to ask you about."

She digressed a little. "Midhurst's a good station," she said, "and we're very happy here. If we can't take it over Mrs. Spears will probably sell it and we'd have to go somewhere else and start again. I'd hate to do that and it would be a great disappointment to Joe after all the work he's put into Midhurst. I'd be miserable leaving Willstown now, because it's turning into quite a fair-sized place, and it's a happy little town to live in, too. I do want to stay here if we can."

She went on, "I know a cattle station isn't a trustee investment, Noel, any more than any of the other things you've let me put my money into. Will you think it over, and tell me if we can have it? If we can't, I'll have to think again; perhaps I could sell or mortgage some of the businesses I've started since I got here. I should hate to do that, because they might get into bad hands and go downhill. This town's like a young baby—I know something about those, Noel! It needs nursing all the time, till it's a bit bigger."

Another ten thousand pounds, of course, would mean that we should have allowed her to invest half of her inheritance in highly speculative businesses in one district, which was by no means the intention of Mr. Macfadden when he made his will. Legally, of course, we were probably safe from any action for a breach of trust by reason of the broad wording of the discretionary clause that I had slipped into the will. I spent a day or two thinking about this before I showed her letter to Lester, and it came to me in the end that our duty was to do what Mr. Macfadden would himself have done in similar circumstances.

What would that queer recluse in Ayr have done if he had had to settle this point? He was an invalid, of course, but I did not think he was an unkind or an unreasonable man. He had not made that long trust because he distrusted Jean Paget; he did not even know her. He had made it for her good, because he thought that an unmarried girl in her twenties who was mistress of a large sum of money would be liable to be imposed upon. In that he may well have been right. But Jean Paget was a married woman of thirty with two children now, and married to a sensible and steady sort of man, whatever his ideas on poddy dodging might be. Would Mr. Macfadden, in these circumstances, still have insisted on the trust being maintained in its original form?

I thought not. He was a kindly man—I felt sure of that— and he would have wanted her to have her Midhurst station, since that was where her home and all her present interests were. He was a careful, Scottish man, however; I thought he would have turned his mind more to the details of her investment in Midhurst to ensure that she got good value for this ten thousand pounds. Looking at it from this point of view I was disturbed at the short tenure of the lease. Seventeen years was a short time for Joe Harman to regain the value of the dams that he was building on the property and all the other improvements that he was making; he could not possibly go on with capital improvements until a very much longer lease had been negotiated.

I showed her letter to my partner then, and we had a long talk about it. He took the same view that I did, that the lease was the kernel of the matter. "I can't say that I take a very serious view of this trust, Noel," he said. "I think your approach is the right one, to try and put yourself in the testator's shoes when looking at this thing. He was quite content to leave the money to his sister without any question of a trust, while her husband was alive to help her. It was only after the husband's death that he wanted the trust. Well, now the daughter's got a husband to help her. If he was disposing of his money now, presumably he wouldn't bother about any trust at all."

"That's a point," I said. "I hadn't thought of that one."

"I don't suggest we disregard the trust," he said. "I think we ought to use it as a lever to get this lease put right for her. Tell all and sundry that we won't release her money till the leasehold is adjusted to our satisfaction. Then, so far as I'm concerned, she can have all she wants."

I smiled. "I wouldn't tell *her* that."

I sat down next day and drafted a letter to her in reply. "I do not think it is impossible to release a further ten thousand pounds," I wrote, "but I should be very sorry to do so until this matter of the lease had been adjusted to our satisfaction. As the thing stands at the moment, you could lose your home in seventeen years' time and lose with it all the money that you and Mrs. Spears have expended on improvements such as dams and other water conservation schemes, which would pass to the State without any payment whatsoever, so far as my present information goes." I learned later that that was incorrect.

I came to the main point of my letter next. "No doubt you have a solicitor that you can trust, but if it would assist you I would very gladly come and visit you in Queensland for a few weeks and see this matter of the lease put into satisfactory order before you invest this money in Midhurst. It is many years since I left England and I have regretted that; I cannot expect to have many more years left in which to travel and to see the world. I would like to take a long holiday and travel a little before I get too feeble, and if I could help you in this matter of the lease I should be only too glad to come and do so." I added, "I need hardly say that I should travel at my own expense."

The answer came in a night-letter telegram about ten days later. She urged me to come to them, and suggested that I should come out by air about the end of April, since their winter was approaching then and the weather would be just like an English summer. She said that she was writing with a list of clothes that I should have and medicines and things that I might need upon the journey. I was a little touched by that.

I saw Kennedy, my doctor, at his place in Wimpole Street next day. "Is there any particular reason why I shouldn't fly out to Queensland?" I asked.

He looked at me quizzically. "It's not exactly what I should advise for you, you know. Have you got to go to Queensland?"

"I want to go, very much," I said. "I want to go and stay out there about a month. There's business I should like to see to personally."

"How have you been walking recently?"

There was no point in lying to him. "I walk as far as Trafalgar Square most mornings," I said. "I take a taxi from there."

"You can't quite manage the whole distance to your office?"

"No," I said. "I haven't done that for some time."

"Can you walk upstairs in your club, to the first floor, without stopping?"

I shook my head. "I always go up in the lift. But anyway, there aren't any stairs in Queensland. All the houses are bungalows."

He smiled. "Take off your coat and your shirt, and let me have a look at you."

When he had finished his examination, he said, "Well. Are you proposing to go alone?"

I nodded. "I shall be staying with friends at the other end. They'll meet me when I get off the aeroplane."

"And you really feel it's necessary that you should go?"

I met his eyes. "I want to go, very much indeed."

"All right," he said. "You know your condition as well as I do. There's nothing new—only the deterioration that you've got to expect. You put ten years on your age during the war. I think, on the whole, you're wise to travel by air. I think you'd find the Red Sea very trying." He went on to tell me what I could do and what I mustn't attempt, all the old precautions that he had told me before.

I went back to my office and saw Lester, and told him what I was proposing to do. "I'm going to take about three months' holiday," I said, "starting at the end of April. I'm going out by air, and I don't know quite how long I shall stay for. If I find air travel too tiring on the way out, I may come home by sea." I paused. "In any case, you'll have to work on the assumption that I shall be away for some considerable time. It's probably about time you started to do that, in any case."

"You really feel that it is necessary for you to go personally, yourself?" he asked.

"I do."

"All right, Noel. I only wish you hadn't got to put so much of your energy into this. After all, it's a fairly trivial affair."

"I can't agree with that," I said. "I'm beginning to think that this thing is the most important business that I ever handled in my life."

I left London one Monday morning, and travelled through to Sydney on the same air liner, arriving late on Wednesday night. We stopped for an hour or so at Cairo and Karachi and Calcutta and Singapore and Darwin. I must say the aeroplane was very comfortable and the stewardess was most kind and attentive; it was fatiguing, of course, sleeping two nights in a reclining chair and I was glad when it was over. I stayed two nights in Sydney to rest, and took a little drive around in a hired car during the afternoon. Next day I took the aeroplane to Cairns. It was a lovely flight, especially along the coast of Queensland, after Brisbane. The very last part, up the Hinchinbrook Channel between Cairns and Townsville, must be one of the most beautiful coastlines in the world.

We landed at Cairns in the evening, and here I had a great surprise, because Joe Harman met me at the aerodrome. The Dakota, he told me, now ran twice a week to the Gulf Country, partly on account of the growth of Willstown, and he had come in on the Friday plane to take me out on Monday. "I got one or two little bits of things to order and to see to," he said. "My solicitor, Ben Hope, he's here in Cairns too. I thought that over the week-end you might like to hear the general set-up of Midhurst, 'n have a talk with him."

I had not heard the slow Queensland speech since he had come to me in Chancery Lane, over three years before. He took me in a car to the hotel, a queer, rambling building rather beautifully situated, with a huge bar that seemed to be the focal point. We got there just before tea, the evening

meal, and went in almost at once and sat down together. He
asked me if I would drink tea or beer or plonk.

"Plonk?" I asked.

"Red wine," he said. "I don't go much for it, myself, but
jokers who know about wine, they say it's all right."

They had a wine list, and I chose a Hunter River wine
which I must say I found to be quite palatable. "Jean was
very sorry she couldn't come and meet you," he said. "We
could have parked Joe with someone, but she's feeding Noel
so that ties her. She's going to drive into Willstown and meet
the Dakota on Monday."

"How is she?" I asked.

"She's fine," he said. "Having babies seems to suit her.
She's looking prettier than ever."

We settled down after tea on the verandah outside my
bedroom, and began discussing the business of Midhurst. He
had brought with him copies of the accounts for the station
for the last three years, neatly typed and very easily intelligible. I commented upon their form, and he said, "I'm not
much of a hand at this sort of thing. Jean did these before
she went into the hospital. She does most of the accounts
for me. I tell her what I want to do out on the station, and she
tells me how much money I've got left to spend. She's got
the schooling for the two of us."

Nevertheless, I found him quite a shrewd man, very well
able to appreciate the somewhat intricate points that came
up about the lease and his capital improvements. We talked
for a couple of hours that night about his station and about
the various businesses that Jean had started in the town. He
was very interesting about those.

"She's got twenty-two girls working in the workshop,"
he said. "Shoes and attaché cases and ladies' bags. That's
the one that isn't doing quite so well as the others." He
turned the pages of the accounts to show me. "It's making a
profit now, but last year there was a loss of over two hundred pounds—two hundred and twenty-seven. But all the
others—oh my word." He showed me the figures for the ice
cream parlour, the beauty parlour, the swimming pool, the
cinema, the laundry, and the dress shop. "They're going fine.
The fruit and vegetable shop, that's all right, too." We totted
up the figures and found that the seven of them together had
made a clear profit of two thousand six hundred and seventy-
three pounds in the previous year. "It'd pay her to run the
workshop at a loss," he said. "She gets it back out of what

the girls spend to make themselves look pretty for the ringers, and what the ringers spend in taking out the girls."

I was a little troubled about the workshop. "Can she expand it?" I asked. "Can she lower the overhead by doing a bigger business?"

He was doubtful about that. "She's using just about all the alligator skins Jeff Pocock and two others can bring in," he said. "Wallabies, they're getting scarcer than they were, too. I don't think she can get much bigger in the workshop. She doesn't want to, either. She's got a kind of hunch that in a few years' time the workshop won't be necessary at all, that the town will be so big that a workshop employing twenty girls won't be neither here nor there."

"I see," I said thoughtfully. "How big is the town now?"

"There's about four hundred and fifty people living in Willstown," he said. "That's not counting boongs, and not counting people living out upon the stations. The population's trebled in the last three years."

"Is that just because of the workshop?" I asked.

He said slowly, "I think it must be—everything comes back to that, when you look at it. It's not only the workshop, you see. She's got two girls employed in the ice cream parlour, and one lubra. Two in the beauty parlour, three in the dress shop, two in the fruit shop, three in the cinema. She employs quite a lot of people."

I was puzzled. "But can twenty girls in the workshop provide work for all these other girls?" I asked.

"It doesn't seem to work that way," he said. "We were totting it up the other day. She's never employed more than about thirty-five girls at any one time, but since she started there's been forty-two girls married out of her businesses. They mostly marry ringers. Well, that's forty-two families starting, forty-two women wanting cinema and beauty parlour and fresh vegetables and that, besides the thirty-five girls that she's still got employed. It kind of snowballs." He paused. "Take the bank. There's two girl clerks there that there never were before, because of the bigger business. The A.M.P. have started up an office, and there's a girl in that. Bill Wakeling's got a girl in his office." He turned to me. "It's a fact, there's something like a hundred girls and married women under twenty-five in Willstown now," he said. "When Jean came, there was two.

"And the babies!" he said. "There's more babies than you could shake a stick at. They've had to send a special maternity nurse to the hospital. That's another girl. She got engaged to Phil Duncan, the copper, last month, so there'll be another one."

I smiled. "Are there enough men to go round?"

"Oh my word," he said. "There's no difficulty in getting men to work in Willstown. I've had ringers coming from all over Queensland, from the Northern Territory, too, wanting a job round about Willstown. There was one chap came all the way from Marble Bar in Western Australia, two thousand miles or so. The labour situation's very different now to what it was three years ago."

I went to bed early that night with plenty to think about. We had a conference next morning with Mr. Hope, the solicitor, in his office, and wrote a letter to the Queensland Land Administration Board suggesting a meeting to discuss the lease of Midhurst. That afternoon we spent in driving around Cairns to see the sights; it seemed to me to be a pleasant little tropical town, beautifully situated. On Sunday we drove up on to the Atherton Tableland, high rolling downs farmed somewhat on the English style.

We flew to Willstown on Monday morning, in a Dakota. We landed at places called Georgetown and Croydon on the way and stayed on each aerodrome for about twenty minutes, picking up and setting down passengers and freight. As we circled Georgetown for the landing I was able to study the place. It was pathetic in a way, for you could see from the air the rectangular pattern of wide streets that once had been busy and lined with houses, now rutted with the rain and grass-grown. A few scattered houses stood at the intersections of what had once been these streets, and they were clustered rather more thickly around the hotel, the only two-storeyed building in either place. Both of these were derelict gold towns.

The people who came to meet the aeroplane in trucks were bronzed, healthy, and humorous; the men were mostly great big tanned, competent people; the women candid, uncomplaining housewives.

I sat at the window studying Croydon as we took off, till it fell away from view behind us. "I'm kind of glad that you've seen those," said Joe beside me. "Willstown was like that, only a bit worse. It's no great shakes yet, of course, but it's better than Croydon, oh my word it is."

We circled Willstown as we came in to land. It stood by quite a large river, and it was queerly like the other two towns in its lay-out. There were the same wide streets arranged in rectangular pattern, but the pattern was filling up with houses here. From the air the glint of the sun upon new corrugated-iron roofs was everywhere, so that at one point as we circled opposite the sun I had to shut my eyes against the dazzle. All these houses seemed to be new, and a considerable number were still in the process of building. In the main street opposite the two-storeyed building that I guessed to be the hotel, a line of shrubs had been planted in a formal garden down the middle of the road, transforming the wide cattle track into two carriage ways, and tarmac pavements had been made in this part of the town. Opposite the hotel I could see the swimming pool with diving boards and cabins and a lawn beside it, just as Jean had described it to me in her letters. Then the town was lost to view, and we were landing, coming in over a brand-new race track.

She was there to meet me in her Ford utility, her own car that she had bought for running in and out of town to see to her businesses. She was more mature now than I had remembered her; she had grown into a very lovely woman. She said, "Oh, Noel, it *is* nice to see you. Are you very tired?"

"I'm not tired," I said. "Three or four years older, perhaps. You're looking very well."

"I am well," she said. "Disgustingly well. Noel, it was good of you to offer to come out like this. I wanted to ask you to, and then it seemed too much to ask. It's such a very long way. Come and sit in the utility. Joe's just getting your bags."

They drove me out immediately to Midhurst. We passed through the main street of Willstown and I wanted to stop and see what she had done, but they would not let me. "Time enough for that tomorrow or the next day," she said. "We'll go to Midhurst now, and you can rest a bit."

I knew the sort of scenery that I should see upon the way to Midhurst from many readings of her letters, and it was just as I had expected it to be. There was no road in the usually accepted sense; she picked her way across country in the car following the general line of the tracks but avoiding the deep holes. When we came to the first creek, however, I was interested to see that they had made a sort of concrete bottom or causeway across the river bed, and this causeway was marked by two massive wooden posts upon the bank at either end. "We haven't got as far as having bridges yet," she said. "But this thing is a godsend in the wet, to know that you won't hit a boulder under water."

The homestead was very much as I had expected it to be, but there was a garden now in front of it, bright with flowers, and there were great ranges of log stockades or cattle pens that I had not heard about. "They've gone up in the last two years," Joe said. "We've got three Zebu bulls now, and you want more stockyards when you start breeding." His Zebu bulls were a cross between Indian cattle and English Herefords. He told me that he was keeping a small herd of dairy cows, too, and that meant more enclosures still.

"How many hands have you got now?" I asked.

"Eleven white stockriders," he said, "and ten boongs. It's almost easier to get white than black in this part of the country."

They would not let me walk that day, but put me in a long chair in the verandah with a cool drink, and I sat watching all the work of the station as it went on in the yard below. It was fascinating to sit there and watch it all, the white stockriders and the black stockriders, the cattle, the dogs, and the horses, and a half-grown wallaby lolloping about with puppies teasing it by playing with its tail. I could have sat there indefinitely watching it all, and watching the grace of Jean moving round the house attending to her children and her Abo women. I did sit there for three days.

She took me into town one morning, and showed me everything that she had done. She took me to the workshop first, and she made me put a scarf on before we went in because it would be cold. It was not cold as we would know cold, but it struck chilly after the warm day outside, because she kept the air conditioner going all the year round. "The girls do love it so," she said. "There's always more of them wanting to work here than I can take on, just because of that." They all looked very smart and pretty in the green smocks, working at the leather goods. There was a long mirror at the end of the shop, and a few pictures of hair styles and frocks cut out of illustrated magazines pinned up upon the wall. "We change those every so often," she said. "I like them to make the best of themselves."

The workshop stood by itself, but she had arranged her other enterprises all in a row as a little street of shops. She had built a wooden verandah over the broad tarmac pavement to shade shopgazers from the sun or the rain. Here she had the beauty parlour with an Esthonian in charge, a dark, handsome, middle-aged woman, beautifully got up, with two Australian girls under her. There were four private little booths, and a glass counter and display case full of women's things; it was all very clean and nice. Next in the row came a little shop with a battery of four Home Laundries, and three young married women sitting gossiping while they waited for their wash. Next was the greengrocer's shop which sold seeds and garden implements as well as fruit and vegetables, and after that the dress shop. This was quite a big place, with counters and dummies clothed in summer frocks, and I was interested to see a small, secluded part served by a middle-aged woman where the elderly could buy the clothes they were accustomed to, black skirts and flannel petticoats and coarse kitchen aprons.

She took me across the road and showed me the cinema and the swimming pool. It was quite a hot day and by that time I had had about enough, so she took me to the ice cream parlour and we had a cool drink there. She had some business to attend to and she left me there for half an hour, and I sat watching the people as they came into the parlour, or as they passed on the sidewalk. There were far more women than men. All of them seemed to be in the family way.

She came back presently, and sat with me in the parlour. "What comes next?" I asked. "Is there any end to this?"

She laughed, and touched my hand. "No end," she said. "I keep on badgering you for more money, don't I? As a matter of fact, I think I can start the next one out of the profits."

"What's that one going to be?"

"A self-service grocer's shop," she replied. "The demand's shifting, Noel. When we started it was entertainment that was needed, because everyone was young and nobody was married then. The solid, sensible things weren't wanted. What they needed then was ice cream, and the swimming pool, and the beauty parlour, and the cinema. They'll still need those things, but they won't expand so much more. What the town needs now is things for the young family. A really good grocer's shop selling good, varied food as cheap as we can possibly get it. And then, as soon as I can start it, we must have a household store. Do you know, you can't even buy a baby's pot in Willstown?"

I nodded at the store opposite. "Doesn't Mr. Duncan sell those?"

"He's got no imagination. He only sells big ones, that'd hold the whole baby."

I asked her presently, "How do all your goods get here? They aren't all flown, surely?"

She shook her head. "They come by train from Cairns to Forsayth, and by truck from there. There's no proper road, of course. It makes it terribly expensive, because a truck is worn out in about two years. Bill Wakeling says the Roads Commission are considering a road from here to Mareeba and Cairns—a proper tarmac road. Of course, he wants to build it. He thinks we'll get it inside two years, because the town's growing so fast. I must say, it'll be a godsend when we do. Fancy being able to drive to Cairns in a day!"

The Land Administration Board answered our letter later on that week and suggested a meeting on the following Tuesday or Wednesday, which suited our air services. I flew down to Brisbane with Joe Harman, picking up his solicitor in Cairns, and we had a conference with the Land Administration Board, which lasted most of one day, settling the Heads of Agreement. Then Harman went back to his station and Mr. Hope and I stayed on in Brisbane passing the draft of the final agreement backwards and forwards to the Land Administration Board with amendments in red and green and blue and purple ink. On top of this, I was in communication with the solicitors for Mrs. Spears over the option agreement for the final purchase of Midhurst; all this kept me busy in Brisbane for nearly a fortnight. Finally I was able to agree them both, after an exchange of cables with Lester, and brought them back to Cairns. Joe Harman signed them, and we put them in the post, and my business in Queensland was done.

I went back to Willstown with Joe and stayed another week with them, not because there was any reason why I should do so, but for an old man's sentiment. I sat on the verandah with Jean, studying her drawing of the lay-out of the self-service grocery. We discussed whether it could not be combined with the hardware store. We went into Willstown and visited the site for it, and I spent some time with Mr. Carter, the Shire Clerk, discussing with him the position in regard to the leases that she held for land. She showed me the swimming pool and we talked about the cost of tiling over the rough concrete to make it look better, and I sat for hours in the ice cream parlour watching those beautiful young women as they pushed their prams from shop to shop.

I asked her once if she would be coming back to England for a holiday. She hesitated, and then said gently, "Not for a bit, Noel. Joe and I want to take a holiday next year, but we've been planning to go to America. We thought we'd go to San Francisco and get an old car, and drive down the west coast into Arizona and Texas. I'm sure we'd learn an awful lot that would be useful here if we did that. Their problems must be just the same as ours, and they've been at it longer."

Jean touched me very much one evening by suggesting that I stay out there and make my home with them. "You've nothing to go back to England for, Noel," she said. "You're practically retired now. Why not give up Chancery Lane, give up London, and stay here with us? You know we'd love to have you."

It was impossible of course; the old have their place and the young have theirs. "That's very kind of you," I said. "I wish I could. But I've got sons, and grandchildren, you know. Harry will be coming home next year and we're all hoping that he'll get a shore appointment. He's due for a term of duty at the Admiralty, I think."

She said, "I'm sorry, for our sake. Joe and I talked this over, and we hoped we'd be able to get you to stay with us for a long time. Make your home here with us."

I said quietly, "That was a very kind thought, Jean, but I must go back."

They drove me to the aeroplane, of course, to see me off. Leaving-takings are stupid things, and best forgotten about as quickly as possible. I cannot even remember what she said, and it is not important anyway. I can only remember a great thankfulness that the Dakota on that service didn't carry a stewardess so that nobody could see my face as we circled after taking off to get on course, and I saw the new buildings and bright roofs of that Gulf town for the last time.

It is winter now, and it is nearly three months since I have been able to get out to the office or the club. My daughter-in-law Eve, Martin's wife, has been organizing me; it was she who insisted that I should engage this nurse to sleep in the flat. They wanted me to go into some sort of nursing home, but I won't do that.

I have spent the winter writing down this story, I suppose because an old man loves to dwell upon the past and this is my own form of the foible. And having finished it, it seems to me that I have been mixed up in things far greater than I realized at the time. It is no small matter to assist in the birth of a new city, and as I sit here looking out into the London mists I sometimes wonder just what it is that Jean has done; if any of us realize, even yet, the importance of her achievement.

I wrote to her the other day and told her a queer thought that came into my head. Her money came originally from the goldfields of Hall's Creek in West Australia, where James Macfadden made it in the last years of the last century. I suppose Hall's Creek is derelict now, and like another Burketown or another Croydon. I think it is fitting that the gold that has been taken from those places should come back to them again in capital to make them prosperous. When I thought of that, it seemed to me that I had done the right thing with her money and that James Macfadden would have approved, although I had run contrary to the strict intentions of his son's will. After all, it was James who made the money and took it away to England from a place like Willstown. I think he would have liked it when his great niece took it back again.

I suppose it is because I have lived rather a restricted life myself that I have found so much enjoyment in remembering what I have learned in these last years about brave people and strange scenes. I have sat here day after day this winter, sleeping a good deal in my chair, hardly knowing if I was in London or the Gulf Country, dreaming of the blazing sunshine, of poddy dodging and black stockriders, of Cairns and of Green Island. Of a girl that I met forty years too late, and of her life in that small town that I shall never see again, that holds so much of my affection.

Author's Note

On the publication of this book I expect to be accused of falsifying history, especially in regard to the march and death of the homeless women prisoners. I shall be told that nothing of the sort ever happened in Malaya, and this is true. It happened in Sumatra.

After the conquest of Malaya in 1942 the Japanese invaded Sumatra and quickly took the island. A party of about eighty Dutch women and children were collected in the vicinity of Padang. The local Japanese commander was reluctant to assume responsibility for these women and, to solve his problem, marched them out of his area; so began a trek all round Sumatra which lasted for two and a half years. At the end of this vast journey less than thirty of them were still alive.

In 1949 I stayed with Mr. and Mrs. J. G. Geysel-Vonck at Palembang in Sumatra. Mrs. Geysel had been a member of that party. When she was taken prisoner she was a slight, pretty girl of twenty-one, recently married; she had a baby six months old, and a very robust sense of humour. In the years that followed Mrs. Geysel marched over twelve hundred miles carrying her baby, in circumstances similar to those which I have described. She emerged from this fantastic ordeal undaunted, and with her son fit and well.

I do not think that I have ever before turned to real life for an incident in one of my novels. If I have done so now it is because I have been unable to resist the appeal of this true story, and because I want to pay what tribute is within my power to the most gallant lady I have ever met.

NEVIL SHUTE.

NEVIL SHUTE

who died in 1960 at the age of sixty, had won distinction in two specialized and demanding careers. As Nevil Shute Norway, aviation engineer, he founded his own aircraft company and worked on the development of secret weapons for the British in World War II. As Nevil Shute, novelist, he had been the author of some two dozen books which have sold over 14,000,000 copies in all editions. Among his novels are "In the Wet," "Trustee from the Toolroom," "The Rainbow and the Rose" and "The Chequer Board," all available in Ballantine Books paperbound editions.